Dale A. Dye is a retired
the rank of private to ca
service. He fought as a
served in Beirut, Leban
rado, and divides his tim
job as executive editor of *Soldier of Fortune* magazine.

By the same author

Platoon
Outrage

DALE A. DYE

Citadel

This edition published 1994 by
Diamond Books
77–85 Fulham Palace Road
Hammersmith, London W6 8JB

A Grafton UK Paperback Original 1989
Published in the USA as *Run Between the Raindrops*

Printed and bound in Great Britain

Set in Times

To Steve, who lives with the painful memory of Hué City in his arm, leg and soul. And to the gallant grunts of the 1st and 2nd Battalions, 5th Marines, both living and dead, this book is lovingly dedicated.

Contents

Prologue

Stereo stethoscope stuffed tightly in both ears. Press the headset till it hurts. Listen for the pulse of this God-damned emotion-drunk pterodactyl that gobbled you up and gave you a double martini before the seat belt sign even went off. Listen hard for that telltale cough, fart, wheeze or whine that means the fucker might fall out of the air. Big silver cylinder stuffed with unstable paranoids who can't imagine there are Friendly Skies left to fly.

Guy in the next seat wearing the wings of a helicopter door-gunner over his Purple Heart. Kept mumbling 'bullshit, bullshit, bullshit' under his breath while a burned-out, over-the-hill Stew mechanically extolled the safety features of the Boeing 707. Tune that shit out, man. Press on the earpieces and seal out the bad vibes with earwax accumulated over what seems like a lifetime in the Land of the Lotus Eaters. Fish-eye view of fleecy clouds through the porthole. Dr Feelgood peering at the patient through his head mirror. All scrubbed up and ready to operate on The World.

Three weeks out of the hospital. Three weeks away from the Great Big Colossal Battle of Hué City. Three weeks to sort it all out and see what it means. Long, lazy afternoon in the hospital solarium, watered and fed like some fucking houseplant. Thousands of thoughts and images in that time. Sometimes you became so absorbed in them that you went slack-jawed and drooled all over your crisply-starched, government-issue pajamas. That pissed the nurses off but they steamed in silence. You don't wake these war-crazy fuckers for the same reasons you don't startle sleepwalkers. No reason to be mutilated by some mindless maniac who didn't realize he was out of the Nam and safe in the lock-step sterility of a military hospital.

Three weeks of glassy-eyed navel-gazing, trying to sort out what the experience meant and what happened to you because of it. Drive yourself to the brink of conclusion and withdraw. *Coitus Interruptus*. Don't want to spawn any monsters that might get you locked in a rubber room and make you miss the Freedom Bird. But the conclusions are welling up to the surface now. One more martini and I can shoot my wad.

Fiddle with the dial that selects programs into the earphones. Muzak to soothe the savage beasts and keep them from ripping off someone's fucking face. George M. Cohan medley. 'I'm a Yankee Doodle Dandy. A Yankee Doodle, do or die.' Shit. Yankee Doodle went to Nam, just to kill the Slopeheads. I am that Yankee Doodle Boy. Yeah. And so is Steve, my partner, my Main Man. Lying back there in the hospital at Yokosuka, shot all to shit and he never even got to ride the pony.

Takes me too far back. Try another channel. *Golden Days of Radio*. Amos and Andy. Fucking Kingfish sounds like Philly Dog. 'Wull, Amos . . . Ah doesn't know perzactly, but look heah . . .' The Dog is dead in Hué City. His gang of South Philly street fighters will want to waste someone when they find out about it.

Maybe some Country sounds. Johnny Cash rumbling about a Ring of Fire. The Southerner: last of the Delta Company Buttplates. Fucker stepped into a ring of AK-47 fire on the wall in Hué. Killed by an NVA officer. He knew it was coming. Said you couldn't run between the raindrops without getting wet.

Rock and roll, man. Gruntspeak for full-auto fire. Is that Joplin? New song; probably banned on AFVN. Too many doper images. 'Freedom's just another word for nothin' left to lose.' There it is. Nothing left to lose and no energy left to hold anything back. Let the images wind up to speed and get it over with. Focus out of the blur. Let it come. Fight off the smeary, insane flashes of action that haunted the hospital nights. Couldn't see the pattern then. No alpha and no omega. Massive mental overload in those first days after Hué. Felt like a kid trying to sleep the night after a first trip to the circus. I could see the lions and tigers; remember the geeks and the headless chickens, but how did I get to the Big Top?

One more channel; one more martini. Show tunes. Reminds me of the innocuous, omnipresent elevator music they piped through the hospital as a relaxant for the twisted, deranged combat veterans. The same inane voices that keyed my first postwar insight. 'There'll be some changes made today! There'll be some changes made.' Fuckin' A, Skippy. Where the hell have they been? The changes have been made, man. That Goddamn Hué City put me through some righteous changes.

Merciless self-interrogation while I lay staring at the soothing, mauve ceiling and walls of the hospital room. How did I get there? Some fucking gook blew two extra navels in my belly during the fight for the walls surrounding the Citadel in Hué City. Why was I up close enough to the fighting to get hit like that? Easy. I lost my war correspondent perspective. No. I gave it away. I volunteered when I realized a King-Hell, balls-to-the-wall war story was really a love story. Where did the cynical, aloof, wiseass, self-centered con man go? He went out of Hué City in a body bag with the poor, suffering bastards he used to ridicule.

Been some changes made, man. And it's time now for some conclusions to be drawn. Whip out the wide-angle lens and take a look at the Big Picture. I can see Hué for what it was now. It was a ludicrous, insane situation in which modern fighting men, possessed of all the highly-destructive engines of war, were ordered to attack a medieval fortress using no weapons that would destroy or harm it. It was ritual suicide made possible by the same insanity that made the Vietnam War a military impossibility.

And it was a metaphor. All absurdity and insanity of the Nam congealed like a giant turd and deposited for consideration and critique by the people who do the fighting and dying. That's what prompted the changes that came over me in Hué. That's what finally cracked Mister Asshole's thick shell and gave birth to Mister Nice Guy. More booze, Goddamnit. I'm unburdening here. 'Dear Sir and/or Madam, your son D.A. was the unfortunate victim of a metaphor. We deeply regret that you may not recognize him when he gets home.'

Yeah. Fucking misdirected metaphor struck me down in the prime of life. Whole Goddamn fight was a metaphor for combat in Vietnam. Began slowly and gained momentum as the shit neared the fan. 'Movement to contact,' the tacticians called it. Grunts called it The Fucker Factor. You walk in the sun and you *feel* it about to happen. Slow-motion effect but you can *feel* it. The foreplay before the fucking. Builds slowly until your balls suddenly slam up into your scrotum and wet, sticky stuff explodes off the walls. That's the way it was in Hué. I can see clearly now.

I began to smell the bullshit when the ward orderly brought the *Stars & Stripes* that morning in the hospital. Banner headline burned right into my eyeballs. Almost puked the pabulum they give a man with a gut wound. Spooning pabulum mechanically and staring at the story that said the gallant ARVN forces finally won the Great Big Battle for Hué City. That's not the way I saw it.

The Walls

Kipling had it nailed down cold. The damn dawn does come up like thunder in this part of the world. Jesus, you could almost hear the roar and rumble as the sky slowly exploded into light. Staring at that crimson orb, spreading streaks of purple and yellow across the horizon as it rose from the South China Sea, you wondered if old Rudyard was really standing on the road to Mandalay when he wrote about it. He could have been standing right there on the southern banks of the Perfume River watching the dawn come thundering up over Hué, the seat of the ancient Annamese emperors.

Nothing – not even the incessant monsoon rain – could take away from the beauty of the dawn. A scarlet sun seemed so warm and welcome chasing away the inky, cloying cold of a wet night. You wanted to zoom out there to sea and sit with your back to the sun where you could see the struggle between light and dark as a prelude to a bloodier confrontation. Out there you'd get a panoramic view of an Asian anachronism.

There's a long stretch of pristine white beach, bisected by the Perfume River which runs into the sea. At the high water mark, a shimmering sand castle, complete with turrets, ramparts and redoubts. All around, particularly on the inland side of the river, there are smaller castles and a gay checkerboard of beach umbrellas protecting their owners from the elements that hang over Hué when the barrier of the Hai Van mountains to the southwest prevents the northeast monsoon from sweeping south over the rest of Vietnam. It was so strange from that angle. Like the topsy-turvy world encountered by Alice on the other side of the looking glass, things seemed curiouser and curiouser. It was almost like watching insects through the glass case of an ant farm. Their actions only have pattern and purpose when you consider the community enclosed in the glass case. The ant farm itself seems to be a living, functioning element of the insect's activity; sometimes cooperating and allowing tunnels to be constructed, sometimes resisting and frustrating the ants with cave-ins or shifting sand.

The bloody sun pumped more light over the city and you could see an army of black ants crawling across the beach to mill around the great walls of the sand castle. Occasionally, a creaky, hard-shelled crab crawled in their midst. They seemed to have their attention focused on an army of red ants which occupied the largest sand castle on the north side of the river. The clacking of mandibles and screaming of wounded ants could be heard far out to sea. Greasy black smoke roiled into the pale sky from the south side of the river behind the ant armies. The clash was horrible there. It would be worse around the sand castle on the north side of the river that runs to the sea. Those great walls would be washed with the blood of the attackers. There was no Joshua there to bring them down with a blast from his horn.

With a final rumble of Kipling's thunder the dawn was over and the yellow sun loomed full circle in the Southeast Asian sky. Pale light gave definition to the insects in Hué. Ants became soldiers and the hard-shelled crabs became tanks. I had to leave my box seat before the sun got much higher. Lingering with thoughts and images was a strong temptation. There would be little enough time for such things during the fight for the north side of Hué and the grand prize trophy of the entire battle, the three-hundred-year-old fortress known as the Citadel.

Maybe just a moment longer. I'd need some color and detailed observations to include in the stories to be written about this battle. If the American military command was cruel enough to order an attack on those great stone walls, the least I could do was try to eulogize the Marines who died in the attempt. There were plenty of civilian reporters who could analyze and dissect the fight from a tactical or political perspective. Someone should say something about the poor bastards who knew little of tactics and cared less for politics. Someone should write about the little guy with the big rifle that was carrying this fight toward an ambiguous conclusion on flat, smelly infantry feet. That someone was me and the other Marine Corps correspondents who lived with the Marine grunts.

It was symbiotic relationship. Grunts were ordered to fight the battles; correspondents were ordered to write the stories that civilian newsmen considered too biased or supportive of the establishment in an unpopular war. The military correspondents got a close-up view of the action which sometimes gave their stories value in the commercial market; the grunts got a shot of self-serving publicity which sometimes made their miserable existence less hard to take.

For most of us, association with the infantry ended when we had a representative sampling of action photos and some eyewitness detail for stories. There was little desire to put up with the misery, pain and exhaustion of the grunt lifestyle on anything but an irregular schedule. An occasional dip in the pool is refreshing and gives you a sense of what fish must feel like. But there's no future in growing gills or drowning while trying to imitate them. After a while – seven months in my case – you developed an emotional callus. Get only so close and then backpedal rapidly; live and tell the story as best you understood it. You developed methods of getting the glory of infantry fighting on film and in your notebooks and then got out of the fight before you realized there really is no glory in it at all. You became a con artist to keep yourself supplied and moving into and out of battles when no one who wasn't zipped into a body bag could get out. And you rapidly adopted the *Code of the Grunt*. Rules to live by, written by outlaws in desperate mental and physical situations.

They don't teach the *Code of the Grunt* in military school. But they do teach military history. And there is a sense of major historical significance in this confrontation between these ancient walls and the modern men ordered to climb them. Students would study this battle someday. I was sure of that. Similar attack and defend situations had fascinated me in a time when I aspired to become a part of military history. It was a time before I looked into my Marine Corps pack and failed to find a field marshal's baton. How would a field marshal handle this?

Throw up the scaling ladders and storm the ramparts? Or maybe ignore the walls. Bypass operation. Let some other poor bastard die for his country. Borrowed a pair of binoculars from an artillery spotter and scanned the looming structure across the Perfume River. Slowly tilted the lenses above a hazy horizon of gunsmoke. There. Your basic fairytale, dope-smoker's pipe dream. Wall surfaces and guard towers. A North Vietnamese flag flew tauntingly from a tall flagpole located somewhere inside. What sort of symbol did Emperor Gia Long fly over those walls when he had them built as a bastion to protect the survivors of the Nguyen dynasty?

Had to be something threateningly nationalistic like the colors that flew over other unconquerable barriers; the

Siegfried line, the massive fortifications of Normandy-Cherbourg, or the complex defensive structures on Pacific flyspecks like Tarawa. Time seemed desperately out of joint here. Modern warriors, fondling automatic rifles and grenades in the same way others must have fondled arbalests and catapults; waiting to be ordered up against such fortifications. Now it was the American Marines. Yankee Doodle in King Nguyen's Court.

Yellow-skinned men moving cautiously along the tops of the great walls. Defenders burrowed like moles into the earth on the surface of the structures. Why? The walls can take care of the situation without an army's help. Walls like this *are* warriors. Like Goliath, a giant sent into the valley to confront David. Who needs an army of Philistines when you've got a giant? To fell this Goliath, Little David would need his best sling and a helmetful of high-explosive, smooth, flat river rocks. But David would not be allowed to use them for fear of damaging national treasures in the fight.

Night yielding to dawn now. Before long, I'd have to take cover. Snipers love to see targets silhouetted against a morning skyline. Babble of voices behind me. Civilian reporters trying to coax stories out of the survivors of the first half of the Great Big Battle for Hué City. What do they expect to get from that? Say Hi to Mom and Dad for me and tell them not to worry despite the fact that I'm scared, filthy, hungry, half-crazy and some gook will probably kill me in the next hour or so. Jesus, who are the real dumb shits? People who ask questions at a time like this or the assholes that bother to answer?

Daylight now. One last look at the Citadel and its walls. They've shouted an irresistible challenge to soldiers over the ages. You can't win. Smug boast. Stone gauntlet tossed to flesh and blood fighting men. No one has conquered these walls in the past and no one will ever do it. Attack these walls and you will die. And the Marines answered such a challenge the only way they knew. We can; we certainly can. We do what no one else has done as a matter of course. Maybe they could do it. I had to see.

More rain on Hué. Same as last night when the wind sighed and coughed, whipping sheets of water through the city and into a window of a building in which we slept. Soaked grunt near the window pulled his poncho tighter around his shoulders and swore at the darkness.

'Ah, Christ. Fucking Hué City. How the hell did we ever get *into* this mess?'

Good question. Just check my reporter's notebook here. Let's see. Yeah. It all started when I didn't go to Hong Kong.

South Side

1
Getting There
28 January 1968

Da Nang

Standard ration of shit from some clerk at the Division Command Post. Christ. Fucking dude with seven months in the bush has got a right to go on R & R, doesn't he?

'Who's going to cover Con Thien while you're gone?' Jesus.

'Here's a dime; call someone who gives a big rat's ass. Got to see the captain when he gets back from the G-2 briefing. OK, OK, don't get your bowels in such a Goddamn uproar. Call me when he gets back. Going down to the hooch and shed some of this slime.'

Rear echelon pogues and their silly-assed paranoia. Gooks moving all over the place. Big push on the urban centers. Don't they realize it's almost Tet, for Christ's sake? Fucking Zipperheads will all be visiting their ancestors and trading money and banging on gongs and barking at the moon or whatever the fuck it is they do this time of year. They can do it without me for five days, by God. Sat up at Con Thien for two months listening to incoming and watching grunts turn to hamburger. Dreaming about this R & R so long I Goddamn near polevaulted my way to the rear.

Shit. Ice-cold water in the showers. At least it's water. Wish it was fucking beer. Won't be long, man. Find a Chinese nurse and have her insert a cold beer IV the minute I get off that plane in Hong Kong. Fucking Hong Kong, man. Just say the word and my crank looks like a boa constrictor with a turtleneck sweater on. Maybe a quick blow-job in the airport. One more quickie in the cab on the way to the hotel and then I can get into some heavy fucking. Should be simple. My shit is organized, Jack. Five bills in back pay, three-hundred-dollar thirst and cheap pussy. Shit. Might even buy a handmade tie or something. Dude up at Con Thien just got back from Hong Kong last week. Gave me the scoop on all the good bars. Even got a picture of a Chinese hooker and a phone number to call so I won't have to observe the social amenities. Just see what the Old Man wants and then let the good times rock and fucking roll.

Do I have any idea why the cooks and clerks are all filling sandbags and running around with loaded rifles? No. Maybe some fucking comedian put 'War of the Worlds' on AFVN. Wrong? Reconnaissance patrols report large elements of enemy forces moving in toward all the central urban areas of I Corps? Da Nang, Phu Bai and Hué on one hundred percent alert for ground attack? Shit about to hit the fan?

'Somebody out there's got a real personal problem, Captain. Check it out first thing when I get back from Hong Kong.'

Shit. Hearts and flowers.

'Yeah, I know I'm needed.'

Right. Move my ass, posthaste, back up north and begin filing hot copy on the latest example of North Vietnamese treachery. Can't be much with Tet and all.

'Can't I just check it out real quick and make my plane? Shit, Captain, I got plans. I don't want to go on R & R next month. Yes, sir. I've been in the Marine Corps long enough to know an order when I hear one.'

Also been in long enough to recognize a cheap-ass rip-off when I see one. Got to find my own way up north also.

'Yes, sir. So what's new? How about briefing me on what you heard up at G-2? Better take your time and give me the full rundown – in detail.'

'Shit, Captain. We've been talking here so long it's too late for me to get a ride back up north today. First thing in the morning. Yes, sir. Be at the aerial port bright and early. Just going down to the hooch to catch up on some sleep and pack my gear.'

Christ. Should have known that R & R was too good to be true. Should have known I used all my Goddamn luck just getting off Con Thien alive. Should have Goddamn known, man. Can't go up north pissed off like this. Hot blood gets you killed. Seen it happen too many times. Got to operate to survive. Maybe spend some of those souvenirs I've been humping around for some booze. Get a few bottles and stay juiced until the next R & R quota comes around. As long as I'm somewhere up north, I'm carrying out the Goddamn order, right? And what the fuck are they going to do to me? Shave my head and send me to Viet Nam?

Freedom Hill PX at Da Nang stocked beer and whiskey for controlled consumption by soldiers, sailors and airmen. Marines barred from purchasing any of it. Commanding General apparently thought Marines had better things to do than sit around drinking. Like fighting the war, for instance. Even the portion of the MACV ration cards that outlined how much booze an American was allowed to purchase per month was removed before any Marine got one.

Prohibition pissed everyone off. Man with an abiding interest in alcohol had to learn to operate within a thriving barter system. Goddamn seller's market for everyone but Marines. Typical shit. Pissed me off to have to deal with these motherfuckers. Feel like a buffoon having to play games with some noncombatant sonofabitch who had all the booze he wanted just because he wasn't a Marine. Great fucking reenlistment incentive. Wish I'd known that before I signed the line. Shit. Wish I'd known they were going to *send me to the Nam* before I signed the line. Ah, hell. Good stories here, I guess. Solid stuff about the guys doing the dying. Better than writing minutes for the Officers' Wives Club meetings. And I know how to horsetrade.

Made it a practice to pick up small items of North Vietnamese equipment that the grunts didn't bother to collect. They ignored equipment pouches, helmets, canteens and entrenching tools. Preferred to race for the SKS carbines and ChiCom pistols. They could claim those as legal souvenirs and take them home. Fuckers didn't realize that other shit was good as gold as trading material. Picked up everything I could carry from the dead gook bodies. Guys in the rear would trade their mothers for a gook souvenir to take home. Didn't make any difference to them how worthless it was to the grunt who picked it up. Souvenirs are relative to your frame of reference.

Threw several items into an old pack and set out on the road, hitchhiking toward the Construction Battalion Compound outside Da Nang. Engineer-sailors were notorious for their ability to drive a hard bargain. Fuckers also had unlimited access to any kind of alcohol a man could want. Figured to get some gin or vodka. White whiskies mixed well with Kool-Aid or the 'bug juice' they served in the field messes. Want to mix that shit. Makes it last longer. Clincher for this deal banged away at my thigh, inside a trouser pocket. Two NVA bayonets. Stripped from an AK-47 rifle, they doubled as wire cutters. SeaBees should go for them like rotation orders.

Early in the day for a crowd. Club manager stood in

the doorway of his facility chewing on a toothpick. 'Whatcha need, Marine?' Crusty first-class petty officer had his leg cocked up on a case of Johnnie Walker scotch.

'Thought I might have a few cool ones with you. Then maybe we could talk about a little trade for some booze.'

Sailor grinned and motioned me into the dark, cool interior of a lush club, built by the SeaBees to their own specifications. Here we go. How much shit am I going to have to take from this asshole?

'You just come in from the bush?'

Popped two Black Label cans from behind the bar. Buying his Goddamn war stories.

'Yeah. My outfit's up on the "Z" and I got back for a few days. Got to go back tomorrow. You might have heard about the big attack that's coming.'

Shared a few more beers. Cheap fucker meticulously subtracted the price from a five-dollar Military Payment Certificate I laid on the bar. Broke out a bottle of Cuervo tequila when I cooked up some bullshit about a bayonet fight.

An hour of beer spiked with tequila. Asshole isn't even listening anymore. Telling me about all his stupid fucking headaches. Guys ripping him off at the bar. Too many inventories. Chief always fucking with him. Dangerous shit. Man might be killed.

'Jesus, I tell ya.' Pouring tequila straight into the beer cans. 'I wisht I could get up there and see some of that shit instead of serving buffalo piss to these guys at the club.' Yeah. Volunteer, dude. Go on up and die instead of ripping off the guys who want to live. OK. One last time.

'Nah, man. You don't want any part of that shit. Stay in the rear, do your time and go the fuck home.'

Nodding at the wisdom of that but the war stories had

gotten to him. Eyeing the pack over in the corner. 'Got some good stuff in there?'

'Yeah. Just some shit I picked up from some NVA we nailed in an ambush last week. Thought I might be able to get something for it.'

'What you lookin' for?' Two more beers hit the bar.

'Need some white stuff. Gin or vodka is best where I'm headed.' Pack open on the bar. Sailor handling an entrenching tool.

'Jeez, man. I don't know.' Slugging from the tequila bottle. Prolonging the Goddamn agony. 'I got a couple of these here items.'

'Hey, man. Enough of this cheap shit.' Steamed from booze and heat. 'I'm tired of your garbage. Here's two AK bayonets. Don't tell me you've ever seen any like them before because you've never even been outside this fucking compound. No more horseshit. Take the Goddamn bayonets and give me four bottles of gin or vodka.'

'Touchy sumbitch, ain't you?' Sailor swept the bayonets off the bar and stuffed them into his pocket.

'Yeah, I'm touchy, asshole. And I don't appreciate being ripped off and fucked around by rear echelon turds. You got what you want now get the fucking booze. And I'm taking the rest of this Mexican mule piss to boot. You want a fucking argument?'

'Shouldn't even let you bush-beasts in here. Can't keep a civil tongue in your head.' Sailors beginning to wander into the club. Getting dark out. 'Meet me around back.'

Lurched off the barstool and out the door of the club. Shit. Fucked up like Hogan's Goat here. Sailor waiting at the delivery door of the club, holding four bottles of Seagram's gin. Sit down right here in the sand and fill these Goddamn canteens.

'Jeez, man. Get that gin and get the fuck outa here

before the Chief comes in for a snort and sees you with club booze.'

'Suppose that Chief might shave my head and send me to Hong Kong? Your Goddamn juniper-berry juice is a poor fucking substitute for my Goddamn R & R. You know that, man? Go on, get out of my life. You got what you want. Now leave me alone.'

Had to sneak through the concertina wire strung around the gate and avoid MP patrols. Only drunks can maneuver properly in these situations. Finally made it back to the hooch and collapsed on a field cot. Alarm sirens and panicky clerks falling all over themselves manning defensive bunkers. Inky night sky lit with parachute flares. Go north, young man. Shit. Which way is Hong Kong? OK. Give it a shot. Get the proper mental set here, man. Might be the Goddamn story of the century up there. Might be a chance to hit the big time with a piece that means something to someone. Stared at the flares for a while. Fucking things look like the nightlights of Kowloon. Felt like puking. Probably the booze.

Dong Ha//29 January 1968

'Now look, Goddamnit. I've got to get north today and standing around here bullshitting with you isn't getting me there.'

Arguing with a fat, sweaty Army corporal behind the booking desk at the Da Nang 15th Aerial Port. Been pissing and moaning for a full hour. Goddamn head full of wet sand and worms. Should be in fucking Hong Kong fucking.

Corporal licked perspiration off his upper lip. He's too short to give a shit. Coloring little squares on a short-timer's calendar. Voluptuous woman, beckoning with one hand and massaging her pussy with the other. Divided up into spaces with numbers in each space corresponding to a countdown for the number of days the owner has left in the Nam. Working on the left tit; doesn't like the interruption.

'You look, dude. You bush-beasts coming in here don't impress me for shit. I'm the one who says *where* you go and *when* you go around here. Word is no Marine birds going north today and that's the way it is. Sorry 'bout that.'

Should slug the bastard. Fuck it. Too hot in here for a man with a world-record hangover. Doomed to rot in a hothouse terminal. Wouldn't be so bad if they had something out on the flight line headed for Hong Kong. Could I tell them I made a mistake and got on the wrong plane? Can't understand this shit. Things usually worked the other way around. Zip right back to the forward areas with minimum difficulty, but just try getting space on something headed for the rear. Much better chance of finding a field grade officer burning shitters.

Had to find a quick way to get myself four canteens full of gin, and a bagful of cameras and film back up north past that uncooperative sonofabitch at passenger control. Jesus. Hotter out here than it was inside. At least there's a breeze. Ah, the pungent smell of the Orient. Delicate aroma of water buffalo dung, wafting gently over the rice paddies. Roaring aircraft propellers. God, my head. Air Force cargo plane taxiing forward toward a stack of boxes sitting next to a forklift. Here we go. Boxes stenciled with the designation of an outfit based at Dong Ha. Get there and I should be able to make Phu Bai before dark. Two infantry regiments headquartered at Phu Bai. If something really was up, they'd be in on it.

Pilot in a jaunty blue overseas cap standing outside the airplane, watching the loading. Better play the game. More bullshit. Lie to this fucker for a ride to a place I don't want to go. Play the fucking clown one more time. *Code of the Grunt*: Do what you have to do. Payback is a motherfucker. Hold that thought. Air Force lieutenant eyed my slovenly condition through tinted flight glasses.

'Scuse me, sir. I got a real problem and I thought maybe I could ask one of you officers for some help. My brother's up at Dong Ha at Charlie Med. He got hit yesterday and I got permission to go up and see him. But the Marines say there ain't anything flying north.'

Officer flashed on an opportunity to demonstrate the Air Force would fly where the Marines wouldn't. 'So you want the Air Force to take you up there, right?'

'Yes, sir. If I don't get up there today, my brother might die and I would never see him again.'

Look at this fucker. Big chance to be a hero. Help out the beleaguered grunts and be remembered as a Good Joe. He bit. Get my gear and climb aboard. Showing me how to strap in on the floor of the airplane.

'When you get up to see your brother, tell him the Air Force got you there on time, hear?'

Sure, asshole. If I *had* a Goddamn brother, I'd pay him to kick your silly ass.

Two-engine transport clawed for airspace over Da Nang. Peculiar sensation. Like the airplane doesn't want to leave the earth and get up there with its ass hanging out. Reluctant little lurch when the wheels lifted off the runway. I can dig it, airplane. Fuck it. Let's go to Hong Kong. On the way north. Hope that short-timer corporal at the booking desk catches a bad burst of clap on his first low-level mission over a broad back in the world.

Stomach woke me from a sweaty stupor. Floor of the airplane dropped and tilted. Red clay patch below. Dong Ha. Pilots taking no chances with incoming artillery. Roared down on the short, bumpy strip and turned into a landing pattern at just the last safe moment. What the hell are they sweating about? Assholes will be back between clean sheets in an hour. Maybe I should learn to fly. Nah. Might turn me into an asshole.

30 January 1968

Doldrums at Dong Ha. Somebody ought to tell these fuckers the yellow horde is about to descend. Single, silent Huey helicopter on the matting in front of the shanty passenger terminal. Two or three Marines sprawled in the red dust beside the building in various stages of stupor. Fuckers are incredible. Manage to arrange their limbs under, over or around sixty pounds of bulky equipment and sleep like babies. *Code of the Grunt*: Never stand when you can sit, never sit when you can lie down, and never lie down without going to sleep.

Familiar form inside the terminal. Tall blond dude arguing with another passenger clerk. Humped enough clicks behind that guy to recognize the rawboned build and tired slouch. What's he doing here? Another kindred spirit looking for the action. One-sided argument at the desk. Slammed his steel helmet down and headed for the door.

'Well, no shit, Steve. They rip you out of that cushy assignment with the ever-peaceful 1st Marines? All ready for World War III?'

'Hey, D.A. I was wondering if I'd run into you on this deal.'

Good dude. Competent in combat. Knew him from duty back in the world too. Things looking up here.

'Been back to Da Nang? They're in some kind of panic down there. Seems the great fucking yellow hordes are about to descend from the north or something. Sent me up here yesterday and I've been trying to get to Phu Bai ever since. Word is the gooks are moving on Hué City.'

'Hué City? Shit. We were there two months ago on a sight-seeing expedition. Remember? Visited Ted Yount at the radio and television station there. Had a *good* time. Christ, there's a whole regiment of ARVN based there and some Army advisors. Vietnamese consider the city sacred or something. Remember he told us about it, kind of like a living museum? Beautiful place, man. Remember that fucking Citadel? Goddamn fortress of the ages. How'd you like to have to attack that? Remember those walls, Steve? I dug those walls, man. Remember?'

14 December 1967

Sight-seeing tour in a borrowed jeep. Half-drunk and half-listening to the historical rap Ted was spouting. Concentrating on tight little asses molded to bicycle or motorbike seats. Winsome gook girls in Ao Dais. Bright colors. Happy people. Everyone seemed to be smiling and no betel-nut stains on their teeth. Different world here, man. Is there really a war going on in this country? Seems like a carnival weaving in and out of ancient ruins. Like Rome, Paris or Athens. People conscious of living in and around their own history. Proud. Happy. Christ. They ought to bring those poor fuckers in from the villages and give them a dose of this.

The Citadel. Fortress, moat and all. Three-square-mile interior occupied nearly half the city. People attacked structures like this one throughout military history. Tremendous sense of historical significance here. Flashing on archers in phalanx, siege engines and boiling oils. Soldier's perspective. What would it be like to attack stone walls, thirty feet high and thirty feet thick?

Culture class continuing. Asian bandits, warring hill tribes, rival rulers and Mongol hordes had attacked the walls over the years. How many thousands had been blown away trying to climb the great stone slabs and get at whatever was behind them? Awesome sight. Ramparts, redoubts and moats. Lichens, mosses and tropical ivy encroached on the walls after three hundred years of nurturing in the hothouse climate of Southeast Asia. Perhaps the walls sprouted a perverse camouflage of their own to hide the ravages of time and weather. Or maybe time itself took a hand in covering the cuts and bruises inflicted by thousands of warriors and weapons over hundreds of years.

Vegetation getting unevenly closer to the broad tops of the walls where bracken and bramble grew wild. In two more centuries it might reach the top. In two or three after that, it might stretch like a lush, living carpet to the 'Palace of Peace,' seat of the Vietnamese emperors. Starting to rain. Tourists want to wind up in a whorehouse. Maybe later. Let me look at the walls some more.

It was the patches of vegetation that gave the stone rectangles their camouflaged appearance. You could sweep the one-mile stretch of each wall with your eyes and imagine the ivy to be the gnarled fingers of attackers who died assaulting a hallowed fortress. Long dead fingers clinging to a wall their owners could not climb. Clouds, pregnant with spume from the South China Sea which feeds the moat around the walls, parted to reveal string-straight streets leading from each of four gates to the inner city. Each street ended in a wooden arc of bridge that was the only entrance to the emperor's splendidly lush gardens. Raindrops wrestled with stray shafts of stormy sunlight to create gemstones embedded in the ornate, upswept roofs of the palace buildings. The fiendish faces of gargoyles guarded every doorway.

Between the great walls and the lush courtyards of the Imperial Palace, four-square blocks of homes had sprung up during the time since the last emperor left and the seat of another dictatorship had been established in Saigon, far to the south. They seemed to be a blot on the pristine palace structures, commingling elements of Asian urban splendor with the tin-roofed squalor of peasant poverty.

God. This place is majestic, beautiful, awesome, frightening.

31 January 1968

Steve swilling gin from one of my canteens.

'Would the gooks really go after Hué?'

'Fuck. I don't know. Best deal is to get to Phu Bai and see what they know around 5th Marines' headquarters.'

'Maybe we can trade some of this gin for a little cooperation from that maggot at the passenger desk.'

'I'll burn in hell first. Had enough shit from these petty fucking bureaucrats. Remember the time we were stuck here for three Goddamn days?'

'You mean the Asshole Aptitude Test?'

'Shit, yeah. Military's got a special Asshole Aptitude Test that they give to everyone. Got to score at least ninety-five to be a passenger clerk in the Nam. Check it yourself. Ninety-five times out of a hundred when you approach the passenger desk at an aerial port, *you will* find an asshole.'

Air Force sergeant playfully goosing a Vietnamese woman in conical hat and baggy, black silk trousers. She pretended to swat at the sweating NCO with her broom each time his thumb jabbed her butt.

'It'll be more than my thumb next time. Har, har.' Slobbering around a soggy cigar butt. 'Whattaya need?'

Definitely asshole material. Probably scored a clean one hundred on the test.

'Any chance of getting out of here to Phu Bai?'

'Shee-it. There ain't a fucking thing flying north or

south. Everything's locked on to standby for combat commitments.'

'What about that Huey parked outside?'

'That's the emergency bird. And it don't go nowhere unless you got an emergency. Which you ain't.'

Serpentine line of Army supply trucks hugging the road outside the Dong Ha terminal compound. Vehicles bearing the tactical mark of a logistics outfit based with the Marines at Phu Bai. Steve strikes a deal with a grizzled NCO. Our taxi awaits. For a canteen of gin we ride up front in comfort with him. Dude can't believe we'd cough up a canteen of gin to get to Hué.

'Ain't you fuckers heard the word? ARVN got caught with their pants down around their ankles up there. And the Goddamn city's only eight miles from Phu Bai combat base too. Supposed to be a ceasefire for Tet and all. But those little dudes up and walked into Hué all of a sudden. Shit. They own the place now. Heard from a chopper crewman that they even got an NVA flag flying over the Goddamn Citadel. Nobody knows how many there are in there but word is they made an attack on the MACV Compound and the ARVN are screaming for the Marines from Phu Bai to come and bail them out of the shit.'

So it *is* Hué. And it *is* a fairly big push. I'll be Goddamned. Steve staring at me, eyes wide behind his glasses. Non-verbal cue. Big-time action. Might even be worth delaying the R & R a month. Christ. Fucking Hong Kong wasn't going anywhere. This deal in Hué is definitely history. And that fucking Citadel . . . if they're in there we might just see the first nuclear strike of the war. A guy could insure his whole future covering a fight like this.

2
Outskirts
2 February 1968

The Canals

Light rain falling at dawn. It will alternate with heavier showers throughout the day. Creates an ambient hiss in Hué. Like a noisy snake undulating through the streets. Musty, cloying smell of wet canvas, mildew, decay. Constant, clammy immersion inside and out of rubber rainsuits. Nagging urge to rip them off and let the spray from the skies wash the slimy sweat from our bodies. Cold for Southeast Asia, but the sweat keeps pumping. Fear and discomfort grip and squeeze it out of the skin.

Momentary dry spell this morning. Woke lying next to a filthy, bearded grunt in a billowy featherbed. No windows in the bedroom. Relatively safe to strip and crawl under the velour curtains we used for quilts. Feathers and velvet sponged the moisture. Wonderful, warm feeling at dawn. And then the burst of small arms and several quick, ringing bangs from grenades. Drenched again instantly.

Not overly interested in what prompted the firing. If it's important, someone will say so. Grunts rolling ponchos; digging in packs for C rations. Drawn-out morning ritual of field troops. No one anxious to go outside, get wet and see what's up for the day. Critical need for coffee. Go for the sensual warmth of a steaming canteen cup. Inhale the vapors and purge the lungs. Little things mean a lot. Borrowed C-4 plastic explosive from an attached engineer. Stuff burns with an intense flame. Coffee water boiling hot in a very short time and no gagging fumes from issue heating tablets. Careful not to roll the doughy little ball too tight. Might blow a finger off just trying to get the engine started.

Bitter C-ration coffee churning around in my belly. Outside into the drizzle. Grunts dragging NVA bodies into a tangled heap. At least some of the dancing shadows last night had hidden enemy soldiers. Other Marines forming up in fire teams on both sides of the street. Squad leader manhandling people out of cover.

'Skipper says we're holding for arty prep from Phu Bai. Supposed to move under it and link up with some people forward of us near the MACV Compound. First Sergeant said more people are comin' into the city. Be a good Goddamn deal, if you ask me. I lost half my fucking squad in that convoy ambush yesterday.'

Three quick explosions from somewhere near the center of the city followed by a sharp exchange of machine-gun fire. Squad leader had been on a reconnaissance patrol earlier this morning.

'That's the MACV Compound. They been catching hell right along. Six says they got a bunch of advisors and Doggie MPs holding the place. Figures them Doggies would get their tit in a wringer.'

Pointed to his helmet. Grotesque caricature of the Marine Corps eagle, globe and anchor emblem. 'Semper Fidelis' replaced by 'Simply Forget Us.'

'Chew tobacco spit. If you ain't a Marine, you ain't shit.'

Fucking poet. Looks like Marines might be shit too. Corpsmen labored over two wounded men under a poncho shelter. One of the wounded taking on the fish-belly complexion that precedes death. Shallow, ragged breathing. Dopey, myopic eyes slowly rolling back into his head. Won't be long now. Morbid inclination to watch it end. What happens in the last moment? Does it end like in the movies? Last gasping message for the girlfriend, deep breath and that's it? Never saw anyone die quietly before this. Mostly battered, shattered corpses with the life blown out violently and quickly by high explosives. Or men riddled by small arms so badly they were dead before they hit the ground.

Lost a bunch like that yesterday. Nasty fight, and looked like worse to come today when they moved on the MACV Compound.

'Well, fuck. Let's get this sucker on the road here. There's an R & R quota out there with my name on it.'

Christ. These communist crazies had to pick this time to pump up their revolutionary zeal. Lord knows, I wished I'd made the flight to Hong Kong with every mile the thrown-together convoy from Phu Bai covered.

Hit the lead truck with a command-detonated mine; blew cooks and clerks all over the area. Headquarters Commandant at Phu Bai had scoured the camp to augment Alpha Company, 1st Marines when they were ordered into Hué. Take the pressure off the MACV Compound and things should slow down. Right. Shit. Things got progressively worse after the mining incident. Grunts and people trying to imitate grunts fanned out to engage NVA in spider-traps and machine gun positions spotted around the outskirts of Hué.

Alpha Company tried through the gathering dusk and rain to form a line and clear the two- and three-storey buildings they encountered. Quickly became apparent that this was no Cavalry-style rescue mission. From the time Alpha Company crossed the first canal leading from the village of An Cuu on the outskirts of Hué into the central portion of the city, it was apparent that Hué would be a tough nut. Marines, fresh from jungle fighting along the DMZ, having trouble getting a coordinated attack going. Frantic calls for reinforcements as the sun went down. Phu Bai scrambling to recover a battalion or two of the 5th Marines and get them ready for a major fight in Hué.

Meanwhile, Alpha grunts desperately trying to deal with a strange sort of fight. Looming shadows, ambushes from above, ducking in and out of buildings. Keystone Kops. Before dark they realized two- and three-man teams were the only workable way to attack and clear fortified areas. Long night, capped by a counterattack in strength. NVA pushed Alpha Company's second platoon back out of a row of three buildings they captured in the afternoon. Back to the canal by midnight. Two hours of terror while the NVA probed and Alpha Company circled the wagons. Enemy suddenly backed off at around 0200 hours. Probably realized reinforcements would be up with daylight.

Time to move the wounded and dead back to An Cuu. Time for sleep while grunts scrambled around trying to establish a bridgehead for the expected reinforcements. Full daylight now and the extra troops had not arrived. Pressure still on the MACV Compound. Alpha Company Commander still figures he can afford to move forward with two platoons and engage the NVA circling the compound. Stupid fucking move if you ask me. Let the Doggies and ARVN hide behind the compound walls until the 5th Marines arrive. Or at least wait until they can get some artillery on the city interior. Naturally, no one asked me.

At the bridgehead position, radios crackled and sputtered. Alpha Six pleading for at least one artillery fire mission and then threatening to move without it. ARVN commanders in Phu Bai flatly refusing to let even one round be stuffed into a tube. Marine commanders argued hotly with the Vietnamese. Paradox developing. ARVN badly wanted the Marines to knock hell out of the NVA occupying the city. But it had to be done *gently*, gentlemen. Despite sound tactical considerations, they flatly refused to approve firing anything heavy enough to do any real damage into the city. No heavy artillery and definitely no air strikes. They expected the Marines to go through the houses and buildings one by one and kill all the NVA without dirtying any carpets or breaking any china in the process.

Initial Marine reaction: No fucking way, José.

ARVN wanted the best of both worlds and they weren't above simpering or wheedling to get it. They made excuses for themselves and heaped praise for the Americans' fighting ability on the Marine generals in hopes of launching an ego trip and getting the job done quickly. Local ARVN commanders are keenly aware of Saigon's displeasure over their inability to prevent take-over of one of the country's most historic sites.

Alpha Six champing at the bit. Attack-trained dog on a tight leash. Snapping at the radio operators and screaming for permission to move into the city. Momentum, man. Got to keep the momentum.

But the ARVN had the upper hand here. Convoluted system of fire support control and coordination for artillery and attack aircraft allowed them to cancel any requested strike on city strong-points before a round was loaded or a jet cleared the runway at Da Nang. Alpha Six screaming that the ARVN can't have their cake and eat it too. Meanwhile, ARVN officers chewing contentedly.

Seemed perfectly logical and fair to Oriental minds trained at the best Western military schools. Weren't these the great American Freedom Fighters who promised to save their country? Didn't they possess special weapons, skills and spirit to defeat an enemy which had foiled government forces for twenty years? OK. Alright. So why couldn't they kill the northern invaders without also destroying the sacred city? Or hurting the homes of the rich people who lived in the fabled city. Massive cross-cultural communications gap. ARVN commanders refused to bridge it. Stalemate would have to be broken over a headquarters conference table.

Alpha Six ordered to wait for instructions. Wait out, Alpha Six. Military version of being put on hold. Alpha Six wants some payback for the punishment he took last night. MACV wants some help with the harassment outside their high stone walls. Preeminent political considerations. Take off your packs. Wait out. We'll give you the word. Company spread out in a half-block of secured houses to sleep and wait for orders. Catch up on some of the sleep they missed last night.

Last night. First full night in Hué. Chinese Fire Drill. Three platoons consolidated by nightfall. Second platoon still probing forward to establish an outpost. Half the remaining Marines on alert; watching the shadowy streets and listening for enemy movement. Distracted and aggravated by the drumming sound of steady rain on roofs and pavements. Alpha Six awake and pacing the CP. Fussing with radios and worrying about his second platoon.

Most of the off-watch Marines made themselves at home in the houses of the well-to-do citizens of Hué. Real beds with mattresses and box springs, over-stuffed couches and chairs. Occupied sector looked like a skid row flophouse filled with filthy railroad bums. Sleep came quickly and comfortably for me and my bed-partner in the first two hours of the wet, muggy night.

And then it started. Second platoon in heavy contact somewhere out there in the inky blackness. Lanky grunt lying next to me on an ornate four-poster bed rolled over wearily and planted his muddy jungle boots on a Persian carpet.

'Shit. Ah mighta knowed it was too Goddamn good to

last.' Several muffled crumps from the alleys between the buildings in which Alpha Company grunts were sleeping or standing watch. Squad leader stuck his head in the door.

'Get on out here. The fuckin' gooks are all over the place pitchin' ChiComs into the houses. Six says hundred percent alert. Don't go outside the building. Pick a window and shoot any fuckin' thing that moves out there.'

Not much to see on the nighttime streets of Hué's south side. Wet pavement glowed in a pale moonlight but no veteran gook would be stupid enough to silhouette himself in the open. Veteran grunts would tell you that. If you were interested in seeing an enemy soldier before he got close enough to rattle a grenade inside your house, you watched the shadows. If one wavered or loomed, you shot the shit out of it. Procedure complicated by low, scudding clouds which drifted across the moon and made shadows flutter. A lot of nervous firing; not much talking. Ears would provide the first warning of an approaching grenadier. You needed to concentrate to stay alive.

Full alert. Shadowboxing. Grunt on the other side of the window from me fondled his M-16 with one hand and his crotch with the other. Frightened and alert. Adrenalin alarm clock keeping him out there on the edge. Pale eyes bugged from their sockets as he searched the shadows for movement. Silenced my only attempt at whispered conversation with an irritated wave of his hand. Shut up and leave the vigilance to him. You'd think the safety of the entire company depended on this one stupid fucking grunt and his lousy space-age plastic popgun. Fuck him. Just like a lot of other assholes in my thoughts lately. Do your job and never mind the Goddamn small talk.

Pre-Nam

Parents, dodging their own brand of threatening shadows. Shut up and do your homework. Shut up and do your chores. Shut up and get a job. Shut up and get grades good enough to get you into military school. Shut up and get promoted. Shut up and be a good soldier.

Didn't matter if what you had to say was interesting or intelligent. No one wanted to hear it. No one had time with all those looming shadows out there. Shit. Had to start writing just to get what I had to say off my chest.

Faggot English professor thought I might have some talent and taught me the mechanics. Wouldn't let him fuck around with me so he wouldn't listen to any small talk. But he did teach me to be an observer; to keep all my senses open and record everything I saw, felt, heard, smelled or tasted when I told a story. Taught me to keep a reporter's notebook and fill it with more than facts.

Hell of a New Year's Eve party in 1963. Tried to talk to everyone. Only the drunks would listen. I joined the drunks. And then I joined the Marines as soon as I was sober enough to sign my name. Ah, Christ. Self-pity in the City. And ain't that shitty. What brings all this on? Muggy night air, pungent with camphor-wood fumes. Dream Smoke.

Boot camp. Parris Island. Psychological warfare. Campus of the Corps. School colors: black-and-blue. Learn to love your fellow Marines and hate everyone else. You are the best there is. You are the elite. You can do much more than you ever thought you could do. Is that clear, ladies?

Listen up. Marines love and respect each other. They depend on each other like family members. No Marine is ever alone if there is another Marine in sight. No Marine ever needs to worry about having to stand alone once he becomes a member of the club. Is *that* clear, maggots? Yes, sir. Kill 'em and eat 'em.

Felt better than I ever had about myself. Found a place

where social intercourse was about as vital to your existence as social disease. Found a place where mavericks were in the mainstream. Pay your dues and pack your load and you didn't need shit from anyone else. Worked the angles; found a job in military journalism. Aloof, cold, professional; a good Marine. Got some stripes. Now all the rest of you assholes shut the fuck up. Remember: A Marine on Duty Has No Friends. Suits me.

Occasionally some fellow writer or photographer who admired my work, or some senior NCO who thought I was an iron-assed potential lifer, made overtures. Easy to handle that phony shit. Pour out the small talk like some twisted, manic tape recording, over beers in the NCO Club. But nothing personal; nothing that might be used to build a friendship. If you get too close to an asshole, you're bound to be shit on. Steve was the only exception in five years.

Probably a perverse case of opposites attracting. He was an educated, clean-cut, all-American type with conservative viewpoints and a loving young wife who wrote homey letters about pots that boiled over and commodes that didn't work. Respected his parents who bragged about their Marine son engaged in the defense of freedom in Southeast Asia. Strong feelings about patriotism and the rightness of American policy. I was none of those things.

There was something about his ability to listen with a sly, understanding grin on his lean face. And there was something about the way he seemed to care – really care – about other people's opinions. There was something about the way he did things for people without waiting around for congratulations or accolades. Couldn't bring myself to tag him an asshole. Figured he must be the exception that proved the rule.

Yeah. Look at this. He wants to relieve me at the

window. Wants me to go back and get a few hours sleep. He'll stand watch. Nice to have at least one flotation device in this sea of assholes.

3 February 1968

Late in the day, but something is going to break. Group of Marines gathered around a lieutenant across the street. Movement order. What will it be, tactics or politics? Lieutenant shaking his head and scratching a torn fingernail across the laminated covering of a street map of Hué. Poorly-scaled sight-seeing guide issued by the Vietnamese Bureau of Tourism.

'Battalion can't get permission from the ARVN to put artillery into the city.' Tight jaws; blank expression. 'We go ahead without it. And when we get across this next canal, nobody stops unless given the order. Six wants to reach the MACV Compound before noon chow.'

Rumble of snide remarks from the assembled squad leaders. Black Marine with a nickel-plated magnum revolver in a shoulder holster figured as much. 'Another dollar job on a dime budget.'

Meeting adjourned. Instructions to attached engineers: assemble some sort of bridge to cross the twenty-foot concrete drainage ditch which led into the central portions of the city. Engineer NCO shouldered through the departing group.

'No sweat, sir. I've got six men on it now and they say they'll have some kind of footbridge up in an hour.'

Engineers had a rickety-looking bridge assembled across the canal. Two-by-fours nailed together and suspended at water level. Engineer testing it wasn't in the mood for critique. Ankle-deep in water but the thing seemed to carry his weight.

'Will that fucking thing hold?'

Bouncing back to the near side to face the sidewalk superintendent. 'What the fuck you want, the Golden Gate? You're lucky I don't set up a Goddamn tollbooth here.'

Joined a squad preparing to go across. Engineers had rope hand-lines above the board bridge. First heavily-loaded Marines began a peculiar sideways shuffle across. When each man reached the opposite bank, he turned to help the next up on to the far side of the canal and then scrambled for cover. Shouldn't take the gooks too long to spot this encroachment.

Finally my turn to try the tricky suspension system. Cautiously negotiated my way across. Clatter of helicopter blades interrupted concentration on the slippery boards. Two Huey choppers roared up the canal. Only about thirty feet off the ground; snouts pointed down in a menacing posture. What's this? Rush to get to the other side. Too many grunts on the bridge. Too much weight. Too shaky. Heavy bursts of machine-gun fire above the roaring noise of the choppers. Jesus H. Christ. Fucking choppers firing on us! Scramble for the far side of the canal. High, sharp adrenalin rush.

'Friendlies, you assholes! Friendlies down here!'

Pressed flat against the concrete of the far bank. Man behind screamed and grabbed my legs to pull himself up off the bridge. Second chopper made its run. Bullets screaming off the concrete; adding to the nerve-jangling panic.

'No, no, no. Goddamn it! We're helpless down here.'

Choppers whining and roaring overhead. Odd markings on the nose. Yellow circle with a black cat in the center. Seen that before. Choppers were from an Army Air Cavalry unit based up in the north country.

Shaking grunts crouched, panting on the concrete ramp leading up from the canal. Squad leaders checking to see if anyone was hit. Helos stuttering away, jinking from side to side as the pilots walked on the rudder pedals. Door gunners leaning out. Stupid fuckers aren't even looking back to see what they've done.

No Marine casualties. Distinct impression from the yelling, cursing grunts that if those Army fliers had been there on the ground, they would quickly have become confirmed KIA. Hué becoming a free-fire zone. No chance to shoot back during the crossing. But the grunts will remember the incident. If Black Cat choppers show up again in Hué, they'll be met by intense antiaircraft fire.

Remainder of Alpha Company holding in houses across the canal. Fire teams sent out to secure the flanks. Teams of two men each flushing the gunners who were blasting away with AK-47s from second-storey windows. Marines advancing cautiously up stairwells to get at them. Classic World War II European Theater gig. One kicked the door to a room open and sprayed a burst of M-16 fire inside. Second man, hugging the other side of the door, armed a grenade and heaved it inside as hard as he could throw. The idea was to make the grenade bounce off the walls which made it difficult for gooks to chase down and toss out a window. Marines learning the tricks of house-to-house fighting quickly.

Still badly shaken; barely able to believe being fired on by American helicopters. Such a helpless feeling. Moment of empathy with the NVA and VC who endured constant air attack throughout the southern areas without the comfort of friendly air cover. What would this deal be like if MIGs suddenly appeared south of the DMZ? Lieutenant trying to explain the foul-up to an incensed infantry platoon.

'Those fuckin' Army turds. I've been on the horn to Phu Bai and reported it, but they say the only Army choppers in the area were supposed to be working west of the city. That's all we would have needed to get some people killed by friendly fire. Phu Bai is all fucked up. They got Army, Air Force and Navy trying to get into the fight. It's a problem but, by God, I promise you, those fucking chopper crews will pay for that crap.'

'Yeah. Well, let me know what the final explanation is.'

Maybe sketch out a story on the engineers who worked under fire to construct the bridge which carried the first combat troops into Hué. Good little feature. The real story was the helicopter screw-up which almost killed Alpha Company's first platoon, but that's not the kind of thing the MACV Information Office likes to see in print.

Moving now; dodging sniper fire, keeping an eye on the black smoke curling up into the wet air over the MACV Compound. Rifle fire to the right. Everyone dove for cover. Just beginning to notice how bloody everyone's knees, elbows and hands are becoming. Scrapes and scratches from throwing yourself down on concrete. Crackle of a radio nearby. In a doorway just ahead, Alpha Six squatted with his radio operator.

'Two Alpha, Two Alpha, Six . . . Two Alpha, Two Alpha, Six, over.' Static. Then the flat, metallic tones of radio communications.

'Six, Two Alpha Actual. No time to bullshit. Wait out.'

Radioman emitted a low whistle between his teeth. 'Those bastards must really have stepped in the shit over there.'

Platoon clearing houses on the right ran into stiff resistance from some NVA in a Buddhist temple. Series of abrupt crumping sounds punctuated by the rattle of gunfire. Grenades. Ringing bark from American frags and a shallow pop from the ChiCom variety.

Firing ceased. Only sporadic, ringing M-16 shots.

Marines crouched on both sides of the street waiting for orders. Ears hurt from the sudden change in sound levels. Radio chatter again.

'Six, Two Alpha Actual. I believe we've got most of them. We're holding in a two-storey building on the left side of the street just across from that fucking temple. Request you send some more bodies over here. We'll play hell holding if they decide to come back.'

Company Commander reached for the handset. 'Two, this is Alpha Six Actual. One Alpha is crossing now. How about casualties?' Pregnant pause and more static.

'Six, Two . . . I've got one Kilo and two Whiskies that I know of. The rest is up for grabs. This place is a cluster-fuck and I don't think I'll be able to find out for sure until help gets here and I can back off for a minute.' One Marine killed and two wounded in the skirmish. Still two city blocks from the MACV Compound.

'Two, Six . . . Roger. Hold on where you are now. I've got two corpsmen headed over there. We should be linking up with you in about one-zero mikes. See if you can spread it out along the first line of buildings and hold. Let me have a confirmed CasRep ASAP, over.'

'Six, Two . . . that's Charles, out.' Tenuous toehold on the city. The movement should be taking some of the pressure off the MACV Compound. As long as there was an external push, the NVA would have to commit some troops to halt it.

Alpha Company began to swing to the right through alleyways; cutting through buildings. Stepped into an alley running east and west, parallel to the axis of advance up the main street toward the MACV Compound. Buildings on either side had iron grillworks closed over their doors and windows. No cover here except flat on the ground. Bad approach, but cutting through buildings appealed even less. No telling what might be inside waiting with a good, tight sight-picture. Fell in behind two grunts. Gate-mouthed asshole grinning at me and my camera.

'Ain't war hell?' His buddy, a squatty little lance corporal with a clipped Bronx accent, pulled back the charging handle on his M-16 to chamber the first round of a fresh magazine.

'Yeah. But dis here combat is a mothahfuckah.' Word games. False bravado? Shit, I don't know anymore. Good snow-job if it is one. Thin line between bravery and bull-goose looneyness here. Maybe the assholes *aren't* afraid. I am.

Down a stinking alley. Camphor-wood smoke from abandoned cooking fires and fish sauce. Marines shouting to keep in contact with others taking the route through the buildings. Occasional grenade blast. Taking no chances. Frag first and ask questions later. Bronx Marine sprawling on the ground every time a grenade goes off. Everyone else following his lead. Strange, up-and-down ballet. No way of knowing which explosion is a ChiCom grenade until the shrapnel blows out your back. Grunts in the buildings should be giving a warning. Grenade exploded inside a building on our left just as the Bronx dude was passing a window. Concussion blew his helmet off and he lost his cool. Spun and triggered a burst of M-16 fire through the window.

'You mothahfuckahs start giving us a fire-in-the-hole before you pitch them frags or I'll blow yer stupid fucking asses away.' Tense, scratchy deal.

Focusing and framing a combat-weary grunt shot when his left arm separated from his shoulder. Automatically kept it focused in the viewfinder. A man's arm, flying through the air, tumbling end over end like it was winding up to toss a softball. Bronx dude slammed up against the near wall of the alleyway. Roaring heat of a B-40 rocket.

'Corpsman up. Gimme a fuckin' Corpsman up here.'

Marines running forward up the alley and piling out the windows of the houses. Street fight in the offing. Impact of the rocket to the rear made forward the safest direction. Run to the sound of firing. *Code of the Grunt*: Charge the fire. You may shock the trigger-man so badly he'll forget to reload and you'll certainly get yourself clear of the impact area.

Broke into another main street just as the second platoon opened up on the Buddhist temple again. Roaring passage of another rocket.

'Where's the gunner? Spot that Goddamn gunner.'

Huge black Marine with a drooping mustache covering his mouth leaning against a concrete wall; laughing at another man who was crouched and peering around a corner into the street.

'Hey, man. Did you see that motherfucker Albritton? That cracker shitheel pissed his pants when that last rocket went over. Hey, did you dudes see fuckin' Albritton's fuckin' trousers? Hey, Albritton. You a loose motherfucker, man.'

Corpsman hauling away the one-armed Bronx Marine. Out of sight; out of mind. Time for other observations.

Rocket burst flayed everyone with rock and concrete. Minor, bloody wounds didn't bother the black Marine. He sucked the blood off a running wound across his knuckles and burst into gales of laughter again. Object of his derision beginning to dig the attention. Laughing and pointing to his dampened crotch.

'Scairt the piss right outa me, man.'

Whole first platoon laughing and jiving in the alley. Fuck the rocket gunner. We got some humor going here, man.

Ripping sound of M-16s on full automatic. Second platoon moving after the gunner. They're catching all the shit. The rest of the company having a hell of a time getting near enough to help. Can't concentrate on the war when you've got people pissing themselves every so often. Snorting roar of small gasoline engines from the direction of the canals to the rear. Curiosity breaking up the show in the alley.

Two 106-millimeter recoilless rifles mounted on 'Mules,' small, four-wheeled platforms designed to move infantry equipment over rough terrain. Some of them had been sent up from Phu Bai when the call for artillery support was denied.

Nearest driver sat behind the wheel completely unprotected except for flak jacket and helmet, steering the Mule into an alley entrance. Huge grin on his face and the butt of a soggy cigar crammed in the corner of his mouth. Grunts began shouting as he braked and jumped off to strip 106 rounds from their cardboard containers.

'Hey 106s! You better get some of those motherfuckers, man. Get Some, dudes.'

Get Some. All-purpose phrase suitable for any violent confrontation. Grunt cheerleader's version of 'Yaaaaaaay, TEAM!'

Driver's gun crew followed him up the street at a run. Now two 106s were emplaced, one on each side of the street. Gook machine guns opened up again. Grunts realized the value of the recoilless guns. Clearing a path forward. Banging away at the gun positions to protect the 106 crews. An occasional rocket roared down the street impacting to the rear. Second platoon still hadn't found the rocket gunner.

Gun crew chief standing on one of the Mules: gazing at the buildings ahead through binoculars. Time for me to regroup. Back down the alley; hoping to find my pack. Dropped it when the first rocket was fired. Didn't need some greedy asshole digging around in there and finding my extra camera body. Radio noise and shouting in a house to the left. Three or four radio operators grouped near a window. Company Commander busily trading handsets and checking on the action out on the street. Map spread on his knee wasn't much more than a pencil sketch. Maps of Hué were in notoriously short supply and most commanders had begun to make their own. One of the radio operators noticed me squatting near the door.

Moved over toward me, his whip-antenna scraping loudly on the corrugated tin roof. Pointed at my pack sitting in a corner. The poncho, hastily jammed beneath the straps that morning, was neatly folded and tied on for easy access. Radioman grinning at me.

'Never hurts to curry the favor of the press.' No signficant sneer or guilty flinch. Camera's probably still in there.

'Got any ideas what the fuck is going on over there?' Jerked my head in the direction of rifle fire and exploding rockets. Radioman piecing together what he could from the traffic with battalion and the maneuvering squads. Apparently the NVA had moved in east of the second platoon with a number of B-40 rocket launchers. Second platoon, reinforced now by the first, was pushing them back to clear an avenue of approach to the MACV Compound.

'Is that what the 106s are for?'

My question lost in the ringing bang of the first recoilless rifle rounds. Better get back out there. Crew-served weapons usually make great action pictures.

Gunners ranging for targets with the .50 caliber spotting-rifles mounted on top of the 106 barrels. Two or three sharp cracks and then the solid boom of the big gun. Steady crumping sounds echoed down the streets as the armor-piercing projectiles impacted concrete. Gun crews working furiously, passing ammo to the assistant gunners who slapped rounds into the rear of the weapon. Oily snick of breech closing.

'Up!' Gunners concentrating behind the reticle sights; elevating and traversing before pulling on the firing switch to trigger the spotting-rifle. When a .50 caliber tracer impacted the suspected location of an NVA gunner, depressed the firing switch and the 106 roared, belching smoke and flame to the rear. Immediately the whole process began again. Crews working with slick precision, showing off for the kibitzing grunts. Gun crew chief scanning the buildings for signs of movement.

'They're moving into the street. Load the beehives.' Beehive rounds. Specially constructed shells containing hundreds of small steel darts. Designed for direct antipersonnel work, they could cut a swath through enemy formations.

Scurrying figures at the other end of the street, running away, carrying the small, tube-like B-40 rocket launchers. The NVA were being pushed from their positions as two platoons of Alpha Company grunts pressed them from the rear and flank. The 106s began firing the beehives. Strange, whirring, buzzing noise like hundreds of pissed off hornets headed for the source of agitation. Gunner nearest me slammed the firing switch and spit out his cigar. Standing, craning forward for a better view. Ringing of the gun still echoing inside my head. Crew yelling and pointing up the street.

All eyes locked on a North Vietnamese soldier squirming against a tree at the head of the street, AK-47 still in his hand. Through the binoculars, a strange tableau. Gook's feet suspended and dangling off the ground. Squirming body riddled with holes which showed through his dark green uniform as bloody splotches. The gunner with the cigar had caught him running from a building and fired as the enemy crossed in front of his sights. The resulting swarm of darts from the beehive round pinned him to a nearby tree like a paper target in a shooting gallery.

Focusing the binoculars for a closer look. The NVA's face suddenly exploded like an overripe tomato. Grinning grunt lowered his M-16 and turned to gesture at his buddies who were just beginning to move back into the street. NVA was still, then. The AK-47 slipped from his grip and fell to the ground below his dangling feet.

Final shot to kill the NVA pinned to the tree seemed to signal a halt to the rest of the firing. Only distant popping sounds of the first and second platoons still moving toward the MACV Compound disturbed the silence. Back to the Company CP. Friendly radioman related that the company was ordered to move west on the outskirts of the city as soon as they reached the Compound. The NVA were breaking their siege and moving in that direction. Reinforcements were already rolling in on convoys from Phu Bai and the Second Battalion, 5th Marines (2/5) were crossing the first canal on the left and moving into the city.

Alpha Six taking a break against a wall. Mission accomplished.

'How can I go about linking up with Two-Five?'

'Hotel Company will be coming forward through this pos. Just hold on here with us for a little while. They'll be our contact relief and you can move on forward with them when they come through.'

Big sigh. Eyes closed. Swan dive into the valley on the other side of Adrenalin Peak. Nodding; head tilted forward as he dropped off to sleep. Hollow clunk as his steel helmet hit the concrete floor of the room. Red-rimmed eyes jerked open. Quick glance at his radio operators and then a slow fade back into oblivion.

Amazing Goddamn act, especially with only about half his unit actually experienced infantrymen. Through the hard fighting last night and this morning he remained calm and collected, running widely-scattered elements in almost constant contact with the NVA. Jumping from one radio operator to the next in an effort to give sensible orders and find out what was happening to Marines out of his sight and personal control. Many sad letters to write tonight.

Shit. Hate to do it, but I need to talk to him. Questions for the story of the Marines' first actions in the Battle of Hué City. Eyes remained closed, but he answered every one. Finished now, he nodded as I moved away and then snapped his head up again.

'Get the story straight. I did a lot of talking on the radio, but those grunts out there bought this real estate.'

Yeah. Noble sentiments for the self-effacing leader of men. Why the Goddamn act, man? You did a fine thing. Shit, it was a heroic thing. I can dig that. Few enough people in this Goddamn war can do what you did with any competence at all. Last cigarette in the C-ration four-pack. Smoke cutting into my lungs. Stale as usual. Alpha Six sprawled in exhausted stupor. Where have I seen something like that before? In a museum back in The World? Yeah. Atlas with the world on his shoulders. Boy, you got to carry that cross. So who asked you to be a fucking officer anyway?

Looking over my notes. Told Steve about the Company Commander's performance. Said it would be a good story. He listened and then said I was finally beginning to see.

'See what?'

'You'll know when your vision gets a little clearer.'

Stupid thing to say. Slightly pissed off at him when we got the word that Hotel Company would be delayed. Find a place to sleep for the night.

Leave him alone. Let him sleep for the first watch.

Wandered outside into a garden where grunts were getting into position for the watch before the sun completely sank below the housetops in Hué. Learned a lesson last night. From now on, listening-posts would be outside the houses where they could stop the gooks before they got close enough to heave grenades.

Smoked a last cigarette before dark and then found a position that partially protected me from the rain. There was another grunt under the shrub staring keenly out into the gloomy night. Too dark to see his face. Tried a few whispered comments about the action that day and followed with a few tentative questions about his hometown.

For some reason he didn't tell me to shut up. Whispered to each other through the rainy night. Nothing very intelligent or enlightening to say, but I kept up the conversation, even when it became personal. Seemed really anxious to tell me about his family and girlfriend. Mentioned his first name but I really wanted to see his face. Heavy shit that morning must be working on my mind. Found myself actually wanting to *know* this guy as we whispered into the night.

If the NVA moved on our position, we wouldn't have heard a thing until the moment before we died. He'd have died happy, thinking of home with a buddy at his side. I'd have died amazed.

The MACV Compound//4 February 1968

God knows snipers have enough targets around this area. Can I afford to fire up a smoke? How bad do you want to burn one, babe? Is the high worth the hurt? Shit. About fifteen more minutes before the sky will be light enough to make it safe. Cough. Goddamn Pneumonia City here. Smoke would be nice but a round full in the fucking face would be rain on the parade. Wait for a while.

Relatively quiet last night. Freshening breeze as the sky grayed around the edges with first light. Yeah. But no silver fucking lining. Breeze brought heavy cloud cover in from the sea and the air turned icy cold. Miserable with chills when the word came to saddle up and move.

Walking toward the MACV Compound, quietly in the musty night before dawn. Steve headed for the Compound gate. Wanted to get inside and talk to the Battalion Commander. Shouldn't be any problem. He moved forward to set up his command post almost immediately after Alpha Company cleared the area around the walls. Now we can get into this shit for real. Heavyweights safely behind stone walls. Grunts can now be moved around with impunity. Well, fuck that. I've got all the story I'm interested in right now. Real question is what Hotel Company, Second Battalion, 5th Marines is facing in *this* part of the city. Gooks pulled back from the Compound, but they sure as shit haven't quit.

Hotel spent most of the day yesterday trying to take the Vietnamese Treasury building. They didn't make it but their attack had done a great deal to protect Alpha Company's exposed flank as they moved on the Compound. Hotel Company hadn't been able to get inside the imposing two-storey structure yesterday and most of the grunts were fatigued and jittery from the daylong futile fight.

Sky flaring into a dull glow. Steve returned just as the drizzling rain started again.

'Looks like we picked the wrong outfit to tie up with. Battalion Six says we're going after the Treasury Building again and this time he wants the fucking thing taken. No excuses. We could split here and stay inside the Compound if you want. There's lots of civilians inside. Six says transportation should be rolling for Phu Bai before dark tonight and we could get some of this early shit out with them.'

'Christ. Let me see. Fucking figures. The plane for Hong Kong left day before yesterday. Nah. We can probably get some good shit up here. Listen, you bundle all the notes and film we've got in some plastic and see if one of the walking wounded will take them back when he goes out. We might as well stick with Hotel. The other outfits could be in for worse shit.'

Wrapping notebook pages and 35-millimeter film in plastic covering from a radio battery.

'You sure you want to do this, man? This outfit got pretty well fucked up trying to take that building yesterday.'

'Yeah. Fuck it. Don't argue. Go on and deliver that shit.'

Raised eyebrows from Steve.

'Yeah. I know what's bothering you, man. Old D.A. acting a bit out of character, right? Not like me to miss an opportunity to take the easy way out of something that might get us killed. Is that what's bothering you, buddy?

'Shit, man. Go on and take that package inside. This is just a good story, that's all. We'll make every fucking paper in the English-speaking world with stuff out of here. Besides, if we go back to the rear, they'll just find some other shit-kicker for us to go out on. Might as well stay here where we know the lay of the land.'

Shrugs. My funeral, right? Steve moved off toward the Compound gate.

Drainage ditch full of slimy water, human shit and Marine grunts all waiting to be flushed into the same sewer. Ripple of bitches from the yawning men waiting for word from their officers to move. Teeth chattering in the morning chill. Must be making enough racket to draw fire from the Treasury Building. Pristine granite façade sparkling with raindrops; half a block away across a wide, tree-lined boulevard and beyond a large courtyard surrounded by an intricately-carved stone fence.

How the fuck could it be so cold in Southeast Asia? Wasn't this the land of tropical jungles and sweltering heat? Smelly water rippled and splashed as a grunt moved toward my position. Wide grin on a filthy, unshaven face. Reached up to scratch at my own prickly growth.

'Where you from in The World, man?' Classic grunt conversational foray.

'Southeast Missouri.'

Light enough now. First cigarette glowing in the gloom. No use telling him exactly. Typical hometown, volunteer grunt. Probably sent postcards from Parris Island which ended up on the bulletin board at the general store. Obviously wanted to shoot the shit.

Flash back. Last night, and the long, rambling intimate conversation with the friendly grunt I didn't know. At least I could see this guy's face. Shit. Think rationally. It's not like you're taking responsibility for a buddy or anything.

'Where you from?'

'Me? I'm from Amarillo, Texas. I ain't never met anybody from Missouri before.'

Kid launched into a monologue about Texas and all the high school girls he'd had before coming into the Marines to 'get me a set of them fuckin' dress blues, man.'

No incoming fire for the past hour. Just biding our time here. Hotel Company leaders still inside the Compound in conference with the Battalion Commander.

More flashes from the past. Grunt's rap opening the time tunnel.

Thinking back to a summer in 1962 in Missouri delta

farm country. Military school as a gift from a preoccupied mother who wanted me to 'do something significant' with my life rather than toss it away like an alcoholic father who committed suicide because he couldn't stop drinking despite the fact that he had no choice if he wanted to live and retain his wife and son.

I did a lot of thinking that high school graduation summer. Trying to latch on to my first piece of ass from a big-titted chick who lived outside the gates of the school. Summer of adolescent introspection prompted by a refusal to surrender her cherry despite romantic, carefree circumstances and gallons of English Leather after-shave. No welcome at home so I stayed at school where I could date town girls and engage in long periods of self-evaluation. During one particularly arduous night of navel-gazing, it dawned on me.

No fucking wonder I couldn't get laid. Shit, the way I acted around people. I was lucky anyone even spoke. Cold fish. That's what she called me. Not willing to commit myself. Yeah. Supposed that was right. Manipulator. Big fucking operator. Get close to people just so I wouldn't miss when I decided to shit on them. How do you solve psychological hang-ups like that?

No psychology classes in high school. But I was smart enough to figure out what prompted the kink. Yeah. I knew then why I was so fucked up and I knew then what I was going to do about it whether the big-titted chick ever let me in her pants or not. I needed a Foreign Legion where they didn't give a shit if you were essentially an asshole. I needed a service that would welcome assholes as long as they were wild ones who could fight. I needed the Marine Corps.

Funny about that decision. Join a lash-up that specialized – even glorified – in death yet it was the sight of death that left me slightly deranged in the first place. Go figure that. It was the summer of 1957 when I had been shuttled off to spend time with my dad who was separated by the bottle from my mom and living with his parents in a small Southeast Missouri town. It was the shotgun blast that I heard from the back of the house and went to investigate. It was the sight of my father, the chunky, intelligent, towheaded Irishman with a heart of gold, a sensitive nature and the ghosts of an earlier war haunting him, that did it. It was wondering who that man with half a head could be. It was watching the crimson blood stream out of his skull, past the barrel of the smoking 16-gauge shotgun and on to my new white tennis shoes. It was the military funeral for a veteran at which they presented me with the flag that covered his casket. It was the weeks and weeks of screaming and crying rather than sleeping.

And most of all, it was the final night when a thirteen-year-old boy woke up dry-eyed and vowed never again to love anyone because everyone either got killed or killed themselves.

Violent death made me the way I was and yet, I sought solace in a service which preached mayhem and close combat as a way of life. Joined a club that played games in the most violent arenas of the world. Driven by one gory death scene, I became part of a legion bound by the nature of its existence to be involved in a war which was filled with death scenes, even during the intermissions. Yeah. But I didn't have to personally contribute to the carnage. There were ways around that shit when you've got a grip on yourself and your life.

4 February 1968

Kid from Amarillo concentrating on the Treasury Building. Nodding and pointing.

'I think I see them fuckers moving up on the second floor again.'

Yeah. Shadows flitting back and forth in the dawn light. If they go after it again today, it'll be the same frustrating shit as yesterday. Lucky to have survived that one. Gooks poured a murderous plunging fire from second-storey windows all day. White pockmarks on the building's façade from Hotel's return fire. Looked like some drunken sculptor had taken a jackhammer to it.

Three dead Marines lying in grotesque postures near the steps of the building on the other side of a broad courtyard. Hotel Company hadn't been able to drag the bodies back after their first attempts to get inside the Treasury Building had failed. Other dead and wounded were evacuated at nightfall, but those three remained to haunt Hotel Marines. When dark closed in, the dead men ceased to be persons and became simple shadows in the dark. When dawn brought the light, they regained names and personalities. Hotel stared and concentrated on hating the gooks who killed them.

Activity beginning now all along the assault line. Officers returned from their conference. Squad leaders briefed. Stirring among the grunts who would make the first rush of the day. Rooster crowed in the distance. Almost like a bugle call. Firing started immediately. Roar of M-16s and M-60 machine guns from both ends of the long drainage ditch.

Six Marines broke cover. Tidal wave of watery slime when they emerged from the ditch. Zigzag-run toward the low gray wall surrounding the building. Grunts coursing water and leaving long trails of wetness as they charged. Action falling into patterns now. Fire and maneuver. One squad keeping gook gunners away from the windows with heavy fire while another moves into defilade or ducks inside the building. Still no return fire. Lead grunts in position behind the wall. Dazed, wondering expressions on their grimy faces. Surprised to be alive at this point. Where are all the fucking machine guns that nearly blew their shit away yesterday?

Two grunts crawled toward an opening in the stone fence which had been blasted the day before by a 106-millimeter recoilless rifle. Last hole that gun would ever punch. Smoking wreckage of the gun, mount and crew, sitting off to the left. Victim of a well-aimed B-40 rocket from the roof of the Treasury Building.

One of the moving grunts hugged an M-79 grenade launcher. Short, widemouthed weapon which hurled 40-millimeter, high-explosive grenades. Grunts called it a 'Blooper' for the popping sound it made when they fired it. Another grunt hugged four slender green tubes. LAAWs. Lightweight Antitank Assault Weapons. Rockets designed to defeat armor until the Marines discovered the hole they could make in a gook bunker. Edging cautiously toward the opening in the wall. Blooper Man dashed across the open space to the outer side. In position to rock and roll on those fuckers now.

Snap of AK-47 rounds. A lieutenant screamed for covering fire. NVA heard reveille. They've spotted the movement. Men in the drainage ditch blazing through M-16 magazines. Machine gun rattling and banging from somewhere to my right. Sparks and rocks flying from the front of the building in a noisy shower. Blooper Man swung around the opening to fire two quick rounds into a second-storey window. Broke open the weapon and inserted a new round so quickly that the two reports sounded like one.

Upper left corner of the Treasury Building exploded. Flash of fire and smoke before the echoing boom. RPD machine gun with gook gunner still attached tumbled slowly to the ground. LAAW gunner stripped another tube preparing to fire again. Rifleman next to him poured half a magazine from his M-16 into the dead gook. Lieutenant yelling again. Up, out of the water and charge the Treasury Building. Grunts blasting away on the run.

'Cut it loose now. Get the fuck up under those guns or you'll die in the streets. No cover unless you go forward.'

Tried to watch the action through the viewfinder of my camera. No good. Too fucking nervous about not seeing the gook who might be sighting on me. Just bang the shutter release and hope for the best.

Fleeting thought of Steve. Still inside the Compound? He hadn't returned when the assault started. No time to worry about that now. Let him stay out of this one. Wish I could. Automatic fire ripping down in sheets. Majority of the grunts made it to the wall. Six, maybe seven lying behind in the street. Lieutenant wanted people inside the building. No one very anxious to leave the relative security of the stone fence. Finally, a squad raced across the open courtyard. Fully exposed and running like hell. Shooting NVA soldiers in spider-trap holes on the run. Rattle and crash of rifle fire from inside the building. Must be two full squads in there now. Signal to move forward. Take up positions in the spider-traps dotted around the courtyard.

'Wait for the all clear. No one goes inside until they get the word.'

Full twenty minutes after the first Hotel Company grunts entered the building before the rifle fire and bang of grenades ceased. Still no return fire from the top floors. Grunts must be getting the best of it. Occupied the time reloading cameras and stripping the gook inside my hole. Never could tell when I might meet a souvenir-hungry someone with a spare bottle of booze.

Movement near the main entrance. Two grunts appeared in the doorway of the Treasury Building walking backwards and dragging two bodies. Slung the rumpled forms and kicked them down the concrete steps. Dead NVA sprawled in the contortionist pose of the stiffening dead. Marines shrugged their shoulders as if tossing off a heavy burden. Other grunts slowly emerged from the courtyard holes. Looks like they own the building. Wonder what the closing costs were?

Along the marble hallways of the Treasury Building, live grunts doing what they always did after a firefight. Smoking or munching on something saved in a pack or pocket. Staring at their boots, the opposite wall or the ceiling. Looking at anything but each other. In another couple of minutes, the ringing in their ears would clear. They'd accept the fact that they survived again. Tough talk would begin. Sarcastic critiques of each other's performance in the fight. Good words; any compliments would be veiled in sarcasm.

Code of the Grunt. Emotion sucks. If you can't say something caustic, don't say anything. Keep the emotions hidden until everyone came to believe you didn't have any; until everyone believed you were just another grunt motherfucker who didn't give a shit for nobody.

PFC in horn-rimmed glasses unloaded his rifle and yelled at another Marine sitting across the hall munching on a C-ration candy bar.

'You the dude that pounded that cocksucker up topside with the LAAW?' Round One.

'Yep. Me and Blooper Man blew that motherfucker right out of his jock. You dudes find the leftovers up there?' Round Two.

'We seen four of them assholes lying around in the area where you put the round. But I don't think they were part of the group that had us pinned down outside yestiddy.'

'Aw, man. Yer fulla shit. How come?' LAAW man

began to see his role as masked avenger of yesterday's insult slipping away.

'Because there's three more of them bastards up there and they smell like they been dead for a while. We must have got them in the first assault that I led yestiddy. The ones you got with the LAAW must have come up to replace them durin' the night.' Round Three.

Another grunt had been inside clearing the building. Thought he had the answer.

'I bet my ass those fuckers who were firing so hot and heavy last night pulled out at dawn and we blew up the sick and wounded who were left to hold us up. That's how come we found three or four live ones when we cleared the upper floors.' TKO.

'Yer dyin' ass.' LAAW man still trying to maintain his image.

Hoots and catcalls from every direction as others joined in to give their opinion of the brief fight for the Treasury Building. Goddamn place had the atmosphere of a locker room the night of the Big Game. Ah, well. What the fuck? Most of these guys weren't that long out of high school anyway.

Steve arrived from his mission to the MACV Compound. Flopped down and began sucking on a canteen.

'What about the copy and film?'

'Got it out with a relatively forthright malaria victim. He promises it'll be in the hands of the Division lifers before sundown.'

Split the gook souvenirs with him and heard the distinct clink of glass when he shoved them in his pack.

'Gimme that. There's a bottle of something in there.'

'Little something I picked up for a few rolls of film at the MACV Compound. A rare vintage which has doubtless graced the palates of European royalty.'

'Yeah. Bullshit. Probably Old Busthead. Vintage:

Tuesday, Three P.M. No. Wait. That's Benedictine brandy. Goddamn. Feels like napalm coursing down my throat. Here, have a hit of this shit. Takes the chill right out of your bones.'

Flaked out in the Treasury Building for the rest of the morning. Trying hard not to drink all the brandy. Might need some kind of self-control in the afternoon. Steve had word an Army contingent was due to arrive bringing their usual mobile PX. Maybe collect more souvenirs and get a resupply train going. Little doubt now that his deal won't be over in a week. Better be fucking over before that Hong Kong R & R quota rolls around next month. Let's see. Should be about fifteen more days before the plane leaves. Maybe take Steve along for grins. Christ, that's good brandy. Nearly gone; replaced by a pleasant buzz.

'Fucking stuff has got a real jolt. No, shit! That's shock wave from an explosion. Goddamn. Booby trap! Or something.'

Jesus Christ, fucking grunts falling all over me. Where's my helmet? What in the fuck was that? Up and running for a doorway to the right. Must have come from whatever's behind that door, hanging open; nearly blown off the hinges by the explosion. Smoke and brick dust boiling up into the hallway. Two Marine NCOs yelling at someone on the other side of the door. Leads to a cellar or something. What the hell was it?

NCOs trying to find out about the blast and manhandle curious grunts back into watch positions. Excited voice wafted up through the smoke and noise.

'Hey, Sarge! C'mon down here. You ain't gonna fuckin' *believe* this shit.'

Whooping and yelling in the background. Lunacy. Maybe the gooks booby-trapped something with laughing gas. Sergeant still reluctant to advance into the doorway and down the stairs. Where there's one booby trap, there's likely two or three more.

'Manero? That you? What the fuck happened down there?'

Steve pushed at my back trying to see through the smoke. What was that? Something sailing up the stairs; landed with a dull thud at our feet.

'Jesus H. Christ! Get down! Grenade!'

Go off, Goddamnit, go off. Can't get any farther away in time. Wheezing breaths. Waiting for the blast. No explosion. Dud? Thank fucking Christ for small favors. Should be a ChiCom rolling around the marble halls somewhere. Get the Goddamn engineers up there. No. Hold it.

Sergeant kneeling over a bundle of paper.

'Here's your fucking grenade. Look at this shit, willya. It's gook money.' Huge bundle of Vietnamese currency in his grimy hand, bound neatly with gummed paper. Top bill was a one hundred piaster note, or about $1.10 in American money.

'Shit. Must be about a thousand dollars there.'

Greed glowing in bloodshot eyes all around. *Code of the American.* Get some while the getting's good. Candy is dandy but cash won't rot your teeth.

Grunts yelled at the sergeant to break open the bundle and pass some of the cash around. Better get below and check this shit out.

'C'mon, Steve. Getting a bad case of greedies myself.'

Smoke made it hard to see down a flight of marble steps. Must be the basement of the Treasury Building. Smoke clearing down there. At the bottom of the stairs an incredible sight.

Huge, iron-filigreed door hung crazily off its hinges and a large chunk of plaster lay crumbled on the floor below where the door must have met the wall. That was before someone decided to gain access via plastic explosive. Beyond the door, what looked like a standard bank vault lined with safety deposit boxes. Any resemblance to a stateside vault ended there.

Three dirty, disheveled grunts sat on the floor wallowing in a huge pile of paper. Awesome sight. Steve swatted at the smoke and stood gaping.

'Do you suppose that all that shit could really be money?'

Grunts throwing bills at each other. Kids playing with the tissue paper from unwrapped presents on Christmas morning. Hard to believe but it looked like piles of piasters.

'Could be our ship has docked and dropped anchor in the treasure cove. Fucking Saigon black market operators couldn't top this, by God. Man with just a small pile of this stuff could bankroll a fucking future, man. Fuck a bunch of Hong Kong R & R. Get through the war, get out of the Goddamn Crotch and go for broke.'

Steve squatting beside one of the laughing grunts. Impossible to count the currency strewn all over the ten-foot-square security area. Steve and the grunts ankle-deep in coins and bills. Must be thousands in there.

'How did you guys find this shit?'

'The sergeant sent us down here to look for gooks.' Grunts busily stuffing pockets with bills. 'And fuckin' Manero over there he looks in here and sees all this fuckin' money lyin' around like the gook bankers was maybe gonna take off for Switzerland before the NVA came in. So fuckin' Manero, he breaks out a quarter pound of C-4 and a cap, see?' Crowd of grunts pushing and shoving down the stairs to see what's causing the commotion. Jealous crowd milled around outside the iron gate to the vault yelling for us to toss some money out to them. Moved inside to hear the oblivious grunt continue his story.

'Anyway, fuckin' Manero rigs up a charge and blows the fuckin' gate off its hinges and when we get inside, here was all this shit. Man, how much you suppose this shit would be worth to a hungry, horny, dried-up dude if he could get to Saigon or someplace?'

Voice from the crowd like a loud fart in a quiet elevator.

'You're never going to find out.'

Grunts looked up from wallowing in cash. Uneasy silence; looks of disbelief. Tense moment until a lieutenant stepped out of the crowd. Strange, electric spark flew between the officer and the recently-paupered enlisted men. Could they get away with it? Could they reach a weapon, blow the dude away and make off with enough cash to buy a new life? Lieutenant staring them down; standing his ground. Officer's Candidate School versus boot camp. Lessons too violently ingrained. OCS wins it by two lengths.

Lieutenant held the original bundle of money the excited grunts had pitched up the stairs. Marine Corps-issue green, waterproof bag in his other hand. Police up the piasters time here. Now or never. Got to make a move or forget about the whole deal. Lieutenant lecturing the milling grunts about looting. Back to the vault. Now. Quietly kick several bundles out of sight behind a row of safe deposit boxes.

Lieutenant addressed the grunts in the vault.

'You people put all that shit in the Willy-Peter bag and be quick about it. There will be no looting in this city by people in my outfit. Get all that cash into the bag and bring it topside when you're through. The Gunny will search everyone before he leaves the building.' Yeah.

Shit., Everyone but me. There's an unbarred window that leads out to an alley.

Officer started up the stairs herding bitching grunts before him like sheep. Steve kicked disgustedly at the piles of bills.

'Can you imagine the fucking R & R we could pitch if we could convert just a little of this shit to greenbacks.'

'Yeah, I can imagine. And I might be able to show you a little of that action on an upcoming R & R next month. Just keep your mouth shut and hang in there.'

Strange look on Steve's face. Didn't notice me cut a chunk out of the pile. Grunts wondering what's going on.

'What's that about R & R?'

Another pauper finishing up the chore of stuffing several million piasters into the WP bag

'Ah, shut the fuck up about R & R. You wouldn't get no chance to spend it anyway. You gonna die in this fucking Hué City.' With loss of assets comes a serious slump in morale.

Code of the Grunt. Don't expect anything because you aren't going to get it. The only ration that won't be short is the ration of shit. Like the buttplate of a rifle, you are fairly insignificant and will get banged around at every turn.

Steve trudged up the marble stairs, leading the trio of bitching grunts who were kicking and cursing at the bulging sack of money. Time to make my move. Stuff this shit everywhere I can find a pocket or fold. Slip out that window and hope no one has a full tally on the take in that vault. Hide this shit in my pack and wait it out for a while. With all the action in this Goddamn place, it should take them a while to get around to counting their money. Hope so anyway. If I make out, might just not come back from that fucking R & R.

Back inside the Treasury Building; resting on the bulging pack. Steve off with the Company Gunny taking pictures and making notes for a story of the brave Marines rescuing GVN resources from the greedy clutches of the communist enemy. Dreamed of disappearing over a verdant green hill somewhere in the mists of the New Territories.

Steve returned, bitching about the lost fortune. Pictured himself making a down payment on a frame house back in The World.

'My Man, you have once again underestimated my cunning ability to analyze a situation and quickly take the correct course of action.' No idea what the shuck is all about. Breaking out a C-ration can for the noon meal.

'Listen. While you were down there weeping over a lost fortune did you notice the tall, skinny guy standing quietly at the back of the vault? That was me. And I managed to get away slicker than cat-shit with several bundles of bread while the lieutenant was warning everyone not to loot.'

Had to wave off his questions.

'Later, man. They're moving on to the streets again.'

Company Gunny said Hotel was ordered to clear an avenue running parallel to the Perfume River which divided the city North and South. Hotel Company Commander took charge of the leading squads personally. Tall, good-looking, blond officer; well liked by the grunts in his line company. Hotel Six indicated a company of ARVN was holding against an NVA assault on an armory near the center of the city. MACV command center anxious that the South Vietnamese received reinforcements before the NVA got their hands on a large stockpile of weapons. Mostly surplus US models left over from World War II and Korea. AKs and B-40s were bad enough.

Hotel fanned out rapidly on both sides of the street. Moving swiftly toward the armory. Six said it wasn't more than three blocks away in an easterly direction. Right flank platoon guided on the river edge; left flank platoon meandered through houses, using a back street as guide to keep them headed in the right direction. Dicey deal. Most of his troops out of sight most of the time. Hotel Six leading a gypsy caravan of radio operators and gun guards.

Drifted off to move with the platoon going through the houses. Steve argued for going with someone closer to the center so we could catch action in either direction when it started.

'Bullshit, man. Payoff starting here. There's valuable plunder to be had in those houses. Got to get your profit motive working. Settle for sixty-five dollars extra a month in combat pay if you want, but I'm taking what I can get my hands on. Beginning to feel like a cossack.'

Third platoon moved rapidly through the houses as the Company Commander talked with them, constantly trying to keep a line and make speed toward the armory. Fucking footrace. Not enough time to look around for the good stuff. Emerged high-stepping from the back door of a breezy-looking porch which rambled veranda-style into a lush garden. Shot cracked by between me and Steve. Sharp, snapping sound of a close miss. Dive for cover. Street to the left erupting with gunfire. Christ. More delays. Two choices here: lie on our face or dig through these houses for valuable items. Got to get someone to get the gooks up there or we get blown away. Simple as that.

'What in the fuck are those people firing at over there? Cease fire, you silly assholes!'

Four Marines, burning ammo in four different directions, turned to see who was giving the orders.

'Can anyone see where that shot came from?' Lanky Marine with tattoos over practically every inch of exposed skin jumped up from behind the stone garden-wall and pointed at a ground floor window. Square of darkness, thirty yards away across the street.

'Yeah. OK, got it.'

Mother of suffering Christ. Burst of AK fire took him full in the face. Deep breaths; trying to puke. Fucker's face exploded like a balloon full of crimson shaving lather. His buddies jumping around in a panic. Puking and brushing at gore. Making sounds like little girls discovering a turd in the punchbowl at a birthday party.

Another burst from across the street.

'Get down, Goddamnit. Wipe that shit off later.'

Ricochets screamed off the wall at our rear. Rock shards stinging everyone.

'Stay down, up there. Goddamnit, pull your buddy back out of there. Don't be afraid to touch him.'

Ah, Christ. Fucking blood in my mouth. Am I hit? Shit. Didn't feel a thing. Steve swabbed at my face with the edge of a battle dressing.

'What is it?'

Dressing came away smeared with blood.

'How bad, man?'

'Fucking piece of rock must have gotten you right on the Goddamn beezer.' Worried look on his face.

'How's it feel?'

'Terrific fucking question. Feels like some asshole just hit me in the nose with a crowbar.'

Nose swelling; hard to breathe through it. More AK fire; more rock shards snaking off helmets and flak jackets. Got to do something before he blows everyone apart.

'Alright, enough of this shit. Did any of you see that little cocksucker fire? Where is he, exactly? Hold your fire.'

Let me think. Got to eliminate that AK gunner. No

telling where the platoon radio is by now. Can't call help and can't move from here while the gook is holed up across the street. Goddamnit. Why the fuck don't these grunt assholes do something? Fucker's got an automatic weapon on the ground floor over there. Field of fire would wipe out anyone who assaults directly. Got to finesse this fucking thing. Shit. Kids have no idea what to do here. That's right, assholes, trust in the cavalry to come charging to the rescue. Lay here until you become another vital statistic.

Wait. Been in a similar position before. Steve and I were pinned down by a gook holed up in a hooch which commanded a trail approach to a village we were assaulting. Bastard killed three of four Marines before we doped out a method for getting to him. Swore I'd never pull that fucking shit again, but something has got to move or he'll murder everyone over here. Might just work. Pulled out a frag grenade and shook it at Steve. Puzzled look until he recalled the incident.

'The old frag-his-fucking-hooch trick?'

'Yeah. Let's try it. Got to do something. Won't be long before he calls his buddies in to shoot the fish in a barrel.'

Stripped two fragmentation grenades from the dead Marine now being dragged to the rear by a corpsman. Crawled to the team of riflemen crouched behind the garden-wall to our front. Faces pale as they watched their faceless buddy disappear, boots bouncing limply over the rocky ground of the yard. Signaled Steve to drop his pack. Hope none of these dudes gets curious and decides to go through mine while I'm away. Got to be loose and unencumbered to pull this deal off. Shouted to distract the frightened grunts.

'Listen. We got to get next to that bastard if we're going to get him. See that doorway over there?'

Grunts followed my pointing finger to an arched

entranceway to the sniper's hideout. Window he fired from was about forty feet to the left. Grunts peered cautiously over the wall and nodded.

'Are you up for it now? You've got to fire cover, or me and my main man are fucked. We're going to beat feet over there and get next to the wall. You pour it on into that window there until we're across and then hold up. And see that everyone else along the line holds up. There won't be any cover out there. Got it?'

Nods and shrugs. Our funeral.

'OK? Now! Open up.'

Grunts banging away at the sniper's window. Vaulted the wall. Up and sprinting for the doorway across the street. Close rounds sound just as frightening going away as coming in. Never noticed that before. Steve had his head down; running with his knees high. Reached the doorway and the covering fire shifted. Quiet along the street now. Lieutenant shouting from somewhere along the row of houses at our rear.

'What the hell are you two doing?'

Steve panted for breath.

'Just fucking delightful. We get to play quiz games with that guy while he announces to the gooks that someone is about to come visiting.'

Peered around the corner of the concrete door frame. Just make out the outline of the sniper's window.

'Ignore the stupid fucker. You want to heave or should I?' Steve considered the earlier experience.

'I got all the speed but you've got the better curve.'

'OK. Shit. Let's get this thing over with.'

Crawled along the base of the building. Hope there are no snipers watching from the other direction. Exposed, vulnerable target out here. On hands and knees. Edged along the sidewalk until I reached a position directly under the sniper's window. OK. Let's do it right now. Signal for the first grenade.

Your average gook is very good at retrieving and tossing live grenades back in your lap. Plan calls for precise timing. Learned that the first time we tried it. Steve pulled the pin on the first grenade in his left hand and hooked a finger into the pin of the second grenade in his right hand. He pulled the pin of the second grenade while simultaneously releasing the safety lever of the one in his left. Lips moved as he counted two seconds before tossing the first smoking grenade underhanded to me. Locked in a baseball catcher's crouch just under the window and out of the sniper's sight line.

Juggler's precise rhythm. Steve let the safety lever of the second grenade fly just as I caught the first one. Tossed the second frag over to his left hand. Precisely two seconds. Fluid motion for the second underhanded toss. Caught the second grenade and flipped it up and over the windowsill just as the roar of the first echoed down the street.

Second bang brought a grin to Steve's filthy face. Going inside the building to inspect the results. Better follow. Could be more than one in there. Steve moving quickly down a deserted hallway. Stopped opposite a decorative screen, perforated like a sieve with grenade shrapnel. Gook sniper should be similarly holed unless we missed the bastard. No. There he is. Back of his dark green uniform shredded and stained black with blood.

'Looks like we got him.' Steve grinned at a crowd of admiring grunts who moved into the building behind us. No kind words. Simple, objective critique of a workman-like performance. That's right, shoot your cheap-assed grunt shit. Dynamic duo in a thrilling brush with death. Kindly direct your attention to the center ring.

'How come you assholes didn't get up and do something

about this fucking gook? You get paid for this shit. I'm just along for the ride.'

Huddled in a building near the armory waiting for the officers to decide how to attack it. Rather, how to attack the NVA who were attacking the armory. Gunfire from the other end of the street was deafening; hadn't slacked for the last ten minutes. ARVN must be firing every weapon they had stacked in that armory. Steve stared ahead out a window. High walls, iron gate and bullets spattering off the stone. No way to see from here where the NVA doing the shooting were hidden. Shit, someone better find out in a hurry. No way to advance quickly except right up the center of the street.

Movement from the armory area. Armored Personnel Carrier roared into the street, tracks clattering and throwing cobblestones. South Vietnamese soldiers tossed or falling off the roof as it roared away from the armory. Black Marine standing to the rear spoke the words softly.

'Ah think the ARVN have just vacated their mothafuckin' armory.'

APC roared by; careening from one side of the street to the other. Like a bucking horse bound to throw its rider. Flash of frightened faces as tiny ARVN soldiers hung on like rodeo cowboys. Eyes wide and white; nostrils flared. Smell of fear mixed with fumes from the APC's diesel engine.

Squad leaders yelled for their Marines to move up both sides of the street. Company Commander and his radio operators crouched in a doorway waving the hustling infantry by and yelling for speed.

'Did you see the Goddamn ARVN? They di-di'ed and I'm trying to get some people into that armory before the gooks get in there and turn it into a fucking Alamo.'

Crescendo of firing on the left in a short block of

houses. One of the Hotel Company platoons must already be in contact with the NVA. If they could engage and hold them, there would be time to make the armory gate.

Sporadic fire still pinging off the armory walls near the front gate. Squad of Marines on the right found a second, sandbagged and barricaded gate and ripped out a passageway. Grunts poured through it to take firing positions along the inside of the walls. Little return fire; no one could spot the NVA positions. But they weren't inside the walls.

CO and his radio operators contacted immediately by another two-man radio team from battalion headquarters. Good news from the Good Guys in the rear. Reinforcements pouring into the city from Phu Bai. All of 2/5 was now in the city along with two companies from the 1st Marines. Battle of Hué City growing by leaps and bounds. And no one across the river with round eyes yet. Clear view of the Citadel looming across the Perfume River from a high vantage point along the armory wall. Blue, red and yellow North Vietnamese flag snapping above the walls in the afternoon breeze. Began to rain hard.

Brief breather; time to question Hotel Six; try to get a feel for what's happening in the confused fighting on the south side. Marine command group, now firmly ensconced in Army territory behind the walls of the MACV Compound, was pleased that Hotel Company beat the NVA to the armory. Now the company was ordered to attack westward before nightfall. Scattered reports of the 1st ARVN Division moving into the city. Vietnamese Rangers and Marines assigned to help whoever got ordered to attack the Citadel. Policy of not firing air or naval gunfire into the city might be modified now that some South Vietnamese blood was bound to be spilled.

Hotel Marines busy rearming themselves from the

armory's huge inventory. Grinning Marines sporting vintage Thompson submachine guns. Browning Automatic Rifles and carbines. Much more dashing weapons than the space-age, plastic M-16s they were issued. Company Gunnery Sergeant tried to get the grunts to give up their prizes, but they were having none of it.

Thompsons were a particular prize. Most of the kids in Hotel grew up on movies which showed the Marines using them to blast Japs in the South Pacific. Picked up one of the last ones left inside the armory along with three 30-round magazines and as much .45 ammo as I could stuff in my pockets. Thinking about the grenade gig earlier. Might need a heavier hammer if something like that happened again. Steve surprised to see the thing hung on an old bandolier around my neck. Mumbled something about 'fucking John Wayne theatrics.'

'Yeah? Shit. How about that brand-new M-2, .30 caliber carbine slung over your shoulder? New toys for the boys. Fuck it. Just because you carry it, doesn't mean you intend to use it.'

Left him playing with the carbine and wandered off around the armory compound. Might be some booze left behind by the ARVN. Nobody in that big a hurry would stop for a bottle.

Raggedy-assed Marines in baggy rainsuits, flak jackets and camouflage helmets. Looked like World War II Leathernecks grinning for the cameras after flushing suicidal Japs out of bunkers on some coral island. Cheeks and chins covered with three-day stubble. Most had battle dressings wrapped around one minor wound or other. Dead beat from almost no sleep in the past three days, but still pissing and moaning at each other. Comparing the new weapons which seemed to have perked their spirits. Most saw the quaint old guns as just reward for hard fighting over the past days. Refused to give them up even with the weight of an extra weapon and ammo. Get these dangerous, dramatic-looking pieces back with them, and they'd mark Hué off as a fair fight despite buddies killed and hardships endured. To the victors go the spoils.

Steve motioning from around the corner of the armory building. Maybe a surprise treasure like a full bottle of something strongly alcoholic.

'Look at this shit.' Pointed to a pile of red and yellow silk which lay crumpled at the base of the armory's flagpole. 'The ARVN di-di'ed and just dropped their flag right on the deck.'

Several bullet holes in the fabric and a stain that looked curiously like blood in one corner of the flag. Unhooked it from the halyard and we held it up. Steve shook his head at the shame of it all. Getting serious about this situation.

'Fuck, man. So what? So they took off without securing their Goddamn silly flag.'

'Those chicken-shit fuckers shouldn't have left their flag like this.'

'Look. Why don't we keep this thing and we can look at it hanging on the wall after the war or something. It may be the only thing we take out of this fucking city if something happens and I lose that pack with the money in it.'

Folded the flag for storage in my pack. Wait. Needs a frame of reference. Took out a pen and wrote in the corner across the yellow background: 'Captured by 1st MarDiv Combat Correspondents. Hué City, RVN. Feb. 1968.'

Steve is confused.

'Wait a minute. Why should we be capturing a *South* Vietnamese flag? They're supposed to be our allies.' Guy has no business sense.

'We might not get a chance at one of those NVA flags.

And besides it may be worth something. In ten years who's going to know one gook flag from another?'

Passed the night in relative peace inside the armory walls. Hotel attacked forward throughout the afternoon; without me. Stayed inside the walls. Thinking about Hong Kong. Thought about a lot of other things too. Mostly death. Nothing new there except that I thought about my own end for the first time since I could remember. South Vietnamese flag made a nice pad inside a pack for use as a pillow. Huge moon finally broke through the clouds and mists about midnight. So bright it woke me from a deep sleep. Stared up at the moon until it hurt my eyes. Closed them again and thought of another flag and what it meant to me when I was a weepy kid at the side of my father's nondescript grave. Somehow the whole incident didn't seem so tragic or traumatic anymore. Lots of people die in lots of horrible ways. So what can you do? You can live with it or you can die with it. It won't change. Never has and never will. So what can you do? Be a fucking monk and take vows. Or learn to live with being close to someone who was bound to die. And let the silly fuckers get close to you if they wanted. What did it all mean in the end? Fart in a whirlwind. Pissing up a picket rope. Hopeless. Maybe just a friend or two to be around at the end.

Started to rain again and a gust of wind blew water over the walls of the armory. Wrapped my poncho liner around Steve's sleeping form.

Cercle Sportif//6 February 1968

Mid-morning. Sixth day in Hué. Rain continues; notebooks getting soaked. Hard to write legibly. Even harder to figure out what was written yesterday. Compelled to get it all down. Everything: sights, sounds, smells, feelings, thoughts. Keeps me occupied and concentrating on being an observer rather than a participant. Strangely compelled to take an active part in the fighting sometimes. More than simple survival it seems. More than: 'If you want something done right, do it yourself.' Ought to know better, for Christ's sake. Hope this part gets wet and becomes illegible. Nearly tripped off the gunline this morning.

Phantom Blooper and his sniper buddy had everyone pissed off and sweating in the cold rain. Holding in a row of houses along the broad promenade that fronted the Perfume River on the south side. Homes particularly well-appointed here. People who lived in them before the NVA came had obviously been members of the country club set. The country club itself was just up the street but the Marines couldn't get in. Membership Committee being chaired by the Phantom Blooper of Hué.

Misty morning filled with arcing tracers and screaming grunts. Hotel Company pushed steadily westward from the armory where they spent the previous night. NVA hiding in the maze of buildings seemed oddly willing to give up their positions with no more than a cursory fusillade before falling back. Near the country club and boat basin it became obvious why.

Company Commander and his Gunnery Sergeant assessed casualties; asking for further instructions near a statue of an elephant carrying an ornate *howdah*. On the Bureau of Tourism map it was marked 'Cercle Sportif.' Marines moving inside out of the rain while Hotel Six checked with the commanders in MACV Compound. Gooks making a habit of tearing down alleys tossing grenades into open windows. More seasoned grunts – the Street Fighters – stayed outside and ate soggy rations. Cold and wet, but they thought it was safer than being enclosed by four concrete walls when a packet of high-explosive shrapnel began to ricochet. That's the reason the Phantom Blooper managed to kill two people with his first round.

Marines on watch heard the coughing bark of an M-79 and assumed it was friendly. No one suspected the NVA might have one of the weapons until the first round impacted in a yard. Two Marines dozing there. They were the first ones to die. Not the last.

Streets in Hotel's sector echoing with shouts for a corpsman. Check the wounded. Six rounds fired in the first barrage. No one took cover quickly enough. Docs trying to come forward toward the wounded. Two more rounds landed. No chance to move until someone locates the Phantom Blooper. Sentry screamed through a doorway to Hotel Six, fighting poor radio reception.

'Some gook sonafabitch has got a Blooper.'

Company Commander wanted it taken out right away.

MACV told him his company would be needed in the southwest sector of the city very soon. No time to be fucking around near the river.

Fire team from a squad across the street detailed to find the Phantom Blooper, kill his ass and repossess the weapon. Donning wet helmets and flak jackets. Tried to take pictures but the misting rain kept fogging the lens. Where's Steve's camera? He sure as hell hasn't been using it lately. Inside now, asking the corpsman for a pill to stop gut-wrenching diarrhea that struck him during the night. Woke me several times when he got up to find an unoccupied place to squat; doubled up with painful stomach cramps. Nervous sentries nearly blew him away. Spirit still good but he's losing perspective. Found him banging away at a sniper position with that Goddamn carbine just before dusk. Blue eyes blazing like the muzzle of the weapon. Said he packed his cameras away to keep them from getting wet. Bullshit.

Staring through the mist at a pristine field of grass. Some two hundred yards from the railroad bridge that connected the two sides of the city. Grass field formed a well-manicured flank for one of Hué's most popular prewar attractions. Cercle Sportif. Laid out in concentric circles. Remnant of French colonial days. Picturesque fountain located at its center. Northern boundary was the Perfume River. On the opposite side, a broad avenue flanked by expensive French houses.

Three broad promenades cut through the circles. Each lined with dwarf shade trees. Promenades were the key to the Cercle Sportif. Each one currently covered by an NVA gunner. Converging cross fires. Fucking meatgrinder. Fire from the mutually-supporting gun positions had stopped the earlier advance. Hotel was supposed to reach the bridge, but they couldn't get by the gun positions. Now the guns *and* the Phantom Blooper.

Fucking gook handled the M-79 like a three-tour veteran. Ace in the hole for an NVA commander who was playing cagey while Hotel Company advanced on his positions in the southeast sector of Hué City. Pulled his men back after just enough resistance to make the Marines think they were in a real fight. Drawing them closer to prepared positions inside the park at Cercle Sportif. Now his back was to the river. Hotel had to come up these promenades to get to him.

Fire team beginning to move along the river's edge. Staying low; out of sight of the promenades. Moving into the Cercle Sportif slowly, cautiously. No one would move further into the park until they nailed the Phantom Blooper. Hotel Six not anxious to advance with a gook popping grenades into his line. Bursts of automatic fire near the riverbank. Cries for a corpsman.

Platoon Commander gathered another fire team and motioned for his corpsman to join them.

'We'll give you a base of fire. Get over there and see what those people stepped into.'

Fire team broke from cover, zigzagging across the street and into the park. Bark of the Blooper began as soon as they sprinted across the nearest promenade. Rounds landed behind the advancing team but short of their original position. Retreat cut off. Fire team leader urging his people on. Christ. Two won't make it. Lying out there in the middle of the promenade squirming. Gut wounds.

'Shit. Sniper. There's a sniper working with the Blooper. Watch for him. Who's hit?'

Corpsman and one Marine both gut-shot. Two more broke cover heading for the wounded. Two quick pops. Phantom Blooper dropped rounds in their path.

Lord. The dip-shits are milling around out there. Where's the fucking lieutenant? Figures. He's the one gut-shot out there next to the Doc. Someone's going to have to take a hand here. Those two cocksuckers are working together. Goddamnit. Can't they figure this shit out? Anybody who tries to reach those wounded gets blown up by the Blooper or ventilated by his sniper buddy. Remainder of the second fire team made it into the bushes across the wide street. No targets; holding their fire. Got to get moving here. Trying to spot gooks in the trees lining the promenade to our right front. Using an old scout's trick. Never stare at anything. Peripheral vision is much better for discerning shape or movement. Keep your eyes moving back and forth across a suspected area until you pick up what you're looking for.

Shit. Moans from the two gut-shot assholes distracting me. Grunts seem mesmerized by it. Phantom Blooper has completely fucked up their composure. Wait. There's something. In the midst of a clump of bushes surrounding a statuette of Cupid. Movement. And what might be the glint of a rifle barrel.

'Hey. I think I see the asshole up there.'

Black squad leader uncased a LAAW. Looking for a target. 'Where at?' Scrambled over near me to sight down my arm. Fucking around trying to see which clump of bushes I mean. Shit.

'Wait a minute, man. Where's that fucking Thompson?'

No. Steve's carbine. It's got a magazine of tracers loaded.

'Listen. I'll open up on that bastard with tracers and you put the LAAW right in where I'm firing.'

Black man nodded and shouldered the tube. Squaddies and two corpsmen moved up behind. Ready to go for the wounded if the LAAW gets the Phantom Blooper. Across the street, fire team ready to take out his sniper buddy when the rocket fires. Squad leader doesn't want any more wounded lying out there in the park.

'You Docs haul ass out there and get those two as soon as I shoot. Get 'em back here as soon as possible. Fire team over there will keep the sniper off your back.'

Four more Marines from the headquarters section volunteered to help carry the wounded. Both men still flopping around in the street. Sniper intentionally shot them in the stomach. They'd stay alive for a while; in agony. Might even entice fresh targets into the open.

Concentrated on the spot where I saw movement. Jacked a tracer into the carbine chamber. Have to pop up, fire and remain exposed, squeezing the trigger until the LAAW fired.

'Ready here.' Black guy picking his nose and glancing around at the people getting set to move.

'Hey! Try not to fuck around too long getting the round off.'

Perfectly calm now. About to take some action.

'Just gimme a motherfucking target and then get out the way.'

Carbine jarring steadily into my shoulder. Tracers streaking into the shrubbery at Cupid's feet.

Holy shit. Must have been hit. No. Alright. OK here. Concussion from the LAAW backblast. Felt like a Goddamn mortar round going off in my hip pocket. Am I hurt? Skin numb; can't tell. What an asshole. Where's *your* camera now, jerk? John-fucking-Wayne stands up in heroic fashion to save the day while getting his ass blown off.

Ringing in my ears. Barely hear the rifle and machine gun fire. Curious. Watching expended cartridge cases pop out of the weapons but I can't hear the firing. High-pitched squeal from the fucking LAAW. Hotel Six moved up. When did that happen? Did he see me pull that cheap shit? Nah. Other things on his mind. Urging his people across the street. Black guy screaming something at me.

'Wait one, man. Can't hear a fucking thing.'

Pounding me on the shoulder and pointing across the street. Jesus. Feel like a fucking frag went off in my head.

What's that? Cupid statue exploded into powder. Two gooks lying face down across the lip of a hole that had been hidden by the bushes. M-79 lying broken open and useless near a chunk of plaster. Phantom Blooper. Spotted by a Space Cadet and laid low by a LAAW Man. Goddamn. Ringing in my ears from the backblast. Can't hear a thing. Ought to go on out of here. Maybe con a MedEvac to Hong Kong where a Chinese hooker can blow in my ears until they clear.

'Take this Goddamn carbine and stick it in your ass, man. Don't even want to see the thing again. And don't bother to talk to me. Can't hear a fucking word you're saying.'

3
Southwest Sector Fight
7 February 1968

The Hospital

Hotel Company on hold. No tinkling Muzak to distract the CO. Wait out. This is a recording. You've reached the MACV Compound but we're busy deciding your fate just now. Please leave your name and number. And don't call us; we'll call you. Suits me.

Stalled since the night of 6 February. Waiting for Echo, Foxtrot and Golf Companies to consolidate positions and form some sort of an assault line perpendicular to the river. Hotel Six anxiously pacing the floor; waiting for word to advance on the City hospital.

CO had his platoons in position but the Battalion Commander wanted the left flank of the assault line secured before he gave the order to move. Steve off in a corner teaching some of the replacements how to make edible potions out of C rations. Seems to be moving away from his job more and more lately. Spending too much time with the grunts. Didn't speak to me at all yesterday until nightfall. Had four frag grenades hooked to his cartridge belt when he came back at dusk. Not a camera in sight.

Occasional burst of fire from the second storey of the building where we waited for word from the MACV Compound. Squad up there keeping gook-sappers honest and under cover. Hotel Six unhappy over casualties from random grenade attacks on dozing grunts over the past few days. And there are plenty of targets over near the four-storey Catholic Hospital.

Wanted to explore this building. It had apparently been some sort of camera supply store, but looters – either NVA or Marines – had carried off everything in the glass cases of the showroom.

'Steve. C'mon, man. No, get your camera, man. Need to expose some film here.'

Embarrassed smile. Oh, Gee. I almost forgot. Yeah.

'Maybe we can find some lenses or something upstairs. Should be a storeroom or something up there.'

What's that pounding noise? Coming from the first landing.

'Ah, shit. Mother of bleeding fucking Christ. Hey. Goddamnit, man. Don't do that. Hold on. Give me that fucking camera.'

Wild-eyed grunt banging away at a wall with a camera he was swinging by the strap. Look at this shit. Goddamn guy is destroying a piece of gear I'd give my left nut to have. I can't stand it. Fucker doesn't know what he's done. Screaming at someone at the top of the stairs.

'You assholes are a bunch of one-way motherfuckers.'

'Pay attention, dip-shit. You know what you've got here?'

'Them cocksuckers found a bunch of good cameras and scarfed them all up while I was on watch. They took all them Yashickers and Cannons and stuff and left me this fuckin' box camera piece of shit.'

'Yashickers? Give me a Goddamn break, man. You have just destroyed a Hasselblad. This particular piece of shit is worth about a thousand bucks. Or it was before you got your dick-skinners on it.'

Asshole is totally amazed. Look at him. Entire background told him the only good cameras were 35-millimeter models like the ones in the PX at Da Nang. Anything else was Instamatic quality and should be destroyed. Hell, there might even be a Polaroid in the next place. Ah, fuck. Why me?

Steve in shock. First the lost fortune in piasters and now this. Grunt breathed deeply through flared nostrils. Still pissed off at his buddies but the mention of a grand for the piece of banged-up junk in his hand slowed him down. Watching the pained expression on Steve's face. Didn't resist when I took the camera from him.

'What'd yuh say this was?' Steve looking at the camera over my shoulder. Lens mounting cracked. Who knows what kind of damage inside.

'It's a Goddamn Hasselblad precision instrument and you couldn't get near it for less than a thousand dollars.'

Grunt grabbed the Hasselblad back from me. Second thoughts.

'Whaddya mean a thousand bucks? Everybody else picked up fuckin' neat little ones that ya can fit in a bandolier and shit. Them's the fuckers that's expensive. I seen 'em in the PX before. This here fucker is just like an old box camera my ma used to have.'

'Believe me, dude. Your ma never had a Hasselblad unless she shot for *Playboy* or some fucking thing.'

Grunt defended his action to the last.

'Well, how the fuck was I supposed to know? You assholes can have all this shit.'

Tossed the Hasselblad to me and began pulling roll after roll of 35-millimeter film out of his trouser pockets.

'Fuck it, man, I'm gettin' me a fuckin' tape recorder from one of these Goddamn places and listen to some jams. Who wants to take pictures of this bullshit anyway.'

Jesus. Another butter and egg salesman from Cornshuck. Save me from badass killers who shit on what they can't find a way to fuck up. Quiet on the stairs after the tirade and shouting match. Put this camera in my pack just in case. Might find someone somewhere who can fix it. Goddamnit. If I'd only been five minutes quicker. This whole fight is turning into one big rip-off. Getting paranoid. Don't want to sound weird but everyone is out to fuck up my profit margin. Steve scraped together a pile of film where the grunt had dumped it.

'That guy has more than one problem. Look at this fucking film. It expired 31 January 1968.'

Area-wide scrounging mission that night. Steve fell heir to two rubber air mattresses. Inflated them under the stars to avoid grenade-throwing gooks. Still drizzling rain but wet was preferable to wounded. Lolled on the soft mattress and thought about the grunt and the camera. Would have hocked my soul for a Hasselblad before the war. Ah, shit. Nothing to be done about it now. Just another grunt motherfucker who don't give a shit for nobody.

Unexpected lull in the fighting at dawn. Patrols, in the streets before the sky lightened, returned to report no contact. No sign of gooks moving through the houses in the areas they had been so anxious to protect yesterday. Marines from Regimental S-2 came up to Hotel Company's position to interrogate two prisoners taken before dark last night. Tough-looking NVA, found dazed by grenades or high explosives. Pissed-off Marines apparently jacked them up a little on the way back to the CP. Bruised and swollen faces. Easy to tell these were no peasant farmers. Tall and erect; well-fed, even chunky, in comparison with the VC in the south. Blood matted in their close-cropped hair. Olive-green uniforms of NVA regulars. One wore NCO chevrons on his uniform collar.

Interrogators speaking Vietnamese they learned in language school before coming to the Nam. Failed to get anything out of the NVA. Preparing to take them to the rear. Good shot at some background information here. S-2 guys indicated the Marines had killed a pot-full of NVA in the fighting so far. Still plenty more occupying the Citadel across the river. Borrowed a pair of field glasses from one of them and looked at it. Foreboding, medieval structure. North Vietnamese flag still rippling in the breeze. S-2 people had done their homework.

'Those fuckin' walls are about thirty feet high; twenty-thirty feet thick, and crawling with NVA.'

'Yeah. I know.'

Still scanning the Citadel when the lull in the fighting ended as it usually did. People resumed dying.

Squad of Marines had been maneuvering forward toward the hospital and were caught by fire from the complex. Battalion Commander worried about momentum. Attack going too slowly. Thinks his people aren't pushing hard enough. Go all out now and take the hospital. Hell with the flanks. Forward with the grunts; shooting frames of the advancing Marines. Steve's camera was out of his pack, but he still fondled the carbine more than he did the shutter release. Damage being done to the lead elements. Two or three grunts lying sprawled in the hospital courtyard; not moving. Zoomed my lens for a close-up look. Worked our way in behind a sandstone wall. Marines all around pumping fire into the windows of the hospital buildings. Heavy return fire. Hotel CO wants to go but the Goddamn street is a meat-grinder.

'Hotel Six, Hotel Six, this is Hotel Two Actual. I've got three KIAs and three WIAs. I need some sixty-mike-mikes to put a hole in the top right-hand corner of the building. They've got a heavy gun in there and we can't get closer until we bust it, over.'

Lieutenant hugging the wall beside his radio operator. Glasses covered with dirt and sweat. How the hell can he see like that?

'Two Alpha, Two Alpha, this is Six, I've got . . .' Remainder of transmission interrupted by a hail of machine gun fire. Spattered the line of grunts hiding behind the wall with rocks and a fine powder. Several of them popped up to return fire. Steve banging away with his carbine. Should have figured that. Cameras hanging ignored around his neck. Lenses covered with a film of fine rock dust like the lieutenant's glasses. Neither fucking one of them could see what was happening.

Team of three Marines lurching toward the wall; carrying a stubby 60-millimeter mortar between them. Steve watching while he reloads carbine magazines.

'Shoot the cameras, Goddamnit. Leave that to the grunts.'

Shit. Ignoring me. Pouring fire at the hospital windows while the mortar crew found a place for their weapon. Other Marines all along the wall hammering the building with rifle fire. Shooting left and right to bring fire from the flanks. Occasional dead NVA tumbled out of one of the upper windows. Hit the concrete with a thump like a bag full of wet sand.

Mortar crew found a position far enough away from their target to allow high-angle field of fire. Two worked over the simple sight. Third man rapidly unpacked vicious-looking projectiles from their fiberboard containers.

One ballsy squad leader took his people into the courtyard right under the gook guns. Big fucking hero? Smart Goddamn move if you ask me. Gooks will have to depress the muzzles of their weapons to get them. And to do that, they'll have to lean out of the windows and make fat targets of themselves. Sharp fucker leading that lash-up. Probably get a medal for being a hero. Right on, man. Get a bunch of fucking medals but I got your number. Dude smart enough to figure the angles like that rates all the medals he can wear.

Squad running all over the courtyard killing NVA in their spider-trap holes. Marines closed to within five or 10 feet of the gooks before they opened up. Two grunts down in the skirmish but the squad is holding the courtyard. Incredibly close combat. Closest I've seen so far. Watched one grunt dive in a hole occupied by an NVA he had just killed at point-blank range and use the body for cover as he picked off two more gooks in holes to his right and left. Each of the enemy died with a single bullet hole in his head. Marine aimed his rifle and fired as though he were on a training range. Calm, deliberate precision.

One of the mortarmen crawled up to the lieutenant with dirt on his glasses.

'Where do you want the rounds, sir?'

Lieutenant sweeping his arm across the hospital and steadying on the top right corner.

'The whole right side of the building is crawling with gooks. Keep popping rounds in there until we get that gun.'

Mortarman scrambled back to his tube and began pulling powder increments off rounds. Stovepipe began to cough and bark with a metallic voice. Watched the rounds in flight as they arched up, almost out of sight, and began a leisurely fall back toward the roof of the hospital.

Working out now. Showing their stuff to the cheering grunts. Get some. As soon as the crew got one round off, gunner twisted the traversing handle and his assistant dumped another down the tube. Steady, staccato racket, almost like an extremely heavy machine gun. Geysers of stone, plaster and debris from the roof of the hospital. New guy on the block. Runner from the Company Commander approached the lieutenant.

'Six says keep the mortars and guns working on this

side. The gooks are comin' out the rear of the building and Golf Company's knockin' the fuck out of 'em.'

Occasional belch of flame and smoke from the third and second floors. Mortar rounds still impacted on the hospital roof but many were falling through previously blasted holes. Lieutenant got new orders over the radio. Mortars, cease fire. Wait one here to see if we're taking any fire from the hospital. Steady firing to the rear of the building. Golf Company in contact. Ought to be able to move inside now.

Marine clutching a 12-gauge shotgun near me got the assignment.

'Take your people in there slowly and see if there's any left.' Squad leader began shouting at his people to fan out and approach the building. Sprinted across the courtyard where they were joined by the squad occupying the spider-holes. No return fire. Looks like they all made their bird out the back. Shit. Too soon. Roaring explosions along the wall. Rockets! Lieutenant knocked flat by the blast of the near one. Gasping for breath.

'Get . . . in there . . . and get that . . . fucking . . . rocket gunner.'

Squads scrambling through doors and windows into the hospital. Shit. What's that? Pistol? Marine from the mortar squad blasting away at the hospital with his .45. Right arm hung limp at his side. Bloody bandage on top of his shoulder. Jaw muscles clenched tight; looked like he had two marbles in his cheeks. Must be in pain. Blood streaming down the injured arm; turning pale rapidly.

'Hey, man. Can't do anything with that pistol. Cool it. Gimme that. We'll get a corpsman up here ASAP.'

Fucker's taking the wound seriously. Big-time gunfighter wants the NVA to come out and face him. High Noon and shit.

'Christ. Corpsman!'

Furious firing inside the building. No more rockets. Gunners must be occupied with the assaulting grunts. Dude with the shotgun waving from the fourth-storey window.

'We've got 'em. Send a corpsman in right away.'

Two Docs shouldered through the crowd along the wall headed for the building. Interrupted in the midst of mortician duties. Wrapping two dead bodies in bloody ponchos. No cheering over victory. Those left behind the sandstone wall staring at the broken bodies of two Hotel grunts killed in the initial assault. No one wanted to get organized enough to finish covering them. Both fish-belly white. Rain splattering on their swollen faces. Steve quietly moved over to finish wrapping them for delivery to the rear.

Softly called my name and motioned me over to the nearest dead man. Shook his head and pointed at the gray-green face.

'Ah, Christ. Might have fucking known it'd be him. Payback is a MedEvac.'

Saw that face before in better, more vital condition. Mouth filled and overflowed with water. Bloody froth around the nose and lips. Last foaming gasp of a grunt shot through the lungs. Last frame for the fucker who destroyed the Hasselblad camera. Fuck. Even this asshole deserved better than this. He didn't mean to smash the camera.

Bulge in his side trouser pocket. Did he find that Polaroid? Nah. Portable cassette tape recorder. Take it with me. He sure as hell won't need it anymore. Finished wrapping his body and then went inside to find a dry place to sleep. Stand down tomorrow. MACV needed more time to assess progress. Why the fuck don't they come up here and see for themselves? Trip to MACV Compound occupied most of the afternoon. More and more civilian correspondents showing up and begging to come forward with the grunts. Situation not stable enough yet. Fuckin' A, it isn't. Got several rolls of film out with one of them and returned to Hotel's position inside the hospital around dusk.

Cushy beds lining the wards but no one wants to sleep on them. Superstition, I guess.

Code of the Grunt. Always look a gift horse in the mouth. Might be a booby trap in there. Remembered the tape machine and pulled it out. Does the fucker work? Might be able to raise a few bucks for it. Might even keep it for some jams in the rear. Never had anything better than a Japanese transistor when I was a kid. Even Chubby-fucking-Checker sounded like Muzak on that. Play-button. Graceful, sometimes strident harmonies of Peter, Paul and Mary surged up through the ward. Grunt croaked from the darkness.

'Shut that motherfucker off.'

'Right, asshole. Can't rock and roll with the commies just around the corner.'

No room in my pack. Fuck it. Toss the Goddamn thing out the window. Recorder went out; chilly, wet night wind came in.

Tried to recall the words of the song. Pictured the Mad Dog Camera Masher shucking and jiving to the tune.

'Kick out the jams, motherfuckers. Got this little box up in Hué City where the war was mighty shitty.'

Leaving on a jet plane. Don't know when I'll be back again. Never, fucker. You'll never be back again. Poor, dumb fucking grunt leaving on a jet plane alright. Won't be any big-titted stewardess to admire his campaign ribbons or Purple Heart on the flight back to The World. Closed-coffin funeral. Poor old Mom wailing for the Marines to open the Goddamn box so she could be sure her gallant son was really in there. Poor old Pop, a veteran of The Big Two, patting her hand and insisting they didn't want to get a last look at their own flesh and blood as just a smelly lump of flesh and blood. Maybe he got some pictures taken by a buddy who kept one of the other cameras. Hard-guy grunt pose. Maybe a dead gook or two in the frame. Big grin on his bearded face and an AK-47 propped on his knee. At least they'd have that.

What would I have if I got blown away in this Goddamn fight? Hasselblad would be gone before anyone knew it was broken. The money would last only as long as it took to open my pack. Nothing else. Rolled over under one of the hospital beds and stared up at the springs. Trying to imagine myself lying in a coffin. Odd thoughts; random weirdness. Funeral parlors smell like jungle rain forests during certain times in the year. Or is it rain forests that smell like flower-bedecked funeral parlors?

Corpse inclines his head slightly to case the joint. Why is it so quiet out there in the funeral parlor? Where's all the pissing and moaning that attends my passing? Oh yeah. There's the assorted gaggle of aunts and uncles yipping and bitching about how I could never stay home and get some shitty, dead-end job like their kids. There it is. Get Some, mourners. Saying I got just what I deserved; just what I asked for. No one who isn't a sinful, indecent loser ever stays in the service. Especially the Marine Corps. Why didn't he go into the Navy like most of the other boys? Or just let the Army draft him and then get some rear echelon job? Or go to college where his poor momma and daddy worked so hard to put him. He'd be alive today. Oh, Lordy. I just knew it would come to this.

Yeah. That's them out there. I can *feel* them gloating. Hear them rehashing the sinful, indecent incident of my mother's funeral. They're saying it serves me right that I don't have any friends here at my own funeral. They're saying any uncouth mongrel who comes home on emergency leave to bury his very own mother and then stays too drunk to attend to all the necessary details, didn't deserve any better. They're remembering how I got shit-faced before the final day in the funeral home and told them all to fuck off. Old Dead D.A. Rated what he got. Fuck him. Let the government give him a headstone and then tell the caretaker to let the Goddamn grass grow over it. Coffin lid closing. Trying to shake off a nightmare. Rolled over, hoping the resurrection would come soon.

Wait. New people coming into the funeral home. Filthy bastards. They stink like week-old corpses. Driving the relatives away from the coffin with bayonets. Look at that one with only half an arm left. Writing something on the casket with a bloody stump. What's it say? Shit. There it is.

My epitaph: 'Here lies one more dumb grunt motherfucker who don't give a shit for no one or nothing.' They're leaving now. Only my family remains, shocked again, as they had been at my mother's funeral, by rude behavior in the presence of the recently departed.

No. Shit. That's wrong. My real family trooped out first, leaving a trail of mud and blood on the floor and a faint odor of decay in the air. I don't know who the fuck these civilians are.

Dream left me chilled through the early morning hours. Lying in a puddle of water when the sound of grunts gathering gear woke me. Deep ache in back and lungs. Arthritis, pleurisy or hair shirt? Fuck it. It'll go away in a while. Work out some of the kinks with a walk up the stairs. Huge hole in the front right corner of the building at the second-floor level. LAAW or one of the sixty rounds that dropped through the roof probably. Stared through it across the Perfume River while the sky blinked yellow and white with scudding clouds. Jesus H. Christ.

More Goddamn rain? Rectangular shape of the Citadel walls loomed out of the dark across the water. Getting close to decision time. North side assault coming up before long. Get involved in that shit over there and there's no telling when you might be able to get back across the water.

Fucking fight over there would be an incestual, cloistered bloodletting. You'd get out of that when the walls fell. Or when you were sufficiently dead to be of no further use.

Goddamn, man. Attack the fortress of the ancients over there. What would that be like? Last night's dream flashing back in filthy color. Goddman fight like that should be a chapter in military history. Shit. Twentieth-century grunts assaulting a sixteenth-century castle. Ah, Jesus, the Siren's Song. Echoing bugles over the desert sands. Robin Hood. Rock and roll in the ramparts and redoubts. The Cisco fucking Kid, man. What we have here is your classic romance-adventure gig. Can you dig it? Sure. Why not? Not like you're shitting yourself or anyone else. No heroics. No duty, honor or great trappings of sacrifice. Just want to be *in* on a gig of this magnitude. Even if I get blown away in the Great Big Famous Colossal Fight for the Citadel in Hué City, there'd be a few more honest tears at the funeral.

Kicked at a swollen NVA corpse. Beginning to stink in the morning humidity. God. Getting tremendously twisted here. Maybe just go with the flow for a while.

Main hospital administration area. Hotel Company Marines from the command group and ARVN interpreters orchestrating a three-ring circus. Trying to sort out panicky patients and staff. ARVN suspected several in grimy white uniforms of being NVA. Screaming interrogation. Patients sick and scared. Most had endured the fighting hiding under their beds. Emerged in the morning, moaning and babbling about aches and pains. Several obviously had recent surgery. Mewling, puking mob. Clutched at bandages covering sutures and begged someone – anyone – to listen to their tale of woe. Many Vietnamese just beginning to trust science enough to submit to modern medical care. This disruption in the routine and the attendant corpses was not reassuring.

ARVN in no mood to pamper sick civilians. When one surgery patient got too vocal, an ARVN sergeant gouged at his incision and ripped the bandages off. Post-op fucker screaming and wailing on the floor. More sound and fury. Marines seem disgusted by the treatment. Many turned their backs and stared stoically out the hospital windows. Navy corpsman tried to intervene. ARVN interrogation team screamed just as loudly at them. Hotel Six finally ordered them to leave everything up to the ARVN.

Senior corpsman huddled with one of the English-speaking Vietnamese doctors. Typical story. NVA took over the hospital six days earlier and moved in their own medical corpsmen and woulded as the battle lines pushed back toward the building. Civilian patients were either bodily tossed out of the hospital or made to work for the NVA. Corpsman said he found several dead civilians in the houses surrounding the hospital where patients crawled in search of shelter when the NVA took their beds.

NVA tried to force the South Vietnamese doctors and nurses to tend their wounded. One or two refused. NVA executed them in front of the remaining staff. Modern medical hiring practices. Sorting process still going on with a great deal of shouting and shoving. Only four more nurses left to be checked for credentials. Two of them bolting for the rear door!

'Christ. Watch it! That one's got a pistol. They're NVA.'

Regular nurses screamed to confirm their identity. ARVN soldiers made a grab and missed. Two sharp cracks from the pistol. Shit. Let them go.

They eluded the grasp of several more ARVN but ran into the arms of three grunts coming in off watch in the hospital courtyard. Pistol shots gave them the picture. Ask questions later. These fucking broads are dangerous. First grunt grabbed the nearest tiny woman by the arms and bent her over backward. Head smacked into the stone floor so hard it sounded like an overripe melon tapped with a tire-iron. Dropped the pistol and fell slack. Grunt danced backward in horror. Shit. That might be somebody's fucking *mother*, man. Second Marine had no such reservations. Sprang to the left as the other nurse tried to race by heading for the door. Unleashed a haymaker from the flank. Sucker-punch. She never saw it coming. Caught her full under the left eye. Knuckle-fucking-sandwich, man. Nurse's head flew back; eyes fluttering up under the lids. Cold-cocked by a running-dog lackey of the Imperialist system that sponsors the Golden Gloves. Marine who threw the punch continued to dance and spar as though he expected the woman to take a standing eight-count and come back swinging. Go to a neutral corner there, asshole.

When she lay still, he danced in and kicked her mightily in the head. Ugly blue welt rose on her temple. ARVN enjoyed the scene immensely. Grunt boxer's buddy retrieved the first woman's pistol and presented it to the Champ. Blowing and snorting around the room now. Ready to take on the next contender. Not me, fucker. Might be time to eat before we move again. Maybe the scenic, open-air balcony on the second floor would foster an appetite.

Flopped down on a pile of rubbish. Dead NVA didn't

smell so bad in the wet breeze from across the river. Steve joined me for breakfast.

'Jesus. Ham and eggs, chopped. Ought to feed those to the Goddamn gooks. Maybe we ought to get out of here today, man. Before that shit on the northside starts. Might not be able to get out once we get across. You dead set on going over there? What's the matter, man? What the fuck are you looking at?'

Face ashen; eyes bulging, staring at something between my legs. 'What the fuck? I leave my fly open or something?'

'Don't move, man. Just sit still and let me see what this fucking thing down here is.'

Shit. What next? Mortar round; half-buried under the rubble pile here, right under my ass. Silver snout protruding from between my legs like a bloated penis. Steve stood to leave.

'Just keep your weight distributed while I go see about getting some engineers up here.'

How about this shit? Fearless Hero of the Great Big Famous Colossal Fight for Hué City gets his shit blown away literally when a live round on which he had momentarily crapped out ignites and runs up his ass. Jesus. Wasn't your whole life supposed to pass before your eyes in these situations? Another cliche bites the fucking dust. Don't care to see mine anyway. Skin flicks get old after the first showing. Seen one; you've seen 'em all.

Steve back from below. Lit a cigarette and said the engineers were on their way. Got to think rationally here.

'What's chances the Goddamn thing is armed and live?'

'Probably is. This is the corner where the rounds were concentrated.' Nodded toward the smelly NVA corpse. 'That's probably one of the victims right there.'

'Yeah. That means it's probably live and that means any screwing around and it will probably detonate.'

Sweat dripping from Steve's forehead. He's taking the predicament worse than I am. Knows the Goddamn thing is dangerous. Won't have a whore's chance in hell if it goes off. Ashen face; wan smile of reassurance.

'Look, man. I'm perched on this cocksucker until it either goes off or some engineer genius arrives to rescue me. Why don't you go on and wait down below?'

Lit another smoke for me.

'That's the logical move. But what happens if I take off and this thing blows before I get out? Who needs to listen to you bitch about how it's all my fault we got into this mess? Nah, man. I'll stick around and write the story.'

At least he's thinking about writing stories again. Conversation interrupted by the arrival of a short, stocky Marine engineer. Whole face looked misshapen by a huge quid of tobacco he worked from cheek to cheek. Spewed a stream of juice on to the dead NVA and looked around the room.

'Where is it?'

Typical engineer. Didn't believe in wasting words. One fuck-up with a booby trap, mine or dud-round and they'd never speak again. Sick Goddamn grin.

'Right here, man. I'm sitting on the fucking thing.'

Second engineer cruised into the room. Assessed the situation at a glance and jerked his head at Steve.

'On your way, bud. No use losing four when three will do.'

Steve glanced fitfully at the door. Shook his head. Told the senior engineer he intended to stay. Not worth an argument to them. Both crouched between my legs studying my perch and the three pounds of volatile, high explosive. Engineers conversing in short, sharp, clinical phrases. Slid down on their bellies for a closer look.

'It's been bruised on the left side near the fuze.'

Engineer Sergeant brushed rubble away gently. Diagnosis time.

'Mah friend, Ah bleeve this here fella is eithuh a dud or hain't never been ahmed.'

'Yeah. How about a second opinion?'

Second engineer slightly more cautious.

'On the other hand, there ain't no use takin' any chances with fuckin' mortars and PD fuzes. They tend to be touchy little motherfuckers.' Sergeant can dig that. Decision time.

'Ah bleeve we kin git you offen this dude, without crematin' the lot of us. Lissen up, now. Mah partnuh here is goin' to keep some pressure on this beauty and while he does that, I'm going to he'p you up from theah. At that time, yoah buddy heah can take you by the hand and y'all can haul ass.'

'Yeah, yeah, OK. Let's do it.'

First engineer designated to keep pressure on the round. Got to rise up out of here like a Goddamn Phoenix. Final instructions.

'When ya come up off there, don't cough, gag, sneeze or fart. Just up and out, understand?'

'Yeah. Let me get my legs arranged here to take the weight.' Engineer reached under my ass to get his hands over the round. Tension getting to me. Nervous giggle. He's not amused.

'You think this shit's funny? I'll just fuckin' leave yer ass sittin' here.'

'No. OK, man. Sorry. Let's go on with it.'

Now. Sergeant had me under both arms. Flex the knees; come directly off of there while the other guy applies downward pressure. Goddamn knees shaking. Legs are asleep. Goddamnit. Move. Now. Final look over my shoulder. Chunky engineer squatted over the round, one hand on top of the other. Looked like he was giving it closed-chest heart massage.

Stumbled down the stairs of the hospital building on wobbly legs. Steve taking most of my weight until we got outside.

'Jesus. Don't let that fucking thing kill those two up there.'

Grunts in the courtyard had all heard about the problem. Alternately laughing and shouting about what silly shitheads we were for getting ourselves into such a mess. Still no explosion from the second floor. Must have been a dud.

Engineers finally emerged from the hospital building. First one carrying our packs and weapons. Second one brandished a mortar round.

'Heah, man. Y'all might want this fuckah for a souvenir someday.'

'Fucking dud? Just like you figured?'

Engineer fingered the olive-drab round examining the fuze.

'Naw. Ah was plumb mistaken about that. This round was live as a Gawgia hooker on payday night. Woulda blowed yo ass sky-high if you hadda fahted real good.'

Numb buzz at the base of my skull. That close, man. It was that close to coming true. Nearly found out about that funeral dream. Feel terrible; almost embarrassed, ashamed. Strange. Remembered I had to take a shit this morning. Probably couldn't bear to squat for a week.

AFVN (American Forces Vietnam Network)//8 February 1968

Mud-spattered jeep coughed to a halt near Hotel Company's Command Post. Festooned with radio aerials. Looks like a Goddamn porcupine in heat. Might be a change of plans in the offing. Can't leave a good thing alone. Platoons sweeping east from the Hospital area since daybreak and no contact so far. Couldn't last. Hotel Six eyed the tall, rawboned figure climbing out of the jeep.

'Jesus Christ. Now the Colonel wants to run the show himself from the front lines.'

Battalion Commander uncoiled from the jeep seat. Sucked noisily on a stubby pipe. Faraway look in his eyes. Headmaster placidly observing his students at play.

'Keeping 'em moving, Captain?' Hotel Six unfolding his sketchy map to begin a description of his troop movements. Colonel preoccupied. Staring at Steve and me. Shit. Hadn't shaved in eight days. Probably look like a couple of wild-eyed Bolsheviks. And officers equate whiskers with communism. Maybe he'll run our asses up on charges. At least we wouldn't have to worry about the north side.

Pinned in position by his glaring stare. Batten down the fucking hatches. Here comes the lecture on field sanitation.

'These the two Division Correspondents?'

Hotel Six winced and looked our way. Poor fucker. Lets us hang around and ends up with an ass-chewing for his trouble.

'Yes, sir. They've been helping out and covering the action. Anything wrong?' Colonel arched an eyebrow. Here it comes.

'Not as yet. You two people step over here.'

Shit. Segregated ass-chewing.

Standing next to the CO near the banks of the river. No indication he's pissed off about the beards. Standing at Parade Rest; staring off at the Citadel. Consulted a soggy notebook.

'You people know anything about an Armed Forces TV station up here?'

'Yes, sir. We visited there a couple of times before the NVA moved in here.'

'Well, I had some visitors from Saigon this morning. They marched into the MACV Compound and started screaming about equipment and personnel that *had* to be rescued.' Scratched his clean-shaven chin with a thumbnail. Preoccupied.

'Can't waste a lot of time or manpower on this thing but we have to check it out for them. You people will be attached to a rifle squad from Hotel Company. Get up to that station, check it out and report to me at the Compound before nightfall. Questions? OK. Here's a list of the things they want to know about.'

'Yes, sir. We've been wanting to get over there and see if our friends got out when the trouble started.'

Ordered a rifle squad from Hotel to take us up to the AFVN station. Good deal. Might find some loose booze around the place. They had plenty last time we were there.

'Oh, I wouldn't worry about your friends. I expect they must have gotten out. When Echo Company swept by there yesterday, they reported nobody in sight and the place all shot-up. The staff probably evacuated when the shooting started and headed for Phu Bai. At any rate, you check it out and make your report directly to me.'

Jeep blatted off in the direction of the MACV Compound. Hotel Six thought the whole deal was a waste of time, but he got his orders. Probably right. Won't be anyone there. Fuckers are all in the rear sucking booze and waiting for the all clear.

Squad leader's name had enough syllables and consonants to make it unpronounceable. Call him Ski. He's not happy with the assignment either.

Doesn't mind being pulled off the assault line, but he's been involved in other 'good deals' before.

'Relax, man. Walk in the sun here. Might even find some shit that makes it worth the effort. Last time I was over there, they were living like kings.'

Suspicious fuckers; rock-hard, survivors.

'What is this place we're supposed to check out?'

'Christ. It's just an AFVN station that used to operate here in the city. You know. TV for the troops and stateside jams on the radio. You guys probably heard them when you were operating out of Phu Bai.'

'I hope that motherfucker who used to yell "Goooooooooooooood Morning, Vietnam" is there. I'll personally cut his fucking balls off.'

'Nah. Goddamnit, that guy's a GI disc jockey who does the morning show out of Saigon. They carry him all over the country on the Network.' He was among the most hated men in Vietnam. Greeted the dawning day as though the Nam was a vacation wonderland. Snappy patter describing the delights of Saigon nightlife. Grunts in northern I Corps had a price on his head.

Ski still not convinced the whole thing isn't a silly-assed stunt.

'Listen. If we get fire from this fuckin' joint, I'm going to haul ass back to the Colonel and suggest he bomb the fuck out of it. I ain't takin' these people into another building unless we got enough heavy shit at our backs to make it worthwhile. This is only one Goddamn short-handed rifle squad here.'

'Yeah, Ski. OK. Just want to check it out, man. Let's get it over with.'

Moved cautiously along the smoky streets. Fires had been started in this area of the city. Cooking or killing? City less torn up than I'd expected. Should have figured. Stone doesn't burn and the ARVN still haven't let anyone fire anything heavier than a 106 yet. Fucking city is a survivor. May be the only one before it's over.

Headed east toward the station. Nice neighborhood. People had some bucks in this area. Wished we had time to take a look in some of these houses. Flashed on the last trip to Hué when we visited the station for the first time. Hoped our buddy was OK. Excitable college boy with a flair for military mischief. Dropped out of a southwest college to join the Marines. First among the stateside crew to get orders to the combat zone. Some envied him the plush assignment with AFVN. Figured he'd spend his whole tour fucking his brains out in Saigon. Good source of in-country R & R with him up here in Hué. Last visit we watched him broadcast the stateside news from a small TV studio in a mobile van parked in the courtyard of the station's compound. Took us on a tour of the city. Chance to walk around the Citadel. Dug that. Gave each of us a bottle of scotch when we left. Really not much of a friend. Don't know much about him at all, but he was willing to share a good deal when he got one. Can't ask much more than that.

Intersection ahead. Steve walked out on point.

'Halt here; got to turn to the right. Station's down that way. Still no incoming fire. Slow it down. That's the place up there.'

Ski fanned his people out along the street in front of the station.

'Take defensive positions and keep your eyes on the high buildings. You two come with me and we'll look this fucker over one time. Watch for booby traps and don't touch nothin'!'

Extreme caution. Place looks like a ghost town or Ground Zero of a nuclear strike. Move slowly and don't be grabby. Never can tell what you'll find left behind by the gooks. Olive-drab TV transmitter vans. A few bullet holes but nothing serious. Big fight must have been elsewhere if there was one. Electronic gear looks intact. Headquarters building.

'Yeah. Here's where the fight was. Jesus. Roof caved in. Probably a satchel charge.'

Bullet holes and shrapnel chinks in the walls. Station manager's desk must have been used as a bullet shield. Finish marred by a row of bullet holes stitched across the front. Wonder who was behind it? Place had been ransacked. Sifted through some of the rubble. Cracked picture frame. Saw that last time I was here. Station manager's wife and family. He'll probably want this.

'Jesus. Wonder if they did make it out? Looked like someone got hurt here.'

Steve called from the rear of the building. More rubble in the area where Ted had kept his personal gear. Locker broken open; gear all over the floor.

'There you go. Full bottle of Cutty Sark. How the fuck did they miss that?'

Steve riffling through a banded stack of letters.

'These are from his family. Not like him to leave these when he took off.'

'Yeah. Unless he was in a big hurry. Or someone ordered him to leave empty-handed.'

Commotion outside the building. What the fuck is going on out there? Two Marines had a Vietnamese pinned to the ground.

'Caught this fucker sneaking around those vans.'

Burly PFC held a .45 to the man's head. Fucker's a civilian. Speaks English anyway.

'No kill me please. Before VC come, I working here.'

PFC unconvinced. 'Sure, fucker. Work on this.'

Pistol cocked and resting on the man's ear. Steve pushed it away.

'Wait. I remember seeing this guy when we visited before. I think he really did work here.'

Marine reluctantly let the shaking man off the ground. 'What happened here, man?'

'Beaucoup VC come here. They shoot everything and put rocket into Station. Most GIs di-di back to Station House.'

'Station House? What Station House?'

'You come. I show you.'

Ski motioned his people back into position.

'Wait a minute. We ain't goin' anywhere with this little prick. He walks us into a trap and we all end up fuckin' dead.'

Wounded dignity. 'Me no VC. No VC stay at Station House. You come see.'

'Hey, Ski. The colonel said he wanted a *full* report. What the fuck we going to tell him if we go back now? We saw a shot-up house and no one around? The list specifically says to check out the living quarters and report any casualties. If they've got another building somewhere we ought to check it out.'

Ski shoved the Vietnamese out the compound gate. 'Well, this fucker walks point.'

Vietnamese dude began to trot up the street, heading back the way we came. Turned right at the intersection of a street that ran parallel with the river. Squad following cautiously behind. Jesus. Look at this. Scorched house with one wall almost completely blown out. Vietnamese walked up on the stone porch and signaled to come ahead. Building a complete shambles. He explained this was where the GIs who staffed the Hué AFVN station lived. Even worse firefight here. Entire roof of the building gone. Misty rain pouring in; soaking the scorched furniture. Looked like someone had tried to erect a barricade. Wooden furniture stacked along one wall near a shot-out window. Machine gun sat atop a dresser.

'How could they have left that here? Yeah. Here's why. Bolt frozen solid, halfway to the rear. Goddamn gun is in shit-shape. Looks like it hasn't been cleaned or fired in a year or more. Hey, man. Where are the people who lived here? Where did the GIs go?'

'VC take them away. Throw bomb on roof. They come out like in cowboy movie. VC take them away. Some GI wounded. Some OK and VC take them away. Maybe go Hanoi.'

Marines clustered around inside the house; eyes searching the area; trying to recreate the fight.

'Shit. You mean they got prisoners, man? Did the VC take away live GIs?'

'They take two, maybe three, with hands tied. I run away before they throw bomb on roof.'

Ski disturbed by the inactivity.

'Outside. And leave what you find here alone. Pick a firing position out in the yard and keep your eyes open.'

'Wait, man. We've got to find out what happened to these people.'

'Hurry the fuck up. We'll wait outside. Don't be milling around. We got to get to MACV before dark and then get back to the company. I ain't walking no Goddamn streets after dark.'

'Yeah. OK. Look, man. Did you know Ted? What happened to the Marines who were here?'

'VC take the lieutenant away. Ted hurt but I not see what happen to him. Maybe he prisoner too.'

'Fuck. OK, man. Where did they sleep? Where is bunkroom?'

There. Pictures of Ted's family on the wall.

'Yeah. Goddamn size thirteen boots. This is his shit. Fucker had the biggest feet I've ever seen on a human.'

No bodies here but blood stains were everywhere. Whoever was in here last was wounded and bleeding heavily. Sheets torn up for bandages. Caked with dried blood and flies. Steve trying to figure out what happened. Gazed through the bunkroom window out across a rice paddy in back of the house.

'Wonder where they took them? Any ideas?'

'Shit. I don't know. Never heard of the fuckers taking prisoners before. What the fuck would they want with a Goddamn bunch of military broadcasters?'

'Yeah. Look at that out there in the paddy.'

Fat green flies buzzed around a long shape about twenty feet away. Something lying out there in the mud and water. Stench of rotting flesh on the breeze. 'Ah, Christ. That's got to be a body. Ski, cover us. We'll go on out there and see who it is.'

Climbed through the blown-out window and sloshed through the slimy water. Cloud of angry flies deprived of their dinner. Yeah. It's a Goddamn roundeye. Face down; hands tied behind with comm wire. Paddy water soaked into the body. Putrid swelling; dead skin trying to burst through a Marine Corps utility uniform. Leeches and maggots feasted in a shoulder wound. Back of the head shattered by a round.

'Shit. Got to be him.'

Steve badly shaken. 'C'mon, man. If it is, it is. Nothing we can do about it now.'

Used my rifle as a lever. Turned the body over. Sucking, vile sound as the muck of the paddy reluctantly yielded to prodding.

'Yeah. Motherfucking Christ on a Goddamn crutch. Should have known it was him. What a fucking mess.'

Steve puked into the paddy. Flies buzzing angrily all over the area. Hard to breathe. Swollen nose and belly heaving so hard the lungs won't work. Goddamn. Got to get a grip here.

Entire right side of the skull blown away. Wrinkled gray matter of the brain clearly visible. Tried to be clinical. First time I ever saw the human brain. Blue eyes stared blankly up into the cloudy sky. All the bullshit really comes home when it's someone you know.

'Remember the serious, concerned look on his face when he did his Cronkite imitation? Stared intently into that tiny fucking camera and pronounced truth for the troops. Got the casualty figures right off the teletype and told the people who were dying how the war was going. Fucking statistic lying here now.'

'Goddamn you, D.A. Stop that shit. He's not a fucking statistic. He's a friend that those dirty bastards assassinated.'

'Yeah, yeah. OK. Can't stand around crying over this.'

Ski walked around the house, sloshing through the paddy; covering his mouth and nose against the stench.

'Executed the fucker, huh?'

'Yeah. This is the guy we told you about. Look here. Hands wired behind his back. Probably thought he was too much of a burden with the shoulder wound. Brought him out here and shot him in the back of the head. Classic Oriental execution.'

Ski unmoved; anxious to get back to the MACV Compound.

'You guys got everything you need here?' Steve glared at both of us.

'We're taking him back with us. Goddamnit. You don't just see shit like this and walk away from it. Someone's got to know what happened. We got to see his body gets home.'

'Listen, man. We'll move it up on the street and wrap

it in a poncho. They'll be along to pick him up after we make our report.'

'Bullshit. Stop playing your fucking hard-guy games with me. He's a buddy. A good dude who liked you despite your cheap shit. Don't listen to him, Ski. I'll take him back myself if I have to.'

Squad leader shrugged. No skin off his ass.

'Suit yourself. But you dudes are carryin' him. And we're leavin' right now.'

'Hey, Steve. Goddamn, man. No sweat here. I'll help you get him back. Don't fucking panic, man.'

Still pissed off at me.

'Shit. Fucking people get killed all the Goddamn time around here. So we knew one of them personally. Dead is fucking dead.'

What the hell does he want from me? Tore a wooden door off the back entrance to the Station House. Made an adequate stretcher. Wrapped the putrid body in a poncho borrowed from one of Ski's Marines. Dude reluctant to give it up. Knew he'd probably never get the rotten smell out of it. Started to bitch but Steve threatened to have his ass court-martialed, or beat the shit out of him. Whichever he feared most.

Tried to close the staring eyes but the lids wouldn't stay down. Rigor mortis. Looked like a clothing dummy, molded into an elegant pose, when we got him up on the door. Heavy bastard. Must be all the rice paddy water that soaked into him. Probably laid out there for a week or more. Stumbled out of the rice paddy and began a straining lurch down the street. Ski's Marines gave us a wide berth. Smell was too much, even for veterans.

High noon when we reached the MACV Compound. Rain had stopped and the soaked streets were steaming in a hazy sun. Still air magnified the stench of the body we carried. Like walking around in the middle of a rotten, green cloud of swamp gas. Doctor at the compound medical station was reluctant to accept the body. He'd have to put the decomposing corpse in his makeshift mortuary among the cleaner, more-recent dead.

'OK, Doc, we'll just let him lay here and stink up the area.'

Started off to find the Battalion Commander. 'Look, it's nothing personal but don't bring any more decomposing bodies back. Just leave 'em lay and get a report back for Graves Registration. I can't have an epidemic back here.'

'Don't see why not. There's certainly an epidemic of dying up there on the line.'

'Yeah. Well. No hard feelings or anything. I mean . . . I know he was a buddy and all . . .'

Steve wanted to lecture. Carrying a Goddamn soapbox around with him lately.

'OK, Doc. Just put him in the reefer. We got the personal effects and here's a dog tag.'

Colonel and his intelligence officer listened patiently to a disjointed briefing. Tried to answer all questions on the list. Upset to hear the NVA had gotten several prisoners, especially an officer.

'Can these people from Saigon move up there and start taking equipment out?'

Steve shrugged and thought for a moment.

'Yes, sir. Don't see why not. Far as we could tell there isn't anything alive around the station, American or NVA.'

'Yes, sir. And it's unlikely as hell anyone will be wanting to watch television for a while.'

'You people get some hot chow here before you go back. And for Christ's sake, get yourselves shaved and cleaned up. There's more press people coming in here than you can shake a stick at. We're going to let them loose tomorrow and I don't want pictures of filthy Marines in the stateside papers.'

Steve mooned over chow. Couldn't see eating a big meal when a friend had died. Whole scene affected him deeply. Stuffed away as much chow as I could and spent some time thinking about my reactions. Am I really fucked up here? Is there a difference between seeing a guy you don't know blown apart in an assault or shredded to death by a mine and finding some dude you know executed? Where's the Old Buddy Syndrome? This isn't how you're supposed to feel. Where's the subtly-macho tear that's supposed to trickle down your cheek? Why aren't you out there vowing revenge on the heathen enemy? Personal perimeter too tight for that. Look behind all the bullshit, man. Fact is, you're *fairly fucking elated* that it wasn't you lying out there.

Zippo//9 February 1968

Just as I suspected. There is a handsome devil under that scurvy melange of beard and shaving lather. Yep. There's an unblemished cheek. Here comes the strong chin. Wait. What's the deal with that little muscle twitching along the jaw? Shit. Stop grinding your teeth. Fucking razor isn't that dull. Probably a reaction to Steve's bullshit. Hasn't stopped carping since he finished shaving. Step to the right half a step and get a look at him in the shard of shaving mirror.

'I'm serious, D.A. You've got to stop all this weird shit and look around at what's happening here. This is no place for cheap give-a-fuck attitudes. You're seeing the essence of what the Marine Corps is all about here in Hué City. Call it cornball bullshit if you want, but these guys are doing the same kind of job that others did at Guadalcanal, Tarawa and Inchon.'

'Yeah, yeah. Goddamn, man. Get off your soapbox. They're good at what they do, but they're still just a bunch of grunt motherfuckers who don't give a shit for nobody.'

'And don't think I haven't been noticing the way you've been acting. You can shit anybody you want except your old *panyo*. I've seen you do your number out there. How about that deal with Zippo? Was that the average D.A. act? I'm tellin' ya, man. Say what you want, but you're getting involved here. You're beginning to see it my way.'

'Your way? Shit. Look who's telling me I'm getting weird. You're the one who wants to blow away the Godless heathen gooks for truth, justice and the fucking American way. I just wanted to get the fuck out of here as soon as possible and see to it you don't get your ass blown away. Don't forget it's a two-man act.'

'Yeah. Well, what prompted the deal with the Zippo yesterday? You want to tell me that? Was that a matter of self-interest or did you want to be in the middle of things? It's pretty satisfying to think of yourself as one of the genuine veterans who faced combat and survived, isn't it?'

'Goddamn, Steve. You're talking like a man with a paper asshole here. This is not The Big Two and the fucking families back home are growing pot in their Victory Gardens. Mom's a hooker on the side and the fucking apple pie gives you ptomaine. You know me, man. I was just trying to see that weasel-assed tank commander didn't accidentally hit reverse when he got called forward. He didn't like the deal at all and you can't grab a tank by the stacking swivel and throw it up into the breech. I went along to make sure we got through the fucking day. That's all. Think about it and you'll see what I did had to be done.'

Just before 1400 hours. Grinding sound of tanks tracks tearing up Hué's pavement. Fire team to the rear as escorts. Tag along to take some tank pictures. Three M48A3 tanks buttoned up, all hatches shut tight. Unusual for Vietnam. Normally tankers rode with hatches open. They prefer a quick exit to the security of being sealed up in a fifty-ton coffin.

Fire team leader. A new guy. Probably never seen a tank up close before. Crouched in a protected doorway, content to watch the tanks idle and sniff the heavy air with 90-millimeter snouts. Doesn't seem to want to move. Shit. Fucking boot camp assholes. We'll be here all day in the midst of three huge Dog targets, if someone doesn't do something. Dip-shit probably doesn't even know about the TI phone.

Shove the kid back into his hole and trot over to the lead tank. Phone box on the rear of the hull provides direct contact with the Tank Commander. There he comes. Dirty as we are. Guess tanks are no better deal in combat. Nice looking Grease Gun he's carrying. Might want to trade him out of that.

Squatty corporal with tattoos up and down his naked arm. Wants to talk to Hotel Six.

'He'll go to the CP with us. Fire team can stay behind and protect the tanks.' Fucking boot doesn't know whether to believe me or not.

'Just do it, man. We lose those tanks and a lot of assholes are going to get blown away today. That might include me, so we will take no chances with the tanks. Just spread your people out on each side of the street and make sure no gooks get close with rockets.'

Tank Commander doesn't like the idea. He doesn't

think armor can be employed safely in built-up areas. Shaky as a dog shitting peach pits. Don't like the feel of that. His tanks can be as much harm as help if someone panics. He didn't give the CO much chance to talk.

'I got to get them tanks into a broader street. Them veehickles cain't traverse or maneuver in fuckin' narrow streets. Ain't supposed to use armor like this at all.'

CO not overly impressed with this dude's motivation but he needs the tanks to crack a strong point. Out comes the tourist street guide again.

'Recon was in this area last night and they say the NVA are holed up in a block of houses surrounding this two-storey structure right here.'

Large building. Full courtyard. Enclosed by two narrow streets and two main thoroughfares with single-storey residences. Certainly wasn't the North African desert. Kid didn't look much like Rommel either.

Hotel Six outlining his basic plan.

'I think we ought to try for the main building first and then fan out to clear the surrounding houses.' Tank Commander squinting at the map and shaking his head.

'Geez, I dunno, sir. If we do that, I got to take my veehickles up this narrow street right here and they cain't maneuver. Maybe we ought to approach from the left over here and try to roll them up from the flank. I got Zippo with me and he can . . .'

Hold it. New deal. Hotel Six didn't know the heavy section of tanks included one equipped with a flame-thrower. He confirmed it with a question. Tank Commander surprised no one knew about the Zippo.

'Yessir. It's number three tank. We always keep Zippo in the rear so he won't be such an easy target. That fucker's got eighty gallons of high octane in the tanks and it don't take much to set it off.'

Hotel Six thinking excitedly now. Massaging his bearded chin and scrutinizing the map again.

'Look. Here's what we'll do with that fucker. I'll send two squads up either side of the narrow street to draw their fire from the biggest building. The rest of the company will advance on line through the houses flanking the street here and here. They'll protect the tanks from flank attack. You send Zippo right up their asses as soon as they take fire and we'll smoke the cocksuckers out in nothing flat.'

Tank Commander unhappy with the plan. Still worried about maneuver room and being trapped with no way to get out. Plan firm as far as the CO is concerned. The two gun tanks will go up the other streets led by his grunts. Flame tank goes right up the middle where the most resistance will be.

Wheels in motion now. Tank Commander admits Hué isn't the Sinai. Grunts to form up in squads on each tank. Steve wants to move with the lead squads. Figures. Probably ought to shoot the tanks from the front. Spectacular photos there. Nah. Shit. No way any flicks of a flame tank will ever see the light of day. According to guidance from the press in Vietnam, the United States does not use flame weapons against infantry troops. Hell, let him go. When we get back to The World we can sell pictures of fried gooks to the cereal company for use in advertising Crispy Critters. Policed up our weapons and gear to get back to the tanks. Still don't like the Tank Commander's attitude. He's an unknown quantity. Maybe I should go along in the turret. If any bullshit starts, I can probably force them to commit to the fight. Better that than having the fuckers balk or hightail it when we need the armor support up front. Might be a shade more dangerous, but we're all fucking dead if the tank doesn't move when we need it.

Crewmen pissing up against a stone wall when we arrived. Zippo. Evil fucking weapon that scares the shit out of everyone, inside, outside or on the receiving end. Employs a high-pressure line, run through the muzzle of the 90-millimeter gun, which can squirt blazing fuel into windows or firing apertures. Hotel Six wanted the Zippo to clear the two-storey building at the end of the street which was the key to the contested block. Hotel Marines lining the streets, eating rations. No use rushing the fight. Gooks going nowhere and neither are they.

Might as well join them. Maybe Steve can concoct something tasty out of this shit. Don't know where he gets that stuff about me acting weird. He's going to fuck around and get his shit blown away before this fight's over. Got to quit thinking like that. No problem there. I just wish he'd stop shooting the shit about changes in my behavior. Probably that . . . uh . . . what the hell do they call that deal? Projection? That's it. He's projecting all his weirdness into me. They'll burst his Goddamn bubble before long too. Look at him over there. Cooking spaghetti and meatballs and shooting the shit with those two black dudes.

'Looks like we're doing the old Quantico trick. Hey-diddle-diddle, right up the middle.'

'Yup,' said the black Lance Corporal around a gap-toothed grin, 'but this time they bringing them fucking rolling Dog targets right along behind. I aint gettin' anywhere near them motherfuckers. One time they had them fuckin' tanks runnin' with us around the Hai Van Pass and the gooks fired everything they had at the fuckin' things.'

'So what,' laughed his buddy. 'At least they wasn't firin' at yo black ass. Shee-it.'

'Shee-it, yo' mothuhfuckin' self, my man. They don't have to shoot *at* you when them fuckin' steel coffins is along. The Goddamn ricochets offa them dudes'll kill you dead as dog shit if you anywhere around 'em.'

So much for my plan of staying close to the tanks. Better go on and ride inside with that shaky-ass corporal. Chow's almost over. Better get over there and crawl inside that Goddamn thing.

Hotel's Company Gunny manhandling people off in the right directions. Company Commander briefing his lead squads. Hotel Six wanted the squads to leapfrog up the street until they came under fire and then he would order the flame tank up in a hurry. The squad leaders were told to load tracer ammo in their weapons and be prepared to spot gun positions with them for the tank.

Someone banging on the turret hatch with a helmet. Hot as hell in here with the diesel rumbling in the rear. Crack of daylight. Tank Commander ready to go.

'Just backin' you up, man. In case you need a helping hand.'

'Look, man. I don't give a shit if you ride but you may miss it all. If they got rockets up there, I ain't takin' this fuckin' veehickle anywhere near 'em. Too Goddamn much fuel and shit in here to be takin' any fuckin' rocket rounds.'

'Yeah, yeah. Just get the fuck in and let's go. You better accelerate like a scalded-ass ape when the word comes, man. Everybody's ass depends on this tank. Including mine.'

Hotel Six on the turret now. Asking for a crewman to carry a radio on the tank frequency for quick communication. Loader climbing out. He'll relay the word to bring on the Goddamn blowtorch.

Maneuvering into position now. Grunts formed up ready to start down the street. Look nervous as shit about the tank and the fire it's sure to draw. Looks weird through this periscope. Like some kind of stretched-out TV screen.

Grunts moving cautiously down the street, dodging from cover to cover and glancing back at the tank. Moving now. Almost an undulating motion. Feels like this fucking thing is sprung with day-old bubblegum. No fire yet. Lead grunts within fifty yards of the two-storey building. Hotel Six shouting into a radio handset. Probably checking the progress of his people approaching on the other streets.

What in the fuck is that? Sounds like some idiot banging on an iron pot with a soup spoon. Shower of shell casings falling down into the turret. Tank Commander triggering long, arching bursts from the .50 caliber up in the cupola. What the fuck is he firing at? Where's a comm helmet?

There. Crackle of static and roar of electronic transmission in my ears. '. . . fucking gook in the upper window on the left side. Might be rockets up there, Six. Better clear to the rear of the veehickle. I'm going to back off.'

Where's the Goddamn intercom switch?

'Listen, man. You can't take this Goddamn tank back now. They're committed. Incoming all over the Goddamn place. They've got to have the tank. You can't back off and leave them out there. Best chance is to get the fuck up there, shoot and knock out any rockets before they can fire. Shit. Make a fucking decision, man. Get the fuck up there.'

Hotel Six giving the double-time signal to his grunts. Christ. They're opening up on the tank with small arms. Sounds like someone banging a shitcan with a bayonet. Gotta go now. Gotta get up there and do it or the rockets will be next.

'Driver. Go, man. They hit this fucking thing with a rocket and we're all fried. Get the fuck up there.'

Grunts peppering the building, concentrating on a second-floor window with M-79s. Firing on all sides.

Sparks and glints of light from the rounds ricocheting off the tank. Hotel Six wants the Zippo now. Running forward and waving at us.

'Go, man. Get the fuck up there before they can get rockets up.'

Muzzle blasts from every window now. Fucking tank sounds like the inside of a popcorn machine. Thank God. Driver made the decision. Gunner traversing the main weapon. Valve to fuel tanks open. Hissing of the pressure lines in the comm helmet. Gears grinding and electric motors whining.

'Shoot, you crazy fucker. Shoot!'

Explosion to our right rear. Brick dust and rubble cascading down all over the vision ports. Tank leaped forward for a moment.

'Rockets. Get that fucking rocket gunner.'

Absolute cacophony of noise in the helmet now. Hotel Six screaming for the flame. Tank Commander wanting to back off.

'Gunner, fire. Goddamn it, man!'

Long metallic roar all around inside the turret. Gunner squeezing his trigger and traversing the turret at the same time. Belching finger of fire tracing a pattern across the front of the building. Billowing ball of flame out of a second-storey window. Gunner traversing; searching for another target. Machine gun still chattering. Guess the Tank Commander decided to join the fight. Ought to get the fuck out of here. Can't get past him in the cupola. Hope they got the rocket gunner. Time to transfer out of armor.

Building boiling with black smoke now. Flaming figure of a man hurtling from a top window. Whoosh of flame when he landed in the courtyard. Greasy black smoke. First time I ever saw a human being burn. Ugly fucking smoke. Bet it smells like shit. Grunts seem mesmerized by the sight. Another burning gook running out the main entrance. Rolling around in the mud. Grunts firing at the corpses. Putting them out of their misery. Tank still squirting flame at the building. Concentrating on the lower windows and arched entranceway.

Tank Commander back on the radio. Sounds relieved. Like a man with chronic constipation getting up off a pot-full.

'Whoo-ee! OK, now. We done it. Driver, let's get back up that street in a hurry. We done it, now. Let's go. Full reverse now. Let's go.'

'Shut the fuck up, man. You Goddamned near chickened out and that would have gotten everyone killed. Your fucking crew did it. You had your way, we'd all be laying out there pinned down or dead.'

Jerking away in reverse gear now. Tank Commander should be observing to the rear and guiding the driver. Shit. He's still popping away with the .50. Trying to keep any rocket gunners from taking a potshot. Fuck this. I'm going out.

Good God. The noise is deafening. Thought it was bad inside the tank. Shit. Feel like a man just surfacing from a deep dive. Better get up forward. Hotel Six inside the main building now. I can hear the tank guns and small arms to the right and left. Must be catching some shit over there too.

Building still billowing smoke. Some return fire from NVA survivors. Foul smell made it hard to breathe. Mixture of gasoline fumes and something else. Sickly, pungent smell like burned sweet potatoes. Squad moved up the marble staircase toward the second floor of the building. Firing rifles into every room along the way. There's the source of that God-awful fucking smell. Smoldering gook rocket team in the corner. Look like burned gingerbread men. Lips burned away so their mouths snarl with bared teeth. Faces completely burned away. Smooth, like the mummy in the fucking horror flicks.

Hotel Six crouched in a corner breathing through a rag held to his mouth and nose. Radio operator can't hack the stench. Just Ralphed his rations into the handset. Infantrymen pouring through the house like maggots through a rotting tree stump. Coughing and wheezing. Firing single shots into charred corpses. Hotel Six can't talk and breathe in the room. Moved outside to check situation on the flanks. Let me get the fuck out into the air. God, what a stink. Like a Goddamn barbecue that got ruined by a gasoline rainstorm. Steve outside; wandering through the smoke and flames.

'Glad to see you took my advice and stayed in the rear for once, D.A. It was fucking incredible up here. The shit flew everywhere. Never got a picture. Ended up firing like a Goddamn crazy man. Shit. It was dicey there for a minute. We thought that fucking Zippo would never come up. And when he did, the motherfucker horsed around for what seemed like an hour before he opened up. Sure fucking glad he finally did though. We'd have been dead meat if he didn't. Just look at this. This is the way to handle this shit, D.A. Gook bastards got a shot of American firepower this time. We ought to stop fucking around up here and bring in a *battalion* of Goddamn Zippos. We could teach these assholes a lesson about fucking around with major power if they'd let us.'

Where does he get the speed? How does he move around with that Goddamn soapbox strapped to his ass?

'Yeah. Guess you're right, Steve. Fucking skatin' in the rear. Old D.A.'s too Goddamn smart to get caught smoking around the fuel farm. Let's get back toward the Compound. Hear there's another battalion coming up. Word is, patrols are going to check out the railroad bridge to see if they can make the crossing on it. By the way, if you're ever thinking of getting into tanks, check with me first. I can tell you what it's like inside Zippo. First hand. One thing you were right about. That Goddamn Tank Commander did try to hightail it just before the Six ordered the Zippo forward. Secure the fucking soapbox! I figured he might pull some shit like that. That's the only reason I'd ever get inside that big-assed box of napalm.'

The north side assault was nearing. Grunt patrols roamed the banks of the Perfume River scouting for crossing points. The most obvious was a double-trestle railroad bridge. If it could be taken intact, tanks and large formations of Marines could flood toward the Citadel in highly-destructive waves. Hotel Six ordered a reinforced squad up the promenade fronting the river to scout the area.

'Shit. There's a Goddamn Christmas present for you. Looks like the same kind of deal the Doggies found at Remagen. Last bridge over the Rhine.'

Squad leader and a few men moving forward to see if they draw fire from the other side. Ought to get over that bastard and try to hold it. If the gooks are smart, they won't leave it standing for long. Radio operator waiting back here to pass the word. We've either got a bridge or we don't.

Runner headed back this way. They must have seen something up there.

'They'se gooks moving on the bridge. Squad leader says to crank up the radio and tell the Six.' Radio operator trying to raise the CP. Firing forward. Rounds striking sparks on the steel girders. Can't see any targets from here. Steve going forward with that Goddamn carbine. Hemingway, the horse's ass. Fuck around and get killed yet. Better follow. Squad leader scanning the spans with field glasses. Waiting for word from Hotel Six.

'There was about six or eight of them fuckers running for the north side just a minute ago. Get that radio up here.'

'There's one of those assholes. Just ducked around a span; headed for the other bridgehead.'

Might have a shot. Hold on him. Full auto. Got to spray the area and hope the cocksucker runs into the burst. Shit. Most of the rounds hit the Goddamn girders.

'Should have *had* that little prick.'

Ah, Christ. Now Steve's watching me. Same Goddamn smug smile on his face.

'Where's your camera, D.A.? How much self-preservation is involved in banging away at that fucking gook on the bridge?'

'Relax, man. Just checking the battle sights on this M-16. Fuck me. Got a little rattled there. That's all. Saw that bastard in the open and just reacted. I'll get the camera out in a little while. As soon as there's something to shoot that I haven't seen four-hundred-thousand fucking times before.'

Gotta find some loaded magazines for this fucking rifle. Shit! Felt like someone kicked me in the Goddamn back! What was that? Blossoms of orange flame from the pilings supporting the bridge. That's what the gooks were doing out there. Crash of the explosion echoing around the buildings like a demented Goddamn subway train. Squad leader can't believe his eyes. Screaming for Hotel Six. Waste of time. Goddamn CO couldn't have missed hearing the blast. Still echoing up and down the river. There it goes. Bridge collapsing into the slate-gray water. Metal dust rising in dirty clouds. Like a slow motion film. Squeals of tortured metal. Huge splash and geysers of dirty water. Whole right side is down.

No, wait. Center of the bridge blown away but only the

right side girders and supports dropped. Skeletal metal silhouette with supporting rails and stanchions on the left still standing. Might get people across, but no vehicles will cross as long as it's in that shape.

'Jesus. Blew that sonafabitch up right under our noses.'

Squad leader receiving orders over the radio. Word is to hold here while Hotel Six informs battalion the bridge is down. He's on his way up as soon as he can get away from his radio.

Clattering chop of helicopters overhead. That didn't take too Goddamn long. Fuckers *can* fly in dirty weather when they want to. Two Hueys orbiting the bridge. One breaking away to make gun runs on the northern bridgehead area. Probably covering for the other one. Passengers leaning out of both doors; staring down at the collapsed railroad bridge. Don't look now, General Patton, but I believe you'll have to swim for it.

'That's got to be the colonel,' said the radio operator. 'Somebody's going to get his balls cut off for losing the bridge before we made the crossing.'

'Fuck 'em,' commented the squad leader. 'The way I see it, the fuckin' gooks did us a favor. How'd you like to be the happy bastard that has to trot across that sonofabitch with your balls hangin' out and all the NVA in the world tryin' to blow them off?' Beginning to put his men in defensive positions now. Hotel Six will be up soon. Fucking comedian. Thinks he's Bill Cosby.

'Captain Giap, this is Captain Jarhead, call the toss, Giap. It's heads; you win. Captain Jarhead, Captain Giap won the toss and he says his people will take up defensive positions on the other side of the bridge where your people can't hit them and you've got to bring your people, bare-ass nekkid, running across carryin' sandbags with absolutely no supportin' fire. Captain Jarhead, you got to run at high-port across the bridge using absolutely nothing for cover until every last one of you motherfuckers is dead as shit.'

Quiet laughter. Graveyard chuckles.

'Shit. That bridge don't mean a fucking thing to Marines.' Cynic. Corporal running a cleaning rod through his rifle. 'Ain't you fuckers heard of amphibious landings? You can bet your ass them dudes wasn't going to have us cross the bridge in the first place or they'd have secured it a long time ago. If you want my opinion, they're going to send us across this motherfucker in assault boats, under fire all the way, so's we can establish a John Wayne-style beachhead on the other side.'

Squad leader didn't like to be up-staged.

'Listen, ass-bag. In the first place, nobody asked for your opinion. You're just a dumb fuckin' grunt like the rest of us. Why the fuck you think they bringin' the fuckin' First Battalion up? They goin' to make the assault while we sit high and dry on this side.'

Heated debate now. Born fatalists. Six to one say they will make the northside assault. Hotel Six in the area. Scanning the collapsed structure with field glasses. Exchanging observations with the circling helo. Weighty decisions being made on high. Helo clattering off now; back toward the MACV Compound. Squad pulling back. Maybe Hotel Six has some word on the north side operation.

'First Battalion is already in the village on the south side of the city. They'll be gearing up to make the crossing. Meanwhile, we've got to secure an area to the west of here. There's still beaucoup gooks holed up in there and it doesn't look like they're going to take the easy way out. Battalion Six says a platoon of tanks is moving up behind One-Five and I'm supposed to use them to take out the pockets over here.'

Should be a while before we move out of the CP again.

Steve has me worried. His Goddamn middleclass morality is going to get him killed yet. Look at him fiddling with that can of C-ration chicken. He's wishing it was Dolly Varden trout from that high, freezing cold lake in Idaho. Ought to force him out of here. Shit. He'll never go on his own. Thinks it's every man's duty to fight and die if necessary. Comes by it honestly, I guess. Swore he was putting me on at first. Seemed like self-righteous jingoism. But it's a real gut feeling with him. He told me about it once, back in the States, over beers in the club.

Came away a little jealous; a little envious. He had a family and strong beliefs. Those things were hard and fast realities to him. Goddamn gee-whiz, pie-in-the-sky bullshit to me.

Raised by a respected family in a small town. Pledge of Allegiance twice a day in school. When the kids weren't reciting they were playing baseball and basketball on organized teams with uniforms provided by town businessmen. Academic atmosphere at home. High school, and he's being pushed in an academic career. Church on Sunday. Philosophical dinner-table discussions about good citizenship and each American's obligations to his country. Pristine dates; chaperoned dances or football games. Good grades in school. Above all, good grades in school which meant admission to college. From there, a certain degree of free choice as long as the selected career didn't take sons or daughters too far from the traditional homestead.

Groping for a rare piece of ass in the backseat of a buddy's car when word of the Marine landings in Vietnam was flashed. That was August 1965. He was in the Marine Corps and on his way to boot camp the next month. Lost one hard-on and gained another. Anxious to lead the Legion parade when he gets home. Shit. *If* he gets home. Good guys are the ones that get it. But maybe I can do something about that. Maybe. If he doesn't do anything too weird.

Better keep him straight. He's the only other human who knows my background. Poor fucker. He had to get saddled with that sentimental shit too. Remember that night I spilled my guts. It was that fucking shotgun.

God, they could have given me a bazooka to carry on guard and it would have been better. Found me in the tent after my tour of duty. Crying like a dumb-assed baby; staring at the shotgun on the deck. Shotguns and whiskey. My fucking downfall. And my old man's. Didn't want his sympathy but what the fuck you gonna do? Can't share shit like that, man. Can't do it. Like reciting wedding vows when you let someone in on that kind of thing.

Rain starting again. Grunts bitching about the stench hanging in the fetid air. It's a cloying, lung-wrenching spoor. Mainly charred human flesh and burned camphor-wood furniture. Wonder who's got the fire insurance policy on this Goddamn city? Probably Thieu or Ky. Bearded hospital corpsman changing a dirty bandage covering a festering shrapnel wound below his knee. Steve helping and trying not to puke at the smell. Wound obviously rotting.

'Doc, you better get back to the rear with that leg before they have to amputate.'

Probing the purplish flesh around the wound with professional interest.

'Got a couple more days before it's gangrene. Till then I better stay up here and put patches on holes blown into the Corps' finest.'

'Christ, another bleeding heart. Look, there's no telling how much more walking we'll have to do today. You'll be lucky to stand up, much less hump around with the company.'

'Don't have to stand and don't have to hump.' Doc

rewrapping the wound. 'I just set up the butcher shop somewhere to the rear of where you all are pissing and moaning. Next thing you know, the grunts come panting in, carrying their asshole buddy who has just been butt-fucked by a B-40 or some such nonsense, and ol' Doc commences to operate and save his misbegotten life. Chalk up another fightin' US Mo-rene who will live to fight another day.' High-pitched giggles. Fucker is strung out like a speed-freak.

Steve coming over. Wanted to get away from the stink. 'That dude and all the rest of these guys are half-fucking crazy. They've had it. This must be what it was like on Guadalcanal or at the Chosen. Too long under pressure. Did it to those guys and it's doing it to us.'

'Here we go again. Better get that Goddamn *us* out of your mind.'

'Goddamnit, D.A. Why don't you come off it, man? We're in this thing up to our assholes. We are they *and have been* since this stuff started. It's time to put up or shut up.'

Have to ponder that for a while. Chicano sergeant looking for us. CO wants to see us over by the CP.

He's in an agitated state. Pacing back and forth across a mud-spattered room while radio operators fussed over their equipment. Turned to face us, glaring and accepting a steaming cup of coffee from the Company Gunny.

'You guys want to know what a fucking zoo this thing is turning into for your reports?' Really pissed about something. Spilled hot coffee all over his rainsuit.

'Remember that block of houses we had such trouble with earlier this week? The ones over near the Sports Stadium? The ones that cost me fifteen dead and twenty-one wounded to take?'

Yeah. Shit. Hell of a fight. Stubborn NVA and a maddening seesaw battle. Got a house or two and held for an hour or so until they pushed us back out. Took two companies eight hours to grab it and keep it.

'Well, the Goddamn NVA are back in there and you can just guess who has been assigned to go back and clear them again. Hell, those houses are six blocks to our rear. What happens to the area we cleared with tanks today? After all the shit I went through, they better not abandon this place.

'It's right on the river, therefore, the First Battalion moves up here to occupy this position. That way they'll be close by the water for the north side assault. Meanwhile, good ol' Tremblin' two-Five goes back the way it came and gets its ass caught in the meat-grinder again. What I'd like to know is where are all the good reinforcements coming from and how the hell are they getting into the city?'

Good questions. Got no answers just now. Been killing NVA by the platoon during the past ten days. You could see and smell their bloated corpses anywhere you went on the south side of the city. No one had bothered to police them up despite repeated warnings from the corpsmen concerning plague and other communicable diseases that attend rotting human flesh.

Hotel Six wired tight, just like his beat-up troops. Too much strain and too many frustrations. Almost makes you feel sorry for them. Almost.

Church Music//10 February 1968

Marine commanders directing the fight in Hué were under increasing pressure from the South Vietnamese government as well as the American Command in Saigon to press the issue in Hué City. What was apparently most galling to everyone not involved in the dirty fight on the south side of the Perfume River was the red, blue and yellow North Vietnamese flag that flew defiantly over the ancient Citadel on the north side.

Rear echelon commanders who visited the city choked on the sight of the enemy flag as much as they did on the fetid air full of stench and rotting corpses. A steady stream of refugees flowed south out of the city and blocked the roads to GVN and American commanders who wanted to see the Citadel, collect their campaign ribbon and offer advice to the Marine Regimental Commander who was running the show.

ARVN officials wanted the Citadel taken immediately, before the NVA turned their possession of the ancient seat of the Vietnamese emperors into too great a propaganda weapon. The Marines and their superiors in the Military Assistance Command were perfectly willing to attack, but they were holding out for air or artillery support to crack the Citadel's thick stone walls. The Vietnamese generals ranted and raved about pressing the attack but they clammed up when the subject of firing on the ancient monument arose. They wanted the Citadel taken. They did not want it harmed.

For their part, the Marines were willing to wait until the Vietnamese relented on the subject. They had enough trouble on their hands on the south side of Hué and they weren't about to attack a medieval fortress without thorough artillery or air preparation. They would continue to struggle on the south side until the GVN decided it could afford a few holes in those ancient walls. Everyone in the MACV Command Post realized the South Vietnamese would have to give in or take the Citadel themselves with their own infantry attempting to breach the walls. Compromise was inevitable. It was simply a matter of time. Meanwhile, the American Command needed a logistics point on the south side to support their assault on the north. The Hué Sports Stadium was perfect for that purpose.

Site of the Vietnamese national soccer tournaments and many lesser competitions that drew throngs of spectators, the stadium was built along the lines of similar arenas in America. It was oval-shaped and ringed by a high wall which was currently festooned with crudely painted anti-American slogans in both Vietnamese and English. There were tiers of bleachers, four entrances big enough to admit trucks and most importantly, a large, flat playing field that was ideal for landing helicopters. All that was needed was to clear the tall buildings surrounding the stadium on three sides to keep NVA gunners from blowing the choppers out of the sky and the Americans had their logistics point for the north side assault.

One long side of the stadium faced the Perfume River which meant casualties could be ferried across the river, given first aid at a Regimental Aid Station that was planned for construction inside the walls and then evacuated via helicopter south to Phu Bai or Da Nang. Ammunition and supplies could be brought into staging areas safely behind the stadium walls and then ferried across to the north side by landing craft. Marine logistics experts, rushed to Hué from Da Nang to run the resupply and MedEvac efforts, realized the stadium was crucial to success on the north side of Hué. All that remained was for the grunts to secure the area surrounding it for the build-up to begin.

Hotel Six can't believe his luck. His outfit drew the easy role in taking the area surrounding the stadium. Chuckling while he pores over a street map. Objective is a 200-yard block of houses fronting the river. Echo and Golf will take the heavy shit this time. They've got to take the high buildings up close to the stadium. Gathering platoon leaders now. Pass the word. Let everyone in on the good news.

Wants minimum casualties. Thinks Hotel will be withdrawn and rested when the north side attack begins. Could be right. First Battalion showed up and moved into the buildings Hotel had cleared. Funny sort of event. None of the friendly shouting and insults that normally accompanies a relief of positions by two Marine commands. All quiet on every front. 2/5 too shot-up to care much and 1/5 too scared to shoot the shit. Simply stared tight-lipped at the filthy, bearded veterans they were replacing.

Crouched near a 60-millimeter mortar crew. Ready to put the tube to work when the word comes. Chopper clattering low overhead. Looking for gooks in the open; flying erratic patterns around the stadium. Won't be long before one of those fuckers draws fire. There it is. Burst of green-colored tracer rounds aimed at one of the Hueys. Lead grunts sprawling for cover. Helo staggering in mid-air. Pilot fighting for control and losing the fight. Grunts up and moving now. Nothing to do but follow. Should be the last hurrah on the south side.

Crump of grenades up front. Firing in earnest from both directions. Lead squads busily kicking in doors and lobbing grenades through windows. Burst of AK fire rattled off the stones to the rear. Vaulted a fence looking for cover. This is the big time. Gooks acting like there's no tomorrow. Maybe there isn't. Shit. This could get out of hand.

'Keep moving. Don't stop now.' Squad leader wanted to get it over with. 'Don't stop. Keep moving through the houses. Shoot the fuck out of anything that moves.'

Grenades flying everywhere. Grunts charging into every house. Lusting for it now. Can't see targets, but they don't give a fuck. Get into it. Pull the trigger. Make it happen. Get it over with, one way or the other. Wild firing. Situation out of control. Stampede now: a herd of angry, frightened cattle spooked by the scent of death and the promise of reprieve. No way I'm following that shit until someone gets those assholes under control. Perhaps a moment of silent meditation and prayer. Ducked into a Buddhist temple with Steve close on my heels.

Christ. Get away from that mob for a minute. Sit and let the coolness of the temple walls soak through our wet uniforms. Look at that up there. Peaceful, pot-bellied Buddha sitting cross-legged on some kind of altar. Serene benediction. How can that shithead be so calm at a time like this? Wonder if that gold leaf is real or painted on? Better get a closer look.

Movement at the rear of the altar. Slight scraping sound like metal against plaster or concrete. Can't wait on this one. Full auto and hope I blow away a car or rat. Burst rattled around the stone walls of the temple. Buddha shattered in large golden flakes. Clatter back there. Hit something that fell hard. Hope it isn't some dip-shit Marine playing Chaplain. Steve sprinting forward to get a shot from the flank. Won't be needed. Fucking gook alright. Looked like a sergeant, lying face up in a pool of blood. Rounds tore out the left side of his face. Dark blood oozing out of several holes in his chest.

Steve sniffing around for others. He won't find any. Not hard to figure this shit out. Gook made himself a last-ditch nest behind the altar. ChiCom grenades and extra ammo clips stacked up there. He was ready to hold out for a while. Wore one of those prized belts with the red star on the buckle. Better get that. Steve dug through the pack he found in a back room. Some letters in there. Look at those stamps. North Vietnamese workers plowing a rice paddy with one hand and brandishing an AK-47 with the other. Stuff those in the pack for souvenirs along with the red NCO collar tabs.

Steve wanted to shove off. He's got the hurry-up fever too.

'Wait a Goddamn minute, man. Look at this temple. Some of the gold leaf on that statue is real. Get a load of the velour wall hangings. Antique brass fixtures for burning incense. These people had some bread. Better check it out. Might be able to find a full collection plate.'

Now he's bitching about booby traps. What's back there? Oh shit.

'Look at that. A brand-new Teac tape recorder. They probably used it to fill in for an organist. Do Buddhists have organ music in their ceremonies? Can't remember if I ever knew. Here's your prize worth carting off back to Da Nang. Guys in the rear giving three or four hundred dollars for a rig like this.'

Got to shift some of this gook money to Steve's pack. Maybe I can stuff this recorder in mine and find a way to get it out and back to the rear.

Steve can't handle it.

'You may have failed to notice, but there's a fucking war going on and this is not the Goddamn PX.'

'Fuck that. You load this loot up in your pack and I'll find a way to fit this deck in mine. When we get to the rear, we're rich.'

Fucker must weigh forty or fifty pounds. No sweat. There now. Swing this thing on to my back. Goddamn. Feels like a baby elephant between my shoulder blades. Got to move slowly or I'll fall and bust this thing to pieces. Nobody said getting rich was easy.

'You're going to get fucking killed humping that thing, D.A!' Steve still wanted me to leave the recorder behind.

'No deal, man. You want me to drop a thing like this, go on out there and find me something lighter and worth more money. Fucking fight won't last forever and I'll never get rich on sergeant's pay.'

Outside the temple, Hotel Company grunts still ran crazily across the street from house to house. Firing sounded like it's all M-16s.

'Slow down, Steve. Want me to fall and break this thing before we can get it to the rear?'

Maybe if I use the rifle as a sort of crutch. No need to zigzag. Goddamn pack pulling me around like a waltzing wino.

Goddamnit. That's all I need. Steve's down. Some of that firing must be incoming. Rolling to the other side of the street. He ain't dead. Better get over there and see how bad it is. Jesus Christ, this tape deck is heavy as an anvil.

'What about me?' Steve dabbing blood away from his nose and left cheek. 'I think I'm fucking wounded.'

'Let me see.' Steve winced as rain mixed with sweat to sting the wound. Looked like a piece of pavement or something hit him. Maybe a ricochet or spent round. Couldn't have been anything else. His face would look like mincemeat pie. Get some water on it. See how bad it is. Not much more than a long, deep scratch. Tie one of these Goddamn calf-length boot socks around his head.

'No sweat. Seen you worse off when you tried to shave with a hangover. Better get on up with Hotel. Fucking tape recorder is kicking my ass.'

Looks like the NVA in this area were fighting a delaying action. Cornered in two houses at the very end of the sector Hotel has to clear. Machine gun fire up and down the street. Mortars popping into action. All out to bust the final stronghold. Need a place to get in out of the rain until those fuckers either win, lose or draw. House up there about fifty yards looks good. Out of the gun-target line. No chance for a short round from the mortars. Got to cross the fucking street though. Better wait until Hotel Six orders his people up. Shouldn't be long. Mortars are popping a heavy barrage into the final row of houses at the end of the street.

Time for another look at this tape deck. What a Goddamn beauty. Best I could afford when I was a kid was a fucking Japanese pocket-sized transistor radio. At least I'll get something tangible and valuable out of this fight. Never had enough money to buy one of these before. Always pissed it away on one thing or another. Took a fucking gift from a gook religious congregation to get old D.A. into materialism. Maybe I won't sell it. Might be great for parties in the rear.

Mortars have done all the damage they can. Other assault companies caught up with Hotel's relatively easy advance. Begining to get dark. Hotel platoons strung out along the street to the riverside of the stadium. Got to get the final two houses on this street before full dark or the stadium won't be secure. Return fire sporadic. Rain getting heavier; making everyone miserable. Grunts in nasty moods; anxious to get it over with and get inside.

Hotel Six senses the end of it. Signaling for the move. Long shadows in the street provide some concealment for the leapfrogging grunts. Machine guns firing long, traversing bursts into the houses at the end of the street. Time to move. Goddamn. Pack feels heavier than before. Better make the CP before nightfall. Should be some word on the north side assault. Get this fucking thing over with and then get back to the stadium. Maybe catch a chopper out of here.

Lurched along behind Steve. Hard to see my footing in the gloom. Moving like a sick drunk up the wet, slick street. Christ. They pick now to start shooting. Tracers whipping all around; making green arcs in the gloom. Shit. Firing at me. Can't move fast enough to keep out of the fire. Fuck 'em. This Goddamn tape deck stays with me. Shoot, you communist assholes. Figures you'd try to kill a man trying to make a fast buck. Story of my dumb fucking life. Ah, Christ. Am I hit? Something knocked me down. No.

'OK, Steve. I'm OK. Go on and get under cover, man. Go on. Those fuckers couldn't hit a bull in the ass with a bass fiddle.'

Made it. Flopped down next to Steve in the building we selected. He's still bitching.

'You fucking idiot. You nearly got killed for humping that silly-assed tape recorder. You know that? You couldn't move worth a shit. God only knows how you kept from getting your stupid ass blown off.'

The man has no nose for economics. Probably have to babysit him through the postwar depression.

'Shit, man. Relax. I made it, didn't I? Nothing to it. This morning I blew away a Godless heathen hiding behind a religious statue and the Creator now feels obligated to protect my ass in times of crisis.'

Code of the Grunt. The good men do keeps them out of body bags. Stop bitching. You've got to start seeing the humor in these things.

Firing dying down now. Enough for a safe move over to the Hotel CP at the southwest corner of the stadium. In the dark of the command post, two corpsmen were working over three wounded men who were hit by small arms during the assault. Wounds were minor. Everyone in high spirits. Regular fucking laughing jag. Hotel took the final objective with no one killed and only five wounded. Company Commander was ecstatic. More sure than ever he would be relieved the next day.

Everyone scrambled to make themselves comfortable. Most could sleep. Grunts from the First Battalion would be involved in the night activities. Hotel could rest for once. Holes in the roof of the CP let in the drizzle and grunts were spread out between puddles trying to fall asleep.

Looking for Steve in the dark. Stumbling over bitching grunts. There he is, cupping a smoke in a corner.

'Let me have your flashlight, man. Time for one final check of the merchandise before I retire.'

'Oh, my God! Those dirty bastards. Those filthy, atrocity-committing motherfuckers. Those slant-eyed cocksuckers shot my tape recorder full of holes. Just look at this shit.'

Plainly visible in the dull red glow of the hooded flash. Three bullet holes dripped copper coils and colored bits of wire. Huge elongated rents were telltale marks of AK-47 rounds. Must have happened when they were shooting at me while I crossed the street. Where's the justice in this Goddamn war? Break my back and nearly get killed just to hump this thing so I'll maybe get something more than a Purple Heart and a pat on the ass out of this fight, and what happens?

Woke Steve from a snoring daze around midnight. Made him promise he'd let me know if he saw any temples on the north side. There had to be another tape recorder in the city.

Helos woke us at first light. First time since the fighting started I could remember loud noises that weren't caused by gunfire of one kind or another. No firing at all. Roaring, whining and clattering from flights of helicopters stacked in vertical echelons and circling over the Sports Stadium, ready to land. Serious business now. Hadn't seen this many choppers in the air since the fighting started.

First of the dual-rotored cargo birds bounced on to the landing surface. Special Helicopter Support Teams scrambled around trying to unload passengers and cargo as fast as the harried crew chiefs could push them out. Looked like the north side assault was underway.

Hotel Company grunts feeling like they're well out of it now. Final phase of the fight for Hué City would be carried by 1/5. Now the hoots and good-natured profanity started. Hotel Company could finally afford a superior attitude. They were already survivors of the Battle for Hué City. Figures I should feel the same way. Something still eating at me though. Can't identify it. Keep looking through the light rain at the Citadel's walls. Am I pressing it to go over there? Look at these assholes.

Steve grinning and jabbering with Hotel grunts about the high weirdness of survival when odds say you ought to be stone dead. Like observing a bunch of African tribal adolescents at a party for the survivors of the Rites of Passage.

'Shit. Let's go on with it. Let's get over there and see what it's all about. Let's get over to that Goddamn fort and see what's on the other side of those walls.'

'Shit. You're like the fucking bear that went over the mountain. Just can't wait to see what you'll see on the other side.'

'OK, Assbag. Maybe you'd like to get on one of those incoming choppers and get out of here. Call it quits and let it rest for a while.' Look of total surprise on his face.

'What? Fuck that. It'd take a cratering charge to get me out of here after I survived this far. I want to see history, man. I want to be part of it.'

'Christ sakes. OK. We go to the north side. Guess I've got a little business there too. But you got to stop acting like a Goddamn shrink all the time. We do a job and we walk. Alright? I'm OK and so are you. Stop acting like an asshole.'

Choppers lifted shakily out of the Sports Stadium landing zone.

'Maybe we ought to be on one of those, man.'

Steve shook his head; looked up from the C-ration coffee he was brewing. Fully adjusted to the decision to go north now.

'Shit, man. Leave it alone.'

'Christ. Should be in Hong Kong drinking good whiskey. No. Had to get up here and see what it's all about. Hope to hell that shit we sent back made it to the rear and got out. Really like to see what the hell some of those shots looked like.'

Got to move. Goddamn helicopters showering us with rain and wind. Headed for Hotel Company, holding in the block of houses between the stadium and the Perfume River. Troops poured into the city. Couldn't tell the Goddamn formations without a scorecard anymore. Everyone spent a lot of time staring across the gray water at the Citadel. Wondering how the hell they're going to do it. Good question. Navy got into the act with a vengeance yesterday. Brought black-hulled Swift boats up to patrol the river from the western outskirts to the South China Sea. Heard them blasting away all last night. Made the grunts nervous and jumpy.

Hotel Company had visitors. Cluster of ARVN officers and US Army advisors. Obviously just in from somewhere in the rear. Spit-shined jungle boots and permanent-press jungle fatigues, still neat and crisp despite the drizzle that turned everything in Hué into a formless mass. Military martinets hated rain. Took the precision crease out of things.

Hotel Six squatted among the newcomers. Talking animatedly; waving his hands and shaking his head.

Looked dog-tired and haggard. Steve tossed off the last of his coffee and pitched the C-ration container into the river.

'Looks like the big dogs have come up from the rear to collect their campaign ribbons.'

Sidled by avoiding the glare of the rear echelon types. Tossed a sloppy salute at the Company Commander.

'Hey, you two. Come over here for a minute.'

Ah, shit. Bet we just got tagged for escort duty. Fuckers are probably from the Saigon Information Office wanting a guided tour of the battlefield.

Stood before the gathering like two street urchins. Muddy, soaked, bearded and ripe. Officers eyed us with obvious distaste. Maybe they'll change their minds about the tour if we keep them downwind. Hotel Six stood to make introductions.

'These gentlemen are from General Westmoreland's staff. And these Vietnamese officers are from the National Police. They're here to investigate a rip-off they say took place when we hit the National Treasury Building last week.'

Americans nodding agreement. Vietnamese squinted and preened. Hotel Six pointed to us.

'These two men are military correspondents. They were present throughout that action. They might be able to tell you something about the missing money.'

Pack on my back felt like it was full of fucking bricks. Would they demand a strip search? Play this fucker right or we are caught. Get caught with a healthy chunk of the national currency in your pack and they might just figure something more for me than a close haircut and a quick trip to the Nam. Jesus. What was that story in the *Stars & Stripes* last month? Fucker in Saigon got twenty years for stealing a Goddamn truck? Bucks or the bastille, man? Think fast.

Hotel Six convinced no one in or around his outfit would steal money. Too busy fighting the Goddamn war, right, Skipper? Not the Marine way to steal.

'If you guys know anything about where a million or so piasters went, I want you to speak up. These officers are prepared to put Hotel Company under mass arrest. They've got the support and authority of the Regimental Commander and they'll begin to interrogate what's left of my command if they don't discover some evidence to indicate we didn't take that money.'

'Christ, Skipper, can't recall anything except your lieutenant collecting all the money that was in the basement vault. Shit. I remember the Gunny searched everyone who came up out of there.'

'Yeah. I already talked to the lieutenant and the Gunny. They told me the same thing and we've looked through all the MedEvac gear. Well, I think it's an insult, but I guess I'll have to ask my people to turn out for interrogation.'

Steve dug me in the ribs and grabbed my elbow.

'Sir, we might be able to turn something on this for you. Can you give us a few minutes to check some sources? We'll be right back.'

Army officer at the end of his tether. Enlisted pukes don't need time to confer. They do as they're told and confess, by God.

'Be quick about it, Goddamn you. We want that money and we want it damned fast or the Marine Corps is going to be mighty sorry they ever got into this fight.'

Hotel Six looked like someone just cut a C-ration fart. 'I'm already very fucking sorry about that.'

Walked off around a corner from the assembled officers. Ducked in out of the misty rain under the roof of a street shrine. Only Buddha to bug the conspirators. We have a genuine fucking problem here. Time for rational thinking. Steve agitated and worried.

'Listen, man. We are fucking caught. Those assholes will strip search every Goddamn Marine in this city and you know it. I'm no plaster Goddamn saint and I would like to get away with that bread as bad as you would, but they are going to look in your pack, man. Sooner or later. We've got to hand it over.'

'Are you fucking nuts, man? We'll go to the Crossbar Hotel for the rest of our lives. They'll put us so far back in the dungeon they'll have to pump air to us. We can hide this shit and come back for it later after they leave.'

'No. Goddamn it. Won't work. Manero and those other dudes know we were down in that vault. They lay that info on them and it's only a matter of time before the fucking rubber hoses come out.'

'Bullshit. We can pull this off if we're cool. You know that. What's the real objection here, man? And don't tell me about a guilty conscience.'

'Look, D.A. You been on the line with these dudes for more than a week now. They ever do you wrong? How many times did they pop up and fire so you could take stupid fucking pictures without getting your ass ventilated? Ever notice that, man? Way I figure it, Hotel has been through too much already to get fucked around by these Slopeheads and a bunch of rear echelon motherfuckers who could give a shit less if they put line grunts in jail for the rest of their lives. Just can't fucking see that, man.'

'Ah, Christ. I could have fucking *owned* Hong Kong. Could have gotten *out* of this green motherfucker and been set, man. Look. I don't figure I owe these people a Goddamn thing, but I don't like the thought of spending the rest of my enlistment in the slammer. And you're right about those assholes. They'll hold up the Goddamn war until they find the bread. And when they find it, they'll sure as shit never rest until they find out who got away with it. So OK. We give it back. But we get out of this with our asses intact. You let me do the talking.'

Slipped the heavy pack off my back. There it is. So long, Hong Kong. Have to rent pussy for a while. Won't have enough to buy it after this last great act of simple humanity. Wooden cabinet under Buddha held joss sticks and incense.

'Toss that shit in the street. Stand over there where you're blocking the view. Put this bread in here and let Buddha guard it for a little while. If it gets ripped off by some money-grubbing grunt we're flat fucked.'

Steve minced around like a burglar with the shits. 'Look. I'll stay here and guard the money. You go back and talk your shit. Tell them we found it or something. I'll back whatever you say.'

'Yeah. Just stand by. Let me handle this.'

Colonel doing the West Point waltz when I got back to the CP. Marching up and down. Not used to waiting on enlisted men.

'Alright. Enough of this cheap shit. If you people know anything about that missing money, you are ordered to tell me what it is; right Goddamn now. Let's hear it.'

'Well, sir. It happens I do know something about the missing money. I'd like to give you a little background on the incident if I may.'

Motioned the entire entourage inside a nearby building. Waved a hand at a thin, bespectacled second lieutenant and a portly Vietnamese officer in a rain-soaked uniform festooned with patches and badges indicating his status.

'You be Goddamn quick about the background. Lieutenant Harley here will translate what you have to say for General Tan.'

Right. Here goes the Big Play.

'It so happens, Colonel, that me and my partner were in the midst of the fight for the Treasury Building. It was a bloody business. NVA all over the place. Hand to hand . . .'

'Listen, you. Knock off the detailed descriptions and tell us what you know about this theft or I will personally see that you are tossed in the slammer for the rest of your misbegotten days at which point you will be turned over to the Vietnamese government for further punishment.'

Impatient fucker. Nodded for the skinny lieutenant to translate the threat for General Tan. Unguarded contempt on that rat bastard's face. OK, shithead. Wait till I get to the punchline.

'OK, Colonel. Here it is. A good buddy of ours was wounded while trying to guard that stash of money from falling into NVA hands. We were trying to keep him alive when we noticed an ARVN squad breaking into the vault and making off with a sackful of piasters. We knew it was a fucking rip-off when we saw the ARVN privates trying to make a getaway without being seen. Hotel Company had already left the area, so it was either do something ourselves or let the little cocksuckers get away with it.'

Apoplexy. Fucker turned the color of stewed tomatoes. Lurched at the translator and slapped a manicured hand over his mouth before he could repeat what I said for the general. Is there a Vietnamese word for cocksucker?

'Are you trying to tell me that ARVN soldiers stole that money?'

Fucker is *enraged*. Spit all over that poor lieutenant.

'No, sir. Not at all. I'm trying to tell you that a bunch of ARVN *tried* to steal the money. So happens, we surprised them and drove them off at gunpoint.'

C'mon, shithead. Grab at it.

'I don't believe this bullshit for a moment.'

Nearly strangled the lieutenant. Finally looked down at

the struggling officer who was flapping his hands and trying to breathe.

'Lieutenant, if you translate one word of this crap to the general, I will personally kill you with my bare hands.'

'It's true, sir. We scared the ARVN off before they could pocket the bread. Been looking around ever since for someone in authority we could tell about it.'

Colonel had the lieutenant nearly bent backwards over his knee; tightening a headlock.

'You mean you've got that money? You personally have that Goddamn money?'

'No, sir. I don't have the money. It'd be stealing if I took the money. But I watched the ARVN stash it. I *know* where the money is right now.'

Lieutenant finally escaped the colonel's grasp and bounded across the room to take shelter in a corner. Look of utter disbelief on the colonel's face gave away to smug contempt. Thought he had me by the balls now. Going to squeeze on me like he did that fucking lieutenant. Shouted over his shoulder at an NCO standing nearby.

'Sergeant, place this criminal under arrest. I intend to have him and his asshole buddy shot. Escort them to where that money is hidden, secure it and return here immediately. Snap to it.'

'Better back off, Colonel. People who point pistols at me bring on amnesia real fucking quick. I'll find that money for you but I do it alone or I don't do it. And if anything happens to me and my buddy, you can forget it.'

Gasping with rage now. 'Don't try to blackmail me, you insolent, thieving sonofabitch. I know Goddamn well you stole that money and, by God . . .'

'Hey. Colonel, I don't give a shit one way or the other what you know or think you know. It's like this. If you want the fucking money, you let me go after it alone. And you give me your word you'll forget where and how you got it once it's turned over to you.'

Hotel Six pointedly ignoring the situation; poring over a map with one of his lieutenants. Colonel looked like a stroke was imminent. Glanced back and forth at the Company Commander and the Vietnamese general.

'How about it, Colonel? Have I got your word? No reprisals?'

Long, hot pause. General Tan stared menacingly at everyone in the room.

'Get the Goddamn money and be quick about it.'

Gaggle of grunts standing around outside the building. They knew the situation. Looked like they wouldn't mind blowing away the visitors. Couple of them grinned and inclined their heads toward the ARVN group.

'Nah. Cool it. I got this fucker handled.'

Steve shivered in the rain. Jumped like a surprised safecracker when I walked up to him.

'What's the fucking deal? Did you tell them?'

'Yeah. Break that shit out of there and stuff it back in my pack. The deal is we stopped some ARVN from ripping it off. Just remember that.'

Two majors opened the pack. Colonel stared coldly from a corner where he retreated to give the Vietnamese general a chance to get his hands on the money. General Tan and his aide licked their thumbs, scribbled figures on a notepad and riffled through the stacks of piasters. When the general finished counting one bundle, he tossed it over his shoulder to another aide and grabbed for more. National Treasury might see some of it but only after he collected a finder's fee.

'Fuck this. Makes me sick. Let's go.'

Turned to leave but the colonel set the hook. Yeah. Knew that cheap fucker would do that.

'Halt. You two are under arrest. When that money is

finally counted, you'll lose a finger or toe for every P that's missing. You Goddamn criminals are going to *jail* for this.'

'Uh huh. What about your word, Colonel?'

'I'm not bound to honor any promise made to a couple of enlisted, criminal thieves.'

'Yeah. Well, you may be forgetting that we're also correspondents; field reporters with contacts in the civilian press. You have us locked up and I'll tell every reporter in sight that we saw the ARVN rip this money off. There's a man from UPI outside interviewing Hotel Company grunts right now. I'll start screaming some shit that will have you explaining to General Westmoreland why *you* shouldn't be put in jail.'

'Don't try that shit with me, you little whelp. I told you blackmail won't work. There are ways to prevent you from talking to the press.'

Hotel Six had enough. Struggled up from his seat in a corner of the room and walked over to face the colonel.

'Mind you, sir, I'm not privy to the thinking of the General Staff, but it seems to me you're in a quandary here. It seems to me field grade officers shouldn't be waltzing into *combat* outfits in the middle of a *combat* operation and start making threats against inncoent *combat* men. There is about half a company of shot-up, pissed-off witnesses outside that would be glad to swear to it if I submitted a report to MACV stating we personally observed ARVN troops trying to steal the money. Seems to me the best move here, now that you have the money back in the hands of the GVN representative, would be to call it a good deal and walk away.'

Colonel stiffened and sputtered. 'Captain, you breathe one word of that lie about ARVN troops stealing this money and I'll see that you're court-martialed. Hell, I'll have you shot too.' There it is. Now it's personal. Get Some, Captain.

'Colonel, why don't you shoot NVA instead of your own fucking troops. You tell your story and I'll tell mine . . . to the press.'

There it is. He's whipped, by God. Colonel sputtered and fumed, looking around the room for support. Staff too busy digging through stacks of piasters to acknowledge the argument. Money talks; not colonels. Kicked angrily at the piles of money, sending a shower of bills around the room. Vietnamese staff officers scrambled to collect them and General Tan screamed a rebuke. 'Police up this crap and get out to the vehicle. We're going back. Lieutenant, you tell General Tan we have discovered that the money wasn't stolen after all. It was . . . was . . . liberated by the Marines for return to his government once the NVA were cleared from the city.'

Rear echelon entourage sidled out into the rain. Hotel grunts formed a silent corridor; contempt on their faces clear to anyone who bothered to notice. But the colonel stared straight ahead until he reached the staff car parked outside the building. Pointed a pudgy finger at me. 'This is a gift. You'll not get away with any more such shit. And if I ever catch you in Saigon, your ass is mine. Remember that.'

Woke Hotel Six from a light sleep just after dark. Steve thought we should say goodbye before we joined the First Battalion for the north side assault.

'You two assholes are really something. I probably should have let that stuffed-shirt sonofabitch cart you away to the brig.'

Yeah. Having trouble understanding that move myself. No doubt about it. Got caught with my ratty-assed trousers down around my jungle boots. Why didn't he just turn us over and be done with it?

'It's not that I approve of what you did. Marines are not thieves unless the mission depends on stealing to survive, but I'll be Goddamned if that pompous Army shithead was going to walk into my outfit after what we've been through and arrest anyone for anything. These bastards in Hotel Company are heroes; not criminals. You fought all the way with us, so I guess you're included. Fucking heroes do not go to jail. That would destroy the moral fiber of the nation. Now, get the fuck out of here and let me sleep.'

Headed for Delta Company's CP to spend the night. Steve exhilarated by the escape. Escape jag. High on getting over.

'Well, shit, D.A. So it goes. To the victors go the spoils.' Hong Kong, man. Hold that thought. Won't be long. Dude doesn't need a lot of bread in a place like that.

'Yeah. You're right. To the victors go the spoils.' Victors fucking Charlie.

Mexican Stand-off//11 February 1968

'You better speak English, motherfuckers.'

Whispering voice from out of the gloom near a stone fence post brought us up short.

'Christ, don't shoot.'

Just *survived* one Goddamn close call. Steve fingered his carbine, pointed at the shadow.

'We're looking for Delta's first platoon.'

Figure formed in the shadow.

'You guys the correspondents, right?'

Delta grunt still hadn't lowered the M-16 pointing at our bellies.

'Yeah. Which way to the first platoon? We're supposed to join up with them for the north side assault tomorrow.'

'Yeah. We heard about you. Fuckin' first platoon is issuing ammo and shit.' Grunt finally shouldered his weapon. 'You guys better not be fuckin' around on the streets no more. Whyn't yez sleep in here with us tonight.'

'Who's us?'

Grunt guarding a two-storey building. Upper windows barricaded with sandbags. Stone façade gleamed white in the moonlight where rounds had torn chunks out of it. Rain starting to fall heavily. Better find some place to sleep in a hurry.

'Corporal Martinez and a squad of rockets from H & S Company. We got some radio operators and S-2 scouts and shit like that inside. But they's plenty of room. And Martinez found a whole shit-pot full of dry mattresses inside here. Yez can have any that's left but try to save me one for when I get off watch. Sure beats sleeping on the fuckin' deck.'

Owed it to ourselves not to refuse that sort of hospitality. Might as well get a good night's sleep. Paid a penny on the south side. Might as well collect some dividends before we go for the pound tomorrow. Followed the sentry's pointing finger through a dark courtyard and into the building. Dim shadows from cooking fires inside. Yeah. South side fight is over. Veteran grunts don't heat chow at night if they're worried about snipers.

Martinez got up from a mattress in the corner. Squatty, swarthy Mexican. Helmet said he was a native of San Antonio. Squaddies called him Ole. Pronounced 'Oh-lee.' Seemed strange until I noticed the intricate sketch of a matador on the back of his flak jacket. Spanish word penned under the drawing: Olé. Fucking Marines must have thought it was his first name. Martinez never bothered to correct them.

Offered us a dry mattress from a pile in a corner. Said we could rack out anywhere we could find room. Walked outside to take a leak. Steve snoring back inside. 2100 or so. Eerie quiet on Hué's south side. Fucking exhausted. Sleep. Worry about what's next when it comes. Mattress felt like a warm woman. Shit. How the fuck would I know? Might have had some basis for comparison if I'd made the Hong Kong gig. Fucking Hué City. Shit's getting tired, man.

Awake in an hour. Listening. Something throbbing in my eardrum. Silent alarm. Closed my eyes. Concentrate. Ignore the soft fingers of foam rubber trying to lull me back to sleep. Nothing. Ragged breathing. Snorts, farts and groans. Natural sounds of night in the field. What else? There. Ringing? Like an alarm clock? Steve sprawled in the same position he assumed five minutes before we got inside. Listen, man. Something outside? No. Nothing now. Sounded just like a fucking alarm clock. Thought it came from somewhere above. Ah, shit. Martinez probably put some of his people up there for security. No, wait. Goddamn entrance to the top floor was blocked, barricaded the same way the second-floor windows were. Sandbags; discarded, shot-up furniture. Remembered seeing that when I went out to piss. Nerves. Worried about the assault tomorrow.

Jesus Christ. AK-47. Gooks. Where? Where are they? Grunts scrambled off mattresses and careened around the room looking for weapons and helmets. Again; another ripping burst. Scream of bullets ricocheting off the stone. Get down, Goddamnit. Martinez loomed up in the center of the chamber.

'Who the fuck is firing?'

Can't figure this shit out. Pushed and shoved the milling grunts. Situation rapidly becoming dangerous here. Grunts fumbling and loading weapons. Another echoing burst. There. Holy fuck! Tracers. Green tracers. Coming down through the Goddamn ceiling.

'Hey, Ole. Who the fuck is on the second deck? Somebody's firing at us from up there through the fucking floor. Saw the Goddamn tracers, man.'

Sprinted over to kneel beside me in a corner. Everyone staring upward.

'What? What? Is somebody topside?'

'Look, man. From up there.'

Another burst crashed down and screamed off the concrete floor. Grunts scrambled and sprawled. Listen.

Rain pouring outside the building. Rattling, cracking sound as it beat down through the foliage in the courtyard. Ole saw the green streaks that time.

'Jesus Christ. Some asshole is up there on the top deck.'

'No shit, man. Didn't you check this Goddamn place out before you moved in?'

'Fuck, no, man. Six tol' us to rack out here and I seen them fucking sandbags and shit, so I figured the top deck was all secure. Who's gonna suspect them fuckin' gooks would hide out up there with a bunch of grunts sleeping down below?'

Marines all hugging the walls; staring up and waiting for another burst. No casualties as yet. Martinez didn't want to take any chances. Ordered everyone out of the building. A few grunts shifted around but none moved for the door. Rain washing off the stone in sheets. Decision time. Live with a trigger-happy gook or spend another night in the rain? Martinez can't understand the reluctance.

'You guys can't sleep in here with fuckin' gooks up there.' No immediate response from the shadows.

Shadow peeled off the opposite wall.

'Ah, fuck them dudes. I come this far without gettin'

killed. And I ain't spendin' another motherfuckin' night in the rain.'

Shadow moving toward a mattress in the center of the room. 'Shoot, you little cocksucker. You ain't drivin' me out in the rain one more Goddamn time.' Stubborn grunt shouted in the dark chamber. Booming echoes as he triggered a long burst up through the ceiling.

'You motherfuckers go on back to sleep. I'll play his silly-assed games.'

Feeble answering burst from above. Two or three rounds. Grunt stood his ground.

'I ain't gonna tell you again, assholes.' Another ringing burst sprung upward. Clanging of the recoil spring in the stock of the M-16 clearly audible. Snickers and snorts from the grunts hugging the walls. Taunting insults aimed up toward the ceiling.

'Hey, Gook. Get offa my cloud, man. Hey, Dude. One man's ceiling is another man's floor. Can you dig it?'

Fucking crazy men. Assholes are going to stay inside with that NVA up there firing down through the floor when the mood strikes. Shadows bobbed and weaved. Grunts pulling their mattresses away from the center of the room, toward the walls. Still vulnerable to ricochets. Seemed to prefer the odds of catching one to another night in the rain.

Fullblown high-weirdness throughout the night. Panic at odd intervals when the gook tenant purged his weapon down through his floor. Grunts taking turns returning fire up through their ceiling. Became fairly casual about it as the sky lightened with dawn. One Marine or another, whoever felt inclined, would roll over and casually crank a few rounds upward. Downstairs tenants banging on the radiator pipes to complain about a noisy party in the apartment above. Weirdness.

Delta Six showed up before the sun, shouting for an

explanation of the firing in a quiet sector. Goddamn people need their sleep. Big job to do tomorrow. Martinez told him about the irate boarder upstairs. Laughing, choking fit.

'That's par for this fucking course, Martinez. You got a Mexican Stand-off here.'

Squad leader didn't see what was so fucking funny. What the hell does he do about it?

'You don't do a damn thing for right now. But before we move out, you find a way to get up there and kill those shitheads.'

Laughed his way out of the building, trailing a bewildered radio operator.

Light enough to see. Soft yellow light filtered in the eastern windows and drove the shadows up the western wall. Martinez had a plan to end the stand-off. Grunts stood aside to give a rocket gunner room for backblast from his weapon. One 3.5-inch armor-piercing rocket round into the barricade. Three volunteer grunts charged up the stairs. Single shot. First man through the door fell back down the stairs. Neat, round bullet hole in the precise center of his forehead. Grunts behind tossed a frag through the shattered barricade and sprayed the upstairs room with M-16 fire.

No one home up there. Sterno stove and a rice bowl sat next to a mattress. Blanket and pillow at one end, neatly folded. Big Ben alarm clock ticked with a hollow sound on a low stool. Grunts piled through the second-storey window on to the surrounding roofs. Searching for the upstairs gook. Alarm set for 0500 hours. Yeah. That matches. Last burst we took through the ceiling was a few minutes after five.

Clock-watching gook got away. Didn't get any on his nightly firing schedule but he made up for that this morning. Jesus. Wake me early, Nguyen. Be sure the alarm is set. Have to get up early and kill some Americans. Downstairs. Waited for the assault boats to arrive. Watched the corpsman haul away the last man I saw dead on the south side of Hué City.

North Side

4

The Citadel

12 February 1968

History lesson from Steve this morning. Full of metaphors and analogies. Bastogne, Monte Cassino, Siegfried line, castles and villas in the mountains above Anzio. Even Corregidor and Tarawa. All fortresses that had to be taken. Modern attackers pitted against the defensive skill of ancient engineers. He sees Hué like that. Figures the fight will go down in history. Become a topic of conversation and speculation among military historians. Might even be a postwar organization of Survivors of the Battle of Hué City.

Tried to tell him it wasn't a passion play. No strategic victory to be won here. Change the Goddamn name. Call it the Great Big Battle of Ego City. Sending Marines up against those walls is the first leg of an all-expenses-paid ego trip for the American Command in Vietnam. Just like it was for the North Vietnamese who took the place and planted their flag where it could piss everyone off from Saigon north along the South China seacoast.

Look at it from the gooks' point of view. Why take the Citadel? There's nothing inside those walls worth protecting. And only a fool of a tactical commander engages in a set-piece battle against numerically and technologically superior forces. It's propaganda in its purest form. Take the one landmark in the one city in both Vietnams that most suggests the decadence of the ancient empires. Show those capitalist bastards in the south that self-righteous socialism can conquer the strongest bastion of the feudal lords. Make a lot of speeches, standing on the walls;

glowing with revolutionary zeal. Free the oppressed masses from the splendor of their surroundings.

Plant your flag in the navel of a decadent, capitalist corpus. Rub the roseate nose of the corrupt Saigon government in it and dare their running dog lackeys to throw you out. Ego airlines paging passengers Ho Chi Minh and Vo Nguyen Giap. Your flight is on schedule.

Also in the first-class cabin: passengers Johnson and Westmoreland. Neither one gave a shit about Hué City or the Citadel. There were less costly, more relevant fish to fry. But this whole Tet '68 business – in particular, the capture of South Vietnam's most revered cultural and historical landmark – was a gauntlet that could not be ignored. In an effort to save face over the loss of Hué and its Citadel, Saigon bared its propaganda fangs and bit the hand that fed them. How could the Americans, in the face of all their claims about superior tactics and technology, take so long to recapture such an important area? How could they balk and dawdle, asking to be allowed to destroy an important piece of Vietnamese history with cannons and bombs? How could they?

Ego airlines announces departure of a special flight to the quaint city of Hué for the Commanding General of the Marines in Vietnam. Please have your personal honor and the reputation of your Corps ready for castigation. When egos clash, innocents die. Check the houses, streets, gutters and alleys of Hué for empirical evidence.

Want to do this thing right? Check history. Short on siege engines? Scaling ladders unsafe? Want to save your finest for bigger and better fights with more at stake? Lay siege to the Goddamn place. Just park around the walls and wait. Starve the bastards out. Shoot the enemy flag down if that's what's sticking in your craw, but don't smear the fucking walls with the bloody entrails of your best troops just because you're in a towering snit.

Got to take an ancient castle? Shit. Do what the people who built such Goddamn things did. Lay siege to the Citadel. Camp all around, bring in the hookers, sutlers and camp followers. Have a big-assed party and wait until the bastards are ready to surrender peaceably. Or let them starve to death, then walk in and police up the bodies. You've got more time than you've got Marines.

Fresh Meat and Plastic Flowers//12 February 1968

Waved us aboard the landing craft. Floating shoeboxes with one end-flap that folded down to make an effective funnel for enemy fire. Bluchers, brogans and penny-loafers inside, ready to dance. First, firsthand impressions in a little while. Spacey thoughts; dumb songs. 'Joshua fit de battle of Cit-a-del. Hope de walls come a-tumblin' down.' Concentrate.

Surprised to note the boat crews were Coast Guard rather than Navy. So much for America's policy of limited intervention. Finally gone and called up the people who are supposed to be manning the lighthouses and guarding the domestic shoreline. NVA might be landing at Pacific Palisades right now. There is no more piss left to pour out of America's military boot. Told them not to write the directions on the heel.

Wonder how many of these poor, scared assholes joined the Coast Guard to keep from getting drafted and sent to Vietnam? Goes to show you. It's not nice – or safe – to fuck about with the Selective Service System. They'll get you in the end and send you someplace where your end will get blown off.

Landing site directly ahead. In an area titled Gia Hoa on the maps. Two city blocks from there to the foot of the walls.

Leaps and bounds. Salty grunts knew how to move in

the city by this time. One man fired cover. Leap. The other fired for him. Bound. NVA were heavily into altitude. Plunging fire from second-storey windows. Ricochets off the concrete street surfaces caused extra casualties. Plenty to deal with before the walls came into play. No future fucking around out here on the street.

Interesting structure to the right, up that alley. Another temple. Looked richer than the first one. Get inside there and check that sucker out. Incense burners and candle holders. Brass. Statuettes looked like they might be antique. Nice tapestries. No Goddamn tape recorder. Must make do with that silly-assed gong over there. Steve called from outside. Shit.

'No tape recorder, huh?'

'Nah. Fucking gooks are just like Baptists back home. Drive Cadillacs to church and put nickels in the collection plate. What's happening on the street?'

'Delta's moving forward. Don't want to lose contact over here, man. First day and all. Wait. Here's a consolation prize.' Yellow plastic flowers arranged in a vase on a fence post outside the temple. 'Here. Plant one of these fuckers in your helmet to demonstrate your defiance of uniform regulations and let's go.'

Flower must have looked ridiculous. Stuck six inches above the top of my helmet.

Strange lull out on the street. Stalemate somewhere. Delta Executive Officer crouched in a stone portico, talking into a radio handset. Assembled Marines glared at the second storey of a building diagonally across the street. High brick wall ran off to the left. Remaining squads of the first platoon hunkered down behind it. Moaning on the other side of the wall. Two voices. 'Oh God. Help me. It hurts.'

Lieutenant waved everyone down. Stay in position. Wait One. Tall Marine with 'Arkansas Angel' imprinted on his flak jacket didn't care for inactivity. Tendons in his jaws stood out like twin tumors.

'I'm gettin' them motherfuckers.' Vaulted the wall; into the street on the other side. Two shots. Helmet clattered on concrete.

Three voices. 'Ah, God. Fucking hurts. Goddamn. Help us.'

Lieutenant waited patiently for a radio message. 'Fucking gooks have got a sniper in that building across the way. Second floor there. On the right. He must have a scope because he places his shots like a real dinger. Shot one guy trying to cross the street in the gut and he's been picking off anyone who goes to help. Asshole doesn't shoot to kill. Shoots to wound so they'll lay out there and beg some other dumb bastard to expose himself trying to help. Whole fucking company will be gut-shot if we don't get him before long.'

Rifle squad maneuvering around through houses on the left side of the street. Trying to flank the sniper and take him out. Quick look over the wall. There it is, at the end of the street up there. The Citadel. Didn't look so bad from back here. Shadows played tricks. Moat seemed wide as a large canyon. Bloody scene in the street when we tore eyes away from the walls. Three very vocal wounded and four very silent dead men out there.

Almost noon. Steady drizzle fell in the face of a pale sun. Lieutenant tried to explain the delay to Delta Six on the radio. Ripping burst sounded across the street. Grunts located the sniper. Others sprang up, shouldered M-16s and prepared to answer.

'Hold it. We got people over there.'

Lieutenant waving two corpsmen forward. Scrunched down behind the wall, they recruited volunteers to help them carry the wounded if and when the maneuver squad got the sharpshooting sniper.

Three quick, ringing shots from somewhere across the street. Stillness; ragged breathing from this side of the wall. Docs and grunts pumping themselves for the big move. Just noticed a steady drumroll of small arms from a distance to our right. No stalemate over there on the other approach to the Citadel. Another 1/5 rifle company in hot contact. Wonder which one? Fuck it. As long as it isn't Delta. Sharp-eyed grunt pointed across the street.

'They got him.' Eyes locked in that direction.

Bearded Marine stood in plain view through a second-storey window waving a sniper's rifle over his head. Lieutenant waved them back and motioned the corpsmen out into the street. Police the bodies. Might as well help.

Steve and I grabbed an end of a poncho, laden with one of the dead grunts. Skinny little dude with cracked GI spectacles sitting askew on his pimply nose. Can't see any wounds but he's definitely not breathing. Yeah. There it is. Under the flak jacket. Ragged purple pinhole. Through the heart, down and out just over his right hip. Dead before the round could travel the length of his body.

Corpsmen talked to the lieutenant as we started to the rear.

'Ain't no BAS set up yet on this side. We'll be taking the wounded and dead back to the LCI ramp where we landed. Battalion Surgeon and a bunch of corpsmen are running a shuttle over to the Sports Stadium from there.'

Lieutenant nodded distractedly. Busy on the radio with Delta Six. Half a conversation revealed the other platoons and companies were having a hard time keeping flanks aligned. Whole sweep becoming disjointed.

Struggled back toward the LCI ramp, dead weight bouncing on the poncho. Fired on several times and we had to drop the body to take cover. Final burst that sent us sprawling just before we reached the street fronting the river was fired by a Marine squad set up in defensive positions around a department store. Machine gun in the display window. Tempted to drop the dead grunt and do a little bargain hunting. Skirmishes in the houses leading up to the massive walls seemed like minor irritants to excited, adrenalin-high grunts.

Quick frag, fire a burst; kill the fucker and get it over with. Get at the Big Enchilada and get it over with. Strange scene. Like kids on Christmas morning. Forced to open all the little presents and deal with them in order. All the while their eyes are locked on the bicycle in that big box over there.

LCI ramp had become the classic beachhead. Supplies and replacements pouring in each time a boat landed from the south side; wounded and dead going out each time one left. Quick, high-speed run across the river. Boats usually didn't bother to turn around. Coast Guard and Navy Coxswains ran them back to the south in reverse. Grunts milled everywhere, helping themselves to chow, ammo, water or anything useful stacked along the riverfront. Assault line was only half a block forward; grunts could resupply themselves at will. Found the medical clearing station set up in what must have been a riverfront newspaper kiosk.

Pile of bloated body bags behind it. Nervous looking boat crews loaded them like rice sacks. Painful expressions on their faces; as though it physically hurt to lift the dead grunts. Drizzle didn't bother the huge black blowflies swarming around the rubber caskets where they leaked blood or gore. Buzzing cloud of angry insects rose each time the sailors lifted a bag and descended again like an animated black shroud when they walked away to load.

Tossed the dead grunt on the pile of bags. No disrespect intended. He didn't care and we had a need to get rid of a heavy burden. Simple as that. He'd have done the same and been glad he was able. Flies blanketed the exposed corpse immediately in a droning frenzy. Sickening sight.

'Well, shit, man. Everybody's got to eat. Hungry myself.'

Steve not in the mood to eat; staring at the pile of corpses.

'C'mon, man. Should be an open case of Cs over there.'

Passed the landing ramp. Two second lieutenants in stateside utility uniforms watched slack-jawed as a corpsman struggled in waist-deep water to recover a gut-shot Marine where he had fallen during the landing. Having a hell of a time with the dead man. Floating intestines undulated in the water like a hungry sea snake. Corpsman cursed and bitched at the dead Marine. Shore Party Marine waded out to help. Grabbed the dead man's boots and tugged viciously until the corpse began to float toward the shore. Lieutenants seemed eager to help but unsure of their role here. Did officers help drag dead men out of the water? Decided on a compromise. Both began shouting suggestions to the struggling men in the water. Corpsman scooped up an armful of intestine and looked up at the officers standing primly on the shore. 'Hey. Whyn't you guys find someplace else to fuck off. We don't need no Goddamn sidewalk superintendents here.'

Taller of the two skinheaded lieutenants stiffened. Looked like he wanted to put the corpsman in his place. His buddy grabbed him by the elbow and led him toward a stack of C-ration boxes away from the landing area. Lieutenants asked if it was alright to help themselves. No one around with a clipboard to record the issue of meals.

'Shit, Lieutenant. Have at it. The only thing they keep track of in this fucking city is body bags. Never have enough of those.'

Tall officer squatted to rifle through the rations. 'You men been here long?' Busy breaking the metal band on a case of Cs with the flash suppressor on the muzzle of an M-16.

'Tell you the truth, Lieutenant. I think we got more time in the Nam than you got in the Corps.'

Jawline firmed; teeth clenched. Had enough of this cheap shit, by God.

'Don't you get smart with me, Marine. You just better watch your mouth.'

'Yeah. OK, Lieutenant. But it isn't my mouth I'm worried about up here. It's my poor little ass that requires all the attention.'

Who the fuck did these boot camp assholes think they were? Cheap OCS bullshit. First thing they'd do is make their people shave and get haircuts. Some saluting drill and then there's time for the war. Somebody ought to melt the starch in these dip-shits before they get some good people killed. M-16 pointed directly at them when I stood to take my licks from the taller skinhead. Easy to blow these pompous turds away and save the gooks the trouble. Steve intervened.

'We just helped bring some dead and wounded to the rear, sir.' Pushed the muzzle of the M-16 away and down. 'I expect you'll be heading up forward yourselves soon?'

Stare-down. Two squeaky-clean shavetails, chests all pumped up and ready to receive a Goddamn medal. First new officers encountered since the fighting began. Obviously new and obviously just out of Officer Candidate School. One of them still had the Military Airlift Command ticket sticking out of his pocket. Probably got in country yesterday.

Shorter of the two lieutenants wanted to defuse the situation. 'Just arrived last night.'

Yeah. Make friends with a veteran. Maybe some of his luck will rub off. Jesus. Cherubs. Lambs for the slaughter.

'Where's your fighting gear, Lieutenant?'

'They rushed us up here so fast we didn't have time to get any.' Taller man chimed in, still pissed off. Had to remind me of his status and place in the military scheme of things.

'We're supposed to get commands in One-Five. Someone from headquarters is supposed to meet us here and take us to the CO.'

Christ. Couldn't they do better than this? One friendly cherub and a knotty-pine fucking recruiting poster. Ah, man. You guys are probably going to die very soon. Try not to take any good grunts with you.

'Listen, Lieutenants. You'll be lucky if you can find the CO in this Goddamn snafu. And if you do, he won't have time for tea and a welcome aboard briefing. Most of these platoons are being commanded by buck sergeants and the last second lieutenant I saw was stiff as a Goddamn board. Let me presume to suggest that this fucking fight up here is a whole hell of a lot different than all that "hi-diddle-diddle-right-up-the-middle" crap they taught you at Quantico.'

Strange stares, wondering if I'm serious. 'And I further suggest that you do a lot of listening and not much talking around the veterans if you want to live through this fight.'

Lieutenants sauntered away mumbling.

'Everyone's down on our case because we're new here. Fucking enlisted guys hate anyone who outranks them.'

No. But we do hate anyone who tries to kill us through stupidity. Life is a prize you have to fight for and hate can be a powerful weapon. It won't take you long to learn, Lieutenants. And you'll learn or you'll die. Simple as that.

Flopped down beside Steve to eat.

'Look at those two, man. Don't have sense enough not to sit around on a case of grenades. Life expectancy up here is thirty seconds or less. I swear to God. Haven't been in country long enough to draw weapons and the Goddamn Crotch sends 'em right up here to fucking Hué City. That's a joke, man. Let's get back up to Delta. Been a lecher so long I can't stand to be around virgin meat.'

Steve shrugged, chucked the rest of his ration and stood to leave.

'No, wait. Goddamn, man. Look at those two. Giggling over what's in the fucking rations. See the looks they're giving that pile of KIAs? Shit. They need every huss they can get. Wait one.'

Pile of bloody equipment stripped from MedEvaced Marines. Picked through it for helmets, flak jackets, rifles, cartridge belts, web gear. Two basic issues for the fighting fucking lieutenants.

Leery glances as I approached carrying the equipment.

'Listen, Lieutenants. I've been in the line a long time. I didn't mean to be fucking with you a while ago. Why don't you take this gear and get used to wearing it. You know, check out the rifles and so forth. You'll need all of it where you're going.'

Tall officer grabbed for one of the M-16s. Squire being presented the sword of knighthood. Take it, Goddamnit. I hereby dub thee Sir Dip-shit. Carry on.

'One more thing, Lieutenants. I suggest both of you take the bars off your collars. This fucking city is full of snipers that can spot an officer from a mile off and kill him from the same range. No use advertising for a bullet in the gourd.'

No dice. One toke over the color-line here. 'We'll decide what's best for us, thank you. We worked and sweated for these bars and we'll survive snipers without hiding our rank.'

'Yeah. OK, Lieutenants. Your funeral. Good luck.'

Sorry, fucker. His funeral was actually eight hours later

just after he'd been given command of a platoon of Delta Company grunts. Late afternoon. Tried to lead the platoon in a charge up the main street toward the walls of the Citadel. Rushed around exalting them all to greater glory. Grunts had enough glory, thank you, Lieutenant. Stayed right where they were. By the time the officer realized he was alone, there were six bullet holes in his chest. Platoon Sergeant couldn't even remember his name to report the casualty. Never saw the shorter of the two again. Guy I talked to later said he lost his legs to a booby trap shortly after he got his platoon. Another guy said he lost his mind.

All the same in the end.

Took Delta all the first day to get within rifle range of the Citadel and tie up their flanks. Battalion stretched and woven throughout four city blocks; angled to face the Citadel's southern and eastern walls. Hold until morning.

MACV searched for one solid innovation to suggest a way across the moats and up on to the mossy walls. Steady downpour at dusk. Hiss of the rain made me drowsy. Flaky state between awake and asleep. Difference between thinking and dreaming. What would it be like to face those walls? What would you do?

Dream: Standing in the shadow, clawing, scratching, screaming and dying. Petitioners at a deadly wailing wall. Killed like a swarm of cockroaches pounded with an insecticide bomb. Thought: All anyone can do now is climb the walls and kill the gooks. Just do that. Worry about the rest later.

Delta positions for the night faced the east wall of the Citadel. From there you could get a lingering look if you felt brave enough to expose yourself for that long. Intense study was dangerous. NVA gunners blazed down at gawkers with machine guns, AK-47s and Rocket-Propelled Grenades. Mortars were set up in defilade at the rear of the wall. Heard the clanging cough throughout the night as they tried to keep us awake.

Several civilian reporters showed up at the house Steve commandeered for our use. Getting dark and the battalion commander didn't want to be bothered with civilians just then. Send 'em up with those two Marine correspondents and don't let them get blown away. Three or four of them competed to compose the most grandiose phrases to describe the feeling they had looking up at the Citadel walls. English exercise; something to occupy the mind.

Steve sat in a corner cleaning his carbine. Something wrong with him lately. Hadn't seen his camera in a while. Said it was broken. Couldn't find anything wrong with it and handed it back. Put it in his pack and picked up the carbine again. Strange emotions; almost embarrassing. Tempted to put my hands on his bony shoulders. Touch him. Don't leave me to do it alone, man. Strain showing. Find a distraction. Explored the dwelling. Wealthy Zips lived here. Elegant rose and teakwood furniture. Polished marble floors with intricately inlaid tiles. Heavy velour drapes. Put this shit to use.

Bone-deep chill when the sun disappeared. Cold wind blowing rain in the shattered windows. Need a Goddamn fire. Grunts all around us and the majority of the NVA burrowed into the Citadel. Should be OK. Fuck a bunch of light discipline. NVA knew Goddamn well where we were and we sure as shit knew where they were. Not a question of spotting our location or theirs. Canteen water warmed over a heat-tab in the living room of the elegant house. Thrashed around in the bedroom breaking up delicate furniture for kindling.

Sounded like a barroom brawl. Had to break up some of the heavier stuff by smacking it with my helmet. In the living room Steve and the others examined a gilt-framed photograph of the Vietnamese homeowner and his family.

Posing with Mickey Mouse at Disneyland. Fuckers must wish they were in Anaheim right now. Armload of kindling and pieces of velour curtain. Fuel for the fire and comforters for repose. Good blaze stoked in a metal trash can. Inky dark outside; no use taking too many chances. Pulled the curtains and moved the fire to a back wall of the living room. Time for talk. Boy Scouts around the campfire. Civilians telling most of the war stories; comparing this fight with all the others they saw. Compared NVA with VC; the Delta with the DMZ in objective, unemotional terms.

Tired but I can't sleep. Cutty Sark we found at the AFVN station gone. Gave half the bottle to Hotel Six before we left for the north side. Might find some shit in this place.

'Steve, give me your flashlight, man. Going exploring.'

Filled my pack in half an hour. Chinese royal guard dog figurine, bronze Buddha, delicate crystal vase. Nothing potable so far. Shit's got to be here somewhere. Tried hard not to dwell on tomorrow. Whole deal reduced to two simple tasks in my mind. Climb the walls and kill the gooks. Get Some, guys. I'll record the events and then we'll all go to Hong Kong. Two simple tasks. Didn't make me think either of them would be easy.

Finally. The family liquor locker. Noticed several etched crystal glasses stacked below a rosewood cabinet. Simple, decorative lock came away with one twist on my knife. Jesus God. Look here. Good booze. Selection dominated by a magnum of fine French champagne. Just crack that fucker right here. Unwrapped the bottle and sweated the cork out with a loud pop. Oh shit. Steve and the civilians dove for cover. Four or five grunts burst in from the bedroom to see about the grenade or booby trap.

'No sweat, people. Relax. Have a snort.'

Strolled into the firelight and proffered the magnum. Champagne bubbles spilled all over my filthy hands. Ah, shit. Audience here needs a little distraction. I pronounce the delicate bubbly of an age and character that makes it fit for human consumption. Delicate nose, full-bodied flavor. Probably from the south of France. Grunts gaped at the magnum as it passed around the circle. Held it about six inches from my mouth and inhaled the wine in a fine stream. Showtime here. Got these fuckers in my pocket.

Grunts made a follow-up pass on the liquor cabinet and brought their horde in by the fire. Gonna do some juicing here, man. God, look at this. Class will out, by God. Probably get them to trade the whole lot for a case of beer. Cheap sauterne cooking wine in slender green bottles, Cutty Sark and Johnny Walker Scotch, Seagram's 7. Apple-cheeked grunt proudly displayed an unopened bottle of Jim Beam.

'This here's my old man's favorite. One of these other assholes almost got it, but I got my hands on it first. Probably save it to celebrate when we get inside that there Citadel.'

Not in this fucking group you don't save anything. Buddy piped up from the perimeter of the circle.

'Shit. You better open that bottle now. You gonna be stone-cold dead by the time we get to that fuckin' wall.'

Apple-cheeks told his buddy to fuck off. He opened the bottle anyway. Good man.

'Yeah. I'll help you drink it. And I'll give you a little lesson in imbibing. Look at this. VSOP Brandy, Five-Star Cognac, dusty bottles of vintage French champagne with elaborate wax seals. You fuckers grab for the $3.98 busthead and pass up all the elegant booze. Wouldn't know fine champagne from water buffalo piss. You know that?'

Apple-cheeks thinks he might have been ripped off. 'I had some champagne once at my sister's wedding.' Apoiogizing for passing up the good stuff.

'Shit, man. That wasn't champagne. That was enema squeezings. This is champagne. Wrap a liplock on *that* one time.'

Popped another cork from one of the dusty bottles. Apple-cheeks and his buddies scampered off after the flying cork.

'Here. Take a hit of this stuff. *This* is champagne.'

Sheepishly accepted the bottle. Buddies urged him on. Fucker turned it up like a cold canteen after a long march.

'Hooooo-eeeee.' Wine dribbling through the peach-fuzz on his chin. 'That shit tickles m'nose.'

'Jesus, man. Go drink your Jim Beam.'

Hué City sank in a quart of some fiery liquid that night. But it resurfaced in the morning.

Head smoking at daybreak. None of the usual promises never to get that drunk again. Packed away the remainder of the booze carefully and promised to do it again as soon as possible. Pain means you're alive to feel things, man. Steve made C-ration coffee. Reporters equally hungover. Greenish-tinted faces. Fucking breakfast would help. No C rations to be had. Someone would have to make the run back to the logistics point near the LCI ramp. Coughing bark of a heavy-caliber machine gun interrupted the deliberation. Jumped violently enough to scald my balls with steaming coffee.

'What the fuck was that? Sounded like a .50 caliber. Yeah. Fucker fired again. Definitely a Fifty and definitely incoming. Anyone see where he might be?'

Outside the house, along a low stone wall, grunts crouched, searching for the gunner. Shitty fucking way to start the day. Hangover hungry. Got to get something in my belly besides this coffee. Another whistling impact. Grunts sprawled and a huge chunk of masonry disappeared from the wall above their heads. Jesus. Sniping with a .50 caliber. Going after ants with A-bombs.

Civilian reporter badly wants breakfast. 'Looks like we go hungry this morning. I'm sure as hell not going out there while that bastard is tearing down walls with a heavy machine gun.'

'Yeah. Well, man. If you want chow, you got to be willing to risk a little. Case of what's worth what, you know? Question is are you hungry and miserable enough to let that fucker shoot at you for a while. Like everything else in this fucking city; it's a crapshoot, man.'

Fuck it, got to get some chow. Shrugged on flak jacket and helmet with the tall, yellow flower attached.

Jesus! Single round as I sprinted out the door and over to the stone wall. Too low to stand. Got to crouch and go for it if I want to eat. Look at the hole that fucker made in a stone pillar. Twelve inches thick, and the round nearly blew the fucking thing in half. Turned to see Steve and the reporters peeking over window ledges at my progress. Yeah, yeah. I'll get the fucking chow.

Within sight of the main street intersection. Another thirty feet or so. Goddamnit! How is that fucker spotting my progress? Couple more of those bastards and he'll blow this fucking wall down. Definitely after me. Buzzing round streaked overhead with a nasty hum and smacked into a building behind. Shower of brick dust and something else.

What's this? Christ. The flower. Fucker must have seen the flower sticking up behind the wall and fired at it. Fucking thing is clipped off about an inch above where my head would be inside the helmet. Shit. Fucking flower almost did me in. Jesus, that seemed funny. Look at those simple fuckers back there. Can't understand why I'm laughing. Can't see anything funny about getting your head blown off by a sniper with a .50 caliber.

Well, shit. Think about it, man. Can you dig the marksmanship of the dude on the gun? Fucker could have fired a burst and caved the Goddamn wall in if he wanted to kill me. Nah. Shit. Trick shot. That's what he wanted. You fuckers out there might be good, but I know a trick. Watch this. How many gooks you know can clip a fucking plastic flower out of a pisspot at this range with a .50 caliber?

I can dig it, gook. Go for the trick shot and show those assholes who's boss. Plenty of time to score later.

Southern Approaches//14 February 1968

Second day on the north side. Frenzied activity everywhere. Grunts tried to get a toehold; a purchase to begin the assault on the summit. Brass hats with faces like Sherpa guides squinted at the walls of the Citadel. In unguarded moments they admitted the whole thing seemed ludicrous. Looking at the mammoth stone slabs from across the river was one thing. Different story when they got close and tried to figure a way to get on top. Most came away shaking their heads and massaging cramped neck muscles.

Why climb the walls? Good question. Let's see. Because they are there? Because someone ordered it done? Yeah. And because there is nothing else to do right now. Climb the walls and kill the gooks.

Moved forward with Delta Company's Gunnery Sergeant. Been trying all day to get his grunts to stop crawling up toward the walls like curious ants. No deal. There was just *something* about those looming sheets of pockmarked stone. Had to get up there and get a look at those fucking things, man. Face the enemy and half the battle is won. Stare down in the center of the ring while both fighters get their instructions. Tall, cold stone. Seemed to lure cautious veterans out of safety like Homer's Sirens. More like a snarling Medusa if you ask me.

Gunny swept the walls with powerful lenses. Ten minutes of silent scrutiny. Whistled softly, shaking his head.

'I've seen some insane shit in seventeen years with this lash-up, but never nothin' like this. How can they ask us to take this Goddamn fort? This has got to be a fuckin' low budget movie, man. This can't be for real.'

Oh, yeah. No doubt about it. Real as rabbit shit in the wintertime. Scaling ladders, ropes, catapults or helmeted heads. Same kind of battering ram. No big deal to Mother Corps. One way or another, take the Citadel. No question about that. Just a matter of finding a crack in the seam. Just a matter of climbing the walls and killing the gooks. When they wanted a Goddamn opinion of how stupid it was, they'd ask.

Look at those fucking walls. Jesus. NVA running from rampart to redoubt. Wonder if they've got boiling oil to pour on the phalanx? Ought to call up the catapults and clobber them with crossbows. God. Take a look at those walls and then take a look at these goddamn space-age, plastic M-16s. Do they have any idea how ridiculous it all seems?

'Subcaliber fucking bang-sticks and a couple of measly-assed hand grenades to pry King Nguyen and his Round Table full of NVA Regulars out of Camelot. Shit. No further advances until they provide a big-assed white horse and a couple of healthy hand maidens.'

Steve popped me on the flak jacket. 'At least they gave you a suit of armor.'

Good news back at Delta's CP. Vietnamese government in Saigon finally decided to allow limited air and naval gunfire strikes in one or two places along the walls. Decent. But no one who saw the walls up close thought it would make much difference in the final fight. Bombers and big guns don't win wars. Sorry-assed infantrymen had to occupy the ground before a winner was declared. Planes and projectiles could punch holes in the walls, but grunts still had to jump through them. And there'd be a pot-full of pissed-off gooks on the other side.

Delta platoons cleared houses to the right and left of the main street leading up to the south gate of the Citadel. Firefights crackled and spat all around. Routine shit for Hué. No one involved in off-loading supplies at the LCI ramp paid much attention. No heavy volume of fire from the walls as yet.

No comfort in that. Delta Six said at least a full battalion of NVA were dug in there. Gooks played it smart. Let the grunts smash themselves against the walls like bugs creaming into a car windshield. Shit, that fits. Everyone acting like a bunch of moths around a porch-light anyway. Yeah. Lay back, Nguyen. Let the fight come to you. You've got the high ground and all the man-made cover your ancestors could provide.

No one very anxious to begin the attack on the Citadel. Look but don't touch. At least not until the weather cleared and the carrier planes could make their attacks. Muggy, misty cloud cover all over the city. Nothing flew in that shit. Not even birds with feathers. Nothing would dry. Grunts stayed soaked all the time. Hands and feet the texture of prunes. Wounds festered almost immediately; even healthy skin peeled off under chafing from packs and equipment. Plenty of time to ogle the crowd.

Patriots out there seethed and fumed over the tattered NVA flag waving defiantly atop a watchtower guarding the Citadel's southern entrance. Began to snort and paw the ground every time they spotted the red, blue and yellow banner flapping in the damp air. Many of them carrying their own US flag in pack or pocket. Tear each other's throats out to be the first one to run it up on the walls. Great deal of speculation and concern over how and when it would be done. Topic of general conversation rapidly shifted from casualty predictions to speculation about raising a flag over the Citadel. Promised to take the picture personally for the first hero who got a US flag up in the breeze over the walls. Least I could do. No joke with some of these fuckers.

Concern with raising a flag on the north side stemmed from a highly-publicized incident on the south side. Hotel Company managed to fly an American flag over the French Provincial Building just about the time the first civilian correspondents were turned loose on that side of the city. Practically every major stateside paper and newsmagazine had carried the picture of Horrible Hotel hauling the flag up a bullet-riddled flagpole. Guys who did the pulling were celebrities among the 5th Marines.

Whole thing probably prompted by Marine Corps history. Two hundred years of tradition unhampered by progress. Ever since the famous flag-raising gig on Iwo Jima during World War II, these guys thought they could insure their immortality by raising a flag within camera range of a reporter or photographer. Theory was good. Certainly enough military and civilian photographers running around begging for the shot. Fell short of expectations in practice. Civilian reporters didn't bother to find out the name of the guy who carried the flag and raised it. They were content with a classic flag-raising photo. 'Embattled Leathernecks raise Stars and Stripes over beleaguered city.' Sufficient, if the photo was dramatic enough.

Resulted in a lot of argument among the veteran grunts about who raised what flag over what battlefield. Seemed like every rifle company in Hué had a guy who was the first to raise an American flag over something. Media took some heavy shots when newspaper clippings showed up in the mail and no names were mentioned. Seemed to be two disparate points of view on the flag-raising issue. Controversy rooted in the way the grunts saw the event and the way the press interpreted it. Infantrymen saw a personal victory in an impersonal war; a chance to be immortalized like the guys who raised the flag on Iwo's Mount Suribachi, and a sterling opportunity to confirm their outfit's contribution to a moment in American history.

Reporters didn't give a shit about any of that. They saw the historical angle alright, but only as the peg that made their photo valuable and saleable. The event was more significant to them than the individuals involved. A classic photo represented a confirmation of their own talent and a chance at front-page, nationwide notoriety. It was a great photo of an emotional moment. That's all. Not a great photo of an emotional moment involving Lance Corporal John Jones of Des Moines, Iowa. Who gave a shit if the guy was with the 1st or 3rd Marine Division? Grunts did, by God. They'd be featured in my frame. Least I could do.

Shitty weather still held. Flag-raisings would have to wait. Let the fliers and Navy gunners blow some holes in those fucking walls first. Can't raise a flag until you own the dirt where you want to plant the pole.

No planes and no replacements, but a shipment of mail came over on one of the LCIs. Sailors tossed it off in trade for twenty or thirty body bags. Looked like a good deal until the grunts got their hands on the post. Fucking junk mail. Typical. Long-overdue correspondence courses, magazine subscription renewal notices, occupant mail and month-old newspapers. Letters from parents, wives and girlfriends waylaid somewhere in the rear. Send up the junk mail so the grunts can have something to read while taking a shit. But don't take any chances on the troops going into a blue-funk over a Dear John letter. Fucks up the morale of the fighting men. Read it and weep.

Pored over a January edition of a weekly newspaper from Fairhope, Alabama. Brief story of the fighting in Hué on page four. Didn't even mention the Marines. Only mention of the Marine Corps was pictures of kids who graduated from Parris Island on page eight and the South Alabama casualty list on page ten.

Delta Six called a briefing. Weather-induced idleness at an end. Company-sized NVA unit spotted to the east of Delta's position; holding in a power generating station outside the Citadel's walls. Power cut off to the city since the fighting started. Marine Command anxious to get it restored. Blow the gooks out of the power station before they fucked up the equipment and technicians might be able to repower Hué in the near future.

Squatty Staff Sergeant toting a Thompson submachine gun: senior man left alive in the second platoon. Orders were to take the gooks out quickly but don't use anything heavier than rifles. Can't chance fucking up the generating equipment. Consulted a pencil sketch of the area; outlined a plan.

'First squad, you'll be base of fire. Move along the riverbank until you're in position between the river and the generating station. Anything moves around that building that ain't got USMC stenciled on it, blow it away. Two Bravo, you set in on this little knoll and do some dinging. Pick off any of the bastards you see. You'll have the machine gun with you. When they come pouring out of there, blow 'em up and don't get carried away with the gun. We don't want to blow away any equipment. Two

Charlie, you move on me. We're going to pop these CS grenades into the building through the windows and then take off to the rear while One and Two pick off the weepers.'

Good plan. Use tear gas grenades to flush the NVA out of the building and let his squads pick them off as they tried to get away from the noxious gas. Should keep the targets away from the generating equipment.

'Good flicks here, Steve. Let's go along.'

Trudged off after the grunts. Down a street which paralleled the Perfume River. Rain and heavy air would keep the gas hanging in one area. Good man with a long lens would get some great stuff of the NVA when they cleared the power generating station.

Carried an M-16 lately. Traded the Thompson from the south side armory to a Delta grunt for a Russian pistol. Get a fortune for that fucker in the rear. Might own Hong Kong yet. Slung the weapon over my back so it wouldn't get in the way of my camera. Steve had no such worry. Still hadn't taken his camera out of his pack; still fondled the carbine. Getting harder and harder to tell the correspondents from the killers.

Station up ahead. Long, low blockhouse affair about seventy-five yards away. Nests of current-currying wires latticed into metal frames on the roof. Strange noise emanating from it. Turbines whirring with a droning hum. Someone was getting power from that station. Staff Sergeant motioned his radio operator over and passed the word to Delta Six. Call back in less than ten minutes. Grunts spread out along the street and watching the station for signs of NVA.

'Battalion Six checked with the S-2 and city officials. They think the NVA are generating power and funneling it to their buddies inside the Citadel. They'll likely put up a pretty good fight to keep us from cutting power to the

Citadel. You proceed as planned, Delta Two. I'll be sending Delta Three along as soon as they get back into the CP.'

OK. Let's do this thing. Staff Sergeant motioned his second and third squads out into the street. First squad hugged the riverbank to get into position as base of fire for the assault. Third squad had the bulbous little tear gas grenades hooked to their cartridge belts.

Shit. They're in there. Fuckers waited for clear targets. Not as many as they expected. See four guns firing from the windows. No other muzzle flashes. Got to get off this Goddamned street. Move. Find a hole. Second squad angling for that grassy knoll on the left. Never make that. Shit. Finding targets now. Two down out there. Better move for the river. Get in with the base of fire. Better angle from there. Goddamn rifle gets in my way.

Second squad on the knoll. That should help. Plunging fire into the power station windows. Here comes the gas. Third squad fired rifles with one hand and ripped at the CS grenades with the other. Roared by the station. Momentary pause to heave the armed gas grenades into any opening. No time wasted. Into cover behind the station; ready to cut off any NVA who decided to leave through rear exits. Cloying, sinus-irritating tickle of tear gas from the power generating station. Slight breeze from inland carrying it toward the river. Hung in the wet air. Grunts breathed in shallow gasps and blinked teary eyes over rifle sights. Gooks should be bailing out any time now. Should be a turkey shoot.

There. Four of them vaulting out the front windows. Holed several times before they hit the ground. Grunts triggering single, well-aimed shots. Rifle range exercise. Good shots through the telephoto. Got some NVA faces. Rare photos in this war.

'Christ. Look over there. Over there. Goddamnit.'

Gook crawling slowly through a side window. Can't they see him? Grabbed the M-16 off my shoulder instinctively. Instinctively? Hope so. Use the fucking camera, man. Plenty of grunts to take care of the killing. Got to stop that kind of shit. Fucking nerves must be going. Almost forgot what the deal is up here.

Like Steve has. Over there banging away with that carbine. Time of his life. Shit. Kid next to me yelling how *we* got some. Slapped me on the back like I did the Goddamn shooting or something. We? We who? Better have a fucking mouse in your pocket, kid.

Third squad opened fire at the rear of the building. More NVA station-keepers trying to duck out the back. And then silence. Six bodies visible in front of the station. Someone reported four more in back. Only ten gooks? Where was the rest of the rifle company supposed to be holding the place? Christ. Too good to be true. There they are. Firing from the knoll above the generating station.

Ambush! That's why they didn't fire when we halted on the street. Remaining gooks got out the back when they saw us coming. Went into hiding on the same knoll the second squad held. Waiting until they had us all in the same area. Sacrificed ten to get us all. Serious trouble for the second squad. Grunts swept up out of cover and headed for the knoll. Needed every gun they could get to save lives up there. Shoot to save, man. Everybody's business to save lives in a fucking mess like this. M-16 jumped and spanged in my hands. Get up on that hill or lose that squad.

Steady roar of gunfire. NVA scampered among the squad positions on the knoll. Clearly visible despite the sting of tear gas that tainted the air. Shit. Wipeout. Only a few of the second squad grunts able to roll over from the prone position in time to return fire. Blazed away in the general direction of the knoll hoping I didn't hit any grunts. Steve on my left slapping a new magazine in the carbine. Out of ammo.

'Anybody got an extra magazine?' Shit. Ought to carry more than one.

Didn't take long for the NVA to shift their AK-47 fire on to us. Pinned down in the middle of the street. No cover. Shit. Got to do something or die out here. Fall back to the river or go for the knoll?

'Get up, Goddamn it. Get up and run for it!'

Under cover with four or five grunts at the base of the knoll. One wounded. He's out of it. Take those magazines. Shit. Not ready for this. What's happening up there? Five . . . no, six, lying in the street bleeding. Second squad couldn't help. Overrun and fucked up totally.

Whining, grinding noise off to the left. Tank. Delta's third platoon fanned out to the rear of it, advancing toward the knoll. Turret swiveling toward the NVA. Can't see over the bank. Targets up there? Let the Goddamn tank do it. Cough of the .50 caliber machine gun added to the din.

Clear to look up there now. Fifty-caliber rounds cutting gooks in half; tossing bodies right and left off the knoll.

'Get Some.'

Four or five took off at a dead run toward the Citadel. Fuckers did enough damage even if they did lose the power generating station. M-16 smoked in my hands. Felt OK. Not so bad. Got the pictures first anyway.

Corpsmen checking out casualties. All eight members of Two Bravo were dead and fourteen more second platoon grunts were wounded. Staff Sergeant down with bullets in both legs. Steve was OK; grinning at the sight of me fondling the rifle.

'Fuck you, man.'

Wounded needed immediate attention to gunshot

wounds. Most of the casualties had ugly wounds which ran the lengths of their bodies. Caused by superior angle of fire from the gooks on the knoll. Rounds impacted at critical angles. Most would die very soon if they didn't get medical help.

Climbed the knoll; tried to shake the buzzing sound out of my ears. State of mild shock, I guessed; mingled with euphoria over survival. Gripped the M-16 tightly. Made my hands hurt. Distraction. Felt like a fucking ghoul standing among the mutilated second squad. Goddamn shame, man. Dudes had the easy trick in the assault. Just a bunch of fucking hamburger now.

Shit. Sharp crack. Like someone bursting a paper bag near my ear. There. Gook on the roof of the station. Happened quickly. No time to think. On one knee with the M-16 in my shoulder. Gook looked like a silhouette target in the tiny aperture of the rear peep sight. Rifle range drill. Snapping in. Front sight post centered and halfway up the aperture. Sight alignment. Hold on his chest. Sight picture. Squeeze. Breathe. Squeeze. Three short, sharp jabs in the shoulder. Gook tossed his SKS carbine in the air and staggered backward into one of the wire terminals.

Watched through the peep sight. Freeze-frame, man. Heard the tank reversing down the street with a bloody cargo of wounded. No one took his eyes off the roof of the power generating station. Dead gook had fallen backward across a live terminal and the jolt of high voltage he received was enough to make him stand rigidly upright. Defying me to shoot again.

OK, asshole. One more time. Steady up the sight alignment. Gook rigid as an ironing board. Silhouette co-operatively standing at attention. Easy shot. Three more rounds and the electrified corpse fell back on the live terminal again. Sparks and the stink of frying flesh.

Turning into a freak show. Gook popped up again, dead muscles rigidly charged with high voltage.

'Crazy bastard. Lay down and be still.'

Third platoon finally decided I needed a little help. Blew the crispy critter off the roof in a vicious fusillade.

Triage

Bothersome, disjointed thoughts on the walk back toward Delta CP. Feelings fighting for control. Can't decide which one ought to win. Grunts shucked on me about the gook on the roof of the power station. Good-natured shit. The kind of thing they do to each other.

'Get Some, Reporter-man. Awright. Fried that motherfucker; then *re*fried his ass. Blew his shit in the street, man. Awright.'

'Yeah. Well, fuck all that. Had to do it, man. No big fucking deal. Won't happen again.'

Steve gloated.

Had to take a civilian correspondent on tour of Battalion Aid Station. Didn't take long to find the place. Follow your nose within a block of it. Stench of disemboweled men and metallic odor of fresh blood provided an accurate guide. Battalion Surgeon and his staff of corpsmen selected a house in the middle of a block now held by Delta grunts. Schoolyard to the rear suitable for landing helicopters if the weather ever cleared. Wide streets in front could accommodate trucks and tanks. Tank which served as ambulance for the Marines hurt in the fight for the power station was parked there.

Wounded Marines strewn everywhere outside the house and on the floor inside. Strangely quiet considering obvious, painful wounds. Some smoked quietly; some stared resignedly off into the distance. Others waited to die, stoically without disturbing others who might live. Pathetic sight. There, but for the grace of God, etc.

Senior corpsman scurrying between wounded that had just been brought in. Checking vital signs and the nature of wounds. Tears streaming down his face; brushing them away periodically with a bloody hand. Tankers and unwounded grunts who brought the shot-up Marines into the aid station standing around smoking nervously. Corpsman occasionally motioned and they sprang forward to carry the man he indicated inside the aid station. Some casualties he examined quickly; shook his head and moved on to another. These stayed outside. Seen this act before. Fucking triage, man. How'd you like to have a horseshit job like that?

Puzzled look on reporter's face. Never heard the term before.

'It's like this, man. There's only one doctor and not enough corpsmen to treat a shit-load of wounded like this. They select a senior corpsman and assign him to triage. He has to make the life or death decision. If the casualty can't be saved, he'll never get inside to take up the doctor's time. If there's a chance, the corpsman has him carried inside and the Doc goes to work.'

He swallowed hard. 'Jesus Christ. No wonder he's crying.'

'Yeah. Triage is not the most popular assignment. Not easy for the corpsmen. But if they didn't do it, we'd lose even more than we do. Story here if you had the place to tell it.' He wanted to talk to the corpsman.

Weeping Doc was a veteran, frontline corpsman. Same growth of beard and filthy uniform that the grunts in Hué sported. Couldn't tell him from the average rifleman except for the crossed ammo bandoliers on his chest. Corpsmen's field expedient for carrying battle dressings.

Reporter approached cautiously. Full-charged, emotionally unstable situation. No telling how the Doc would react to a civilian's questions about what he was doing. Looked up blankly at him. Picked up an old, bloody battle dressing and wiped his face and hands with the clean side.

'Fuckin' A, I'll tell you about triage. Come look at this guy over here.'

He and the corpsman walked over to a sagging stretcher near the wall of the BAS; sheltered from the drizzling rain. Skinny little Marine lay in a pile of bloody rags. Breathing raggedly; eyes closed.

'I got him shot so full of morphine he's not sufferin', but he ain't got a whore's chance in hell. I didn't even bother to put an IV in his arm.'

Corpsman fighting tears. Breathed deeply several times but the tears came and made wormy streaks on his dirty cheeks.

'You want to see the kind of shit I see every day in the fuckin' city? Look here and maybe you'll understand why this poor asshole never got to see the surgeon.'

Fetid, sickening odor drifted up from the wounded man. Reporter started to retch into his handkerchief. Corpsman didn't notice. Locked into a clinical briefing. 'This man was hit by three rounds of an AK burst at close range. One round apparently got under his helmet and took the top of his skull off causing massive brain damage.'

Corpsman pulled back the battle dressing covering the top of the grunt's head. Brain was a pulsing, red-tinged mass, spurting frothy blood where cranial arteries had ruptured. Entire top of his skull had been taken off by the enemy round. More diagnosis.

'A second round entered the chest area under one arm and exited here.' Doc pulled another battle dressing away from the left side of the man's heaving chest. Heart and lung, both bravely pumping through a churned and torn mass of rib bone and gristle. As he inhaled, a putrid foam spurted from the exit wound. Corpsman replaced the battle dressing to keep him from losing any more blood.

'Finally, the third round caught him almost full in the navel. Look at this shit.' Peeled away a large bandage covering the grunt's lower abdomen. Shiny intestine surged up like bloated blood sausage through a huge rent in the man's belly. Nauseating smell. Similar to human shit but much stronger. Smell of waste, decay. Smell of violent death.

Enough for the reporter. Staggered away retching; vomited violently, supporting his heaving body against the tank. Corpsman watched him reel off.

'How the fuck do you think I feel? I got nothing left to puke up anymore.'

Reporter wiped his mouth and walked back over to the glaring medical man. 'Look. I'm sorry. I know it's tough on you. I'm just not used to it yet.'

Corpsman kneeled beside the skinny grunt who was rapidly losing color. Breathing becoming more labored. 'He's about gone. Poor little fucker. Look here.' Corpsman grabbed the man's right forearm and turned it so reporter could observe the tattoo. Gruesome skull pierced vertically by a bayonet which bore the inscription USMC on the handle. Words emblazoned across the skull in crimson and blue: 'Death Before Dishonor.'

Choking sobs from the medical man. 'Ain't that a fucking joke? Sure hope he didn't dishonor himself or the raggedy-assed fucking Marine Crotch, because he's about to be dead. I'd say he's about nineteen, no more than that. Probably ain't even had a good piece of ass yet. This shit's a real fuckin' shame. You know that, man?'

Reporter nodded. Calming hand on the corpsman's

shoulder. Too shaken to say anything more. Wounded grunt's eyes flickered open suddenly. Pleading stare up into the filthy, bearded face of the man who sealed his doom.

'OK, Babycakes.' More tears ran down the corpsman's face and disappeared into his beard. 'It's OK, man. You're going to be OK, hear? No sweat, man. You got a ticket home. Just lay back. It's OK, man.' Grunt slowly reclosed his eyes.

Corpsman whipped a battle dressing out of one of the bandoliers spanning his chest and blew his nose. Stood up to go inside the BAS. No more life or death decisions to be made just now. The surgeon would need his help. Final word to the wounded grunt.

'Just go on and die quick, Babycakes. Let go and get the fuck out of Hué City.'

The grunt did as he was told.

Southwest Corner

Beer is beer. And looters can't be choosers. Fucking Ba Muoi Ba swill running search and destroy operations on my kidneys. Ought to walk up there and see if I can piss over the fucking walls. Should be glad the cowardly gook bastard that owned the liquor store left anything at all. Certainly wasn't any hard booze left. Finally managed to shoot the lock off the shuttered storefront late this afternoon.

Second week on the north side of Hué. Getting God-damn desperate. Had to have a snort or two; say goodbye to a buddy who left yesterday. Make that two buddies. One without a face and one without a head. Could be three buddies but Steve might drop out of the fighting fucking infantry if I could talk some sense into him. Like to have at least one buddy left in this maggot-infested, shot-up excuse for a no good motherfucking city. Ah, shit. Let the booze work.

Up jumped the devil. Late yesterday. All fucked up; wounded. Just left the African headhunter who lost his head on the Goddamn wall and stumbled on the faceless kid from the south side. Big-ass hole blown in his gut. Wouldn't live for more than an hour or so. Wanted a fucking smoke so I gave him one. Asked me where I was from in The World, man. Fucking guts swelling out of his belly; and about to burst like putrid Polish sausage and he wants a smoke and shoot the shit about hometowns. Something familiar about his voice. Even with the morphine mumbles, heard him say that same thing somewhere before.

Told him southeast Goddamn Missouri and he reached out for my hand. Said we were Goddamn buddies. Said we spent a night together on the south side. Said he felt better with a buddy near him. Then he fucking died.

Best buddy I ever had when I didn't see him in the dark. Told him more about me than anyone else – in the dark – when I didn't have to know who he was.

Don't think this old cheap shit will work anymore, man. You either are or you ain't. Either alive or dead. Can't fiddle-fuck around on the perimeter. Want to rock and roll, you got to pay some group to play. Might as well be the Marine Corps. Cue the Lonely Hearts Club Band. Hard to piss with my hand all fucked up. How did it get that way?

Yeah. Goddamn weather. Rain and clouds. Planes couldn't fly that morning. Visit by the battalion brass. Said this final phase of the Battle for Hué City was just *taking too fucking long*. Charlie Company supposed to probe for a way up on to the Citadel's walls. Christ, what an abortion. Thought they found a chink in the NVA's stone armor.

Residents of a clutch of houses outside the Citadel walls near the southwest corner had either built or allowed to stand a mound of dirt between the back of their homes and the western wall of the ancient fortress. A man standing on top of that mound would be within five or six feet of the top of the wall. Even a dog-tired grunt could jump or climb that far. The idea was to take two Charlie Company rifle platoons and see if they could do it.

NVA troops still crawled around outside the Citadel in some areas of the north side. Operated in squad-sized formations. Like phantoms, reoccupying buildings previously cleared. Sniping at the advancing troops from the rear. Harassed units at night and kept commanders inside the Citadel walls aware of every move the Marines made.

Delta Company probed to find the Phantom units. Steve moved with them. Left his fucking camera with me. Gave me all his film. Said good luck. He didn't want to see anything more through a lens. Yeah. I can dig that. Maybe I'm just starting to dig it. Wanted to go with Charlie Company; try to get up on those walls, man. Might as well go for broke. Hong Kong half a fucking world away. Hadn't taken a picture in nearly two days. Camera hung around my neck like a benign tumor. Learning the f-stops on an M-16. Couldn't remember where my notebook was. Not thinking right half the time anymore. Pocketful of frag grenades. Couldn't remember where or when I got them.

Charlie Company Gunnery Sergeant led the element. Three city blocks to cover before the southwest corner of the wall. Couldn't afford to lollygag down the streets. Had to move through the houses in each block. Shaky business. Watch for booby traps and avoid contact; keep the NVA from knowing we were moving on the walls.

Sweated and bitched under my breath in the heavy air.

Threw a leg over a windowsill and cautiously stepped into an abandoned living room. Nice looking vase on that coffee table. Wonder if the bastard's booby-trapped? Jesus Christ! Standing on something soft. Shit. Don't let this be a booby trap. Might be pressure-release. If I shift my weight, it goes. Maybe if I just heave my ass back out the window. Nah. Shit. Can't outrun an instantaneous detonation. Gooks are too smart to fix any fuze delay to booby traps. Just glance down easy here. See what I've got. Christ. Dead gook. Standing on the bastard's belly.

Should have my picture taken like this. Great White Hunter poses in triumph over his vanquished quarry. Get on in here. Back against the wall; looking for any live ones. Eyes adjusted to the gloom. No one else in sight. Get a look at this porcelain vase. Looks clean – and expensive. Wrapped it in a towel and shoved it in my pack. Another grunt came through the same window. Glanced over his rifle sights, waiting for me to wave him inside.

'OK, man. Nobody in here but me and old Luke the Gook lying there. I'm still alive and he ain't. Come on through but watch where you step. Should have some respect for the dead.'

Grunt in a hurry to move on. 'Fuck a bunch of dead. As long as they're gooks. Better hurry up, man. I'm the last one in the squad.'

'Yeah. Be right with you.'

Wait. Something weird about that dead gook. Eyes adjusted further to the dark inside the room. Took another look. No rank insignia. Basic gook trooper. Pack, helmet and SKS carbine stacked against the wall. Looks like he put them there and decided to take a break. Crew cut. Well-fed. Death bloat swelled his body to the point of bursting through the dark green uniform. But you could tell he was no peasant rice farmer. Must be about eighteen years old. Hard to tell with gooks. Probably on watch at that window waiting for us. Wait. Look at his hands.

Moved closer to get a better look. Can't delay too long and get left by the advancing grunts. Pastel square of light from the window revealed what seemed so strange about his death pose. Shot in the back. Probably some Marines burst in on him while he was watching the alley. Unusual. Not many of these hard-core bastards would face away from an enemy hunting for them house-to-house. But this fucker obviously had other things on his mind.

Right hand wrapped tightly around his penis. Guy's crank swollen like a fat sausage, bloated and bruise-blue. Left hand wrapped around a photo; crushed in a death grip. Pried his hand open; flattened the picture and held it to the feeble sunlight. Pretty Vietnamese girl, framed from the waist up with her breasts exposed. Nipples gorged and prominent like two Bing cherries. Poor Private Dip-Shit. Got blown away while beating his meat.

No wonder he got it in the back. Hope he came before his killer did. Jesus. How can a guy flog his fucking log with enemy soldiers in the area? Stupid question. Groped my own crotch a few times while mortars or artillery dropped all around. Never thought of an NVA possessing sexual drives, though. Shit. Wasn't all that displaced by revolutionary zeal or party doctrine or some such shit?

Killed in mid-masturbation. This fucking fight was getting weird. Hope he got a final nut. His girlfriend won't be getting one for a long, long time. Nah. Hell, she's probably already fucking someone in the Hanoi Home Guard while her boyfriend lies dead in Hué City with his dick in his hand. Better take the photo along. Never can tell when a man might need some inspiration.

Row of ramshackle houses fronted the hillock which should provide an access to the top of the Citadel's southwest wall. Nervous silence from everyone staring at the ramp of dirt. Company Gunny motioned to hold position and crept out the back of the hut to direct another squad into position. Plan was simple. Have them relieve the assault squad at the facing windows. Then they fire cover while the first squad rushes up the hillock and over the top. Must be what bailing out of an airplane is like. Just leap through the door and hope like hell nothing happens on the other side that will kill you.

No sense in delaying the inevitable. Charlie Six got two machine guns in position, motioned a third gun team to go with the assault squad and sent them off toward the hillock. Best get on with it. First ground-level look at what's on top of the walls. Had to see that. Wait around here and I might get confused by a burst of common sense.

Fully expected the NVA to pop up shooting when the first Marine stuck his helmeted head out of cover. No time to delay. No time to go slowly. Get out into that exposed area; run like hell and don't stop until you're under cover again. Just keep your head down and hope for the best. Don't look up for gook machine guns and they won't be there.

Code of the Grunt. There's no cover between Point A and Point B, so don't bother looking for any. Grasp your ass at high port and go for broke.

Grunts gasped for breath atop the hillock; hugging the wall. Feels strange up here. Not a shot fired by either side. Grinning with our backs to the wall like a bunch of silly assholes. Nervous giggles. High on undetected crime. Same sort of feeling a kid gets when he rips something off from the corner Rexall and manages to elude the pursuit of a salesclerk or the cops. Just sit there breathing hard in some dark alley, marveling at what a slick bastard you are. Hell of a high, but CO wanted more.

Waved frantically at us from a window in the row of houses. Don't stop now, you dizzy shitheels.

'You got that far, get the hell up on that wall.'

Other grunts moved out of the houses now. Still moved cautiously and slowly across the open ground. Might be we just had beginner's luck.

Two Marines grabbed opposite ends of an M-16 and held it level near the wall. Portable catapult. You stand on the rifle and they boost you up to level with the top of the wall. No one wanted to be first. Grunts with the rifle-stepladder grinned back at the crowd like wolves. Smart enough to dream up the elevator idea; no fucking way they're going to stick their heads up over that wall and get their faces shot off.

Scrawny Boston Irishman with a huge shamrock on the back of his flak jacket pushed through the gaggle. Stepped up on the rifle.

'Yez arseholes don't be too fuckin' fah behind.'

Elevator operators hoisted him up on the rifle. Watched his skinny ass disappear over the artificial horizon created by the lip of the wall surface. Should be a burst any minute now. Should come flopping back over shot full of holes. Nobody else waiting to follow. Shit.

'What's happening up there?'

Irishman high as a Goddamn kite. Can't believe he isn't dead.

'You pussies gonna come up heah with me or wuz yez plannin' on stayin' down theah all fuckin' day?'

Toehold on the wall. Long way from final victory. About twenty-five grunts crouched, tucked tightly into the southwest corner of the Big Enchilada. Below on the hillock, Charlie Six radioed Battalion. Adrenalin-high; kept repeating himself.

'Banyan Six, this is Charlie Six. Be advised, we are on the wall. Negative incoming, negative incoming.'

Christ. Don't cream your jeans, Captain. This won't last long.

From the corner to the north and east wound two separate, thirty-foot-wide paths of uneven dirt. Earthen fill between the exterior and interior stone slabs of the walls. Guys on the left flank whispered they could see another moat to their front beyond the interior wall. Ornate building over there surrounded by gardens. Must be the Imperial Palace.

Guys on the right said they could see the guard tower from which the silly-assed gook flag flew. No NVA in sight. Something is definitely wrong. Feel shit like that as plain as a rock in your boot. Charlie Six on the wall now. Spread out and move east. Capture a street-level entrance for the battalion to enter. Maybe even get at that gook flag. Wonder how many of these dudes have got an American flag along?

Small bushes and mounds of dirt marred the surface. Gooks should be there. Hold it. There. Behind that dirt mound. A green-clad figure stood, yawning and stretching. Stepped out from behind the mound, reaching for his fly. Going to take a leak. Spotted us. Jesus. Look at that. Crotch area and one leg of his trousers turned a darker green. Fucker pissed himself. Screamed a warning. Crop of helmeted heads topped with Russian-style helmets and camouflage netting sprouted from nearby mounds.

AK fire ripped through our line. Three grunts down before anyone could recover from the surprise. Grunts pulling pins and popping frags toward the mounds before the gooks had burned through their first magazine of ammo. Couple hit the mark. Squad in position to deliver flanking fire. First roadblock removed. Only six gooks. But they knew we were here now.

Dropped into the smoking holes. No Goddamn wonder the gooks didn't see us coming. Each mound of dirt formed the rear embrasure of a five-foot-deep fighting hole. Gooks were dug-in facing the southern approaches to the wall. Looked like they didn't believe anyone would try another route. So much for a tactical blunder. Wouldn't be long before their buddies moved over to do something about it. Puny-assed reconnaissance party might just get blown completely off the wall.

Company Gunny figured we hit a flank outpost. Wanted to continue east and locate the main defenses. Corpsmen taking dead and wounded to the rear and down off the wall. Sergeant squad leader argued for holding in the line of fighting holes and bringing up reinforcements to secure what we had. Said we might be able to take the whole sector and open the area up for the rest of the battalion.

Sounded sensible to me. No one asked for my opinion. Continued to move cautiously along the wall toward the guard tower which straddled the southern entrance through the walls. About nineteen left in the platoon after the wounded were taken off to the rear.

Didn't take long for the NVA to acknowledge our presence. Rattle of rifle shots from another line of mounds to our front. Big time now. Main body or a strong flank of the unit guarding the Citadel. ChiCom potato-masher grenades cracked in the midst of the squirming grunts. Small arms fire sang and thudded into the dirt around us. Here it is. Final fucking act. Got our ass cold up here. Probably die right here. Never been in a heavier shit-storm. Grunts dying all around me. Plenty of time to observe. Can't move an inch in all this incoming. Why the fuck haven't they hit me yet?

Never noticed how mundane getting blown away can be. Not very dramatic at all. You die very simply in the prone position. No expansive falling or flying through the air when the rounds hit. No indicative death rattle or scream of pain. Fuckers just lay there and get killed. One minute you're alive and the next you're dead. Maybe a slight involuntary twitching of the muscles. That guy's fingers dug a little deeper into the dirt. But that's it. Only your corpsman can tell which twin has the bullet in his gourd.

No way out of this other than getting killed for real or fooling the NVA into thinking you were dead. Rattling sound of M-16s to the rear. Return fire. Thank bleeding Christ. Someone coming up to help. Hadn't been hit yet. Probably meant the gooks thought I was already a corpse lying out here. No use disillusioning them at this late stage. Lay here and wait for the fucking cavalry to charge.

Sounded like the Company Commander screaming over the gunfire.

'Pull back. Pull back and get the fuck out of there.'

Right, coach. Any idea how the fuck I can do that with all this shit flying? Raising up to run made about as much sense as trying to get a close shave by sticking your Goddamn face into a buzz saw. Tell the fucking gooks you're firing cover so they'll get back in their holes.

Barking roar of an M-60 machine gun to the rear. Sounded like the muzzle blast was getting closer. Assault fire? Shit. No Goddamn gunner in his right mind would stand up and walk through this. No telling exactly what frame of mind the machine gunner and his assistant were in. Who cared? There they were. Standing up and blasting away at the line of gook bunkers. Vile sneer on the gunner's face. See them clearly off to my right just by turning my head. Assistant gunner working his jaws on something. Praying, cursing or begging the gunner to be sensible and lay down? Shuffled through the prostrate forms, intent on closing the line of gooks.

Too Goddamn amazed to get up and run for cover. Big gun bucking and chattering as the gunner fired from the hip. Assistant had extra ammo belts draped all over his upper torso. Struggled to link them together on the move. If the gun ran through a belt before an additional one could be linked on, their bravery would buy them nothing more than a bellyful of return fire. A-gunner seemed slightly concerned with it. Fucking gunner didn't seem to give a shit one way or the other. Look at that silly asshole. Had enough of being pinned down. If the gun ran out of ammo, he'd club the fucking gooks to death.

NVA blasted into shock. Can't believe this fucking pair either. Incoming slacked off to a trickle. Time to leave them with it.

Two or three remaining who could navigate got up and sprinted to the rear toward the first line of fighting holes. Jesus. Never thought I'd get out of there alive. Maybe fifteen grunts in position here, cranking away to try and keep the gooks down and let the machine gunner do his incredible thing. Look at those two. Hard to judge bravery and insanity.

Gunner closed to fifteen yards of the bunker complex. Assistant began to jerk on his trigger arm. Showers of tracer and ball ammo sprayed wildly off to the right. Christ, leave him alone. He's doing great. Gunner standing still now. Pressing his luck. Fucker wants the gooks to get up and fight; wants more targets. Assistant gunner finally whacked him on the back of the head, sending his helmet flying. Screamed at him to break the trance.

'That's all, you dumb shit. Let's get the fuck out of here.'

Gunner looked around him. Wild-eyed, intense expression. Cold hate and common sense struggling with each other out there. Hadn't been alone more than two minutes. Gradually began to realize his predicament. Amazed at his own audacity.

'Sheeeee-it!'

Common sense won. Gun team sprinted to the rear, stumbling over the belted ammo dragging behind them.

NVA's turn then. Shot-up reconnaissance force mustered along the first line of dirt mounds. About 200 yards of open ground between us and the hillock where we got up on the wall. Charlie Six had a decision to make. Badly wanted to get out of there before the NVA decided to counterattack. If we ran back for the southwest corner, we'd be naked targets for the length of time it would take to cover the 200 yards of open ground. And we'd have to leave the dead and wounded – if there were any out there – behind on the wall. About ten dead Marines visible out on the killing ground.

Charlie Six chewed his lip, hunkered down behind a dirt mound. Probably thinking of Chesty Puller. Revered Marine General who pulled all his dead and wounded out of Korea's Chosen Reservoir despite pressure from several Chinese Divisions. Marine doctrine said no dead and wounded were to be left on any battlefield. Breach of faith that would not be tolerated. Charlie Six would have to do a lot of explaining if he left dead Marines behind. Even in this weird war, Marines don't leave dead or wounded Marines lying on a battlefield.

CO pointed to six or seven shaky grunts crouched behind the dirt mounds. Decision made.

'You people. When we open up again, you get the hell out there and drag those Marines back here.' Selected grunts took it stoically. Knew it was probably coming. Shrugged off any item of equipment that might slow them down when they got out into the killing ground again. What the fuck? Run out there and die or sit here and die. What's the difference?

Charlie Six in desperate radio contact with battalion. Mortar fire promised to cover the withdrawal. That would take a while. Dead and wounded to be policed up before an escape could be made.

Time now. Open up. Now. Get out there and get them. Designated grunts dashed out toward the silent, bloody forms. Not much time to think. Scared, stoic men rounding up errant club members so they could be buried in the club's private plot where other club members could weep and wail over their sacrifice. Raggedy asses disappearing over the dirt mounds. Typical perspective. Everybody shows me their ass. Constantly seeing these fuckers from the rear or through a long lens. My perspective on the world. Would they come after me? Did the assholes owe me anything for considering them assholes? Would I get up and do it for them?

Yeah. Shit. Got to start somewhere, sometime, man. Got to either shit or get off the pot here. Got to get off these one-way streets. Set me free or get the fuck off my back.

Worked quickly out there. Shoulders hunched against the inevitable burst of fire. When it came, we'd be just as dead as the dudes we were trying to retrieve. Grasped a decapitated black Marine under the shoulders. Heavy bastard even without a head. Shout from the bunker line.

'Mother of fucking Christ. There they come.'

NVA troops streamed out of their bunkers. Bayonets. Good God. No. Wait. Where's that fucking rifle?

On us too quickly for us to get away back to the dirt mounds. Grunts to the rear held fire. Had to. Either that or blow us away along with the NVA. Swarming all over the Goddamn place. How many of them? One charged at me and the headless corpse. Stood there like a groom holding a new bride on the threshold. Wicked-looking triangular bayonet pointed directly at my throat. Three more steps and I'd be skewered on that fucking thing. Got to do something NOW.

Heaved the Marine's dead body up and toward the screaming NVA soldier. Shuddering jolt and hollow thunk as the bayonet pierced the corpse. Tore the black man's body out of my hands. Shield down. Gook struggled with his rifle. Trying to dislodge his bayonet from the dead man's chest cavity. Rolled away; scrambled to my feet.

Jungle rules now, man. Grunts and NVA tore at each other's throats. Hand-to-hand. Fucking gook had his bayonet free. Here he comes again. Got to be a Goddamn weapon around here somewhere. Is that a rock? Black dude's head lying there near my left foot. Eyes big and white, staring off into the distance. Looking for something to stem the ooze of blood and gore dripping from his shattered neck. Nearly on me now. Where's the fucking helmet? There.

Scooped up the black dude's helmet. Swung it at the NVA's bayonet. He spun around with the impact. Pulled the rifle back into position for another thrust. Crush his fucking head or I'm a dead man. Sounded like a sledge hammer splitting a wooden tent peg when the helmet hit the side of his face. Went down like a wet sack of rice. Finish the fucker. His own bayonet through the throat.

Magazine in this weapon. Why didn't he just shoot me instead of fucking around with the bayonet? Other guys not doing so well in the melee. Cranked off a few rounds to see if I can break it up a little. Here comes help. Rest of the recon party headed for the center of the ring. Gooks had enough of close combat with bigger, heavier, more desperate men. Headed back for their bunkers. Time to get the fuck off this Goddamn wall. Charlie Six back in the saddle. No time to dwell on the hand-to-hand fight. Had the bodies; get the hell off the wall.

'Toss the bodies over and jump after them. Get moving.' No one challenged the order. Any way off would do. Broken leg from a thirty-foot drop is better than a body bag.

'Here you go, black dude. Geronimo, or whatever.'

Black dude cushioned my fall. Shit. Even without a head, the fucker was still in the fight. Ought to get a medal. Shit. Ought to get two or three. If I *ever* write another newspaper story, it'll be about him. Swear to God, man. That's a promise. Rounds thudded all around as we fell or leaped off the wall. Heard the fuckers whistling by as I fell toward the moat. Below the southern wall. Grabbing and scrambling to police up the dead bodies for the second time. Where the fuck are the mortars? Another dude hit. Survived the jump and got his back shot out down here.

'Enough of this shit. Sick and fucking tired of getting kneed in the balls by those cocksuckers, man. Sick of this shit. Sick of it. Goddamnit!' M-16 lying there in the mud.

'Get out of here, you motherfuckers.' Pointed up and pulled the trigger. Kill some sonofabitch, by God! Blinding flash in front of my eyes. Jesus fucking Christ. Maybe a jammed round. Pain in my jaw. Feels like a Goddamn bayonet in there. What happened? On my knees flapping at the blood flowing from my chin with the left hand. God. Look at that. Fucking hand is all torn up. What happened? Thumb's nearly gone from my fucking hand. Shit. Blood all over the area. Hit, man. I'm hit. Or the fucking M-16 blew up in my hands. What happened? Christ, I'm going to bleed to death out here.

Distant crump and rattle. Mortar fire on the walls. Finally. Lay down out here, man. Got to stop the bleeding. Hand mangled, useless. Feel . . . good? No pain. What the fuck? Did I pass the initiation? Blood all over. Not thinking right. Blood-red fucking fraternity pin?

Fraternity brothers scooped me up under the shoulders.

Wall getting smaller. Headed to the rear. Face the fucking enemy, by God. Half the battle there.

'Where are we going, Goddamnit? What happened to my hand? Don't forget to get the black dude, man. Owe him. Owe that dude. Can't leave him out there. Make sure that fucking black guy – the one without a head, Goddamnit. Make sure he gets out of there. Yeah. Get him too. Carry him out or I will. What the fuck happened to my hand? Can't see anymore. Did they get my eyes?'

Somehow, despite the ambush, attack and counterattack, bayonet fight and dangerous leap off the southern wall of the Citadel, thirteen of the original Charlie Company reconnaissance force lived to fall or be carried, shivering and gasping, back into the battalion command post on the north side. That's where we were when I could see again.

Head wrapped in bandages. Thought it was my Goddamn hand, man. Yeah. That too. Corpsman worked on the thumb. Jesus. Felt like I went one-on-one with a fucking tank. Steve hovered over me, bitching at the corpsman.

'Yeah. I'm awake, man. What happened? What did they get me with? Did that fucking M-16 blow up or what?' Corpsman pressed down on my chest with his free hand.

'Don't move your left hand. Got to stitch this thumb back on or you'll lose it.' Steve had other concerns.

'You Goddam near lost the whole fucking chicken ranch out there. You're a mess.'

'Yeah. But what kind of mess? What happened? Did anybody see it?'

Corpsman got a fresh purchase on my hand. 'One of those dudes brought that M-16 in. Looks like the gooks were trying to pop you one in the gourd and missed. They hit the fucking rifle right in the receiver group instead.

Fuckin' Mattie Mattel rifle shattered in your hands when the round hit it. You got a good-sized chunk of plastic stuck in your chin when the stock shattered. The pistol grip blew up and damn near took your thumb off. Ask me, you got away clean as a whistle. That round could have turned the other way and blown your head off.'

Steve tried to convince the corpsman to send me out on the next boat. Thumb had been badly gashed. Should have the wound treated. Yeah. Should go on out. Get well enough to make the Hong Kong gig next month. Flash my Purple Heart and fuck myself back to health. Strange feelings. No pain. Sort of an elation. Something's different now. Feel light and warm. Morphine? No. Something else. What? Can't think right. Did I pay dues to join something here? Badge of honor? Dueling scar? Funny thoughts now that I'm definitely alive. Feels like getting laid after beating your meat for too many years. Not thinking right. No time to make decisions.

'Nah. Thanks, Doc. Not going out on this boat. Maybe later. Just get up here and see how I feel.'

Policed up my gear and washed some of the blood off in the Perfume River next to the LCI ramp. That's where I met the faceless buddy from the south side. He died but I got his name. Got my buddy's name, by God. Went to see my other buddy then. Formless, headless lump in a green plastic body bag. Know how you feel, man. Loaded both my friends in an LCI. Have to make new ones now. Goodbye, dudes. Good luck. I know how you feel now. Know exactly how you feel.

'Let's see if we can find some fucking booze, man.'

South Side

Street Sweepers

Misty morning in Hué. Glowering clouds finally receded. Heat from a pristine sun caused steam to rise in spidery white wisps off the pavement and stone. Grunts exposed their wrinkles and festering sores to the sun for the first time in two weeks.

Warm, fuzzy feeling. Like after you get laid. Stripped nearly naked in a courtyard. Fuck a bunch of snipers. Assholes wouldn't dare kill a man on vacation. Respite should last until the fliers and shipboard gunners can lower a drawbridge into the Citadel. Break in the dirty weather meant Hué could be seen clearly from the air.

At the battalion CP this morning. Jubiliant atmosphere. Carriers already steaming into position to launch the fighter-bombers. Closer to the beach, cruisers and destroyers maneuvered to bring their heavy caliber guns to bear. Ringside seat for the action up here. Just sit back and watch the flyboys and sailors pound hell out of the walls without having to do anything but cheer or bitch, depending on their accuracy.

Picnic spread in the courtyard of a house near the northern bank of the Perfume River. Stripped to skivvies. Gear laid out to dry in the sun. Musty smell of wet canvas. Steve cooked an elaborate C-ration banquet. Coffee smells enough to give you a hard-on. Strange things going on with him. Disappeared all day yesterday. When I looked for him, a platoon sergeant said he was leading a patrol. Leading a Goddamn patrol? Won't talk about it at any length. Said he's doing his part.

'How about your fucking job, man? How about doing your Goddamn job?'

Shakes his head. Says he can't believe a guy who saw what I saw up on the wall would ask that question. Shit. Got to do what we have to do. All of us. Maybe the change in the weather will affect him; get him back on track here. Worked wonders for me. Going to survive this Goddamn fight, man. Bloodied but unbowed, by God. Get the final frames when the flag goes up and walk away to tell about it. Shouldn't be long now.

Navy officer and two Marines packing long-range radios approached from the direction of the LCI ramp. Set up in our courtyard. They'll direct the naval gunfire on to the walls. Steve walking around in green skivvy shorts. Pale, grimy skin poached white from the cloying humidity of a rainsuit. Thin legs sticking out of green underwear reminded me of bone showing through the rent of a bad shrapnel wound. Had a clutch of pseudo-grunts clustered around him. Mortar men, truck drivers, supply men, rocket gunners; all pressed into service as riflemen. Steve had a squad. Won't admit it, but he's gone over the edge.

Said he's just helping out where he's needed. Bullshit. Cluster of dudes with rifles is a rifle squad. And the asshole that gives them orders is a squad leader. Who's he trying to shit?

Spent some time trying to rebandage my wounds. Worried about the thumb. Left hand and forearm throbbing like there's a pissed-off python in there. Jaw muscles and throat sore as hell. Must have gotten torn up inside when the corpsman pulled the sliver of plastic out.

Christ. Don't know why I'm worried about Steve. He's alive and functioning. Should be worried about myself. Always have been before. Beginning to shift focus. Look at this shit. Carrying a Goddamn M-16 everywhere now. Notebook soaked through. Didn't wrap it in plastic. Been carrying one of these bastards for seven – no, eight – months now and never forgot before. Lost half the names and notes in there. Fuck it. Seen this shit so many times I can make up names and fill in the blanks. Stories all the same after a while. Camera's been dead Goddamn weight for the past three days. Look at that counter. Ten fucking frames exposed. Three days of fighting and I exposed ten stupid frames of film. Slowing down, man. Or I'm easing over the line too. Got to stay away from the fucking booze. Leads to bad thoughts which leads to bad decisions.

Sorry about the headless headhunter and the faceless fucking grunt. Got to get back on my regular perch here. Grunt shit is a one-trip pony, man. Take you there, buck you off, crap in your face and leave your ass lying in the dust. One-trip pony always trots back to the barn riderless. Been through too much shit in my time to take that ride.

Feel better now, man. Yeah. I can handle this shit. Just stay away from the booze and self-pity. On to other things. Better do something about these bandages before the Doc comes looking for his Unit One medical kit. Christ. Hard to bandage a wound on the point of your Goddamn chin. Guess I'll have to settle for sanitation over esthetics. Look like I got some kind of weird white beard. Hand's the real problem. Got to wrap the bandage tight enough to let me fire a rifle in case I need to. Plan to do more shooting with a camera than a rifle, but you've got to be ready to open up when the situation requires 5.56 over 35-millimeter.

Gunfire teams barked into their handsets. Navy officer anxious to show us his shit.

'The USS Boston is on station. In just a few minutes,

she'll bring the eight-inchers to bear. We'll see how Luke the Gook likes flat-trajectory, high-velocity naval gunfire.'

Jesus. Spare us the promotional announcements. Just blow a hole in those fucking walls.

'Fucking gooks will be lucky if they can stand up after we get through pounding them.'

Real good, Lieutenant. Should have been up here to hear all the other guys say that. They're mostly dead now. Hide and watch. Fucking sailors will be lucky if they figure out how to get the gun loaded.

Must have figured it out aboard the cruiser. Coughing roar over our heads. Grunts winced and ducked. Few had ever heard that sort of sound before. Frightening sort of Doppler effect. Like standing too close to the tracks in a subway. You know you're safe but the sheer volume of sound causes a dissonance that scares the shit out of you. Hope it scares the gooks just as badly.

Impact of the first round was spectacular. White phosphorus. Willy Peter. Smoking, sparking spears of burning chemical arching through the air. Navy officer observing the strike through field glasses. Calling corrections to the radio operators in contact with the ship. Got the range. Air filled with roaring, rushing sounds and thudding, booming explosions. Too much for the nervous grunts. Shells aimed at the enemy but nothing that noisy could be safe no matter how accurate.

Code of the Grunt. Avoid loud noises and you decrease your chances of getting nailed. Very few silent killers in the Nam.

Shelling continued for nearly an hour. Silence seemed nearly as loud as the barrage when it was over. Grunts crawled from cover to assess the damage. Hoped to hell those walls have been reduced to rubble. Sounded like they ought to be. Goddamnit. Fucking figures. Some craters in the surface of the walls. Some chips and dents in the exterior lip around the top. But no pathway to glory. The Citadel's drawbridge remained up and locked.

Navy officer wishing he hadn't bragged on the might of his guns so loudly. Gunfire team slunk away back toward the LCI ramp. No celebration aboard the cruiser tonight. Nice try but no cigar.

'What we really needed was a battleship with 16-inch naval rifles.' Staring at the minor chips his guns made in the walls of the Citadel.

'Or maybe if the ARVN let us fire a few more rounds. I don't know. Those Goddamn walls are incredible. Wish the gun crews could see the size of those fuckers.'

Guy is totally destroyed. Came in here expecting to be the savior of the raggedy-assed infantry and had to go home with his tail between his legs. Paranoid masonry of the ancient engineers took one of modern technology's best shots and shrugged it off like a bothersome insect.

'Maybe you tore up some of the gook defenders, sir. Anything that reduces the number of NVA up there is a good job.'

Bright smile. That speculation will be carried back to the ship as consolation prize for the gun crews. You're a nice fucking guy, D.A.

Airspace over the Citadel clear of projectiles. Attack aircraft have a clear look at it. First flight on station before the sailors were out of sight. Screaming over our heads; making dummy runs, trying to draw fire from the top of the wall. Pilots wanted to know if the gooks have AA weapons or missiles tucked somewhere behind those walls. Roaring, swooping passes. Taunting the NVA to poke a muzzle skyward. Green-clad figures scrambling away from perches in guard towers. Fuckers know what's about to happen.

Better get dressed and repack the gear. Navy planes dragged a mass of scudding, dark clouds with them on the flight in from the coast. Delta Six passed the word. Be ready to make a quick run for the walls if the planes managed to do what naval gunfire couldn't. If we get an assault ramp, we go balls to the wall. Literally.

In the concrete doorway that served as Delta CP, Company Commander obviously unhappy with the order to follow air strikes so closely and quickly. Hoping for replacements before he has to try for the top. Delta only about fifty percent effective after days of housecleaning and the first wall fight. Jets circling in regular patterns. Arming the ordnance hanging from wings and fuselages. Bombs and rockets looked like clusters of grapes or bundles of ripe cigars. Delta Six outlined the game plan.

Smoothed a small-scale tourist map on his knee. Long John Silver briefing a crew of brigands on the location of buried treasure.

'It looks like this. We are the left flank of the assault line. Our objective is to clear the buildings along the street to our front here, get on the wall and then seize and hold the southeast sector. On our right in the center of the assault line is the third ARVN Regiment. The Vietnamese Marines are on the right flank. If the planes can blow a hole in the wall suitable for us to gain access, and if the gooks don't have too much strength on this side of the wall to hold us up, and if we don't get blown off the wall once we get up there like Charlie Company did the other day, we might just have it in hand by nightfall.'

Does he really believe that shit? After what we've seen for the past few days?

'Fuck, no. I'm giving you the party line for publication. There are too many gooks and too few Marines left. S-2 says the major portion of the NVA Sixth Division is still operating over here. Now Two-Five and the 1st Marines managed to kill about a thousand of them on the south side. Do your arithmetic. How many does that leave running around over here?'

'Let's see. Average NVA infantry battalion has about three hundred men. Scratch two battalions blown away on the south side. Leaves about eight battalions of NVA or about two-thousand-four-hundred gooks, I guess.'

'You guess about right. And I've got one shot-up company of weary-assed grunts. The other companies are just as short. Shit. Half the fucking battalion is walking-wounded and the other half will be shortly. We just have to hope the air strikes do some significant damage.'

Won't be long before we find out. Live runs going in now. First jet peeled off from altitude. Fuselage glinting in the sunlight. Dived for the wall like a thrown dagger. Grunts in courtyards and doorways craned their necks to watch the show. Nose up now. Paddle-shaped air-speed brakes sprouted from behind the wings. Makes it a more stable platform for pinpoint bombing. Scream of jet engines hurt the ears. Pulling up now. US NAVY painted on the underside of the wings. Grabbed for altitude as two cigar-shaped objects snapped off the wings. Projectiles sprouted fins and flew into the surface of the wall.

Booming explosions cracked and echoed off the façades of buildings all around. Grunts screwed up faces against the blast and opened their mouths to ease the pressure of the following shock wave. Good shit, man. That might get it. Snakeye bombs. You could tell by the stabilizing fins. Know what that means. Napalm is next. Nape on the walls. Great faith in that shit. Should make it a little easier. Grunts had seen this sort of thing before. Nape follows Snakeyes in most aircraft ordnance loads designed for close air support. Usually loaded in mixed clusters. Great for opening defensive positions. Blow a hole with high explosive and let the jellied gasoline seep into it.

Flights of fighter-bombers roared over the wall in a continuous cartwheel. Where's the nape? Looking for that familiar black and orange fireball and listening for the whump and whoosh of a napalm strike. Grunts seemed fascinated. Cheering the scene. Get Some, Zoomies. Greatest show on earth as long as you don't have to stick your head in the lion's mouth. Fourth pass; featured act about to begin. Jet jinked away from the formation and kicked right rudder. Barely missed the tall guard tower. Looked like he was too low. There it is. Stand by, gooks. Two silver cannisters tumbled from beneath the wings.

Cannisters hit and burst. Impact area flooded with volatile napalm. Microsecond delay. Entire area on the wall's surface blossomed into ugly, roaring flames. Grunts ecstatic. They'd seen nape strikes before. Not much survived. The whole wall fight will be just a matter of policing up the crispy critters. Maybe. But don't hold your fucking breath. Seen gooks walk away from B-52 strikes before. Been with outfits that lollygagged into an air strike zone and got their asses kicked by gooks who couldn't possibly have survived. Goddamn NVA are veteran survivors. Been doing it for twenty years.

More Snakeye bombs and napalm cannisters. Whole wall sector to our front on fire. Roiling with greasy black smoke from the nape. First flight of jets turned eastward. Low on fuel; back to the floating bird-farms. Second flight roared in low to replace the first. How much of this shit would the Vietnamese allow? Air strikes damage real estate. Nape strikes continue much longer and there's going to be a lot of splash-over into the nearby terraced courts and wooden structures on the other side of the wall.

Flights of fighter planes approaching from the beach. Rocket and cannon fire rattling all over the wall area.

Making clouds of mud and chopped vegetation as the planes made their passes. Grunts grooving on the show. Fuck with the bull and you get the horn, man. Those badass airplanes tearing it up. Get Some. Rocket and gun runs over now. Air still for the first time in nearly two hours. Not a sound from the grunts. Everyone waited for gook bodies to come tumbling over the walls and fall at our feet. No such luck. No one wanted to queer the possibility by talking about it. Drone of a single-engine aircraft approaching. What the hell is this? Somebody miss formation?

Prop-driven aircraft banked overhead. Pilot angling for a good look at the target. Reconnaissance?

'Nah. Fucking AD Skyraider.'

One of the WW II attack planes resurrected when jets proved too fast for accurate close air support in tight situations. 'Look at the size of that fucking bomb he's got hung.'

Word passed from the CP. Get down and stay under cover. Skyraider will be dropping a heavy bomb in the area. Last gasp. Final attempt to bust that Goddamn wall and make a hole suitable for passage. Target area is a stretch of wall fifty yards to the left of the guard tower straddling the southern gate. Here's something you don't see every day. Can't say I've ever seen one of these blockbusters dropped. Focus the camera on it.

Skyraider wheeling and making dummy passes overhead. Try the telephoto lens. Shit. That bastard has got ARVN markings. Wonder what prompted that? Probably figure if their national artifacts have got to be fucked up, they ought to do it themselves. Piston engine snarling and ripping. Steady whine. Increased the pitch on his prop. Here it comes. View through the range finder. Squatty airplane bounced in the air when the fat, black bomb dropped away from the centerline of its fuselage.

Shattering roar rolling down the street. Concussion blew helmets off several curious grunts. Fuckers couldn't resist the temptation to see if the blockbuster would work. Windows in the house to my rear shattered and blown inward by the force. Nearly everyone stunned by the violence of the blast. Grunts closer to the wall unsteadily weaving back toward the CP. Blood streamed from their ears and noses. Too close to the shock wave. What size was that Goddamn thing?

Must have been at least two thousand pounds. A fucking ton of high explosive. Skyraider nowhere in sight. Carried only the single bomb. He could get away now. Grunts would live with whatever impact he made on the fight. Dust clouds obscured everything along the wall. Even the tall guard tower disappeared in the smoky aftermath. Full attention focused on the wall. Was the drawbridge finally down? Hell, yes. There it is. Stiffening wind blew most of the dust away. There's the path. Blockbuster worked. Section of wall caved in, filling the moat with rubble and stone.

Strange reactions from the grunts. Mixture of glee and disappointment. There's the route. What's the hang-up? Grunts waiting for word. Orders were to exploit the air strikes. No one wants to move. Nervous glances in the direction of the Company CP. Clouds moving back in from the sea. Started to rain again.

Grunts ordered forward. Better get along if anyone wants to get up on the wall today. Can't believe any gooks could be left up there. Wishful thinking. Steve waved his clump of riflemen forward.

'Hey, man. Goddamnit. Where's your camera? Not your fucking job to be toting a rifle up there with the assault element.'

Calm, resigned look on his face; grim smile. Pitying me.

'D.A., it's a shame to watch all this shit through a lens. Does looking through that Goddamn camera make it less real for you, man? Do you get some kind of dispensation from responsibility because you observe through fine photo-optics instead of doing your share? You can keep a Goddamn telephoto between you and the war if you want to, D.A. But your fucking time will come, my man.'

Slammed a fresh magazine into his carbine and turned to walk toward the walls.

'Hold it, man. Goddamnit. Come to your fucking senses here. You can't go loping your fucking mule up there. We got a job to do. You forget about that? What the fuck are you going to tell them back at Division when you come back empty-handed?'

'It's a personal thing, D.A. I don't give a shit about all that anymore. You better come along and see. You'll understand in a little while. Face the gooks; face yourself. In the end it's all the same.'

Shit. No way to stop him. No one to turn to for help. Betrayed by his own background and upbringing. Betrayal begets betrayal. He'll find that out. If he lives. Goddamn him. Silly turd's going to get us all killed.

'Alright, asshole. Go on. Do your own ego trip. Get a medal and they'll let you lead the parade. But don't come crying to me when they won't even buy you a fucking beer or listen to your shit. Go on, Goddamnit. I'll cover you until you get us both blown away.'

First teams of Delta grunts cautiously approaching the wall. Ducking in and out of doorways all up and down the street. Rubble-strewn ramp just to the left of the southern gate. Crossing the open ground between the last row of houses, across the street which paralleled the wall and across the moat to the ramp, would be a bitch-kitty. Can't piecemeal a move like that. Need to get enough people into position to put a sizeable force into the rush. Steve wants to be part of the action. No way to talk him out of it. But he'll need someone to save his ass. Yeah. OK. But I go only so far, man.

Sporadic gunfire forward. Momentum increasing. Grunts sprinting from position to position. NVA firing heavily now. Plenty of small arms and at least two machine guns. Hear them distinctly. No way to move any further forward. Duck into the doorway where Delta Six is screaming into his radio. Wanted mortar fire on the wall in a hurry. Bullets splatting and whining off the concrete outside. Wheeled to glare at me as I ducked into cover. Nearly jerked his radioman off his feet. Pissed off and disgusted that the NVA weren't wiped out by the air strikes.

'How the fuck could they have survived those Goddamn strikes? How the fuck could there be that many of them left?'

'Got no answer for you, Captain. Shit. I always said you shouldn't presume anything with these fucking gooks.'

Muzzle flashes winked like fireflies all along the surface of the wall. Jesus. These NVA must have moved into the area from somewhere else after the planes did their number. NVA in the guard tower doing the most damage. At least five or six grunts lying dead or wounded out in the street. Still no mortars. Rocket gunner in the upper portico of the tower and a machine gun firing from the window below him. Elevated positions gave them excellent opportunities to kill Marines. Delta Six wanted mortar fire on the guard tower. Ask me, he's lost the surprise or shock element needed to exploit the break in the wall. No one could make it to the ramp unless some of the rocket and machine gun fire could be suppressed.

Cough and bang. Mortars. Finally. Distinctive sound. Hear it plainly over the roar of gunfire. Explosions on the wall. Sound rushed up and down the street, blatting like an unmuffled engine. Incoming slacked off a little. Better go now if you're going to go. Delta Six stood to give the signal. Big mistake. Sound like someone thumped on a watermelon. Saw his knees buckle sharply. Oh, Christ. What's this shit that hit me in the face and helmet? Bone, pieces of hair and scalp. Brain tissue. Feels like hard sponge. Radio operator puked into his handset; crying with the transmission key depressed.

'Stop that shit, man. Go get the Gunny. Hurry up.'

Delta Six had been hit in the middle of the forehead by a single rifle round. Neat black hole. Ghoulish caste mark. Steve advancing forward out there.

'Wait a fucking minute, man.'

Christ. Entire back of his head blown away. Must have been cranial fluid that splashed all over me. Pulled him further into the doorway. Where was that fucking Company Gunny? Poor fucker's skull is totally empty. Won't see his people get on the wall. *If* they get on the wall. Radio splitting static. Battalion Commander trying to raise Delta Company.

'Wait out, Goddamnit. Busy up here.'

Company Gunnery Sergeant sprinting up the street. His outfit now. No officers left. Handed him the radio handset and he recalled the mortars. Where the fuck has Steve gone? Better try to find him. No one near the ramp yet. Must be holed up somewhere along the street. Mortars beginning to pop and burst on the surface of the wall. Better hurry if they intend to get up there today. Can't be much more mortar ammo left. There they are. Steve and his clutch of antsy grunts in a house across the street from the moat. Mighty Goddamn close, man. Wait for me.

Race is on. Machine guns still winking fire up and down the street. Mortars aren't hitting the tower. That's where the Goddamn guns are, man. Hit the fucking tower. There they go. Sprinted across the open street. Tumbled into the muck of the moat. Just enough time to get across behind them. Out of fucking breath, man. Made this deal on a dead run. Only twenty feet to the edge of the ramp. Waiting for more grunts to get in position. Need massed firepower up there.

'No. No.' Company Gunny screaming into the handset across the street. 'Don't stop now. Goddamnit, get some more ammo quick. We need mortars. We're almost there.'

No more explosions on the top of the wall above us. Steve glancing around to see if I'm there. Gave me a weak smile. Fuck that.

'Goddamnit. You wanted to be up here. You got us into this shit. Now what?'

Grunts confused. Some still trying to worm their way toward the wall. Others running back for cover. Most of the runners got shot. Best to lay low and hope they find some more mortar ammo in a hurry. Just a few more rounds.

Too late. Past the shock point. Gooks on the wall have figured it out by now. No more mortars. They can come out and start shooting again. Delta grunts to our rear popping away with rifles and machine guns, but the gooks aren't deterred. AK rounds smacking into the brackish water at the bottom of the moat and singing off the pavement to our rear. Shit.

'That's enough, Steve. Now we get the fuck out of here. Grenades. Heave 'em up as far as you can. Go for cover across the street when the first one fires.'

Two men cut down as they stood to throw grenades. Tumbled into the moat while we threw frags like pitching machines. Grenades banging to our rear. Fire still incoming hot and heavy. Nothing to do but turn your back, hunch your shoulders and run. Four more grunts picked off in the moat. Somehow Steve made it back to cover in a house across the street without being hit. No inclination to police up the dead this time. No crowbar inserted into the Citadel. Walls win another round.

Company Gunny yelling for his people to pull back. Doubtful if Delta had enough Marines left to make another assault on the wall. Still, there would have to be an accounting. Time to count heads. Steve grinning at some inside joke. Smug, self-satisfied smile. Almost exhilarated; thrilled with survival and participation.

'Goddamnit, man. That's enough of that shit. I mean it.'

'Funny feeling, D.A. Knowing you have to go up there; you can't lay back and look through a lens. You really get a taste of how these guys feel.'

'You're really out of your fucking mind. You know that? Who the hell said you *have* to go up there? Huh? You're *supposed* to lay back and look through a lens. It's your Goddamn job, man. Now don't give me any more of this shit. I don't *want* a taste and feel of what asshole grunts feel like. Stop acting like an asshole before you get both of us killed.'

Head-count complete. Company Gunny railed at the Battalion Commander over the radio about the lack of mortar support and the twenty additional killed and wounded in the abortive assault. Delta Company now a platoon-sized unit. Gunny wanted replacements before dark. Battalion said more mortar ammo was on the way from Phu Bai. Any replacements that could be scrounged from the rear would be sent directly to Delta.

Grunt observing the wall from outside the new CP area yelled for the Gunny.

'Jesus Christ. Look at this. Fuckin' Rodrigues got left

out there by the wall. Look at that little turd, will'ya? He's waving at us.'

Grunts clambered for a place from which to look at the wall. Gunny shoved the man with the best view aside and focused his field glasses on the figure to our front. Skinny Puerto Rican standing flush against the wall with his back to the masonry. Gunny got his bowels in an uproar.

'Holy shit. Was fuckin' Rodrigues up there with you?'

One of the survivors considered.

'Yeah, Gunny. I think he was. Shit. I thought he was one of the two that got dinged when we pulled back and the gooks opened up again. What the fuck's he doin' up there?'

'Looks like he's got his ass in a crack.' Gunny trying to figure all the angles. 'He can't get back to us. If he moves out, away from the wall, the gooks will get him for sure. He's OK right where he is now, though. The gooks either don't know he's there or, if they do, they don't want to expose themselves trying to aim a rifle down at him.' Rodrigues' squad leader piped up.

'Whut we goin' to do about him? Can't leave his ass out there.'

Company Gunny made a quick decision. 'We move up through the houses. You people saddle up, lock and load. We'll try to create enough shit and mass confusion up there so he can make it back into the first row of houses across the street. We either get him back in, or that crazy shithead might take a notion to storm the walls all by himself.'

Steve slung a bandolier of ammo around his neck and stood.

'That's it, man. Go on by yourself. Look at my fucking hand. Bleeding all through this pile of bandages from that last excursion. You don't need to go up there with them. And if you do, by God, you go by yourself.'

Same smug grin. He's going to go. Well, shit. Not likely to get hurt creating a diversion. Got to try to rewrap this hand.

Two squads bulled their way forward through the houses toward the wall. Had to be careful not to accidentally dart out into the street which ended in the barricaded south gate of the Citadel. Took them about fifteen minutes to get into positions from which they could put fire on the wall. Rodrigues skylarking. Waving wildly at the grunts he can see spread out in two houses which directly faced the wall. Gunny waved back and signaled for Rodrigues to stay put. Made motions with his rifle trying to communicate the plan to create a diversion.

Rodrigues digging the whole thing. Flashed a brilliant smile and waved again. Turned around to face the wall and extended the middle finger of both hands upward over his head. Hoots of laughter from the grunts observing near me.

'Fuckin' dip-shit. He's flippin' the gooks the bird. Man, he don't know what kind of shit he's in out there.'

Guess not. Goddamn guy has to be fucking crazy. Look at that shit. Rodrigues prancing up and down along the wall in an exaggerated close-order drill. Every few steps, he faced his buddies and waved. Thinks the whole thing is a great Goddamn joke. Digs grab-assing around right under the nose of the enemy. Macho deal. Like waving the red cape at a fighting bull. Only the strong survive. Figures the gooks won't try for him with grunts up there in rifle range.

Company Gunny failed to see the humor. Getting red as a Goddamn beet; trying to signal Rodrigues to stop his clowning and get ready to run. Fucking Crazy Man just grinned and waved back.

'That motherfucker done tripped off the gun line again.' Rodrigues' squad leader told the story of the Puerto

Rican's previous escapade on an operation in the An Hoa region of central I Corps. Story went that Rodrigues stood up in front of a machine gun which was pinning the company down and began to do some sort of weird salsa dance routine, singing in Spanish at the top of his voice.

Squad leader swore the gooks were so surprised and amazed at his audacity that Rodrigues was able to dance right up to their position and toss in a frag. Gook machine gun crew died wondering what kind of crazy assholes the Americans were sending to fight the war. Rodrigues supposedly laughed and spoke to himself in rapid-fire Spanish for several hours after the event. Didn't think there had been anything unusual in his behavior.

Punch line was the Company Commander was going to put Rodrigues in for a medal but he was afraid the crazy fucker would drop his trousers in front of the general who presented it or some such weird shit.

Whatever the truth of the matter was, Rodrigues was doing it again. Company Gunny swearing loudly now; trying to figure out what to do about the Company Clown and his precarious position. Asshole couldn't be rescued unless he knocked off the shit and cooperated.

No need to worry. Goddamn kid took things in his own hands. Took two frag grenades in his own hands, in fact. Pulled the pins and held the grenades out where everyone could see what they were. Big shit-eating grin. Heaved both grenades up into the air behind him and over the lip of the wall. Crazy Man laughing and shouting at his buddies in Spanish. Great Goddamn joke on the gooks.

Bad joke. Kid should have known gooks don't have a sense of humor. Grunts shouted a warning. Two seconds after he pitched the frags, he got a return on his investment. His grenades came flying back over the wall in formation with three ChiCom potato-masher grenades. Five for two. Best deal in town. If you're looking to get killed in the transaction. Grunts screaming at the Crazy Man to warn him. Followed pointing fingers and looked up just in time to grasp what happened. Big white smile drooped. But not much. Laughing Puerto Rican had just enough time to dive into the moat before the two original grenades went off in midair. More subtle bangs from the ChiComs followed. Nice shit-storm you created for yourself out there, kid.

Gunny screaming to be heard over the din of firing.

'Get over here, you crazy bastard.'

Rodrigues sprinted up the near side of the moat and scampered into a nearby doorway out of the line of fire. Gunny tried to chew his ass but gave up. Kid raving to himself in Spanish again.

Grunts on their way back toward the temporary CP. Got good news for them. Came in on the radio from battalion while they were rescuing the Crazy Man. No more assaults on the wall today. Dig in for the night and wait on replacements and resupply. Gathered up film from Steve's unused cameras. Fucking thing is still in his pack. Christ. If he keeps this shit up, I might as well put mine away too. Goddamnit.

I swore this shit would not happen to me. I swore it. Now look. Can't decide for myself anymore and I'm letting someone make the fucking decisions. Better get what exposed film I have back to the LCI ramp. Maybe the last journalism I do.

Near the LCI ramp. Looking for someone to take the film back on the next boat. Two quick shots off to my right. Grunts, corpsmen and Shore Party people dove for cover. Everyone searched nervously for a sniper. Rounds weren't incoming. Half a block up the street a tall, lanky black grunt stepped out into the street. 'No sweat, y'all. Jes' ol' Philly Dog blew away a fuckin' gook ovah heah.

Jes' one. And the Dog put his shit in the street. No problem ovah heah.'

Heard that name before. Another legend in the 5th Marines. Philly Dog. Stocky, coal-black street fighter from South Philadelphia. Called himself 'The BADDEST mothafuckah in the entire Mo-rene Corps.' Dog ran with a buddy from New Jersey named Willis. Both carried straight razors tucked into their jungle boots. Gold teeth flashed viciously when Dog mouthed his famous lines.

'Fuck wit' Philly Dog, dudes, and you get cut every way but loose. Ol' Dog cut ya t'ree ways, mothafuckahs: long, deep and con-tin-u-ously.' Philly Dog made good on his claim in a number of rear area fights but he was loyal to the grunts in his company. They liked him too. But they gave Philly Dog and Willis a wide berth. Everyone did.

Dog felt he needed to get his name and picture in the *Philadelphia Inquirer*. He cultivated me every time I showed up with a camera. Glad to find out the badass was still alive. Get up and shoot the shit with them. Get away from the high weirdness.

Willis sitting in a doorway. Long, skinny legs stretched out in front. Filthy like all the other grunts in Hué, but still talking his brand of shit.

'Ain't *dis* a kick in the ass. Dog, look whut's comin' up the mothafuckin' front drive heah. Got to be the reporter-man, dude. Watcha hear from the *Inquirer* and the *Newark News*, my man? They readin' all 'bout the exploits of Willis and Philly Dog back in The World?'

'Nobody'd believe your cheap shit, Willis. Let me sit down and . . . Jesus Christ, Dog!'

Philly Dog sat on a freshly-killed NVA soldier. Nearly sat on the asshole's face. Shit. Philly Dog's gold teeth flashed in a wide grin. Basso voice rumbled in the dusk.

'Da fuck is a mattah wit' ya, dude?'

Perched sedately on the NVA's sunken chest. Gook

had been shot twice at close range. Almost directly behind the left ear.

'Spotted dis heah mothafuckah peepin' round the area. He a mothafuckin' officer. Ain't that right, Willis?'

Willis pulled a pair of red and gold collar tabs out of his pocket.

'Major. Ought to turn that dude over to S-2. They don't get many field grade gooks.'

'Ah will. Ah will.'

Far be it from Dog to violate regulations or procedures.

'But first I got to get me a little use out of him. Fuckin' piles been bleedin' from settin' round on all this Gahdamn concrete, man. B'lieve I jest rest my ass for a little while on a mothafuckin' field grade officer. Can you dig it?'

Wanted their picture taken with the dead NVA. Dog managed to beat Willis to the prize souvenir of the encounter. Big gold grin. Held up a smallish Russian pistol and a shiny leather holster for my inspection. Willis had to settle for the cloth belt and silver buckle embossed with a red star. Said he'd give me the belt if I would take their picture before it got too dark. Had to promise I'd send it to the *Inquirer* and the *Newark News*. Boys on the block got to check out what's happenin' in the Nam, man.

Fucking waste of time. No atrocity shots ever get by the censors in Da Nang. Fuck it. Maybe I can get a print for them back in the rear. Hard to focus in the gathering gloom. Hand hurts like hell trying to hold the camera. Both men gamboled and posed with the dead NVA. Dog lit a smoke and poked it in the dead man's mouth. Willis insisted I take the belt. Stuck it in my pocket to keep the peace.

'Let's get this Goddamn major down among his fellow officers at the Battalion CP. Dog, you still carrying that fucking razor, man?'

'Jes' like my dick, my man. Ah ain't dressed wit'out it.'

Willis lacking attention. 'Fuckin' blade ain't no good in this Gahdamn Hué City.' Philly Dog highly incensed.

'What you sayin', Nigger? Ol' Dog show you jes' how fuckin' good dat blade be right heah in dis street. Dis is *my* place, baby. Watch dis shit.'

Propped the dead officer up against a tree. Dog's gold teeth flashed in the first moonlight. One fluid motion: razor out of the boot top; blade open with a mean snick. Willis high on all this shit.

'Well, go on, man. Get Some.' Dog dropped into a knife-fighter's crouched stance before the dead NVA officer.

Three clean, quick passes over the corpse's bloating stomach area.

'Fuckin' Zorro done been heah, man.' Cold blood oozed from the perfect Z. Second, underhanded swipe at the corpse. Left ear laying at my feet.

'How's dat, Reporter-man? Have the Dog lost his touch with the blade?'

'No, man. You still got it. No doubt about that.'

Offered to do more cutting. Willis wanted to show off his moves. No thanks. Seen enough blood today. At the Battalion CP, Philly Dog asked about Steve. Surprised to hear he gave up the camera. Hard for him to understand why anyone would do that. Shrugged and grinned brightly in the night.

'We go on back to Delta wit' ya, Reporter-man. Might have to be some cuttin' done up on them walls.'

Hard-shelled Crabs//18 February 1968

Everyone in Hué walking around with his ass hanging out of ripped and ragged clothing. No replacements. Incessant rain rotted jungle utility uniforms. Rocks and rough-hewn stonework reduced rags to tatters. American modesty made it a point of some concern. No one wanted to be found wiped out with his weenie waving in the breeze.

Spent last night and most of the morning scrounging through likely-looking homes. Hoping to find something that would fit and keep the rain off puckered carcasses. Grunts showed up for the day's fighting in garish costumes. Another assault on the wall. And they'd make it looking like the lost command of Coxey's Army.

Grunts standing around, waiting for the order to advance; giggling and hooting over their get-ups. Bigger guys had to settle for baggy, black peasant pants. Nothing else would fit their frames. Smaller grunts fell out strutting in multi-colored tweeds and gabardines. Several found gaudy, hand-painted neckties which they wore as sashes or strung around the rim of their helmets. One Marine clipped an intricately embroidered kimono from the bedroom of a former Hué City resident. Rampant, raging dragons up the barrel sleeves and across the silken back. Samurai girded for battle. Gaily-printed silk scarves, sleeve garters and even chintz curtains tied across broad shoulders like a cape. Gooks should have no trouble getting a bead on anyone in this lash-up.

Warming a C-ration breakfast when the Company Gunnery Sergeant returned from the Battalion Command Post with the word on today's operations and five or six scared-looking replacements. Fright nearly became panic when they got a glimpse of Delta's weird appearance. They were issued to the remaining squad leaders. Veterans eyed their fresh-scrubbed faces and new equipment with suspicion.

'What you do for a livin', man?'

Squad leader interrogated one of the new guys. New man gripped his M-16 tightly. Obviously terrified of the band of filthy, bearded Gypsies.

'I'm a baker. They policed my ass up out of Division

headquarters yestiddy and said I was goin' to Hué. Thought they was goin' to assign me to a fuckin' field kitchen or somethin'. I don't know much about this grunt shit.'

Squad leader shook his head disgustedly and pulled a crumpled notebook out of his flak jacket pocket.

'What's your name, baker?'

'That's it.' Replacement grinned nervously; knuckles showing white on the grip of the M-16.

'That's what?' Squad leader poised over his notebook.

'That's my name. See, when I come in the Corps after graduatin' from high school. Uh, I went to DeWitt High in Des Moines . . . that's my hometown, see. Well, fuck, when I come in the Corps I was only seventeen, see? And they seen my name was Baker, so they naturally . . .'

Disgusted squad leader snapped his notebook shut.

'Hey, man. Don't tell me all that shit. I don't give a fuck and neither does anyone else here. If you make it through this fight alive, you'll be Goddamn lucky. If you're alive tomorrow, Newbie, you can tell us all this background shit. Meanwhile, stay close to one of us and do exactly what you're told.'

New guy would have to pay some dues before the veterans would admit him to their closed circle of death and destruction. Anguished look on his face. Wasn't sure he could afford the price or wanted to pay it.

'Relax, man. Nothing you can do about it now. If you make it through the day, you'll start to become one of them. Then it won't be you and them. It'll be us. That's the only way you can live with it, man. If you live. Want to handle all this shit in your own mind, you've got to become one of us. Outsiders like you see this shit and they don't understand. Most of 'em go crazy.'

Steve still played the leader to his nondescript squad of pseudo-grunts. Only four of them left after yesterday's fight. Being briefed just like any other unit leader now.

Won't be long. Soon as replacements come up, he'll fucking volunteer to take a squad. No doubt in my mind.

'Seems they brought more tanks across the river last night. They want to try and bust a hole through that barricaded gate. That way, we can rush the wall, through the gate and up the ramp at the same time. Might even be able to drive some armor through to the inside if they can bust a big enough hole in the gate.'

'Very professional sounding, Steve. But you're supposed to be writing about it, not leading it.'

Corpsman fussing with the wounded hand. Lean back and stare at the south wall through a gap in the stone fence. There's the south gate and the end of the street. Shot-up jeep blocking the moat bridge in front of the southern portico. Junky barricade stuffed into the arched gate area. Tanks, shit. Don't mean a fucking thing. Just like the naval guns and the airplanes. We still have to climb the walls and kill the gooks. No other way, man. Ain't nobody leaving this fucking city until that's over with; I don't give a shit if they use tanks or tactical nukes. Steve still up and into his total involvement trip. Drawing assault diagrams in the mud. Can't conceive of it anymore, man. Vietnam *cafard*.

Last living corpsman unwrapping the filthy bandage from my left hand. 'That gash on your thumb is infected.'

Doesn't seem to give a fuck much. Unable to work up much enthusiasm or sympathy for something smaller than a bullet wound or disembowelment.

'Stinks like shit and all I got is sulfa powder to put on it. You're gonna lose it if you don't get out of here and back where they can shoot you up with antibiotics.'

'What fucking difference does it make? Might fuck up my hitchhiking? Just put some powder on the cocksucker, change the bandage and forget it.'

Corpsman shrugged and began treating the hand. Jesus.

Depression City. Feel like all my give-a-fuck drained out with the blood. Steve walked over to watch the operation. Napoléon checking his troops before Waterloo. Shit. Same smirk on his face.

'What the fuck is the matter with you, man?'

'Just checking to see how you are, man.'

'Fine. Goddamn hand is fine. Be beating my meat again in no time.' Smug grin again.

'No, man. I mean how you're doing in your mind. Can you dig it yet? Can you see what we've got to do here?'

'C'mon, man. I'm doing what the fuck I'm supposed to do. Leave me alone. I'll be there when you need me. Don't fucking worry about it.'

Fooled around with my cameras for a while. Shit. He's right about one thing. Cleaning Goddamn lenses seems irrelevant. Who's going to see the pictures? More importantly, who's going to give a shit? Who can understand this shit without being here? Comes a time when you can't be an observer anymore, I guess. But when is that time? Got to confront memories and nightmares if you want to live with them. Yeah. I can dig that. But when, man? When?

Understand the torment and you can live with it. Basic fucking psychology. Steve's got it psyched. Stopped looking at Hué City and the asshole grunts through a viewfinder. Faced it; got involved. Doesn't bother him anymore. When he's helping he can't be hurting. Simple as that.

Steve ambled away to talk to the Company Gunny. Know what that's all about. He smelled the rotten hand. Saw it in his face. Wanted the Gunny to order me evacuated. Fuck that. Got to learn to live with it too, man. Take a walk and get away from this.

Tank engines. Throaty roar to the rear. Won't be long now. Have to find me to fuck with me. Maybe today. Tanks bust through and I can hit that Hong Kong R & R, man. Ten days if my calendar is right. Nurse this hand along until then. Let those fuckers try to keep me off an airplane.

Staring at the barricaded south portico. Street entrance cut through the walls of the Citadel. Started to laugh. Jesus. It's fucking funny, man. Cold rain dripped off my helmet and down my back under the flak jacket. Taking a Goddamn shower with my clothes on. Christ. Hilarious. Look up there. Gooks drove two Peugeot taxis crossways at the gate to form the base of the barricade. Must have moved through the high-class homes on the interior of the walls like a swarm of termites. Every conceivable form of furniture stacked and stuffed around the autos to complete the block. Open spaces closed with odds and ends and household junk. Complete barricade looked like an idiot's impression of ultra-modern sculpture.

Must be several tons of assorted junk piled in there. Take some doing to blow it all away to the point where a fifty-ton tank could roll through. Nguyen, bar the door. Here come the crazy fucking grunts again. Does it make any fucking difference if I'm with them? Biggest Goddamn move I'll ever make here and I can't seem to work up a good give-a-shit about it. Reaching critical mass here, man. Control rods all shot to shit.

Street rumbling. Tanks pivoted and wheeled into the avenue. Going to do it now, man. Climb the walls and kill the gooks. Icy feeling in my lower back and legs. Like standing in ice-cold water. Fuck. They say the water isn't so cold if you jump in all at once. Passing the word up and down the line.

'Don't move out of cover until the tank is past your position.'

Maybe just a piece of the action. Maybe just concentrate on doing one bit. No orders, no assault. Lone Ranger after one bad guy. Get my man and call it even.

Dues paid. You will receive no further notices in the mail. Do that and keep my eye on that crazy fucking Steve.

Pile of discarded weapons and gear back there. Smorgasbord for anyone who wants or needs new tools. Blooper and a demo-bag full of rounds. Go after the gooks in the tower. That ought to get it. Lay back and pop rounds up there. Like artillery. Rear echelon support. Have to do for now. Just keep an eye on Steve and try to get the range of the guns in the guard tower.

Heavy machine guns spat at the tanks. Steve and Delta grunts forming up to move forward. Back off from there, man. You ought to know ricochets can kill you just as dead as direct fire. Make nastier wounds sometimes. Covered position in a stone portico on the right side of the street. Lean out and fire the Blooper left-handed from here. Should make it easier.

Tanks moved forward, crawling with a high-pitched whine; transmissions in ultra-low gear. No place for sweeping armor assaults. Can't get too far ahead of the foot troops. Heavy .50 caliber slugs whacked and whined around me. Must have seen me duck in here. No way I can fire for a while. Mind games. Gunner timing his bursts to when he figures I might stick my head out of cover. Fuck him. Let the bastard shoot. Wait until the tanks get up here and he shifts his fire. Little Kentucky windage; little luck; might take that gunner up in the tower out for good.

Clank and creak of tracks. Diesel engine snorting, drowning out orders from squad leaders. Hey-diddle-diddle-right-up-the-middle. Tank angled for a head-on cannon shot at the barricade. First tank braked, rocking while the gunner sniffed the air with the cannon muzzle. Looked like a cautious elephant cow testing the air for danger. Lead caroming and splatting off the tank in sheets of sparks. Sounded like someone heaving ball bearings at a steel drum. Elephant images keep coming back. Big bull reacting to a violation of the territorial imperative.

Here comes the charge. Gunner got the sight picture he wanted. Lead tank taking virtually all the fire. Remainder of the herd idling noisily at the intersection to our rear. Spout of flame and gassy smoke. First round on the way. Too much fire to stick my head up and observe the effect. Company Gunnery Sergeant talking to the tank commander on the T-I phone at the rear of the vehicle. Craned his neck around an armored fender to observe the strike of the first round. Chance for a quick look. It passed directly through the barricade. Only a small hole. Shit. Might be a very long day. Lead tank fired twice more with similar results. Three small, round holes in the garbage pile blocking the street entrance to the Citadel.

Grunts holding positions; exchanging disgusted glances. Expected much flashier results from the tank fire. Most of them knew it was inevitable. Nuke the fucking place. Won't make any difference. Grunts will still have to climb the walls and kill the gooks. Shit. Can't we do any Goddamn thing to make this easier? We? There it is again. Put up or shut up. Fire a few M-79 rounds up at the tower. Participate, man. Hard to manipulate the shotgun mechanism with this fucking club for a hand. Not much movement left in the fingers.

Tanks through wasting time. Lead vehicle slowly reversing back down the street. Heavy machine gun in the cupola spitting lead at the guard tower. Grunts scrambling for other cover. Tankers must be embarrassed.

Wrong. Tankers must be dead.

Spout of flame from the guard tower. No mistake about that. Seen it often enough before in this fucking Hué City. Wonder if the tankers saw it? If they did, it probably didn't make the antitank rocket any easier to take. Would you have time to anticipate something like that? No way to maneuver or avoid the impact. Grunts poured fire at the rocket gunner's position. Popped the Blooper a few times, but couldn't get the range. Not enough; not in time. Rocket team got off another round and dove for cover behind the wall.

First round hit with a ringing bang near the commander's cupola. Boring action of an enraged termite. Not much to see from the outside. Neat pinhole when the dust cleared. All the killing going on inside the tank where molten metal was flying around like a gale of razor blades.

Second round struck with a piercing clang. Internal explosion. Probably ammo in the ready racks around the turret. Fifty-ton tank rocked on its tracks like a cow struggling to escape the slaughter pens. Eerie reverberating explosions. Like a huge, heavy-gauge spring struck with a ball-peen hammer. Turret hatches blown open by the concussion of the internal explosion.

Bloody hand and arm slowly reached out of the tank commander's turret and flexed as though the owner was trying to get a grip on thin air and pull himself out of the mortally wounded tank. Delta Company's Gunny screaming for covering fire and trying to climb on to the engine deck. Someone running from the crowd on the other side of the street to help.

Shit. Steve. Trying to get the crew out of the tank. Waste of time. Damn dangerous waste of time. Crew would have been killed by the first AP round or certainly by the internal explosion. False bravado. Leave it the fuck alone, man. Wait. Driver's moving. Pulling himself out of a hatch directly under the drooping muzzle of the tank's cannon. Blood streaming from his mouth, nose, ears, eyes. Looked like something out of a horror flick. Beware, earthmen. This will happen if you resist the power of the invaders. Got only part of the way out of the vehicle before he fell forward. Lying draped over the sloped front of the smoldering vehicle. Like a mutilated discarded rag doll.

Grunts still firing at the top of the wall and the offending guard tower. Added a few Blooper rounds to the din. Great deal of pain and fumbling breaking, loading and cocking the Blooper. Watched Steve and the Gunny standing exposed to return fire on the turret of the dead tank. Gunny shaking his head violently. Pushed Steve off the tank and yelled something. Steve slid off the engine deck and ran to the front of the tank to help the driver.

Wrong move, man. Puts your back to the walls. Irresistible target. Steve grasped the bleeding crewman under the armpits and yanked him out of the driver's seat. Covering barrage made NVA return fire, inaccurate but there were still plenty of rounds chipping concrete as they disappeared to the rear. Gunny jumped down off the tank. Sprinted to his left and ducked into my covered doorway position.

'Holy fuckin' Christ.' Gasping, panting for breath. Smell of cordite and diesel fumes. Motioned his radio operator forward. 'Them Goddamn tankers is hamburger in there. Looks like your buddy got the driver out. If he's alive, he's the only survivor. First round caught the TC full in the gut and damn near cut him in half. Second took the gunner's head off and went right on through the loader. Looks like a big bowl of fuckin' strawberry jam inside that tank. Hope to shit it don't decide to detonate and burn.'

Naturally, it did just that.

Black smoke boiling out of the open hatches of the tank as the company radioman reached our position. Tongues of flame licking upward from the commander's cupola. Oh, shit. That fucking thing is going to go. Gunny kicked his radioman out of the protection of the doorway and sprinted back down the street calling for people to back off and take cover. Better split for high ground. Grunts poured out of doorways heading for the main intersection and safety.

Just short of the end of the street. Tank exploded in a final, spectacular death spasm. Ammunition detonated in loud explosions. Searing heat from the fuel supply. Smoke and flames boiling up through the rain. Delta Gunny on the horn to battalion CP explaining recent events on the street. ARVN troops on the right flank having similar problems. Rattle and roar of heavy firefights from that direction. Gunny warned his remaining grunts.

'Don't go anywhere out of this area. Soon's this fucking bonfire goes out and they can send another tank up we're gonna try it again.'

Yeah. So where the hell is the hero? Probably looking for a well to make his death wish. Can't keep doing that shit if he wants to live. Maybe we can both live through this fucking thing if I can talk some sense into him.

Found Steve near a jerry-rigged aid station half a block away from the main intersection. Probably ought to set the example for him. Tossed the Blooper aside and picked up my camera. Pictures and questions for the tank driver. Poor fucker was sitting up; being ministered to by several corpsmen. Steve looked surprised when he heard the shutter click. Shook his head and stood away from the wounded driver. Grabbed my elbow and walked off a distance from the corpsmen.

'What the fuck are you doing, man? Don't you know that's senseless anymore? What kind of picture can you take that will make any difference up here?'

'It's my fucking job. Shit. It's *our* job, man. Don't you realize that anymore? No. Guess you don't. We aren't fucking grunts. You're the one that ain't right anymore, pal. Our Goddamn job is to take pictures and report what these guys do. Not do it for them. Don't you remember?

We've been doing that for the past eight months. What the fuck is wrong with you?'

Smug smile over his shoulder. 'That what you were doing up there with the Blooper today, D.A.? Taking pictures with an M-79, man?'

Heat from the burning tank dissipated. Waiting to make another assault. Company Gunny talking animatedly to a second tank commander. Next batter. Second M-48 rumbling and creaking forward. Barricade has to come down. Tank sat idling at the crossroad. Waiting to make the fateful turn into the elephant graveyard.

Gunny briefed what remained of Delta Company. No grunts lost in the first assault. Tankers only. Fairly good spirits for the moment.

'Nobody moves until the tank has made a hole in the barricade. He's going to run up behind the dead tank and use it for cover. This time they're loading all HE rounds rather than armor-piercing. We know that don't work worth a shit. The TC over there figures rapid fire HE until he runs out of ammo then he's going to reverse back down the street where he'll be away from the rocket gunner but he can still fire cover for us. Questions?'

What the fuck's to question. Let's go. Gunny gave a hand signal. Tank Commander spoke into his handset, slammed the hatch closed and roared away, turning into the street. Tank committed full on. Firing from the wall increased. Everyone waiting for the whoosh and bang of the rocket gunner's weapon. Not yet. Nothing but small arms over the roar of the tank diesel. Top speed, roaring up behind the dead vehicle. Gunner ranging for a sight picture as soon as the tank braked. First round off and into the barricade. Second crew was good. Regular, smooth tempo of fire from the cannon and machine guns. Large rents torn in the junk-pile barricade. Plenty of room for two men abreast to get through there. Second tank finally had most of the way cleared for an assault. Reversing, transmission whining, back down the street. Hull down. Firing machine gun cover without being exposed. Clear for an infantry movement. Assault forces should be able to get at the gooks from two directions. Up the ramp and through the gate.

Dual attack routes ought to get it. Gunny waving everyone forward. Cautious, rapid walking assault. Hoped the tank machine gun would keep the gooks' heads down. 1400 hours. Fine time for an afternoon stroll along the avenue. Delta moving on the walls again; leapfrogging in and out of doorways along the street. Grunts planned their rushes easily. Into alleys or behind stone fences. As little exposure as possible. Infantry training exercise. If you shitheads don't get it right this time, we'll do it again and again until you do.

Rounds from M-16s and the tank's heavy machine guns kicked white sparks and stone-dust where they struck the wall. NVA strangely silent. Will we make it this time, man? Hyperactive gunners in the guard tower haven't fired. Did they split? Will we finally get on that Goddamn wall? Nearly to the street on the near side of the moat. Going to make it, man. Going to make it. Steadily accelerating rush. Momentum increased with every bound. Company Gunny standing exposed in the middle of the street. Only a pile of rubble at his back for cover. Looked like a harried, filthy traffic cop. Directing two assault groups. One on the left side of the street, set to rush the ramp. The other one the right side, set to charge through the open gate, across the moat and into the Citadel.

Shit. There it is. Too Goddamn good to be true. Gunny lurched forward. Burst caught him in the small of the back. Hips thrust forward obscenely by the force of the rounds. Wave of fire, lit by bright green tracers, swept the street around the surprised grunts. Gunny lying in a pool of blood. Rounds blew the belly out of his hard, old veteran's body.

Half of the assault groups had begun to cross the street when the gooks finally responded. Mousetrap. Pinned down if there happened to be cover handy. If not, dead before they could hit the ground. NVA growing weary of fucking with Delta Company along this street. Held their fire until they could be sure of wiping out the whole bothersome bunch. Debilitate the ranks to such an extent that they won't be back.

Along the brick wall near the curb. Fifteen or twenty Delta grunts lying dead or bleeding. Major perpetrator in the slaughter was a gunner in the guard tower. Machine gunner this time, rather than the rocket team. Swept the street, searching for any living grunts. Blowing extra holes in dead ones. Just a matter of time now. No way out. Living grunts could never survive the exposure of a retreat under that gun. Have to lie where they are until dark. Or die.

No more fire from the tank at the intersection. Why? Where the fuck is he? Glance to the rear. No sinister snout peeking out from the corner of the intersection. No matter. Tanks couldn't pull us out of the fire this time. But Delta had at least one more trick to play.

Weird to watch from a street-level angle in a shallow ditch. Up the middle of the avenue: Squatty, Italian, 3.5-inch rocket launcher gunner and his lanky assistant. Shoulder-fired stovepipe resting casually on the gunner's broad shoulder. Didn't seem to be bothered by the incoming fire at all. Out for a stroll. Calmly walking up to a practice range at Camp Pendleton. Going to toss a few antitank rockets into some rusting armored hulk down range. No big deal.

Rocket team stopped in the middle of the street near

the burned-out tank. AK and machine gun fire whining and popping all around them. Fucking gooks must have terrible sights on those things. How could they just stand there like that without being blown away? Little time to contemplate. Gunner quickly dropped to one knee and shouldered the tube-like launcher. Round already in it. Assistant merely flipped the firing switch and tapped his buddy on the helmet. Up. Clanging bang and a tongue of flame shot to the rear of the gun team. Debris and rubble blew to the rear down the street.

Huge chunk of the guard tower crumpled to the top of the wall in a shower of stone. Neither member of the gun team paused to observe the effect of their fire. Lanky assistant armed another rocket, inserted it in the back of the tube and repeated the ritual of tapping the squatty gunner on the helmet. Up again. Whoosh and roar as the rocket sped away to take another chunk out of the guard tower.

'Get Some, Goddamnit. Get Some.'

Impact of the second round was directly below the lower window. Firing port for the NVA's heavy machine gun. Flash of detonation. Heavy gun barrel spiraling up into the air.

Two more rounds loaded and fired at the guard tower. Now full of holes and ready to topple. Gun team probably would have kept it up until the rounds ran out, but the remaining Delta grunts – no more than eight or ten who could still move – ran to the rear taking advantage of the respite. Broke the gun team's concentration. Both men laughed and pointed at the guard tower. Still hadn't moved from their exposed position in the middle of the street. NVA stopped firing for a moment. Won't last long. Won't take them long to figure out they won. More fucking heroes determined to die out there in the street. Shouts sounded loud in the momentary lull.

'Goddamnit. Save yourselves. Get up and run.'

Gun team laughing and pounding each other on the back. Screamed at them and waved my arms. No deal. Grooving on the holes they made in the guard tower. Fuck this.

'Get out of the Goddamn street. Get out!'

Grabbed the gunner by the launcher and spun him around facing to the rear. Still laughing hysterically.

'Got another target? Got another target?'

'You got 'em, Goddamnit. Go. Get out of here. Let's go now.'

Both men trotted docilely down the street behind me.

Delta's last dance of the day. Battalion Commander waiting when we got back off the street. Counting heads. Motioned to a first lieutenant. Staring open-mouthed at our bloody, bearded, filthy, shot-up group of survivors. Someone said he was the new Company Commander.

'What fucking company he gonna command?' Philly Dog was among the living. Willis lay dead in the street.

'Ain't no fuckin' Delta Company left.' Battalion Commander cringed.

'You people have done an outstanding job but we've got to have more Marines if we're going to walk over that wall. I've brought a new officer and there'll be replacements coming across the river tonight. Get some sleep now. I'm damned proud of all of you and I'm terribly sorry for all the shipmates you lost out there today. We're getting stronger fast over here. You won't have to do so much with so little anymore.'

Getting stronger. Shit. Where's he been all day? We get nothing but fucking weaker. Sap drained out of Delta. Nothing left.

'Colonel, we're still going over that wall, aren't we? No change of plans or anything?'

'That part has not changed.' Speaking quietly,

resignedly. Bearer of badass tidings. 'No. There's been no change in our mission. We still take this sector of the wall.'

Yeah. That's all there is now. Can't take that away from us too. Dog had Steve in tow; headed for shelter. Raining again. Blank look in Steve's eyes. Like the colonel when I asked him if we go back up against the wall.

Senior corpsman and two assistants strolled up to the two houses we had set up in for the night. They were looking for the rocket gunner and his assistant. Both had made it off the street. Said nothing in response to kind words from the remaining Delta grunts. Said nothing at all. Except to each other. Weird pair. Hadn't made a sound since the incident, except to giggle over some private joke. Both asleep inside one of the houses with the rocket launcher tucked securely between them.

'Watcha want wit' them heroes?' Dog held the corpsmen in position on the porch of a house. 'Shit. Dem two fuckers are stone dangerous.'

Corpsmen convinced the gun team is inside the house.

'They were MedEvaced for cracking up yesterday. Turned that fucking rocket launcher on the Battalion Commander's jeep and damn near killed him and his driver. Then they tried to blow away a couple of ARVN vehicles over on the right flank before some of Charlie Company grunts knocked them out and brought them to the rear. We was keeping 'em under sedation at the LCI ramp but they got away and took that Goddamn stovepipe with them. We got to find 'em before they really do kill someone.'

Dog emitted a bass rumble. 'They killed a whole shitpot of gooks today.' Doc unmoved.

'Don't make no fuckin' difference, man. You never can

tell when they'll flip out again and start killin' Marines. We got to take 'em back with us.'

Flash of gold teeth. Dog drew the razor out of his boot and began stropping it across the palm of his hand. 'Naw, I don't think so. I b'lieve y'all better just leave that fuckin' gun team alone. They stayin' wit' us for now. Ain't no cause to worry. We prob'ly all be dead tomorra anyways.' Corpsmen wanted to argue.

'We owe dem boys somethin' for this afternoon. And Dog always pays his dues. Y'all go on back to BAS and tell 'em you can't find no fuckin' rocket team. Hell, tell 'em they's dead. Sure as shit ought to b'lieve that.'

Corpsman eyed the razor moving slowly and steadily across the black man's milk chocolate palm. 'Your fuckin' funeral.'

Dog laughed into the night. 'Shit, man. We known whose funeral this is since we come into mothafuckin' Hué City. We even got us a dude here trained to write the o-bit-u-aries.'

No, man. Don't think I'll be writing anything at all for a while. No obits. Nothing.

5
Jericho

Hey-Diddle-Diddle

Shaky clutch of twenty or thirty nondescript new guys arrived last night. What remained of Delta was asleep. Didn't notice they'd been reinforced. Sleep seemed more important. Survivors came groggily awake with the dawn. Splash of stale urine drizzling with the morning rain. Another miserable day. Glad to have it.

Strong temptation to roll over and tell Mom you've got a stomachache. Can't go to school today. Too sick to climb the walls and kill the gooks. Steve already awake. Running a toothbrush aimlessly across his carbine. Swan dive off the deep end. Keeping him out of trouble would be tougher today.

Delta veterans finally noticed the shining faces and new, complete combat uniforms of the replacements. Seemed to scare the shit out of them. Most moved away to huddle under a porch out of the rain. Walls only a block away at their backs. Nice place to keep cigarettes lit. Nice place to eye the new guys. Slight, towheaded private with a bloody bandage covering one ear elected himself spokesman.

'They's two ways a'lookin' at this. Either them's a buncha hot-shit heroes a'gonna take the walls fer us. Or they's a buncha rear-area dip-shits who'll fuck up just bad enough to get us all killed.'

New lieutenant broke away from the group. He got the same suspicious treatment from the Delta survivors.

'Wish to hell they'd let me evacuate all of you. God

knows, you've had just about enough.' There might be hope for this commissioned asshole.

'I asked the Battalion Commander about it this morning. Word is you are going to have to hang in here and try and keep all of us new guys pointed in the right direction. The ARVN aren't making any more progress than we are and MACV wants that wall bad . . . today.'

Nope. No hope. Same old subterfuge. Look at that. Shy grin. Just the right touch of dignity and superiority tempered with humility. Keep the new guys pointed in the right direction. Shit. How about letting some of us old guys point in the other Goddamn direction and get out of here?

I know. I know. Never happen. There's medals to be won. Careers to be made. How many chances does a brown-bar get to command a company in combat and lead them to victory in an historic fight? Can't pull that off without the vets, can you, Lieutenant? As they say in the fighting Fleet Marine Force: fuck you, very much. Here's one Goddamn veteran you won't march to victory over. Got my balls back after a good night's rest. One more suicidal incident and I'm getting the fuck out of here. Take Steve with me, too. May have to shoot the stupid shit myself, but he goes when I do.

Veterans took in the short speech through dead eyes and ears. They expected as much. They'd leave Hué when the walls were taken or they were poured into a body bag like tomato puree; no sooner. Lieutenant apologizing again.

'I know how much you all want to hang together, but I got to break you up and mix you in with that lot over there. We got enough for six or eight full rifle squads, so I'll try to put as many veterans in each squad as I can. Now let's see the hands of any NCOs.'

No one over-anxious to inherit a squad of boots. Finally

three grimy paws appeared above the group. Shit. Figures, one of them would be Steve's. Going all out now. Leaped right into the breech. Leader of men. Fuck that. Let him think I'm a slick-sleeved private. Tag along with General Steve over there and shanghai his ass as soon as the first stupid move is made.

First fucking guy goes down; we go out, General. You hear that? No more fucking wounded out of Hué. Had a bellyful of that shit. Dead ones are lucky; well out of it. See these assholes go out of here minus eyes, arms, legs or other parts necessary to lead a normal life and it makes you want to puke. Off they go, bouncing on stretchers; back to a country that hates their stupid guts for being wounded. Hates the stumps and glass eyes and prosthetic devices because they are reminders of a war no sane or civilized person could want.

Fuck 'em, guys. Give the pukes what they expect. Act insane and uncivilized. Wear your uniforms a lot and stick your stump in their faces every chance you get. Act fucking crazy and have a hell of a time.

Assault orders down from battalion. Go up the street again. Only this time, *get on the Goddamn walls*. Keep things simple. No tactical sweeps or envelopments. Just get the lead out of your ass, get up that street, climb the walls and kill the gooks. Is that clear, girls? It's clear, sir. Clearly fucking ridiculous. Veteran grunts slowly shuffling over to the batch of replacements carrying rusty weapons and tattered combat equipment. New men split into eight rifle squads. Delta still desperately undermanned. Fresh meat only brought the unit up to fifty percent of normal combat strength.

New officer arguing with Philly Dog. Bad move, Lieutenant. May mean a short career. Dog singled out to be a squad leader even though he's only a private. Had one of the biggest and baddest gang of cutthroats in South Philly, but he wanted no part of a clutch of boot Marines. Dog's idea of effective leadership is holding a razor to the throat until he gets his way. Might need that sort of inspiration for this fiasco.

'Go ahead, Dog. Save their asses for them.'

'Fuck you, man. Hey, Lieutenant. Reporter-man over there, he a sergeant. Now, he oughta have a squad. He seen plenty of shit. Ol' Dog follow him easy. How 'bout you make Reporter-man squad leader?'

'Piss on that, Dog. Just here for the ride, man. You know that. Got a different job to do, man. Can't be fucking around with a bunch of boots and do my job, dude. Go on, Dog. Paint some kind of emblem on the back of their flak jackets and play like it's your old crew from South Philly.'

Lieutenant's eyebrows went up when Dog told him I was an NCO.

'You a sergeant? Where's your rank insignia?'

'Shit, Lieutenant. Up here you don't advertise for a fucking sniper round. I'm a Division correspondent assigned to cover Delta in this operation. Orders come directly from the Chief of Staff. We get the stories and photos and get them back by the most expeditious means.'

Dog panicky. Didn't quite understand all that, but he heard the Chief of Staff mentioned. Might fuck around and lose this one if he didn't do something quick.

'Don't know nothin' about that shit, Lieutenant. But they'se another reporter-man already got him a squad over there. This here sergeant, now he oughta have himself one too. Sergeants is supposed to have squads. Fuckin' privates ain't. Ain't that right?'

Lieutenant pursing his lips; considering. Should he challenge the venerable authority of the Chief of Staff? Fuck him. He's in Da Nang.

'Look, Sergeant. This company is undermanned and

shot all to hell. These replacements won't hack it without someone who's got experience leading them. I realize it's not your job, but I'd like to appeal to you to help out. Just take one of these squads until we get some replacement NCOs.'

'Fuck that, Lieutenant. I'm on my way out of here around sundown today. Got to do my job or I'll be in a world of shit.'

'We're all in a world of shit up here, Sergeant. Your job is first to be a rifleman. You ought to know that. Every Marine is primarily a rifleman. Now just take the squad for today's action and I'll see about relieving you tonight so you can get out.'

Ah, Christ. 'Yeah, Lieutenant. OK.'

No use fucking arguing with him. Fucker would probably have me court-martialed. Shave my head and send me to Nam. Ought to back out and tell him to shove it. Never said it was a direct order, did he? Well, shit. Do the one trip. And then leave it to them. Steve smiling at me from the middle of his new squad. Fuck off. Do as I'm told for one day. Send these assholes up as directed. Leadership is based on survival of the leader.

Get on with this shit. Ten new men and Philly Dog.

'Sit down. Give your names to Dog here so he can write them down. Forget squad tactics and all that shit. Today out on that street, you key on Philly Dog. If he's down or out of sight, you keep your eyes on me for directions. Don't do anything on your own that we don't do first unless one of us tells you to do it.

'The idea is keep moving forward and firing cover for your buddy while he moves forward. We need to get enough of us near the wall so we can finally get up on that cocksucker and blow the gooks off. Check your weapons and ammo. Dog, you see to resupply. I'll get the details on this circus.'

Shit. Better get rid of this Blooper if I'm going to play field marshal. Get that M-16 from the new guy.

'You know how to use an M-79? Here, then. You stick close to me in case we need direct fire support.'

Lieutenant briefing all the shanghaied squad leaders. Should have saved the energy for the walk over here. It's hi-diddle-diddle, right up the middle again. Move up to assault positions near this end of the street and wait until they run a little more arty and mortars on top of the wall. Then we try to get up into an area where we can rush the ramp and the gate again. Same old shit. Move out just before noon or whenever the arty and mortars finish.

Not much to say to my newly-acquired herd. New guys full of questions. Answer the important shit like which end of the rifle does the bullet come out of. Ignore everything else. They'll find out all the details in a little while.

Moved to the mustering area. Divide the squad up into two-man teams. Only way to work on the street. Worry about squad integrity if and when we get up on that wall.

'This is your buddy now. You fire cover for him and he fires cover for you. If one of you goes down, don't panic. Just join up on someone else and keep moving.'

New guys didn't seem overly pleased with such simple advice. What the fuck do they want from me? A fucking five-paragraph field order? Guys like me ought to be sergeants in peacetime and privates at war. Better yet: civilians. Let's get this shit over with and let me get out of here. Steve's squad mustered across the street. Seems calm and purposeful. Got to keep an eye on him too. Busy as a twenty-peckered billygoat in a pen-full of pussy. New guys pale and sweaty despite the chilly rain.

Arrived in our preassault area. Mortars coughing and banging in on the wall. Check weapons and equipment. Maybe say a word to some of them sweating the worst.

Mixed squads in holding positions along the street paralleling the Perfume River; facing the Citadel.

'Wait for word, then we all move forward along a straight axis of advance toward the walls.'

Some squads would move up through a block of houses and yards. Their main problem would be any gooks left in the area to delay the advance. This squad and Steve's drew dirty deal. Duck and weave from doorway to doorway, breaking cover every time we moved, and advancing straight for the Citadel gate.

Company strength slightly skewed to the left to put more men into the assault that should eventually reach the ramp area. If things went well, some would be on the walls this afternoon. One way or the other, orders were *not* to pull back to the river area. Even if we didn't get on to the walls this time, we move off the street and form a line in the houses and buildings to our right and left facing the walls. If we fuck it up, there will be a great deal of embarrassing questions asked about our inability to make progress. Therefore, we *would* make progress. Even if it was only a matter of holding a line closer to the walls. On the map used to brief reporters back at MACV, it would appear the Marines were advancing steadily.

Heavier rumbling in the air from artillery. Watched the explosions along the top of the wall, hoping they meant something more than postmonsoon plowing. No one harbored any delusion that arty and mortars would take out the defenders. Not after the Goddamn fiasco with the air strikes. No use telling the new guys that, but we knew. When the smoke cleared, they'd be there. Waiting for us.

More new men just before noon. Three civilian correspondents wanting to go along with the assault teams. They went over to Steve's squad. I didn't want them around while I had to do this number as squad leader.

Shocked them a little to get the cold-shoulder from a guy who's supposed to be a correspondent himself.

'Sorry 'bout that. This is fucking conscription, guys. Bastille or body bag? Hobson's choice. Go on over and see Steve. He'll give you a good ride.'

Might even bring him to his Goddamn senses. Man from *Time Magazine* hung back to ask questions.

'What are you two doing as squad leaders?'

'Had to quit our jobs it seems. Today, we're both genuine, certified, Mental Category 4 US Marine Corps grunts. You guys will have to do all the reporting and picture-taking by yourselves today.'

'What's the deal?' *Time* guy had worked with Steve and me before. Probably smells a story. Headlines: 'Reporters Pressed Into Service In Hué. Marines Badly Mauled, etc.'

'No fucking deal, man. No fucking deal at all.'

Carried away Steve's dedication and objectivity in a body bag four days ago. Got to see himself as a sort of festering scab on the grunts. Decided he couldn't live with that and got involved.

'I am currently an indentured servant of the Corps under threat of brig time. Watch for the big mutiny after we get this shit over today. You can buy me a bunch of beers back at the Press Center.'

None of the civilians knew how to take that. They had been counting on our company. Fuck 'em. Let them move with Steve. We'll compare war stories later. Artillery lifted just before noon. Lieutenant running up the street dragging his radio operator by the handset. Up jumped the Goddamn devil.

'Here we go. On your feet. Lock and load. Remember to move in leaps and bounds. Fire cover for your buddy even if the gooks haven't opened up yet. Don't stop for any-fucking-thing unless you get the word. Dog, you go up the middle. Blooper, pop a few rounds up the street. Let's go.'

Machine gun fire. Dog pointing to covered positions. Sending two teams of two men up toward them. Break cover now. Get into that storefront. Position to observe. Push 'em, don't pull 'em. Lead horse always breaks his leg. Fuck that. Just get through this one and go. Roar of gunfire swept the streets. Jesus God. Sounded like a heavy storm crashing down out of a clear sky. Rattle and whine of ricochets. Can't tell which way those fuckers are going to go. Sounded like squads on the left were into some heavy shit moving through the houses. ARVN must be catching hell on the other side. Whole fucking world is firing at something today. Rockets ripping down the streets. Running forward. Look at that shit. Everyone sprinting but it looks like slow motion. Never noticed that before.

Steve's squad keeping pace on the left. Civilian reporters fanned out to the rear. Shooting pictures of the people shooting at the people who were shooting at them. Dizzy fuckers. What kind of life is that anyway? No radio with this squad. Used two replacements to keep in touch with squads on the left in the houses. Got to keep a solid line and get maximum strength forward for the rush on the walls.

Gooks must have moved a pot-full of people down off the walls and into the houses fronting the Citadel last night. Most of the fighting seemed to be on our left. Good deal. Maybe we can waltz up this street and get it over with in a hurry. Kept a steady volume of fire on the top of the wall hoping to keep NVA gunners under cover while we move. Replacements slow and unsure. What the fuck do you expect? Gun in the beat-up tower was not replaced apparently. Out-fucking-standing. They put another gun up in what's left of that high position, and we're all fucking chopped liver out here. Most of the fire seemed to be coming from covered positions along the surface of the wall. Reached cover about halfway up the street. Nobody down yet. Might just make it today. Can't understand about that Goddamn guard tower. There's enough standing to cover an automatic weapon. Why didn't they put one up there?

Just found out. Bastards are tired of wasting ammo trying to hit guys scrambling in and out of gunsights like ducks in a shooting gallery. Set up two machine guns in commanding positions at the top of the street. Cross fire could spray rounds directly into hiding places. Gun on the left kills the men on the right. Gun on the right kills the men on the left. Checkmate.

One gun in sight. Hear the other one ahead of me. Sounded like 12.7 millimeter. Big fuckers. Gooks had the guns placed on the second storey of the buildings at each corner of the main street nearest the Citadel. New guys caught in mid-bound by the first bursts. Shit. There's the first suicidal incident. Which way out of this fucker?

'Stay down, Goddamnit! Get under cover and stay down. Those fucking guns are killing us. Hold what you've got until I can figure something out.'

Shit. What now? Pinned down Goddamn flat. Machine guns poked and probed into doorways and hidey-holes like anteaters looking for lunch in a tree stump.

'Get into the houses on the left. Hurry up, Goddamnit. Into the houses. Get out of the line of fire.'

Ah, Christ. Two more of those silly assholes down. Should have told them to stay down. Steve's squad already out of sight in the buildings on the right side of the street. Same idea as I had, but he did it sooner. Shit. At least ten bodies out there. Street rapidly becoming a graveyard again.

Squads trying to fire out the windows at the guns. No

Goddamn use. Gooks have got the commanding positions. Got to expose ourselves to aim upward. That's suicidal. Got to do something about this shit or I'll never make it out of here tonight. Fucking lieutenant ought to be somewhere near that alley on the left. Cut through the house and find him.

'Can't move in that cross fire, Lieutenant. Got to get those fucking guns or the whole thing goes down the tubes.'

Lieutenant calm despite the seething action on all sides. Might live to get his medal.

'I'll get some of the people engaged on our right and try to get up on the roofs where we can get at them. You hold here and keep fire on the gun positions so they don't see the movement.'

Right, coach. Best fucking news I've had all day. Hold here. That's as opposed to running out in the middle of the street and waving my skivvies at them, right? You got it.

Send two of the replacements across the street to tell Steve the plan. He'll send some people through the houses on his side, up on the roofs and after the gun over there. Hope he doesn't decide to do it himself. Shit. He probably will.

'Goddamnit, wait. When you get over there, you tell the squad leader the lieutenant said he's to send some of his people up on the roof. Not go up there himself. He's to stay down here and keep his eyes open so the assault line doesn't get out of whack. Got that? Now, go.'

Good deal. Both made it across. Not much action on the street. Gooks waiting for better targets. No stalemate on the right and left side of the street. Firing so long and loud on our flanks it hurts the ears. Can't fucking think in all this racket. Shit. Should be used to it now. Probably never noticed it before because I never had to think before. Fuck a bunch of leadership. Movement out there. Goddamn. Hope that isn't those silly-assed messengers.

'Stay over there until I call you back!'

No wait. Holy shit. Look at those dizzy bastards. Rocket team again. Can't believe that. Same assured, business-as-usual stroll as yesterday. What the fuck are they doing? Goddamn machine guns will kill them out there. Same two. Short, dark rocket gunner and his freckle-faced assistant out for another crack at the heathen slant-eyes.

'Fire cover! Fire cover! Put some rounds up there on that right side gun.'

Steve's squad followed suit. Cross fire going up at the guns. Hope it does some good. Those two insane fuckers shouldn't die. Fucking lunatics. Not much we could do for them but try to keep the machine guns from blowing them away. Civilians shouting and shooting pictures of the rocket team from covered positions on the other side of the street. Hope they live to read about themselves in the dispatches.

Laughing at some private joke out there. Seemed to be a disagreement over which gun position to attack first. Gunner down on one knee; aiming at the right side window, the one containing the gun which fired on Steve's squad. Shit. Gooks have got their number. Rounds spanged off the pavement all around them. How the hell do they keep from getting mowed down out there? Gunner took careful aim and squeezed the trigger of the launcher. Flash and roar of the rocket soaring upward. Grunts scrambling to escape the debris of the backblast. Orange flash and boom of echoing impact. Hit just above the gun position. Bricks and debris clattered to the street.

Both NVA gunners down inside their cover now. Goddamn crazy men have got them cowed. Lord must protect drunks and fools. Assistant gunner chewing his partner out for missing with the first round. Second rocket gripped in his hand. Using it as a pointer showing the gunner where to aim the next round.

'Keep firing at the windows, Goddamnit. Stop gawking at them and bust caps.'

Oh, shit. Second gun up and firing. Assistant gunner down and bleeding. Maybe a sniper. Can't see or hear in this shit-storm. He's still alive. Crawling over toward his buddy. Get the hell out of the street! Gunner dropped the tube from his shoulder and grabbed for his crazy friend.

Rocking back and forth in the middle of the street trying to wipe away the blood oozing out of his buddy's chest and shoulder. Screamed something at the NVA. Got a stupid pistol out now. Butch Crazy Man Cassidy and the Insane Sundance Kid. Pistolero hit in the arm and shoulder. Lord may protect drunks, but fools get hit. Cloth and flesh popped outward from a dark pool of blood. Gunner fell back across his assistant.

Both machine guns shifted fire from the middle of the street back to the sidewalks. Rocket team taken out. No need to waste more ammo. Shit. Stay still out there. Both crazies snuggling and whispering to themselves now. Might be able to save their asses if we can get them off the street in a hurry. Better check my Goddamn pockets for mice again. I go out of here tonight and it won't be in a body bag. Jesus. Someone do something. They should live. Who cares if they're crazy? We're all fucking crazy in one way or another. Maybe someone should study these two guys. Maybe someone could certify once and for all which ones are the real whackos: the ones who act like it in combat or the ones who don't.

Whine of a heavy-duty transmission coming up the street toward the wounded rocket team. Bright blue civilian van commandeered as a make-shift ambulance.

Black holes and ragged rents appeared in the bright paint job. NVA gunners on the walls and in the buildings shifted their fire. Some dip-shit hot-wired a local delivery truck and decided to come after the wounded. Good deal.

Windshield of the truck exploded in a shower of glass shards. Driver's challenge being met. Truck swerved into a tight left turn. Tires smoking and collapsing loudly. Broadside in the street; horn blaring away like an air-raid siren triggered by the first falling bomb. Driver didn't make it.

One more dead hero. Hold that count. Someone sprinted from the other side out toward the disabled van. Shit, that's Steve's squad.

'No, no, Goddamnit. Get back inside!'

Steve and two civilian reporters running for the truck.

'Fire cover for them. Pour it on the walls. Now!'

Christ, they made it. What now?

'Stay down out there. Stay down!'

Truck short of the rocket team by about ten yards. How the hell do they expect to get out there to them? Don't try it, Steve. Rifle fire loud once again. One of the civilians pulled the dead driver back away from the horn. Drumming sound of steel-jackets slamming into the truck body quite audible. What the hell are they doing? Checking out the dashboard and controls. Will it still run? Get in the fucker and get the hell out of here. Meet you in the rear shortly.

Real-fucking-good. Steve crawling under the truck. Field expedient. Repair the axle in the field. No. He's crawling out the other side. Going after the rocket team.

'No, Goddamnit. No, leave them there.'

Don't need to know about craziness that bad. No, stay down. Rocket gunner aware of something happening behind him now. Hasn't moved. Crying for someone to come get his buddy. Shut up, crazy man. Don't encourage them.

Shit. They're going to make it. Only a few more feet. Stay low, man. Stay low. Where are the machine guns? Not that much cover fire in the world. Maybe they can't see for paying attention to other targets. Fire still snapping in here and across the street. Where the fuck are the guys who were supposed to get at them up on the roofs? Christ, he made it out there. Get back, man. Steve grabbed the gunner's assistant by the ankles. Man from UPI had hold of the gunner's flak jacket. They began to scoot backwards under the truck. Looked like two lifeguards backstroking drowning victims to the beach.

They made it. Fucking Steve will get his medal for sure now. Maybe we can get out of here. Wonder what they'll give the civilians. Probably an exclusive interview with the Battalion Commander. He better not try to shit those guys. They've seen the elephant. Trying to load the rocket team into the truck. Goddamnit. Two of my replacements running out there to help. Probably figure they can get on the truck too.

'Get back here, you assholes. Don't go out there.'

Ah, shit. Told them so. One's got a round in the leg. That's it. Don't stop. Pick him up and get the hell behind that truck. Five of them out there now. Bound to draw fire. Got the engine started anyway. Maybe they'll make it.

Small arms heating up on the truck. NVA are suspicious. Might be a heavy weapon in that thing. Truck engine whining and coughing. Activity at the back of the truck. Loading the wounded. Guess everyone gets out but me. Shit. A spout of flame lit a portion of the wall near the guard tower. Ripping sound. Rocket. Impact near the rear axle. Truck seemed to lift off the ground at the rear end like a bucking horse under spurs. Vehicle parts and bodies springing away from it. One wheel bounding up the street toward the Citadel's moat. Rolled right up to the gate and across the moat bridge. Might be the only thing that gets that far today. Watched it for a long time. Didn't want to swivel my head right and look at the carnage. Steve would be smoldering in there somewhere.

Neck muscles stiff as a board. Don't look and it won't be there. *Code of the Grunt*. No, no, Goddamnit. Don't look over there. Strain, man, strain to stare at the walls. Head coming around now, slowly. Can't stop it. Like a Goddamn tank turret. Whirr of gears and squeak of joints. Go ahead, man. Look over there at that. That's what you get when you dive off the deep end. That sack of smoking meat over there is your buddy. What's that happening down in your guts? Attack of C-ration shits coming on?

Light feeling coming off the deck. Same sort of sensation you get when you drop a heavy pack after a long march. Feels like you could just float right up to the sky with all that weight gone. Where's the old anchor, man? Shouldn't be running out here. Can't see anymore. Just pain like a broken rib sticking into a lung. What for, man? Why did you do this? Why did you do this to yourself? Look at you, man. I liked you. I really did. That cold-shoulder shit didn't mean anything. Just stupid me and my stupid fucking paranoia. You're my buddy, man, and now look at you. You're almost dead, man. Don't know if I can save you. But I want to try.

I'll take over from here, man. Finish up whatever the fuck it was you wanted to prove. Owe you the cliche, man. Owe it to you to react like it says you're supposed to react when a buddy goes down. I will. But first get you out of here so you can live.

Civilians hanging over my shoulder, breathing fear into me.

'Get the fuck out of here. Get to the rear and get a corpsman quick.'

Rocket gunner and his assistant both dead. Two other grunts – my grunts – lying in contorted postures under the truck. Both dead. Fuck them. See to Steve. Left arm shattered at the elbow. Left leg torn from thigh to knee. Bone shining white through the pulsing blood in both wounds. Out cold and fish-belly white. Shallow breathing. At least he was breathing. Got to stop that fucking blood. Battle dressings from one of the dead men's cartridge belt. Might work on the arm wound. Leg wound is hopeless. Like trying to put a Band-Aid on a disembowelment.

Got to get him to an aid station. Can't carry him. Too slow and the gooks would have another clear shot. Got to find another vehicle. Where the fuck are those civilians with a corpsman? Shit. He's coming around. Stay under, man. You don't want to see it. Let me handle this. Glasses gone in the explosion of the rocket. Staring up at me myopically.

'God, it hurts, man. I think they blew my leg off.' Mouth gasping for air like a beached fish. On the verge of shock.

'Leg's still there, babe. You're hit bad, but you're going to be OK. Nothing's missing. I promise.'

Gripped my hand with his good arm and closed his eyes against the pain. Shaking his head back and forth trying to deny the hurt. Grabbed his chin. Fight the shock.

'Hold on, man. I'm going to get something to get you out of here. Just hang on. Be back in a few minutes.'

On my feet, headed for the intersection. Philly Dog standing at the curb directing cover fire.

'Stay with it, Dog. Got to get something to get Steve out.'

Welcome to the Goddamn war, man.

Cut left at the intersection. Headed for the ARVN sector. There's what I need. Parked up there about a hundred yards. Camouflage-painted ARVN six-by truck waiting for someone or something alongside the street which ran along the Perfume River. Driver and his buddy in the cab seemed content to sit and wait. No way they wanted any part of the immense volume of fire coming from the streets all around them. Either stationed here or waiting for orders to move. Orders coming right up, assholes. Driver recoiled from my face poking into the cab. Must have looked crazy as a loon and Vietnamese are afraid of insanity.

'Get out! Get out! I need your Goddamn truck. I'm taking your fucking truck.'

Driver staring wide-eyed. Scared shitless by the crazy, holy man.

'No, no. We wait. Beaucoup VC. Beaucoup VC. No take truck.'

'I know there's beaucoup VC, you slopeheaded dip-shit. That's why I need the truck. Now, get out. Di-di, motherfuckers.'

Neither man wanted to give up his seat. Cocked pistol in their faces should fix that.

'Get the fuck out of this truck right now.'

They tumbled out of the opposite door to get away from the lunatic with the big gun.

Truck started and ground into gear. Diesel gunning loudly in the roar of gunfire and grenades. Into the street and run through the gears. Can't this fucking thing roll any faster? No need to plan now. Just barrel this fucker up the street behind the other truck, load Steve in the back and get the fuck out of Dodge. If I get lucky, Philly Dog and the rest will get the drift and fire some sort of cover. Covering fire hadn't done much good before, but it might give me just enough time. Fuck it. One way or the other. This is the big cliche, man. Buddy goes down and the other buddy vows vengeance. Got to get Steve out of here.

Intersection ahead now. Wind this fucking diesel up tight. No use down-shifting for the turn. Need speed, not power for this run. Into the street, dual road wheels sliding on some rubble. Straighten this fucker out. Just head right for the wall. Shit. Round hit the windshield. Spray of tiny glass shards stinging my face and hands.

Where's the covering fire? Fuckers have got my range. Kicked open the driver's side door and leaned out of the cab. Steer with my right arm and keep my foot jammed down on the throttle. Just enough crack between the open door and the frame of the cab to give me a view ahead. Stay down here until I reach the other truck. Might make it.

Half a block to go. There's Steve. Pool of blood underneath him getting wider and darker. Grunts on both sides of the street returning fire now. Right up behind the civilian truck and jam the brakes. Out of gear and let it idle. Can't take a chance it won't start again. Christ, they're shooting the shit out of the cab. Into the street. No time to be gentle. Got to be more rockets up on that wall. Just pick Steve up under the armpits and heave him in the back of the six-by. Someone shouting. Philly Dog sprinted over toward the wreckage.

'Get him in, man. Get him in. Ah'll he'p.'

Got Steve's body into the truck. Nerves chattering loudly up and down my spine. Big adrenalin rush. Waiting for the one that's bound to come. Keep wanting to look over my shoulder and see it coming.

'Get dis 'chine movin', Reporter-man.'

Dog leaped up beside Steve in the truck bed.

'Ah'll fire cover from up topside.'

Dog's M-16 cranking on full auto. Time to get the fuck out of here. Where's the nearest Goddamn aid station?

Gear box protested going into reverse. Painful jolt when the clutch grabbed. Jerked and bucked backward. Didn't bother to turn around to see where I was steering. Stared straight ahead at the receding walls and the muzzle flashes of the people trying to kill me for saving my buddy. Dog yelling and screaming as he fired over the cab. Burning up that Goddamn weapon up there. Tinny rattle of empty magazines falling to the truck bed as he dropped them and reloaded. Truck geared very low in reverse.

Seemed to take forever to swerve and jerk the half-block back to the intersection. On the way, rocket gunner tried to put another notch in his launcher. Ripping sound and searing blast. Over and right. Mash the fucking throttle. Next one might be dead on. Swung the truck right at the intersection and offered a broadside shot. No takers.

Jammed the shift-lever into a forward gear and aimed the truck down the street which paralleled the Perfume River. Should be an aid station up ahead. No veterans left to guide my squad back there on the street now. They would live or die on their own. Had to get Steve to medical attention. Dog and I would police up the survivors later.

Idiot bastard. Tried to flag me down near the LCI ramp. Fuck him. Blasted the horn and nosed the truck through a sandbag barricade. Dog firing again from the truck bed. Shit. Hope he didn't decide to kill the guy. Should have known better. Dog aiming at other targets. Three NVA scampered into the street. Christ. AK fire all over the Goddamn place.

'Get 'em, Dog! Can't stop this fucking thing now.'

Must have broken through the Delta squads sweeping the sector.

'Get down and hang on, Dog. We're going through. Duck down!'

AK rounds popping all over the Goddamn place. Sharp jolt. Must have hit one of the fuckers. Christ, twist the wheel. Rolled up on the left side tires. Don't turn over, Goddamnit. Sit down, sit down. Brief glimpse of two mangled bodies as the truck righted itself. Third gook lying across the hood of the truck. Blood from his crushed head blowing back through the remains of the windshield.

There's the aid station. Jam the brakes; let the engine die.

'Corpsman! Corpsman! We need a Goddamn corpsman out here now!'

Two of them up in the bed of the truck examining Steve. Cold-blooded fuckers.

'Get away from him. Don't give me your cheap triage shit. He's goin' inside to the surgeon. Get the fuck out of my way. Where's the surgeon in here?'

Doctor rose tiredly from another casualty and pointed to an empty stretcher.

'There you go, man. Surgeon's coming right over. Just hang on.'

Corpsman inserting an IV into the whole arm. Tried to shove me away and out the door.

'Leave me the fuck alone or I'll blow your ass away. Swear to God, man. I'm staying until I see if he's OK.'

Doctor staring at me with a sour look on his face. No fear at all.

'If you don't put that away and wait outside, I won't work on your buddy.'

Got to get a grip here, man. Not much more I can do. Outside and get a smoke. Still raining. Shit. I never noticed that before. Must have been coming down all day. What the fuck time is it? Wonder how the kids are doing back on the street? Great fucking squad leader. Tell them not to panic if someone gets wounded and then I take off and leave them high and dry when my buddy gets it. D.A. the Great Grunt. Shit. They'll probably shoot me when I get back.

Get back? Get back, Loretta? Get back and live out the old bromide. What should I be saying now? I'll get you for this, you dirty Huns, Japs, Gooks, commie rat-bastards? How you gonna act, my man? Trot your ass out of here? Or go on back up there and do something stupid?

Do something stupid, of course. *Code of the Grunt.* You will do something stupid every day of your miserable life. If you cannot find something stupid to do on your own, you will be ordered to do something stupid.

Code of the motherfucking grunt.

My code.

Nearly dark now. Full pack of butts scattered around me outside the BAS. Still some firing to my rear. But the main thrust was over. Tell by the sound. Win or lose, we were pulling back and disengaging. Wonder how far up the street we got this time? Doctor kneeling beside me, wiping his bloody hands.

'Listen. Your buddy is going to be alright. He's shot up bad in that arm and leg but he won't lose them. As for walking and using that left arm for anything but an ornament, I just don't know. We pasted him back together and he's going out on the LCI run tonight. Incidentally, we want to use that ARVN truck to take the wounded down to the ramp, OK?'

'Sure. Have at it. I don't give a shit. Can I see him now?'

'You can go in there if you want, but I've got him so shot up with morphine he won't hear a word you're saying.'

My God. He looks dead. Ashen and frail. Tagged for immediate evacuation. Jot a note where he might see it.

'I'm OK. See you soon.'

He won't believe that. Maybe I don't either. At least one of us was getting out of Hué alive.

Time to go back and see it through. Climb the walls and kill the gooks. Nothing else left to do, man. Not for a fucking grunt. Corpsmen loading wounded in the back of the ARVN truck.

'Hey, man. Why the fuck didn't you tell us about this guy back here?'

Manhandling a cold, stiffening body down from over the side of the truck.

'Ah, Christ. Philly Dog, man. What happened?'

Shit. How much fucking more, man? How much fucking more? Dog shot through one eye, throat and upper chest. Purple, black man's lips pulled back over his gold teeth in a snarl.

Shit, Dog. Not you too, man. Alone in Hué City. Have to make some new buddies now.

Dog can't answer. What the fuck could he say if he was alive? What can I say, man? Deep voice pounding your ears; gold teeth flashing. Corpsmen having trouble getting his big feet into the body bag. What's that?

Off-white gleam of Dog's ivory-handled straight razor sticking out the top of his boot. Take that with me back up to the walls. Dog gone now. Zipped in a body bag and no razor to cut his way out. So long, South Philly street fighter. You were a bad, bad motherfucker, man. Loved you too, man. No shit. Razor cold and brutal-feeling in my good hand. Blade glinted in the nightlights.

'I know the rap, Dog. Cut 'em three ways: long, deep and con-tin-uously.'

Right-up-the-Middle//20 February 1968

Balls to the wall now. Put your back into it, people. Ball's in your court. Run for daylight. Hang tough. Push 'em back, push 'em back; waaaaay back. Assault through the objective and consolidate.

Cliches rebounding off the walls like berserk basketballs. Locker-room pep talk from everyone clustered around the Battalion Commander. Pucker-factor exceedingly high. Pump 'em up and send 'em out there to KILL, by God. Adrenalin rush has everyone high; grinding teeth and swearing king-hell vengeance.

Strange sights from up on the rooftops, looking down on the walls. False sense of superiority. Seems so simple from up here. Climb down from the roofs, climb up the walls and kill the gooks. Victory. Being swept up in the Goddamn thing. Heart rapping against my ribcage like there's a speedy welter-weight in there working up a training lather. Got to slow fucking down here, man. Got to think through this thing.

Rooftop assaults worked well enough to save about a third of Delta's combat strength. The rest is lying down there in various shapes of dead. Grenades through the firing windows took out the guns that had been cutting us apart all day. Extra dividends once the guns had been silenced: fine field of fire from up here to cover a walking assault on the wall. For once in Hué, we held the high ground. Took a while for the attackers to realize what they had. When that was done, the temptation to relish the flavor of escape and survival was strong. Finally, some grinning grunt bothered to look over the edge of the roof and discovered he was perched twenty feet higher than the top of the Citadel wall. When the tactical significance of that dawned, they called the Battalion Commander up to have a look for himself.

Gooks plainly visible, hunkered down in their fighting holes and eyeing the streets for signs of action. Battalion Six knew what he had here. He had a key to the final assault. From the rooftops he could finally cover a move on to the walls of the Citadel. He could finally crack this fucking nut and get enough force up on that wall to push the gooks off. Quick rooftop conference with what was left of his battalion staff. All very low-key and quiet. God help us if the NVA discovered what we had on them. This deal had to go down just right. It had to hit them like a frightening shit-rain. They had to be killed in place. Wouldn't mean a fucking thing if they got away over the back side of the wall.

The plan: scrape up reinforcements from wherever possible; all but emergency wounded would have to wait while LCI ferried more grunts over to the north side from across the river. Move cautiously and quietly with no visible action out on the street. New men shuffled into the remaining veteran squads in positions on the ground floors of the buildings facing the walls. No unnecessary noise nor any movement that would alert the gooks that an assault was massing under their noses.

Machine guns, M-79s and LAAWs, as many as we could muster, quietly positioned on the roofs of both corner buildings facing our sector of the wall. Gunners would remain hidden until word came to rush. When the whistle blew, they would pop up and lay into the gook defenders from superior firing positions.

The results: If it went right, the NVA would be so busy trying to protect themselves from the overhead fire, they'd have no time to fend off the Marines rushing across the street and into their midst. If the people firing cover timed the lifting of their fire exactly with the emergence of the assault force on the wall, the gooks should have no time to recover before they died in their holes. If. Shit. Toss it up and swing at it. No place to go from here but up. Up the Goddamn walls and kill the gooks.

Just a jangled moment to breathe deeply. Fight the deadly rush; try to stop grinding my teeth. Get a grip on this thing. Delta seething with blood-lust when I got back from the LCI ramp. That place was a beehive of silent activity. Replacements moving up. Led by veteran guides to join Delta and Charlie Companies in our sector.

Steve moving steadily to the rear away from all this shit. Philly Dog in a bag. Probably still lying on the ramp. No room for corpses. Wounded ones to the rear, live ones forward. Like a Goddamn Detroit assembly line. Hit the new ones a lick with the polishing rag and roll those suckers south to the showrooms. Recall the lemons and make modifications. Don't let the line stop. Getting ready to come back up with Dog's razor in my hand. I felt like a thousand-mile demonstrator. Thousand miles of bad-assed Goddamn road. She ain't pretty, man, but she's reliable transportation. Performance tested.

Gunny manhandling troops and issuing ammo recognized me and handed over a gaggle of twenty replacements for Delta Company.

'Just get 'em up forward to the last line of houses and don't get anywhere near the street. The lieutenant will meet you near there and give you the rest of the dope.'

'Hell yes, man. Might as well. Make myself useful.'

Get right into this mind-bending shit-storm with both feet. C'mon, you assholes. Let's all go on up there and get our asses blown full of holes.

'Check your Goddamn equipment. Make sure nothing rattles or bangs around. We'll be crawling in and out of windows and doors to get where we're going. Don't want to advertise our progress.'

Pitch dark and raining again. Goddamn. Will this fucking rain *ever* stop? Yeah. Can't last forever, even in this stinking place. Probably break with a bright, fulgent sunshine and rainbows while we're up on the top policing up the dead. Like to see that.

But I probably won't. Well, fuck that. Just fuck it and

let's get going. Can't get a hit if you don't step into the batter's box.

Replacements are getting lost and separated in the dark. Goddamn daisy-chain going through here. Like a bunch of blundering baby elephants. Signal for a halt. Got to put a stop to this or we'll have boot replacements wandering all over the place yelling for help by dawn.

'Pass the word. Everyone come forward to the alley. Muster on me. OK. That's all twenty. Now grab hold of the next guy's cartridge belt. Don't let go, no matter what.'

Trunk to tail now. Move through the alleyways and up toward the assault positions. Noisy fucking conga line, but it was better than letting them wander off into the houses alone and shoot the shit out of some Goddamn shadow. Can't blow this gig now, man. Got to roll. Now or never.

Glow of a red-lensed flashlight ahead. Flickering on and off. Should be the lieutenant or one of his guides. Yeah. It's the towheaded Southerner, one of Delta's last remaining original veterans. Dull glow of light in my face.

'That you, D.A.?'

'Yeah. Where you want all these newbies?'

'Shit, we all thought you bought the fucking farm someplace. You better get in and see the lieutenant. I'll take these maggots up into position for ya. You got Ol' Dog with ya back there somewhere?'

'Philly Dog got blown away this afternoon on that MedEvac run. Where's the lieutenant?'

'He's right up yonder inside that building with the wrought iron gate, man. Shitfire. That right about the Ol' Dog? Guess you and me must be about the last ones left. Sure hope we still around after tomorra. They goin' to get that fuckin' wall tomorra, man. Ain't no doubt about it.'

Fucker's stoned on adrenalin. Didn't realize how heady

the rush could be until I got a look at the top of the walls from the rooftops. But it was time to see the Man. Find out how I could make myself useful in this deal. Lieutenant crouched in a corner with a group of NCOs. By the dim light of hooded flashlights, they pored over a pencil sketch.

'I'm back. Brought about twenty replacements. Looks like I'll be with you for the duration. For the record: I'm a sergeant and I'm ready to do whatever you need. Combat Correspondent status hereby voluntarily suspended. I'm yours.'

Lieutenant looked like he just won a minor mental victory. 'Good to see you back in one piece. Afraid there's not much left of the bunch you went up the street with this morning. Maybe one or two are left. We had to evacuate the rest.'

'It's OK, Lieutenant. Didn't have any of their names anyway. Philly Dog had a list with him. But the Dog is dead. I forgot to get his notebook out of his pocket before they zipped him up.'

Blank stares from the new NCOs. Pissed me off. Fuckers didn't know the Dog and didn't give a shit if he was alive or dead. Delta might make the wall tomorrow, but it wouldn't be the same outfit. Might as well call it Epsilon or Omega Company now. The old Delta had died fighting for the fucking walls these new assholes would take. Just imagine the fucking sea stories these guys would tell. If they lived, they'd claim to be Deadly Delta 1/5, the heroes of the Citadel Fight. Shit. Delta Company *died* to get them this far.

Lieutenant obsessed with his pencil sketch. Team captain trying to diagram a complicated play in the schoolyard dirt.

'Listen up. We'll need your help come dawn.'

OK, man. You guys block and I'll go along. Right

down the sideline, catch the E Bus and climb the walls and kill the gooks. Shit. I could run this bastard in my sleep. What's the deal?

As soon as it was light enough for the rooftop gunners to see targets on the walls below their perches, they'd open fire. That would be the signal for the rush in strength. Gunners on the roofs would keep the gooks hiding while we go up on the wall and then lift their fire so we could go to work. The reinforced company would be split in two: one half moving west and the other east to take out any opposition they encountered. We were to occupy the holes we cleared and tie in with Charlie Company on the left and the ARVN on our right. We would stretch our sector as far as we could until it got dark or we got the word to hold. Very simple. Neat and tidy. Very logical. Hard as a petrified donkey dick to pull it off. But very simple and logical. Lieutenant delivering his own version of the halftime pep talk.

'Nothing is going to stop us this time. Is that clear?'

Wide-eyed stares from the new leaders. Stifled a yawn and tried to pay attention. Determined look on the young officer's face. Stone fucking serious now. Locking eyeballs with each of us; searching for reassurance. We either get up on that wall or we all die.

No doubt in *my* mind. Climb the walls and kill the gooks. KISS. Keep It Simple, Stupid. Maybe it should be Keep It Stupid, Simple. No matter now. My own battle for Hué City should be over tomorrow, one way or another.

Assigned two squads to lead up the ramp at dawn tomorrow. One of the other NCOs took me over to the area where the squads were waiting, trying to sleep. Ran into the towheaded Southerner on the way.

'Y'all don't mind, I'll jes join up with you for the doins' tomorra.'

'Glad to have you, man.'

Felt like putting my arm around his scrawny shoulders, so I did. Maybe we can get through this fucking thing together.

'About yoah buddy . . .' Southerner had something else on his mind.

'Yeah, man. He's hurt, but not dead. Doc said he'd be banged up pretty bad but he wouldn't lose anything.'

'Guess he's lucky then. Least he don't have to run up into that fucking meat-grinder again. Wisht I'da got me a wound like you did t'other day. I'd been outa this mammy-jammer like a fuckin' shot.'

Southerner in the low valley on the other side of his adrenalin peak now. Having second thoughts about tomorrow's activities.

Comment reminded me of the throbbing I had been living with all day. Left hand swollen to twice normal size. Burning pain throbbed up my forearm to jangle nerve centers somewhere under my helmet every time I tried to use the hand. Probably lose the thumb. Maybe the whole hand if I lived through the fight on the wall. Can't seem to work out a good shit about it. Is it because I didn't think I would live through the assault or because I figured the least I could do was sacrifice a hand when everyone else seemed to be sacrificing so much more? Piss on it. Maybe a hook. Should be a great conversation piece down at the Legion Hall. Southerner trying to get around to something.

'Looky heah. Ah don't want you to get the wrong idea about this, but Ah got yoah buddy's pack over theah with my gear. Truth of it is, Ah thought he was daid and wouldn't have no more use for them cameras inside theah. It wasn't like Ah was stealin' nor nothin', man. You better take the pack now that Ah know yoah partner is alive. He's gonna want them cameras to take pictures of all that pussy runnin' around in the hospital.'

Code of the Grunt: Never steal from a buddy, or anyone who might turn out to be a buddy. But dead men don't need what they had when they were alive. Take what you need from the dead and welcome to it. If a resurrection occurs, there's an element of embarrassment to be dealt with. 'I ain't dead, man. Gimme back my fucking skivvies.' Tough not to grovel in that situation.

'No sweat, man. I'll take the pack to him. I know you weren't stealing anything. Shit, I'd do the same thing.'

Southerner broke into a huge grin. Nobody thought he was a thief. Honor restored. He tagged along to introduce me to the senior man among the replacements that suddenly belonged to me.

Set of gleaming white teeth in the gloom. Eyes dilating to deal with the dark. A hawkish face emerging. Seen this black dude somewhere before.

'Yeah. We been together before. Name's Sims from Sarasota, Florida. You did a story on me during some op out on the Cau Doi Peninsula 'bout three months ago. Got hit before the op was over and they sent me to the hospital ship. Had to come back and face this shit. Shoulda jumped ship in fuckin' Hong Kong.'

Yeah. Remember the guy now. Took out a gook bunker that was holding up our advance with a satchel charge.

'Good to have a veteran. Any more bush vets come back with you?'

'Maybe one or two. We didn't have much time for reunions, so I ain't sure. Most of 'em is fuzzy-assed boots, but I expect they'll do alright if we keep close tabs on 'em.'

'Fucking right, man. I'll need your help with that. How about shifting around to these guys and making a list of their names for me.'

Shit. Same job I gave to Philly Dog. Hope it isn't a bad omen.

'No sweat, man. Got to stick together in the grunts.'

Never questioned my new role. Never asked why I was now the leader and not the reporter. Took the whole Goddamn thing as a matter of course.

Code of the Grunt: Don't question realities. Deal with the situation and get on with the war or mark another day off your short-timer's calendar or whatever. Don't waste time questioning what you can't change unless it might get you killed. In that case, find an angle and work it like hell.

Got my list. Southerner acting like my bat-man. Probably remnants of guilt about taking Steve's pack and cameras. A pair of ponchos for us to sleep on in a dark corner. Four more hours until dawn. Better concentrate on some kind of bare bones plan. Might not be time for that kind of thing in the morning. Southerner and Sims gathered around a hooded flashlight in our corner.

'Here's the deal. We break for the wall in two teams of ten each. When the first team is together at the base of the ramp, the second team crosses. First ten then rush up the ramp and spread out to cover the second team's movement on to the wall. Play it by ear from there. Southerner leads the second team. Sims and I move with the first bunch. Put 'em down and force 'em to rest.' Tell 'em about the *Code of the Grunt*: Never stand when you can sit; never sit when you can lie down; and never lie down without going to sleep.

Pale dawn spreading over Hué. Pushed by a chilly wind. Drizzle still falling. Crack in the sky at the eastern corner of the wall. Pastel dawn-colors flowing through. Strange observations at a time like this. Why do I give a shit about skies and colors and rain when we all stand a good chance of being dead shortly? Do doomed men have a proclivity for noting irrelevant details? Shit. It's fucking beautiful.

Kipling must have looked at something like this somewhere over there on the other side of the horizon. Then he sat down and penned a lilting, rhythmic thing like 'Road to Mandalay.' Will I ever write anything like that? Will I ever write anything again?

No matter now. Fat moving slowly toward the fire. We may all get burned in the first burst of grease. Or we may all get greased in the first burst of fire. Ah, shit. Just look at the dawn. Don't think about anything else. May not see another one.

Ribbons of orange, pink and red unraveled in a widening pattern across the wall; sparkling where they touched dew-damp stone and vegetation. Crickets or chirping birds would have made the pastel scene perfect, but they had long since left the fields and trees to higher animals engaged in the bloody business of killing each other.

Grunts moving quietly in the buildings facing the wall. Heavy, rapid breathing for men just waking from restless slumber. New guys trembling noticeably. Veterans chewing on their lips and fondling weapons. Few of them enjoying the dawn like me. Got to concentrate here, man. Some engaged in a quiet preassault shit. Many pissing against the stone walls back in the alley where the gooks won't notice the build-up of men. Said everything I needed to say last night. Communication this morning limited to whispers, hugs and reassuring touches.

Jesus. Will someone with enough brains and formal education in sociology ever join up or get drafted and let himself observe this shit? Goddamn social phenomenon that needs to be examined and explained here.

Seems this brand new, unblooded Delta Company had been forged into a family unit by the sheer enormity and risk of what lay ahead. Faced with imminent death or disfigurement they felt an intense need to be among brothers.

Code of the Grunt: When you need a brother and you don't have one, you just fucking make one. Or a squad-full. Or however many you need to get you through the shit-storm you're facing.

Much more frightening to face wounds or death among strangers. Adopt a family overnight. No need for fanfare or social intercourse. Such a simple fucking thing. And so important to survival when your ass is on the chopping block.

The Volunteer//21 February 1968

Circulated among the twenty or so grunts I would lead. Jesus bloody fucking Christ. Frustration here, man. These were human beings but no one knew their fucking names except Sims. Am I expected to feel sorry or write maudlin, sentimental letters to their parents or wives if they get blown away up on that wall? Who the fuck were these people? And what, beyond following orders, were they doing here? They are all Marines and I could use that title in place of a name, but I felt like I should know more before I ordered them to place their balls in the breechblock.

Sims followed me from man to man. Holding his scribbled sweat-stained list. Whispered a name to me as I checked each man's equipment and weapon. No idea among them about the big picture. Only glimpse is the snapshot they can see in the dawn out the windows and doorways of the buildings. Many questions. Most deal with exactly what they are supposed to do this morning. No time for details.

'Just do what Sims or me or the Southerner tell you. We climb the walls and we kill the gooks. You'll get the hang of it quickly. Go when you're told to go and shoot anything that moves up there. We're going to take and hold a sector of the wall. Now you know as much as I do.'

Enough for most of them. Frightened eyes locked on to the objective. Not much peace left now.

Almost full light. Lieutenant slipping along the line, in and out of buildings. Telling leaders to get ready. Soon now. Grunts crouched in position like football linemen waiting for the snap signal. Sims and I on either side of an arched doorway.

Thirty yards across the concrete avenue was the moat. Beyond that, the ramp. Sims whispering nervously.

'You got to lead this lash-up. I'll go first up the ramp to see what we gettin' ourselves into and you be tight on me.'

'OK. Sounds good. Let's get it on. Where's the fucking covering fire? Light enough now.'

Booming, rippling wave of fire from the roofs above and across from us. Blood pounding in my ears. Strange echo effect. Tough to breathe normally. Feels like my diaphragm is squeezing up on my lungs. Can't get enough air. Out of the doorway. Running hard. Eyes on Sims' ass and churning legs. Shit. What about the others? Faces scrunched up around wide, white eyes. Fidgeting with weapons and waiting for an order. Christ. There are no fucking orders for a deal like this.

'Go, Goddamnit it, go.'

Fuck it. Just spin around and follow Sims. Either they decided to follow or it's Sims and me alone. Nothing I can do about it from out here. At the moat now and scrambling down the near side. Thank shuddering Christ. Here they come.

Landed on Sims' back. Screaming to be heard over the din of rifle and rocket fire from the rooftops. Gook defenders haven't fired a round in return as far as I can tell. Sims climbing up out of the moat. Using his rifle as a prop. Extended a huge hand down to help me up beside him. Other Marines scrambling up to crouch at the base of the ramp. Some sprinting across the street at our backs. Other assault teams making progress to our right near the gate area. Fucker's rolling now. This one will go all the way. Finally, climb the walls and kill the gooks.

Strangely calm. Concentrating on the action. No time to dwell on anything but the job. Another Goddamn cliche, man. All the old vets talked about it. No time to dwell on fright when the shit has hit the fan. But wait till it's over, man. Hits you like a large jolt of DC in the balls.

Second echelon clear of the moat. Grabbed a grenade from the pocket of my flak jacket. Showed it to the first team. They got the idea. Eyes focused upward. Can't be heard over this Goddamn din. Shake the grenade at each of them to get their attention. Got to do this deal now, Goddamnit. Pulled the pin and let the grenade go over the wall in a long upward arc. Watched the arming handle fly off and hoped the fuckers followed suit. OK. Good deal. Get those frags up on the wall.

Southerner across the moat and kneeling beside me.

'You hold here, man. We're going up. Don't move until you get a signal and then get up there in a big fucking hurry. Take your team to the left. We'll be moving to the right.'

Nod and silly-assed grin. Lips bleeding. He's been chewing on them for the past hour. Moved away to huddle his people at the base of the ramp. Things moving too Goddamn slowly.

'Let's go! Up on the ramp. Let's go now!'

Pointed up the ramp with my M-16. Pain in my hand intense and distracting. Squeeze on the pistol grip. Maybe the pain will be enough to conquer the adrenalin-high craziness.

Sims and others like fucking rabid animals now. Making strange noises deep in their throats as they stepped up on the ramp. Some screaming until their voices crack. Some making whimpering sounds. Like Goddamn starving dogs held away from food on a leash. Leash snapped now. Time to salivate, snap and tear with our teeth. In a running crouch just behind Sims. Background before my eyes changing from brown dirt to blue sky. Sims was on the wall. Slight pause to get his bearings. Jinked to the right, jerking on the trigger of his M-16. On the walls myself now. Looking around for something to kill. Roof-top gunners lifting or shifting their fire. Rattling din from AKs and M-16s. Sims on my right, firing full automatic into a hole in the top of the Citadel's walls.

Movement on my left. An NVA cautiously poking his head out of a log-reinforced bunker. Helmet looks like an emerging mushroom. Barrel of his AK swiveling toward Sims.

'Behind you, Sims!'

Fire from the hip. Rounds tore into the firing aperture. Gook's face exploded like a ripe tomato. Grunts surging up on to the wall behind me saw the threat also. Sims motioning me forward. Trotting toward the guard tower about fifty yards to our right. Grunts stopped; staring around at the top of the ramp. Can't believe they've made it this far.

'Clear the fucking holes, Goddamnit! Signal the second team up. They'll be moving to the left of you when they get up here. Clear the holes on the right. Go on, Goddamnit.'

Glimpse of the Southerner's flak jacket as I moved off to the right towards Sims. Fucking Confederate Flag. Grab a piece of the walls, boys, the South will rise again. On top now and leading his people off to the left of the ramp access. Burst of fire everywhere around us here. Muffled crump of grenades making me flinch constantly.

Sims halted, crouching ahead. Behind a mound of dirt, waiting for me. Giggling and flashing his brilliant white smile.

'I'm the first man on this motherfucker. You gonna write up a story about that, ain't ya?'

'Yeah. Later. Let's get this fucking sector secured first.'

Jesus. This Goddamn adrenalin high was a dickhead. So fucking relieved to be alive that everything – even killing other people – seems downright hilarious. Shit. Dirt mound in front of us exploded. Incoming rounds. From where? Sims had it spotted. Over there on the left. Up and running toward a row of bushes and triggering long bursts from his M-16.

Better get after him. Shit moving fast up here. Got to keep up with it. Shift off to one side. Might get a flank shot at whatever's got us spotted. Something got my foot. Falling into a hole. Seems like fucking slow motion. Trying to keep my head up and keep an eye on Sims. Christ, falling like a crippled kid. Can't get my rifle up with this Goddamn hand. Gook standing up; taking a bead on Sims.

'Gook, man! Gook to your left!'

Sims couldn't hear. Never saw the badass who killed the first man on the wall in Hué.

Sims went down hard. First rounds of the burst caught him full in the chest. Shit. Tried to catch myself with this gimpy Goddamn hand. Bleeding again. Jesus, Sims! Flak jacket seemed to explode outward with the impact of the rounds. That's all, man. That's got to be all. Rolled backward and came to rest on the lip of the hole.

'CORPSMAN! GODDAMNIT, WHERE'S A FUCKING CORPSMAN?!'

Better make it to the interior edge of the wall. Looked

like Sims was gone. Fucking bushwhacker disappeared. Got his quota for the day. But I'm still short. C'mon, fucker. Stick your Goddamn head out here and let me take it off for you. More vengeance trip now, man. First Steve, then Philly Dog; now Sims. Some evil motherfucker was going to pay.

Holy shit. At the edge of the wall now; looking over at the gook who shot Sims. He was squatting on a pile of rubble, reloading his AK-47. Struggling with the bolt. Head on a level with my feet. Easy fucking shot. But wait. This fucker needs to know; needs to be aware of what's about to happen.

'Hey!' Gook spun around dropping the jammed rifle. Cringing now. Looking up at me with dark, frightened eyes. Expression melting. Fucker can't figure out why he's not already dead.

Kill the fucker, man. No, wait. Look at that asshole. Look at the Goddamn fear in his eyes. Staring at the muzzle of my rifle. Christ, how long have I been standing here? Am I enjoying this? Why don't I just shoot the cocksucker and have done with it?

Savoring the moment, man. Digging it. Feeling it over the pain in my hand. Feeling the strength and power it brings to my arms and chest. Muscles tightening slowly. Focusing through the peep sight now. Just like a camera. Photographing every microsecond of this scene. Kill him slowly and watch the fucker die. Enjoy the payback.

This is the moment I would remember if I survived the war. When the memories and nightmares began, I could conjure up the image of this particular gook's death at my hands and live with it. This is my weapon against whatever the war does to me, man. Got to know your weapons. Intimately.

Delay bringing the gook out of his initial shock. Thought he got a reprieve. Thought he was a POW.

Wrong. Single, sharp jolt following a slight pressure on my trigger-finger. Full in the fucking face. Bone, brain and fluid spewed out the back of his head. Bullet went into his face right on the tip of his nose. Dead immediately, but that's no escape. More frames to expose on this roll of film. Full auto now. Walk a burst across the chest and down into his belly. Bolt smacked to the rear. Empty magazine.

Get down there on that mound and take a close look. Let this shit seep into my senses. Sticky-feeling blood pooling around his body; dripping off my hand. Memorized the color, smell and taste of it. This is my contribution, man. There are many others like it, but this one is mine.

Grunts screaming and firing above me. Clearing shell-shocked NVA defenders from the holes. More war to be fought. Better make a few more contributions if I want the dividends. One final look at this gook. Fucker seems harmless now; vulnerable and unreasonably harmed. Like Steve looked lying out there in the street yesterday. Fuck this. Take the Goddamn green cloth belt and red star buckle for a reminder. Fuck this.

Pattern forming out of the chaos on top of the wall now. Short, sharp firefights between sweeping grunts and NVA trying to hold on to their barricaded fighting holes. My team getting experienced. Working in groups of four or five. Spotting a hole, flanking it, getting the occupant with close range rifle fire or grenades. Each hole covered by grazing fire from two others. Casualties coming among grunts who forgot to check their flanks before moving from cover.

Southerner says the corpsmen have set up a mini aid station and casualty-clearing post in the shadow of the guard tower. Trying to organize the teams into a systematic search. Fuckers are running into each other's fire.

Chaos up here whenever someone finds an occupied hole or takes incoming rounds. Lieutenant looking for me. Thought I had been hit when I disappeared over the backside of the wall to kill my gook.

'I've got a CP and some security set up between you and the guard tower. That area is pretty well secured. You need to move left now and tie in with Charlie Company. They came up the west side this morning and should be sweeping this way now. I got them on the horn and told them to be looking for you.'

'Yeah. Shit. OK. On line now. Move slowly to your left and watch for Charlie Company grunts coming your way. Let's go.'

Nothing fancier than an on-line sweep occurred to me. Fuck it. Let's get over there and get this over with. Charlie Company in contact somewhere ahead of us. Gunfire rattling between us and them. Smoke and dust boiling up over there. Got to clear that patch before we can link up. Can't afford the threat of a counterattack through the gap. Watching for any telltale movement ahead. Everyone's eyes locked on the ground. NVA smart enough to let us walk right up on them before they open fire.

Firing on my left. Two Marines pouring rounds into a hole. Must be a dead one. They're making sure. Smart move. Southerner yelling something; shouldering his rifle. There it is. Just at the base of that bush. A firing aperture. Gook inside with an AK at his shoulder. Shit. Something weird here. His Goddamn eyes are wide open but he hasn't fired. Dead? What the fuck? Rounds blowing through the aperture. Gook jerked backward without pulling the trigger. What's wrong with these assholes? Southerner shouting again; reloading his weapon.

'That dude had us dead in his sights. Shit, we either a

bunch of lucky mammy-jammers or them gooks is deadass stupid.'

Firing into several holes ahead now. Only an occasional sporadic round returned. Getting giddy with success. Dangerous business. Marines shouting and laughing about walking right up on live gooks behind heavy machine guns and never having a round fired back at them.

'We smokin' these motherfuckers, man.'

'Yeah. Don't get rammy.'

Weirdness will kill you if you don't learn to suspect it every time. Something strange here. Go slow. Shit. Hard lesson to learn. Moving easily across the gap toward Charlie Company. Grunts don't argue with success.

Charlie Company coming into view. Their grunts seem to be meeting the same passive resistance. Fuck. This deal is turning into a turkey shoot. Get a bead on the fish down there in the barrel and blow his ass away. Simple as that. Only an occasional AK or light machine gun burst. What NVA opened up did so almost reluctantly. Fuckers seemed to be fatalistically resigned to what was happening. Only three of my people hit. Sims the only KIA that I knew of for sure. Got to tally up here. What's that?

Mother of shrieking Christ. Look at this shit. Foot nearly in a spider-trap. Fucking gook inside fondling an SKS carbine. Look at that. Fucking spit dribbling down his chin.

Quick concentrated look at him over the rifle sights. Bastard's moving in slow motion. Looks like a manic drunk concentrating on a sobriety test. Trying to swing the rifle up and point it at me. Fucker's eyes look like two pissholes in a snowbank. Facial features seem loose and somehow out of focus. Looked like he knew he was supposed to kill me but wasn't sure exactly how to go about it. Must be shell-shock. Fuck him and his head trips. Half a magazine blew away his neck and chest.

Southerner trotted up behind me; whistled at the dead gook only four feet away.

'Shee-it. This is some weird doin's. I jest kilt another one a them assholes from the same distance. They's somethin' fucked up about all this.'

'Yeah. Right. Something fucked up. The fucking gooks are fucked up on something.'

Charlie Company Commander yelling to form a line. Put one of mine and one of his into a hole together. Link up completely. String the rest of mine into a line leading back toward the guard tower. About three hundred yards of wall now in our hands. Goddamn. C rations and ammo coming up the ramp. Bitching grunts pressed into service as porters. Should be a Goddamn counterattack. They can't give up this easily. Heavy fighting on the right yet. Should be more to it, man.

Been trying to get up here for nearly a month and now everybody's perfectly content to sit around and chew on fucking ham and eggs, chopped. Is the taste of victory the same as the taste of Goddamn canned pig-shit C rations?

Numbness in my hand. Numbness in my head. Feel like the drooling gook. Just lay back in this hole. Shove the dead gook over and lay back for a while. They'll come again, man. Got to get over this fucking numbness. How can you go through something like this and then not have any thoughts at all. Fucking zero. Zip. Can't say I don't give a fuck. I do. Don't want to die now. Why can't I think of something? No images. This is probably what it's like to be dead.

Nearly 1400 hours now. Things quiet all along the wall. No action since the link-up with Charlie Company. No thoughts either. Where's the heavyweight, king-hell recriminations? Where's the adrenalin high? ARVN still banging and thumping away on the other side of the guard tower, but nothing over here. Lieutenant heading for my position. First thought: Will he want some of this C-ration cracker laced with pimento cheese? That's it. I'm fucking nuts. Or dead.

'These people are from S-2.'

Two relatively clean, enlisted Marines stood staring down at me and the dead gook in the hole.

'They're going to look over the bodies in this area and pick up whatever they can. You go with them and watch for booby traps or any live ones that are left.' Yeah, yeah. OK. Might find some thoughts out there.

'Guess you all ought to start here where we linked up with Charlie. There's at least fifteen or twenty holes or bunkers leading off to the right toward the guard tower. My people are in some of them.'

OK with them. Fuck it. Might as well go along and see what this fucked-up vanquished enemy had on its mind when we blew 'em away. Shot-up spider-trap to our front. Dead gook inside but the S-2 guys didn't let that stop them. One searched his body and the other looked through his pack.

'Careful. There's a lot of ChiComs in these Goddamn holes. Don't fuck around with them. They're touchy and we don't need any more Goddamn casualties now.'

Not interested in grenades or weapons. Seen all that shit before.

'We're looking for maps, orders, diaries and that sort of shit.'

One of them found something in the dead NVA's pack. Clear plastic bag with some white powder shit in it. And a plastic case. Looks like the kind of thing old safety razors used to come in.

'Uh huh. Yep. That's what I thought.'

Senior S-2 guy seemed to have been expecting the find.

'What is that shit? Looks like sugar or salt.'

Jumping from hole to hole now. Finding packets of that stuff in nearly all of them.

Southerner occupying the fourth hole they checked. Dead gook private lying outside the hole where he'd been tossed when the Southerner decided to move in and make himself at home. Contents of the NVA's pack strewn on the bottom of the holes at his feet. Busy stuffing what he wanted to keep in his pockets. Discards ended up in a pile outside the hole. What's that shiny deal in the discard pile? Looks like a bent, metal spoon charred on one side. Jesus. A fucking eyedropper-type hypodermic syringe too.

'Smack! That fucking powder is heroin, man.'

S-2 guys nodding and smiling. 'You got it. We got this outfit's war diary and expected we'd find this sort of thing. Appears their unit commander was killed during one of the artillery attacks and they requested permission yesterday to pull back off the wall. Hanoi said no dice, so they all shot up and waited for us to come and get 'em.'

Well, fuck me. The Big H, man. Pure as the driven snow from the looks of it. Uncut and suitable for a hundred mile day-trip at the pop of a vein. No Goddamn wonder these bastards didn't open up or come out of the holes after us. Southerner totally stunned. This sort of weirdness is not on the daily agenda in Tupelo.

'Shee-it. These fuckers was noddin' on Horse when we come up here after 'em.'

Fondling a large bag of heroin. 'Hey. How's this shit work anyways?'

S-2 man knows the drill. Wonder where he learned it?

'They put a little of the powder into this spoon here, see? And then they heat it over a match or candle until it melts into a liquid. Then they suck it up into this syringe here, pop up a vein and squeeze it right in.'

Something still bothering the Tupelo Flash.

'Naw, man. Ah know how they shoot it. What Ah want to know is what it does to you.'

Southerner staring down into a half-empty C-ration can of coffee. S-2 guy can't figure him out.

'Shit. You saw what it does to you this morning. It makes you nod off and dream. If you're in combat, it makes you a cooperative target. Fucking defenseless.' Southerner definitely worried now.

'Aw shee-it. Ah think ya'll better get me to a fuckin' corpsman right away. Ah thought that shit was sugar and I done dumped some of it into my cawfee.'

Christ. What fucking next? 'Go on, man. Get over to the surgeon with these guys and tell him what you did. You'll be OK. In fact, you might learn to like it.'

Southerner drifting and giggling away toward the aid station. 'Oh, mah God. This fuckin' Hué City done turned me into a stone-assed fuckin' junkie.'

S-2 guy thought it was hilarious. Maybe we should all shoot some of this shit and let it rip. Shouldn't be hard to talk these fucking people into a little escapism.

'Some of these other fuckers may not be so naïve. We won't be going anywhere tonight since they want to get ammo and replacements up here on the wall while they can. You better go on around and police up any of that shit you can find and bring it back to the BAS. I'll tell Charlie Company to do the same.'

Right. Round up all the Horse. Corral that shit before one of these strung-out fucking grunts decides to take a ride. Spent the next two hours scouring all the holes and tossing little packets of Smack into an old NVA pack. Grunts didn't seem interested in keeping any once they knew what it was. Most of them had figured it out long before I arrived. Didn't feel like hassling them. If they keep some, so fucking what? New guy from South Bronx tossed me two bags he found.

'Yez can have this shit. But if I find any grass around here, don't expect me to toin it ovah wit'out a fight.'

Right. Real good, dude. Get your head all fucked up and sleep through a counterattack. That kind of act is terminal up here. Look around you.

Mid-afternoon when I finished my rounds. Had to inspect each hole carefully in case of booby traps or dud ChiComs. Fucking pack stuffed with heroin. Get back to the guard tower and turn this shit over to the Battalion Surgeon. Feel like a Goddamn smuggler approaching customs with a stash up his ass. Surgeon busy with a casualty. Motioned for me to deposit the load on a pile of plastic bags growing out of a nearby hole. Jump down into that fucker and I'd be knee-deep in Skag. Jesus. Incredible.

Had to check on the Southerner.

'How's the junkie, Doc? Should be OK? Good deal.'

Made him puke it up and then gave him a sedative. Sleeping over there in a mud puddle. Let the fucker rest. Look at that Goddamn pile of Horse. Jesus. How much would something like that be worth on the streets back in The World. Doctor eyed the pile of plastic bags, cooking spoons and spikes.

'I did my premed and residence in East LA. Believe me, I've seen a lot of junk and a lot of junkies, but nothing like this. I'll bet that pile of Horse has got a street value of five or six million dollars. Too bad we can't take it back and sell it legally to hospitals or something. That much money would make losing a son or husband easier on a lot of families.'

Yeah. Shit. 'Billy's blown away, sir and/or madam. Enclosed please find a check from the sale of the heroin he helped liberate. Sincere condolences, etc.'

Getting dark. Better wake up the Smack casualty and

get back to the holes. Lieutenant intercepted me. Southerner still shaky on his pins. Hope the fucker doesn't decide he likes the pony rides.

'Get 'em ready for tomorrow. The fucking ARVN didn't make it up on their sector of the wall today. We go over into the attack and help them take the Eastern sector. Your people will lead.'

'Whatever you say, Lieutenant. But after today, I think you should realize *my people* may very well tell you – and me – to get bent. Fuckers figure they've got their fight won. Let the ARVN get hot or get killed.'

Crickets returned to Hué last night. Buzzing chirps droned over the walls of the Citadel and echoed through the empty streets. Strange, peaceful sound. Everyone noticed it. Restful after weeks of nights filled with ominous silence or deadly noise. Bugs and animals, man. They get the feel of a situation through their senses. Crickets probably sensed the end on the north side. Or maybe they simply wanted to reclaim the old orchestra pit where they used to serenade the emperors. No matter. Nice to hear them again.

Replacements arriving on the wall throughout the night. Lucky to have the chirp of the crickets to cover their blundering. New guys can be noisy as hell when they're trying to find a sleeping squad in unfamiliar terrain. Inky darkness complicated matters. Half the Marines who survived the assault on the walls that morning were awake and watching. The other half let the crickets lull them into a fitful sleep. Whispered directions hissed along the line of positions. Veterans trying to guide replacements to the appropriate units. Serenity shattered when a new guy stepped into a hole and wound up hugging a cold, dead NVA. No response to apologies or whispered questions. Ear-piercing shriek when the new guy discovers why and vaults out of the hole to flounder into another. Sometimes a burst of M-16 fire when a new guy gets his first taste of action by killing a corpse.

Crickets don't seem to mind the outbursts. They hang in there. Keep the bass line pumping under the song of war. NVA had their own arrangement. Some probing counterattacks further down the line from us. Command post security taking most of the pressure. They were dug in between us and the unsecured sector on our right. Defenders knew they were flanked. We had a chunk of the western sector. The ARVN would be back in strength at dawn and the Americans would attack from their right side. They were probing for a way out of the vise.

Flares. Shimmering, ghostly glow over the walls. Grunts popped them like roman candles when it sounded like the gooks were moving. Most of the enemy – in groups of two or three – were cut down before they could do anything more than burn through a magazine or toss a grenade. Not much action. Not much to be gained by counterattacks. Before dawn it was clear they'd have to stand and fight.

Southerner crawled up to my hole. Fucker's convinced heroism is a Yankee plot to destroy clean-living Southern gentry.

'Looky who's heah.' Shit-eating grin glowing in the light of another flare. 'Ol' Doc Toothpick done come back as soon as he found out most of the fightin' was over.'

Rangy hospital corpsman covered with tattoos slid into the hole with me. Popping sound as he squirted tobacco juice over the side out into the darkness. Noisy replacements still stumbling around in the dark. Shit-heels didn't even have sense enough to get down when a flare popped. Doc working a quid around the other side of his clean-shaven jaw.

'How you doin', Reporter-man? Hear you been playin'

grunt. Squad leader and all. Thought you'd be dead by now. Or at least made your bird back to the Press Center.'

Goofy fucker. Veteran medic. Slightly wounded on the first day of the north side fighting. Old Delta Company hand. Always carried a huge razor-sharp 'Arkansas Toothpick' knife. Cut boots and gear off a wounded grunt so fast and clean it was scary. Used to take bets on when he'd slip and castrate some poor fucker.

'How ya doin', Doc. Been climbin' walls and killin' gooks, man. Shit. Nothin' to it. That's all there is to do for excitement in this Goddamn burg.'

Doc settling in. Looked like I had a roommate. 'Listen. I never got completely out of the city. They policed me up to work in casualty-clearing on the south side and I seen your buddy come through. He was conscious and sent you a message. Said to get one for the cripple. Shit. He ain't so bad. I seen plenty others worse off. They're sendin' him to the Naval Hospital at Yokosuka.'

Southerner still hanging over the edge of the hole. 'Shit. He done *got* one. Fact is, he got a whole shit-pot full of 'em yestiddy. We all been tryin' to convince him to go back to carryin' them cameras and makin' us all famous, but he's a hard-headed fucker.'

Code of the Grunt: Never back off once you commit. Indecision causes blue balls or death. Once you got a hard-on, stroke that sucker until you get a nut. Only way to go.

'Just till this one is over, man. That's the end of this grunt shit for me.'

Spent some time arguing about it last night. Fucked up my head very seriously. They wanted me to quit. Wanted to see someone who *could* get away do it. Wanted to see me live and tell about their part in the fight. Tempting. Very tempting. Shit. Waste of time. Not enough talent in the world to make anyone who hadn't seen what went on here give a shit.

In the end, a simple decision. Stay and see it through. When this one's over, hand me a discharge from the grunts. Just one more assault left anyway. Should be a piece of cake compared with getting up on these walls. Southerner still convinced I should pick up the cameras.

'Shee-it. You done missed all the good flicks while you was fuckin' around playin' grunt, man.' Toothpick worrying his mouthful of tobacco.

'Yeah. And you keep fuckin' around with the grunts in this city and you may not make it through to the end.'

Spent most of the night shooting the shit about dead and wounded. Southerner's close brush with the Big H. Stoned NVA nodding in dope's dream. What a fuck story. Who had the balls to try and tell it down at the VFW? High weirdness, man. Maybe the gooks in the eastern sector will be stoned too.

22 February 1968

Not a junkie among them. Dawn. First full day on the walls. Lieutenant briefing me on what my two beefed-up squads are supposed to accomplish.

'ARVN couldn't get to an access yesterday. They spent the whole day pinned down, exchanging fire with gooks on the wall. The NVA came up with some mortars and stopped their advance which was headed for the southeast corner where they can get up on the wall. They're going in again this morning and we're supposed to keep the gooks' attention focused in the other direction while the ARVN mass some attack strength.

'All you've got to do is engage them and keep in contact. We're sending what strength we've got behind you but Charlie Company will hold this sector so they won't be coming along. Bring your people up here and spread out along the area of the guard tower. I'll give you the word when to move out.'

OK. One last shot, then we get it. Piddle around with a little long-distance firefight and then back to the rear. Decision is made. Just lead this one because they need an old hand and then back down off the wall. Back to sanity. When I snap my fingers, you will wake up feeling fit and refreshed. You will remember nothing about what went on while you were under. Is that clear? Right, got it.

'Let's move out. Up to the guard tower and get down behind something. Move on line when I give the word. Keep it down now. Let's go.'

Southerner and Doc Toothpick got them ready. Simple move here. Didn't take long to explain the situation. One squad on line and sweeping east; the other following in trace to assault through any contact. Shit, man. I'm getting good at this. Fine plan for a final plan. Move up there now. Christ. Look at the sky. Another one of those rose-petal dawns. NVA flag flying from a pole in the courtyard of the Imperial Palace. Just a small one but it grated on the grunts. The big flag that flew from the walls and pissed off so many people who didn't have to take it down was removed. Someone would get this other one today.

Doc Toothpick wanted to talk. Dropped in beside me while I scanned the rubble-strewn terrain to the east of the guard tower.

'You know, I seen an awful lot of shit in nine months over here. I seen whole companies damn near wiped out in one action, but nothin' like this fuckin' Hué City. I mean, it was ridiculous workin' over there on the south side and seein' the wounded and dead come out of here. You know Goddamn well that except for me and the Southerner and maybe three other guys, we lost the entire

Delta Company. And I hear the other companies is just as bad.'

'Christ, Doc. Gimme a fucking break. Goddamn pain in my hand is killing me. Feels like there's electric eels crawling around inside there. Can't even figure out what you're saying, man.'

'See, me and the Southerner was talkin' last night about the odds of gettin' through this entire fight without gettin' blown away.'

'Well, what did you figure? And maybe you ought to give me some of those horse-pill tranqs you got in that bag. This fuckin' hand is really gettin' bad, man.'

'Well, we figured a lot of examples for hopeless. Like havin' hookers in heaven or findin' a PFC in the Pentagon. But mostly we agreed that gettin' through the Battle for Hué City without bein' blown away was like gettin' caught in a storm and tryin' to run between the raindrops without gettin' wet.'

Great coughing laugh. Fucker spit tobacco juice all over me. There it is. But maybe I beat the odds. Just tripped, stumbled and fell right through the shit-rain and never got any on me. So fucking slick, I ran right between the raindrops.

Signal to go now. Move out. Out of the shadow of the torn-up guard tower, away from the CP and over on to the east side of the wall. C'mon, ARVN. Get your asses up here and get it over with before the rain starts again. Point ahead about fifty yards now. Wait. He wants us to halt. Get down back there. Pointing to an area about thirty yards ahead of us. What's that?

'Looks like they's a nest of radio antennas or somethin'.'

Yeah. Right. Several narrow-gauge wire antenna grids poking up through the branches of some scraggly trees up there.

Get the Southerner forward. He can figure out what's up there without dancing on his dick.

'Careful, man. Just want to know what it is. We'll decide what to do about it later. Move a little closer and get another look.'

Yeah. Sandbagged bunker on the other side of the trees. Used to be covered and hidden by dirt. Rain washed away most of the camouflage. Southerner very close to it.

'Looks like a command bunker or somethin'.'

'Yeah. OK. See if you can get up near the hatch and have a frag in there. That's it. Careful. Get the grenade ready but don't arm it yet. Just pull the pin and hold on until you get a better look.'

Shit. Gooks! Open up. No, wait. Christ. Two of them. Running for the lip of the wall. Officers. Pistol snapping tinny-sounding shots at us. Christ, not now. Southerner caught by surprise. Couldn't use his right hand to raise his rifle while he held on to the armed grenade. Get away, man. Get out of there. Rifle jarred against my shoulder. Long burst of fire into the two gooks. Too fucking late, man. Too fucking late.

First NVA twisted in his tracks and smacked into the bunker's sandbagged wall. Bullets tore into his body and held him pinned for a long second. Second one not hit. Pumping nasty little rounds into the Southerner's body. Grunt on my right tore his chest apart with a ripping burst.

'TOOTHPICK! DOC! GET UP HERE QUICK!'

Southerner trying to stand. Toothpick barreling up from the rear. Nearly by me and headed for the bleeding Southerner. Jesus fucking Christ. The grenade. Snag Toothpick's boot and knock him down. Screaming and bitching. Doesn't know about the frag yet. Southerner twisting; falling on his left side. Hollow snap as the arming handle flew off the grenade. Blast sent rocks, dirt and shrapnel singing all around us. Held on to Toothpick's jungle boot to insure he stayed down. Explosion seemed to trigger the action.

Gunfire rattling all around. Incoming from a line of dirt mounds at our front.

'Get up there, Goddamnit. Get up there and return fire.'

Moving up now. Blowing the tops off the dirt mounds. Burning through magazines. Machine gun opening up to the rear.

'Hold that fucking gun, Goddamnit. We got people moving up here.'

Toothpick squirming forward to look at the Southerner. 'Grenade tore his fucking arm off. But I 'spect he was dead before that. Fucking gook hit him seven times in the chest with that Goddamn popgun.'

Toothpick crying. Crawled over to the dead NVA officer. Prying the nasty little pistol out of a dead hand.

'I been wantin' one of these fuckin' things as a souvenir for nine Goddamn months. Now I wouldn't have it on a bet.' Chucked the pistol over the wall and picked up the Southerner's bleeding corpse.

'Goin' to take him to the rear. Then I'll be back. I told him you couldn't run between no Goddamn raindrops and not get wet. I fuckin' told him that, didn't I?'

No more, man. I don't want anymore. Let's get this over with. Where the fuck are those slimy-assed ARVN? Squaddies leaping between dirt mounds up ahead. Firing on the bounce. No fucking stoned NVA here, man. Looks like a Goddamn roving area defense based on counterattacks. Gooks leaping and bounding between the mounds also. Jesus. Looks like some kind of fucking weird ballet. Goddamn armed men jumping up and down and shooting at each other like deranged dancers. Look at that shit.

Fascinating, man. Another buddy shot to shit and I've got to lay here and watch these assholes perform. There's an uncontrolled *pas de deux* right into the footlights. Fucker caught a bellyful of lead.

Better choreograph this shit before it gets any further out of hand. We're starting to shoot at ourselves here.

'Pull back to the dirt mounds!'

Sprayed fire around to the front. Cover the withdrawal.

'Pull back, Goddamnit. Get behind the dirt mounds and get a line.'

NVA moving in similar short rushes. Two lines now on either side of the dirt mounds. Stalemate.

Maybe we can wait it out here until the ARVN can get up and take the pressure off. Nope. Shit. No trench warfare this morning. ChiComs winging over the line of mounds. Don't have the range yet. Most of the potato-masher-style grenades landing to our rear. Shrapnel stinging us but nothing serious. Can't let this go on much longer.

'Frag 'em back! Lob frags at 'em! Shit.'

Wrong thing to say. Some arming their own grenades; others scrambling to police up the ChiComs and hurl them over the line. Banging grenade explosions everywhere. Sounds like the whole fucking place is under artillery fire from some rapid-firing mini cannon.

'Watch that shit. Use your own frags, Goddamnit.' Risky business with those fucking ChiComs. No telling how long the gook held it before he heaved it. Given the standard four-to-six-second delay, not much time to ponder the issue. Either you do or you don't. You either catch him with an air burst from his own grenade or you get your fucking arm blown off.

No stopping the action now. Christ, this is ludicrous. Looks like a bunch of kids tossing snowballs at each other from behind the walls of an ice fort. Grenades everywhere. Can't tell who threw what at whom anymore. Grunts still scrambling to return ChiComs.

'Use *your* frags!' Shit. At least three or four with bad shrapnel wounds. Should be getting the better of this. Return tosses had to be quick and there was little time to aim.

Goddamn gimpy left hand made me useless. Christ, keep yourself busy. They won't listen. Adrenalin-high, flat-out fucking craziness on every one of them.

'Here, man. I'll roll these over to you. You just pull the pins and heave.'

Shit. What's that? Smoking ChiCom lying near my right boot. Looked like a green-painted tin can mounted atop a hollow stick handle. No time to roll out of range. Got to get this Goddamn thing back over to the other side. Reach for it with the closest hand. Jesus bleeding fucking Christ, that hurts. Barely grip the fucking thing with the bandages. So little time. It's going to go off before I can lash out with this clubbed-up Goddamn hand. Squeeze hard, man. Squeeze! Blood bursting through the bandages. Fuck that. Get rid of this thing. Heave, man! Trail of blood followed the frag over the mounds. Made it. Air burst.

'Ah, God. CORPSMAN!' Feels like my fucking hand went with it.

Can't hear me over the grenade explosions. Here comes Toothpick. Carrying two Unit One Medical kits. Must have seen what happened. Explosions slowing down now. Toothpick flopped down breathing hard.

'The ARVN have broken through. They're on the wall behind the gooks now. Six says to stay down and hold until he passes the word to pull back. They're gonna let the ARVN take these bastards out now.'

'Fuck the ARVN, man. Do something about this God-damn hand. I know, I know. You told me so. Never fucking mind. Go look at the shrapnel wounds. Anybody has to get to the BAS right now, let me know.'

Christ. Look at this fucking mess. Nearly everyone in the squads hit with shrapnel. From a ChiCom or one of ours that got sent back. Threw every Goddamn grenade we had and everyone had six before we moved out this morning. Must be twenty ChiCom duds lying around to our rear. Don't get near those Goddamn things. Duds made the difference. About half of theirs didn't go off after they were armed. Looks like we got the best of the exchange. Shrapnel wounds don't bleed much. Doesn't look like anyone is going into shock.

Toothpick coming back to have a look at the hand. Blood dripping steadily through the bandages now.

'Goodbye grunts, man. You know I can force you out of here by telling the Six you're a liability, don't you?'

'Yeah. OK, Doc. Let me get organized here and I'll go back to the BAS and let the surgeon see it. Where's that corporal who came back with the MedEvac last night? Hey, man. You got it. Just hold 'em here until the Six says to pull back. And don't take any fucking chances. Let the ARVN climb the walls and kill the gooks for a while.'

Surgeon worked for quite a while trying to cut the sticky bandage off my hand. No idea what to expect when he exposes it. Haven't seen the fucker for days. Probably fall off when he gets the wrapping cleared. Fuck it. Smell from the wound is bad. No feeling in the thumb or fingers. Pain centered around my wrist. Evil looking red streaks running the length of my forearm. Surgeon shaking his head and making clucking noises.

'I got some antibiotics here but you need a good cutter in an operating room to work on that thumb if you're going to save it. Look, you aren't an emergency but you ought to go on out of here on the next LCI. It doesn't look like they need you anymore. Get your gear. I'll do what I can and then tag you for Evac.'

Half-hour of intense misery. Cleaned the wound of dirt and dead skin, shot me with a local anesthetic and resutured the gashes on my thumb and palm. Tried to get my mind on something else. Sweating heavily with the hurt. Did these fuckers need me in the first place? Stupid question at this point.

'Thanks, Doc. Let me get my gear and I'll be right back. Just over to my hole over there.'

Serious pain, but the mild narcotic he gave me was beginning to help some. Delta Six motioned me over to the CP area.

Smiling and exuberant now. ARVN finally getting their act together. Wanted the battle to be over for his people. Doesn't want any more death. Welcome to the Hué City Veterans' Club, Lieutenant. You just said the magic words.

'Word is they're going to pull us out before long.' Big grin and solicitous questions about my hand.

'It's OK. Going to the rear tonight with the rest of the MedEvacs.'

'Yeah, well. There's one more thing I'd like Delta Company to do and I could use your help. I'm going to send a patrol into the Imperial Palace to cut down that gook flag and raise ours. We need someone to take some flicks and, well, you are a reporter.'

'Look, I, uh . . .' Ah, shit. Why not? I can focus the fucker with one hand. Immortalize the final flag-raising. Sure. Fuckin' A. Let me get a camera. Freeze-frame: One genuine American flag, flying over the Imperial Palace, in plain sight of the crush of brass that would be here soon.

Flag raised by Delta Company, 1/5, Heroes of the Citadel fight.

'Means a lot, huh? Well, just let me get a Goddamn camera.'

Patrol made up mostly of walking wounded. Some headquarters people who could be spared away from the radios. Line grunts would have to hold their positions on the wall. Sounded like the issue between the remaining NVA and the ARVN had still not been settled conclusively.

Staff Sergeant who claimed to have the world's worst case of amoebic dysentery would lead. Simple gig. Move into the courtyard, lower the NVA flag, raise one of ours being carried by a limping lance corporal with shrapnel wounds in the butt and legs, take the pictures and split back to the CP where most of the patrol would be evacuated. No sweat.

Moved out along the cobblestone streets of the Citadel's interior. Grunts staring around in awe. Houses along the string-straight streets a mixture of Asian urban splendor and tin-roofed peasant squalor. Big shit-rain here not long ago. Houses closest to the walls shot-up and chipped from artillery and air strike blasts. No people. Or none that were then living. In several yards there were shot-up corpses. Bloated, turning purple. Ripe stench of days-old death in the air.

Through the first block. Why the fuck did the NVA put up such a big fight to hold this place? Why would they leave us alone to stroll toward the main attraction? Still heard fighting from the wall to our rear and some distance off toward the northwest. Yeah. That's it. Keep us out of the Citadel by manning the walls. If we got across them, the fight was lost anyway. So why bother to defend the interior? Made sense. Still, keep an eye out for snipers.

Gone too far over too much bad road to die for a fucking photograph.

Final corner. Facing an interior moat guarding a lush garden. Emperor's courtyard beyond there. That's where the offending flag flew. Beyond that, the gilded square of the Imperial Palace. Huge, delicately crafted exterior. Tiled roof with upswept corners and snarling gargoyles guarding each entrance to the throne room. Left half our strength at the foot of an arched wooden bridge. Move slowly now. Nearly home.

Over the bridge and through the courtyard gate. Still no sign of gooks. Flowers are fucking beautiful. And distracting. Must be the Goddamn dope. Tempted to groove here for a while. Delicate blossoms in brilliant colors, dripping rain. Courtyard a barren, typically Oriental rock garden. Rough-hewn stones, polished and placed in geometric patterns. Beautiful fucking place.

Also devoid of cover. Hope to screaming Christ the NVA don't have a bunch of fanatics in the upper reaches of the Palace building. God. Look at the fucking splendor. Almost hurts the eyes after weeks of looking at devastation and ruin. Is this the same Goddamn war in here? War can't exist in here. That's what the walls are all about, Goddamnit. War will not be tolerated within sight or hearing of the Throne Room. Let the peasants maim and tear at each other out along the walls, but no such shit in here, by God. Here one sheathed the bloody sword and grounded the battered shield. Here one stood in awe of the emperor and the splendor of his domain. Jesus. That's good dope. Got to get some more of that when I get back.

Staff Sergeant getting antsy for several reasons.

'You guys spread out in them bushes and look around real good before we go for the flagpole. Jesus, I got to shit again. Don't move until I get back.'

Poor fucker. Lurched toward the interior moat, scratching and clawing to get his trousers down in time. Lame lance corporal still has a sense of humor.

'Ain't this the shits.' Unpacking his flag for the final act. 'We get all this way only to be stopped by a bad case of Hershey Squirts.'

Leader's back, pale and worn. Looks like he tried to shit his brains out over there. Jesus. Let's get this over with. Warm glow from the dope fucking up my depth of field. Moving toward the flagpole. Lance corporal untying the halyard. Gook flag on the deck in a tattered pile. Moved around, shooting different angles. Fucking hand making it hard to work the camera controls.

Time to work the magic; time to raise the American flag here. Christ. Everyone crowding around trying to get into the frame. One fucking round would get them all. Fuck it. Burn the Goddamn film. There it goes. Big finish. Cue the fanfare. Stars and Stripes flies over Hué. Marines ecstatic. Or something. Shit, let's go.

Marines staring at the flag snapping in the wet wind. Another anticlimax. No one knows what to do now. Should be more to it than this. Is this how they felt on Mount Suribachi? Like a bunch of kids who just painted obscene graffiti on the town water tower in the middle of the night. *Getting away* with something here, man. Where's the thrill of victory? Feel like a bunch of juvenile delinquents pissing in the open window of a cop car. No cheers. Just the popping sound of the American flag flapping at the top of the pole, spanking tight with rain. Staff Sergeant wants to go. Thrill is gone – if it was ever there.

Lame lance corporal wanted to press the issue. Brave little fucker. 'Wait a minute. We've come a long way to get here and I'd sure as shit like to get a look inside that

Throne Room in there.' Popular support for the proposal. Staff Sergeant went for it reluctantly.

'OK. We look around for ten minutes and that's all. Then we split. Don't get lost and stay together.'

Up the marble steps. An intricately-scrolled corridor marked a twisting trail leading to the Throne Room. Entrance to a huge, vaulted chamber partially blocked by a Chinese silk screen painted with charging warriors and rearing horses. Just knock those fuckers aside and get a good look at the place where the ancient rulers of Annam and Cochin China held court.

My God. Look at that fucking place. Can't go in there like this. Filthy-assed, bearded barbarian. Maybe if I take off my helmet. Muddy Goddamn boots squishing smelly water on the hand-pegged floorboards.

There's the throne. Sitting on a three-tiered dais off to the right. Huge, beautifully woven tapestry as a backdrop. Strange looking chairs. Should be high-backed and imposing like the ones you see in the movies. Look at that. Two thrones really. One slightly smaller. Probably for the empress. Very low backs; sort of semicircular. Intricate carving on the side and legs. Covered in gilt. They glistened even in the midday gloom.

Grunts couldn't resist the temptation to sit in them.

'Take some pictures of this shit, man. What's that on the left?'

It was over there near the screened chambers where the emperor's bodyguards stood, ready to leap out and behead anyone who misbehaved in this hallowed chamber.

Gooks! Get down. Single echoing blast. Sound still rolling around the vaulted hall. Grunts spraying fire into the antechamber. Delicately carved wooden doors shattered with the impact of M-16 rounds. Staff Sergeant highly pissed now.

'Goddamnit, I knew we shouldn't have fucked around in here. Get in there and check it out.'

Two grunts darted from behind the throne. Careful. Might be a shit-pot full of bodyguards in there.

Shit. Don't let them catch us in here, man. Wait. All clear signal from the chamber.

'Just two. Can't see any more in here. Looks like these two was the fucking palace guards. They're both dead.'

Staff Sergeant emerged from behind an ornate pillar. 'That's it for this shit. You people muster out here now. We're going back right away.'

Leery grunts shuffling out of hiding places. Looking around for a portable souvenir they could lift to prove they'd actually been inside the Imperial Palace. Staff Sergeant groaning; doubled over with another attack of dysentery.

'Oh, Jesus. I got to shit again.'

Sympathetic grunt saved the day. A huge, delicately-crafted porcelain vase came sliding across the floor toward the tortured NCO.

'Here, Sarge. Try this for a chamberpot.'

No time to argue. Pulled his trousers down and plopped his ass on the vase. Fluid squirted noisily into the porcelain receptacle. Horrible sight. Everyone trying not to watch. Christ, the weirdness is upon us. One fucked-up Marine squirting his guts into a hundred year old receptacle that was probably designed for sunflowers or peacock feather fans.

Now he wanted toilet paper. 'Any of you guys got shit-paper? This business makes a God-awful mess and I used my last shit-paper back there at the moat.'

No shit-paper. Hadn't planned on taking a dump in the middle of a flag-raising. Wait. We can handle this.

'Use the Goddamn gook flag, man. Wipe your ass with

this, babe. Show 'em what you think of their stinkin' fucking country.'

Grunts got a great boost out of that action. Wash that fucker off in the moat and take it back with me. Might be used shit-paper, but Steve would like to have it. And it looked like I might live to see him.

Different route through the Citadel back toward the wall. Brace of huge brass cannon near the western wall. Very ancient. Designed to fend off attackers who had the audacity to challenge the fortress of the emperors. Grunts enthralled.

'Goddamn. Wouldn't them cannon-cockers from 12th Marines love to see this shit.' Gun-crazy. Fuckers would put a sling on one and carry it off if they thought they could lift it. Fucking things must weigh several tons each. Twenty feet long and etched with scrollwork obviously accomplished by skilled artisans.

Beautiful, useless machines of war. Pointed impotently up at attackers who scorned such things as outmoded. Shit. They had cannon that could fire faster, quicker and more accurately. Not so pretty, but they killed more people. That's the nut. In the end – despite the craftsmanship of the ancient armorers – you had to use a modern yardstick.

Grunts climbing all over these curiosities from bore to breech. Shot a lot of pictures. Cameras beginning to feel comfortable again. Back to observer status. Fucking right, man. Time to get the fuck out of Dodge. Few more pills from the surgeon and I'm gone from Hué City. Kindly stick these finely-crafted old cannons up your ass.

Nearly dark when we got back to Delta's position on the wall. Fucking progress hampered by two assholes that couldn't resist trying to carry off two of the sixty-pound brass cannonballs, from the stacks near the brace of cannon. Christ. Should have walked back here by myself. No cheers. Everyone avoiding our return.

Code of the Grunt: What you don't see or acknowledge isn't there or didn't happen. What is the sound of one hand clapping? Talk to the fucking Chaplain.

Lieutenant apologizing: 'Turns out I sent you all on a Goddamn wild goose chase. MACV saw the flag and so did the ARVN. We been ordered to take it down right away. The ARVN are beaucoup pissed. Seems they made some kind of deal somewhere and only their flag will fly for the photographers.'

'Well, fuck me blind. OK, Lieutenant. Got the pictures right here. When I get to the rear, I'll make some prints for the civilians and tell 'em what happened.'

Another cringe. What now? 'Shit. I forgot to mention that. Looks like you'll have to stay at least one more day. Battalion sent word up that all the LCIs would be tied up this evening evacuating ARVN wounded. Seems they got the shit shot out of them during the assault on their sector.'

Uh huh. Don't stick it in and wait. Twist the fucker. More dope please, Doc. Wake me when our gallant allies have been thoroughly taken care of.

23 February 1968

Chemical dawn. Fucking tequila sunrise. Here's the deal for sure. Kipling was hitting the opiates when he looked across and saw that meatball sun leap up over the mountains. Had to be. Fucker is glorious this way. Almost audible. Cracking, creaking sounds like the squeaky hinges on the door to the inner sanctum. Whoosh and steady buzz while the pastels pour out. Sizzle like pancake batter hitting a griddle. Looks like that too. Off-white covering the black surface of the sky, slowly; in great spouts of brightness.

Almost over in Hué City. Delta grunts making themselves at home on the walls. Dead NVA tossed over the side into the moat. Let the fuckers rot down there. Acrid smells from C-ration coffee and heating tabs beginning to penetrate the musty stench of rain and decay. Extreme caution influencing what tactical decisions were left to be made.

Activity limited to patrols directed against dwindling enemy strong-points in the interior. Link-up with the ARVN and the Vietnamese Marines completed. Solid line along the wall. Word is an Army Air Cavalry unit is moving toward us from the northwest sector. Catching and killing slugs of NVA trying to escape the city. Only the southwestern sector of the wall remained relatively unexplored. Fuck that. Let the Army handle it.

Flag situation all squared away this morning. Crimson and yellow South Vietnamese colors hanging wetly from the flagpole in the Emperor's courtyard. Got our flag back last night and raised it over our sector, but they told us to take it down again. Press people all over the Goddamn area. ARVN posing with their flag and stacks of dead NVA we killed. Should show up in all the papers as a great victory for the South Vietnamese. Fuck it, man.

When the life or death struggle ends, it's time for political football. Who cares at this point? Got to deal with it. Washington wanted the nation convinced the ARVN could win. Saigon said Hué was to be made to appear primarily an ARVN victory. The realities of the matter, including all the dead and wounded Marines, were neither here nor there in the political scheme of things.

Rear echelon ARVN troops flooding the north side. Appearing in trucks along the silent streets. Crawling through the homes outside the Citadel like maggots through a rotting tree stump. Look at that shit. Full panorama from up here on the wall. ARVN scouring the streets. Stopping to loot each likely looking home. Just look at that shit. Laughing and giggling. Armloads of clothing, furniture, food and keepsakes. Nothing will be left when the homeowners return.

Tax man been here, lady. Had to collect a penalty because you let the NVA occupy your house for a while. Got to pay a fortune for that mistake. The revenue will not be shared.

Grunts on the wall intensely pissed off by the whole scene. Doesn't matter that *we* looted with gay abandon just two or three days ago. Looting by people who fought for the privilege was one thing. Unwarranted rip-offs by rear echelon assholes who hadn't heard a shot fired in anger was another matter entirely. Victors should have the Goddamn spoils. Not the vanquished who couldn't keep the fucking enemy out of their most hallowed ground.

Well, let 'er rip, man. Fuck that. Color me gone. Gear all set here. Gave my rusty M-16 to Doc Toothpick last night. Never want to see one of the motherfuckers again. Rain turning this Goddamn place into a swamp.

'Let's go, man. Get this MedEvac on the road.'

Grunts rigged their ponchos over remodeled NVA fighting holes. Sound of rain on canvas was an irregular drumroll. Made it through the raindrops. That's what Doc Toothpick said. South side, north side; all around the town. Ran between raindrops and didn't get shot down. Take another pill here and let's go.

Toothpick and some last-minute hassle. 'See you're back in the correspondent business.' Cameras slung around my neck; wrapped in plastic against the rain.

'Yeah. Gonna live with it now. Did what I could.

Doesn't seem like enough. Everyone's dead, man. Except you and me. Didn't make much difference in the end, did it?'

Heavy hand on the shoulder of my flak jacket. 'Listen, dude. What you did was stone fuckin' crazy to begin with. But it helped get the job over and done with so no more got killed than were goin' to die anyway. That's the way it is.'

'*Code of the Grunt*: There ain't no fuckin' Superman that can save us all. You do what you can and then you go home and try to live with the fact that it wasn't half enough.'

'Yeah. Well, goin' home now, Doc. No more to say. Tell the lieutenant I'm leaving so he can report it to the rear.'

Patrol assembling to move toward the northwest sector of the wall. Walking-wounded and sick men lining up to go along as far as the southwest corner where they would split off and head for the LCI ramp. Lieutenant sipping C-ration coffee in the rain. 'You can go along with them or you can wait around until they bring trucks up for the litter cases.'

'Fuck that. Time to go. Maybe get some final flicks on the way.'

'Yeah. That's decent. Maybe you can get me some prints later.' Name and address scribbled on a dry piece of C-ration box.

'Before you go, I want to say thanks for turning grunt. We needed veterans bad but I know you didn't have to do what you did. I'll be sure something goes up to Division headquarters about what you did here. We need to crank out a helmet-full of decorations for this fight.'

'Yeah. Well . . . goodbye.'

Handshake. Patrol walking off. Is that all there is to say? Can't think of anything more. Goodbye. Get on out of here now. Take care. All that shit. See you later, in the rear with the gear. Yeah. See you then.

Grunts moving cautiously still. Spider-traps and bunkers on the other side of Charlie Company's area that could have been reoccupied. Careful up there. Don't blow it now. Charlie Company can't man all the holes to the corner of the wall and there's NVA all over the city looking for someplace to hide. Smart patrol leader. Ordered his people to frag the holes as we went by. Don't want any fucking surprises. Good final photos. 'Fire in the hole' to warn Charlie Company and pitch in the smokin' frag.

What? Ah, shit. Not now. Shooting on the right front. Point spotted three NVA running from a bunker over there. Headed for an escape route in the same area where Charlie Company's recon patrol had been ambushed last week. Point man's got them pinned down. Patrol moving forward to finish them. Good action here, man.

Final frames. Mopping up stubborn resistance on the wall. Get up there and focus tightly. Good stuff. Fucking wide angle lens. Got to get closer. What's that in the corner of the frame? That movement on the left? Something at the base of a pile of rubble which included broken furniture, discarded crates and boxes. Probably a rat foraging for food. Concentrate on the frame here.

No wait. There it is again. Shit. Pile of garbage has got a broken, bent bicycle with mangled wheels on top pointing up into the grey sky. Remember that much clearly.

Jesus. Heard it. Heard it happen. They say you aren't supposed to hear the one that gets you. Maybe I heard the four or five that missed me? The ones that hit hurt deeply. Looking up at the sky. Can't lift my head. Pain surging up from my gut forcing my head back into the mud. Choking. Can't breathe. No. That's puke. Puking my breakfast all over myself. Someone screaming for a corpsman.

Better now. Just a throbbing ache from my knees up to my armpits. Wonder where he hit me? When it's numb I'll be dead. Remember that much from before. When I was dead before. Ah, mother of tortured fucking Christ. Just lay here for a while and sleep. Raindrops feel cool and comforting on my face.

Pain focused and intensified. Not numb. Not dead. Gut-shot. That's it. Please God, don't *let* it be in the nuts. Please God, don't *let* this fucking war emasculate me. Please God. Ah, fuck You, man. How did you let this shit happen *now*?

Four grunts puffing and wheezing around me. What's with the Goddamn roller coaster? On a poncho; litter-borne commando.

'Jesus! Be careful, you assholes.'

That Doc Toothpick yelling over there? Was he with the patrol? Hey, man. Oh shit. Puking some evil-tasting shit all over myself. Halted now. There's Toothpick. Fucking around down there near my belly.

'What's happening, man? Get me some fucking water before I choke on my own puke.'

'No water, man. The asshole got you with two rounds in the gut. Water will kill you now. You understand that? Just hold on, babe. We've only got a few blocks to go to the LCI ramp.'

Doc picking up one corner of the poncho. Gimme fucking water, man. Can't die thirsty like this. Sending a grunt off to order a boat for an emergency MedEvac. Heard that, man. Emergency? It's bad. Don't let it be my nuts or my dick. God, You motherfucker. I'm serious, man. Make them give me some water. Rain still falling. Wet as hell with raindrops here. Open my mouth and let 'em run in.

Toothpick and some other asshole leaning over me. At the LCI ramp now. Hear the fucking diesels? Who is this other dude?

'Tag him emergency and tell the casualty-clearing station to get a helo in the air from Phu Bai. Make sure they tell the corpsman on the bird that we've got a stomach wound.'

Damned decent of you, whoever you are. Doc's crying, man. Never saw him do that before. Must be rain.

'Them fuckin' raindrops got you, man. Them fuckin' raindrops.'

'Ah, shit. Don't use that Goddamn knife on me, you asshole. No. Wait. That's the needle. Morphine, man. Give me some water and I'll go to sleep, Doc.'

'Lay back and take it easy now. You're going to be OK, Reporter-man. You're going out on this boat right here.'

Buzzing in my ears. Bass line for the gurgle of the diesels. Smell that? Engine exhaust. Boat's backing off. Got to sit up and take a little inventory, man. Just get the elbows under me. Morphine heaviness in my arms and legs. One last look here, man. Toothpick standing in water up to his knees back there. Raindrops splashing off his helmet.

'Get in out of the rain, dip-shit. Can't run between the raindrops and not get wet.'

Shit, that's funny. Only hurts when I laugh.

Who's this bearded geek with the soggy smoke hanging out of his mouth? Fucking Coastie rolling up the ramp.

'Gimme a smoke, man. Come here, Goddamnit. Gimme a smoke. Listen. Lift that fucking battle dressing. Take a look and see if they shot my balls off. C'mon, man. I want to know.'

Doesn't want any part of this deal. Might be bad news.

Might kill the poor fucker if he found out bad news. Jesus, finally.

'You got balls, man. Do I?'

'You got away clean in that department. Not a scratch on the family jewels or the scepter that goes with 'em. You'll be fucking your brains out back in The World in a little while.'

Big laugh. Hurts when I laugh. But I got to share the joke. Morphine rush, take me away from this fuckin' Hué City. Walls receding in the distance. Squeezing in from the sides of the frame. Silly-assed fucking sand castle, washing away in the tide.

Post-op:
Ward C – USNH Yokosuka

Morgue or mausoleum? Couldn't decide which for the first few days in the hospital. Drug dreams and brief, panicky periods of frightening lucidity. Painful plastic tubes protruding from my nose when the dope wore off for the first time. Moaned and cried and tried to sneeze them out. No one came to help. Peered into the gloom, looking for some assurance that I hadn't been shoved into a corner and left for dead. So sorry for myself. Loud sobs and pleas for help answered only by the metallic swish and thump of machinery off somewhere to my left.

Sometime later I pissed all over myself and realized I must be alive. Corpses don't urinate. Seen enough to know that. Tried to move away from the puddle. That's when I noticed the other tubes. One in each arm and three or four others protruding like tapeworms from a huge white bandage covering my lower belly. Surrounded by bottles and jars. Not much pain in my belly. Terrible, dull aches where the tubes go in. Or come out? Couldn't tell but I knew I was alive then. Corpses don't get fed either.

Piss-puddle made me uncomfortable enough to stay awake until the ward orderly came to change some of my bottles and jars. Starchy, businesslike Navy nurse told me I was on a post-op ward at Yokosuka, Japan. Been there nearly a week, she said. Not to worry, she said, clucking over having to change my sheets, tubes would come out on Saturday. Had to come out, she said, they needed room in post-op and I would be moved out into the corridor temporarily.

Corpsmen took the feeding tubes out one morning just after I discovered why no one else on the ward ever cried or made any of the terrible blubbering sounds I did during the night. Most of the mummies left lying in rows on my right and left had head wounds. No faces in this place. Bumpy bandages sprouting tubes where the heads and faces should be. Shouldn't be here, man. Put me in with the rest of the belly wounds. These guys are going to die. Most head wounds do.

Real pain came in the corridor. Left hand wrapped in a clumpy mitten. Tubes in my belly feel like moray eels burrowing into my intestines; trying to bite their way through to my asshole. No more dope, Doc. Got to start dealing with this situation. Apologies for the inconvenience of having to put me in a corridor. Too many casualties coming in for them to handle. Goddamn, that's funny. Nearly blew the tubes out trying to laugh. Corpsmen backing away from the lunatic.

'Shit. Only hurts when I laugh, man. What the fuck are you guys saying? Sorry? Sorry for what? I'm alive. These are clean, white sheets. This place is not Hué City. This is not the Nam. Put me outside in a shit-can, man. But don't apologize for this. Don't you see? No one wants to kill me here.'

On the mend, the doctor said. Put me in a room soon and get me well enough to go home. Meanwhile, I played games out there in the corridor, trying to keep my mind off Hué, the Nam and the pain. Name of the game is *Guess What Gottem*. At odd hours, day and night, they wheeled wounded in and out. Flat on their backs usually, with intravenous bottles dripping solution into arms tanned only from the elbow down. You could tell the ones from Hué. Their skin was marble white and shriveled from the rain. Look at the wounds. If it's gunshot, you look at the angle of penetration, the area of the body and you can construct a scenario. Angled entry wound in the upper body: sniper. Multiple entry wounds in a horizontal or diagonal line: machine gun. Shrapnel wounds were even easier. Small, clean punctures in the legs or buttocks: grenade. Ragged, tearing wounds in the groin, belly or chest: mine, probably a Bouncing Betty.

Brought a wheelchair one day in the middle of the game and told me my room was ready. Had seniority by then. And they needed the corridor space for overflow from the operating rooms. Two wheelchair trips per day to the solarium or the reading room. Between times, I stared at the mauve walls of the hospital room and tried to deal with the changes in myself and my outlook. Tried to take it all the way back to the beginning of the Battle for Hué City, but that seemed so long ago.

Drift factor was hard to deal with when I tried to remember. Found myself remembering that hard-luck shithead from Kilo Company. When he got back from the hospital after his third Purple Heart he bitched for two days straight about tiles. Said he damn near went ape-shit lying on his back with nothing to do but count tiles. Everywhere he looked there were tiny, six-sided porcelain tiles. Said he had nightmares where the tiles came down off the walls and ganged up on him. Lucky bastard. A man could deal with marauding tiles; but I was having more difficulty with my nightmares.

Between wheelchair rides I swooped between fits of depression and wild elation. The corpsmen who came to feed me and change the bed linen whispered to each other that I should be topside – on the nut ward. I agreed. Didn't feel as though I had any control at all over my thoughts or emotions. Red Cross ladies came around and noticed my injured left hand. Could they write a letter or two for me?

Sure they could. I dictated long, rambling, bitter letters to parents and wives of my friends from Hué. Even dictated a profane eulogy for Philly Dog that I wanted to send to his Bro's back on the block. Red Cross ladies blushed but kept scratching away at the paper. Anything to appease the crazy bastard. Swished away in a huff when I told them I didn't have any addresses or even last names for the people I was writing.

Felt better after my daily outings. When the Red Cross lady with the cocker spaniel eyes and the beagle face came back, she let me cry into her soft tits for a while and then went away. No more letters. I began to concentrate on going home, wherever that was going to be. Hué was fading behind me now. I could accept most of it and live with it. I had done what I could. It wasn't half enough, but it was all I could do.

There was a real world of clean people who didn't get up every morning looking to kill each other. I wanted a piece of that action. No more wars; no more for a while. Let someone else live with it. Let someone else tell it like it was.

Casual Quarters

Scheduled for a flight back to The World in two days. Still wasn't allowed to walk around but they moved me to a staging ward with others who had recovered sufficiently to leave the Western Pacific. Most of them had what were called 'wounds of the extremities.' Arms and legs. At night they hobbled or gimped their way to the Enlisted Men's Club on the base and came back singing and puking. Gloriously drunk. I wanted to go. They wanted to take me. They didn't know me, but they were my friends.

Entertained them all one rainy night when they lurched back in with a bottle of bourbon. Sing along with your old buddy D.A.:

'They called for the Army to come to Hué City,
The Army they quickly said No.
I'll tell you the reason, it isn't the season;
Besides they've got no USO. Fuck 'em all, fuck 'em all . . .

'They called for the Navy to come to Hué City,
The Navy appeared with great speed.
In sixteen different sections, from fourteen directions;
Oh, God, what a fucked up stampede. Fuck 'em all, fuck 'em all . . .

'They called for the Air Farce to come to Hué City,
The Air Farce appeared on the scene.
They bombed out two bridges, four tanks and three ridges,
And seven platoons of Marines. Fuck 'em all . . .

Corpsman brought a uniform and a newspaper the morning of our flight back to The World. Glanced at the *Pacific Stars & Stripes* while trying to struggle into my trousers.

'ARVN VICTORY IN HUÉ DECLARED TET TURNING POINT.'

Tore the paper in half and threw it against the wall. Corpsman flinched and shook his head.

'Jesus. Remind me never to deliver newspapers to you

Goddamn Bush-Beasts again. You're the second guy this morning that went ballistic over that headline. Other guy said he was a correspondent in Hué and he knew damn good and well the ARVN didn't do shit.'

'What? A correspondent? Where is he?' It had to be Steve.

He was tucked away in a corner of a ward with one leg propped up and his arm strapped to a board. Pale and angry; still smarting from reading the newspaper that morning. The tears started again. Both of us crying and blubbering; standing, afraid to come together. And then I hugged him. It hurt when the bubbling laughter came surging up from my belly.

He was giggling and weeping. Trying to wipe his runny nose with a pajama sleeve. Nurses shushed us angrily and a corpsman was tugging on my arm. One hour till plane time. Our hooting laughter increased and echoed off the sterile hospital walls.

'See, man, see? See what I told you?' Peals of insane laughter. I looked at Steve for the first time then.

'We are victims of those insidious raindrops, man. Tried to run through those bastards without getting wet and got our asses soaked. So it goes for grunts or guys who take pictures of grunts and write bullshit about grunts.'

Roar and hoot. Corpsman bitching about catching a bus to the air terminal.

'You realize all that now, do you, D.A.?'

'Got a firm handle on that sucker, my friend. Haven't thought it all out yet, but I can live with it. So can you.'

'Did you climb the walls and kill the gooks, D.A.?' Had to back away then. Time to catch a plane for The World.

'Not me, man. We *all* climbed the walls and killed the gooks. You and me, and all the others in Hué. We all climbed the walls and killed the gooks. And they killed us. As it was in the beginning, is now and ever shall be: kill or be killed. Amen, man.'

'Amen.'